HOLMES
ON THE
RANGE

A Novel of Bad Choices, Harsh Realities
and Life in the Federal Prison System

Dan Holmes
and
Sam Skinner

CCB Publishing
British Columbia, Canada

Holmes on the Range: A Novel of Bad Choices, Harsh Realities and Life in the Federal Prison System

Copyright ©2013 by Dan Holmes and Sam Skinner
ISBN-13   978-1-927360-66-8
First Edition

Library and Archives Canada Cataloguing in Publication
Holmes, Dan, 1954-
Holmes on the range : a novel of bad choices, harsh realities and life in the federal prison system / by Dan Holmes and Sam Skinner.
ISBN 978-1-927360-66-8
Also available in electronic format.
Additional cataloguing data available from Library and Archives Canada

Original cover art design by Jinger Heaston: www.jingraphix.org

Disclaimer: This is a work of fiction. Names, characters, places and incidents are products of the authors' imaginations or are used fictitiously and are not to be construed as real. Any resemblance to actual events, localities or persons, living or dead, except as noted, is entirely coincidental.

Extreme care has been taken by the authors to ensure that all information presented in this book is accurate and up to date at the time of publishing. Neither the author nor the publisher can be held responsible for any errors or omissions. Additionally, neither is any liability assumed for damages resulting from the use of the information contained herein.

Publisher: CCB Publishing
British Columbia, Canada
www.ccbpublishing.com

Dan Holmes:
To all those who have supported me since my release.
You have shown me amounts of Love and Kindness
that words cannot adequately describe.

Sam Skinner:
Take heart fellow felons and never despair,
Whether you've been caught yet or not, life's just not fair.
And when you're down and out and think of pushing up clover,
Just realize that, if you never give up, the game's never over.

In the not-too-distant-times of past, if there was a teenage pregnancy, a divorce or a bankruptcy in your life, society deemed you to be an outcast and banished you from respectable circles. But the worst stigma occurred when you were accused of a crime. That's why the "perp" covers his face as the policeman puts him in the squad car or as the Marshal Service leads him out of the courtroom. I should know. I descended from a young, up and coming, highly respected lawyer to shielding my face with a towel when I was handcuffed by a U.S. Marshal, dragged from my office and escorted to my new home at the Federal Penitentiary-Leavenworth, Kansas.

A Brief Overview

Did you ever wake up on Christmas morning; sneak downstairs before anyone else and realize that all of your Christmas wishes had come true? Well, it happened to me except Saint Nick arrived in the middle of July, 1987. I awoke at three AM and slumbered into the Queen Ann chair in our Master Bedroom. There wasn't a sound in the house. I relaxed there and realized that at age thirty-three, I had everything that I ever dreamed of. I lived in a thirty-five hundred square foot house that was recently constructed on a five acre wooded lot. I had three children who were still toddlers and, thank God, healthy. They were my pride and joy. They were normal and well adjusted. They played sports each season and attended private pre-school. My wife and I were deeply in love. She was the most wonderful, caring person I had ever met. In addition, she was a loving mother who devoted her life to raising our children and she did a marvelous job. I was a lawyer who was the managing partner of a small but rapidly growing law firm. I had all the trappings of a major law firm except I practiced on a smaller scale. As I sat there in the dark, I thanked God for all the blessings that He had bestowed upon me.

My thoughts then turned to the distance I had traveled since my youth. I was raised in a row house that contained two bedrooms and one bathroom. Now, I owned three houses: the gentleman's farm in southern New Jersey; the summer house at a Jersey shore resort and a winter house in Phoenix, Arizona. The houses, though, were just the beginning. There was expensive furniture, fast cars, designer clothes, private school, exotic vacations, theatre, sporting events and so much more. But beyond the personal possessions was the gratification in knowing that I wasn't that geeky nerd who was the object of everyone's jokes anymore. Now, I was on the Board of Directors of several non-profit corporations; I was an advisor to the Mayor of the town where we lived and I was being "groomed" for a judgeship. As I sat there, I realized that my reality was better than my dreams. The best part was that the future was only going to improve.

But what I didn't envision was that the quality of a man is not in what he "owns" but in what resides within him. In my case, it meant that I was still haunted by a past that was dominated by the demons of loneliness, humiliation and fear. They were dormant at the time but were lurking within me. Then, one day, when my practice was struggling and my marriage crumbling, they seized me and my personal "Pearl Harbor" ensued. All along, I thought that money and friends and status would insulate me but I was wrong. Suddenly, I was emotionally propelled twenty years back in time when I was alone and scared. Even though I was outwardly successful, the fears of loneliness and failure choked me until I prayed for death. Now, not only did I suffer, but I dragged my wife, my children, my mother, relatives, friends and clients into my emotional quagmire. The trip to hell lasted 18 months, and in that time, I forced countless victims to endure an emotional upheaval that totally blindsided them. I don't know if they'll ever recover. I can only ask for forgiveness. More accurately, my personal voyage to Hades lasted the aforementioned 18 months and the additional ninety-six months that the Honorable Court imposed so that I would not be a detriment to society.

The Journey Begins

It has taken me a long time to write this story. That's not unusual because countless times when I had to write a paper in college I couldn't start it until the night before it was due. I kidded myself back then by saying that I worked better under pressure. I've come to learn that the statement is not true. I was really afraid of failing.

I have a dream that haunts me where I'm running to a college English class so that I can take a test. I arrive at class and, of course, fail the test miserably. Then I wake up in a cold sweat and "feel like a failure" except that I graduated from college over thirty years ago. That's why writing this beginning part is so difficult because it forces me to reface my indiscretions (in reality my failures). There was no reason for the disaster that I caused. I had the world in the palms of my hands and I screwed it up. As I think about whose fault it is, I realize that I faced him this morning when I shaved. I want to slit his throat. But suicide would be the easy road and I don't want the story to end that way. I want my dad, my mom and my three children to be proud of me.

So, who am I and why did I crash and burn? The technical answer is that I'm the product of my upbringing and my surroundings. On the "upbringing" side, my father was the typical Irish patriarch who was forty-six when I was born. He was the breadwinner and the king of his castle. His words were his bond and his steely eyed stare reflected the intensity of his words. Formal education ended with the seventh grade so his employment opportunities were limited. He earned a living as a manager of a policyholder service department of a life insurance company. My most vivid memory of his attitude toward work happened one day when it was snowing so hard that the public transportation system was shut down. He came down to breakfast at the usual time and my mom asked where he was going. He said, without emotion, "If we want to continue to eat, somebody in this house has to go to work.

If I have to, I'll walk." And that's what he did. He must have frozen in that bitter winter storm. It took him three hours to make the trip. He was sixty-four years old.

Since I was born so late in his life, my dad's agenda was fairly fixed. He had his own schedule that didn't provide much time for me. As a result, he never came to watch me play sports. When it was time for the father/son games, he claimed that he was "too old for that." For a lot of years, we lived in the same house but had little interaction. I stopped trying to impress him because no matter what I did to garner his attention, it never worked. Eventually, I gave up. I finally became a part of his world when he was seventy years old. His passion in life was golf. He loved to play and/or watch the game and one day, I started playing. Then we became closer than ever. He would never stop buying me golfing gadgets to help me improve my game. He even introduced me to his golfing buddies and I joined their club. Hearing his friends tell me what a great guy he was, provided me with an understanding of who my dad was and what he was all about. I worked hard to become a decent golfer. At first I thought I did it because I loved the game; later in life I admitted to myself that it was because I loved him. I wanted to be like him; a guy who overcame a poor background to support his family and give them more than he had. He was a man of his word and his world was black and white. Over time, I had nothing but the utmost respect for my dad. The saddest day in my life was when he died. He was seventy-six. We had six good years together. Didn't seem like a lot but I've cherished those years to this day.

My mom was a stay at home mom who birthed me when she was forty. I was ten pounds, seven ounces and twenty-one inches long. The delivery techniques were a lot different back then and the pain of child birth was like the Bill Cosby joke "take your bottom lip and pull it over your head." Considering my size and her age, she must have been a strong woman. In our family, her job was to tend to all the matters of the house. Since we never had a lot of money, she would stretch everything as far as she could. Nothing was ever thrown out. If I ever complained that I didn't have enough of something, she would calmly say, "There are people that don't have any." Mom was the quiet type who everyone in the neighborhood went to for advice. She was a very generous woman whose best attribute was her willingness to listen to the other person's troubles. As with my dad, mom never saw me play sports either. I wanted her to come but she was always going to help out a neighbor around their house. I never understood how great my mom was until my dad died because she was the one who glued me together and was a source of strength for the family. Over time, I watched her evolve from a person who played second fiddle to my dad into a person who handled the bills, maintained the house and car, and watched over her family. But, what impressed me the most was that my mom developed a close connection with her grandchildren. For example, when she came to our house to babysit, she'd sit on the floor and play games with my oldest child for hours. The loving devotion she bestowed upon him was why he adored "his nanny." It was one of the greatest lessons I ever learned.

I have two brothers who are seven and fourteen years older than me so I rolled through life being an "Oops." They were out of the house before I started first grade so I had very little interaction with them. I don't remember sharing holiday meals or taking vacations with them so I guess they didn't happen. We never played games, or tossed a ball, or even talked. It seemed like all we shared was a last name.

Well, what were my "surroundings?" I was born in 1954 and my first memories were of the sixties. You've heard of them. A President was killed by a Russian (or the mob or a Cuban-they still aren't sure); Civil Rights were prominent; there was a war with the "yellow man"; protest songs abounded; there was a violent outbreak at the Democratic National Convention; the British invasion shook the music scene; drugs and sex or was it sex and drugs; black and white TV; man walked on the moon (and then he hit a golf ball); Ed Sullivan and American Bandstand; Elvis; Marilyn Monroe; The Tonight Show; Mr. Ed; all this and more. Sad part is I missed it. You see, while all that was going on in the world, I was born and raised in a quiet section of Philadelphia, Pennsylvania. Back then, the city was comprised of neighborhoods and each neighborhood had a different ethnic flavor. The rule was that you didn't leave your area. My family was Irish, so we lived in the Irish section where we attended the Irish Church and grade school. We only hung out with our Irish neighbors and stayed on "our" block. If a Polish kid drifted into where we played, one of our mother's would march out and order the Polish kid to "get back where he belonged." It didn't matter if we were playing with the Polish kid; you stayed with your own kind. You went to church with your own kind; you went to school with your own kind; you vacationed with your Irish kin; you shopped at the stores owned by Irish proprietors. You get the idea. Great parties—lots of beer but not much integration. Diversity was lacking. You can figure out that since we didn't hang with non-Irish types that we didn't know what a black person was. Forget Hispanics and Asians. Nope, my world consisted of "Irish only" and didn't extend beyond a city block or two. To me, that two block area was my whole, wide world.

But by far, the biggest, non-family influence on me was Catholic school. I survived the eight years of pain and mayhem but it didn't go well. I encountered the Nuns in first grade and worked my way through to the eighth grade by staying out of the way. The key to my academic success was that my mom chauffeured the Nuns wherever they had to be driven and I think the good Sisters were afraid that my mom wouldn't drive them if they flunked me. Good thing for that because I was petrified of the Nuns and the beating you absorbed if you didn't do what they ordered you to do. Fear gripped my body like a vise and often caused me to freeze when I was called on to answer a question. One time I was told to go to the blackboard to diagram a sentence and stood there like a mummy. I didn't know where to begin and the Nun screamed at me to "get moving." The more she yelled, the "more scared" I became. She ended the standoff by walking over to me, grabbing me by the ear and dragging me back to my chair. I wanted to screw myself into the floor to avoid walking home that day. I knew my classmates would tease me to no end and that's what happened. Homework projects and book reports overpowered me and I never knew where to begin. My work product resembled a disorganized and jumbled mess and my grades reflected it. I was labeled, for eight consecutive years, as "slow."

High school represented a continuation of the educational hell that commenced in grade school except it was located in a different place. To travel to school, I rode on public transportation to Center City where a whole new world awaited me. High school was in the middle of the City of Philadelphia where cars and people moved much faster than I had experienced before. My sheltered upbringing didn't prepare me for the increased, impersonal pace. I was forced from my Irish cocoon into a world where Priests replaced Nuns and lunch ladies served up cold pizza and burned burgers instead of mom's home cooked meals. The first couple of days I was lost as I wandered from classroom to classroom in scared amazement. Everything was bigger and moved faster than in grade school. Walking to different classes, while I bumped into other students in cramped hallways, was unnerving. Where was room 24 anyway? Also, terminology was different—instead of being a grade schooler, I was now a freshman who was to report to D-3, whatever that was (ended up being my homeroom). Plus, I lost a physical comfort in that I was one of the bigger eighth graders and suddenly, I was one of the smaller students in my class. I was intimidated and scared. There was no one in my house who could help me with the adjustment and consequently I was forced to tackle the newness by myself. I stumbled for a short time until I found some friends that I rode with on the bus. They weren't Irish but at least they were in the same boat as I was and, while they didn't have all the answers, there was comfort in that I wasn't the only one lost.

There were two things that I encountered early in my high school career that expanded my worldly horizon. The first was the exposure to African-Americans. There were only twelve of them in a school of a thousand but they dominated the environment. They were the tough guys who had more street smarts than anyone else. They weren't afraid to confront the faculty and there was a cold harshness to them. They seemed to be mad that their ancestors were slaves. I couldn't understand the logic since neither I nor my ancestors had anything to do with slavery. But my rationale didn't quench their anger. To survive, I stayed away from them. I was scared of their hostility and I didn't know how to handle it since I had never encountered it before. The other eye popper was the ladies clothing store across the street. No! I wasn't into the dresses, but I fell in love with the PYT who changed the manikins every Wednesday during math class. Sadly, the school uniforms worn by the Catholic school girls didn't prepare young men for the emotions that were generated when they saw a young lady dressed in a mini-skirt. All I know was that the manikin changer was "hot" and she wore the skimpiest mini-skirts that I ever saw. Just seeing her gave me feelings that I never felt before but when she bent over, oh my God, it was "ride 'em cowboy" time.

That was as close to sex as I would come in high school. Simply put, I didn't fit in. I was a round peg in a square hole. There were three main, social groups in high school and I didn't qualify for any of them. I didn't have sufficient school spirit to be a "yahoo;" I wasn't smart enough to be a "brainiack;" and I didn't know what drugs were so I wasn't a "head." On weekends, I reverted to my grade school crowd that more closely resembled "male nerd bonding." Our group consisted of my former grade school classmates who didn't fit into the other mainstream high school groups. We were a group of "losers." While the "in" crowd went to parties with girls or hung out by the creek drinking, we went bowling or watched movies. One of the guys claimed to have felt a girl up so we elected him as our leader even though we knew that he was lying. We were that desperate.

In high school, since I was so awkward, I was picked on by the "in" crowd and ended up being called "goofy" whenever I ate lunch with them. To avoid that slap, I ate by myself and the vulgarity changed to, "Hey, Homo." You can envision the joy of hearing that yelled all over the lunchroom when I entered. The insult took on a life of its own as students I didn't know picked up the chant. I finally stopped eating in the lunchroom and just went to the library.

I didn't do very well academically in high school either. I was totally lost in most of the classes. I couldn't figure out what Greek mythology was all about and couldn't keep the names of the different "gods" straight. On top of that, there were classes that we didn't have in grade school like science and foreign language and I was unable to grasp the material. I prayed that I'd never be called on. Tests were worse because I'd panic as soon as I didn't know the first answer. Then, one time in my junior year when I studied very hard for a

French test, I was accused of cheating because I achieved the highest score in the class. The teacher made me sit in the library during my lunch period and retake the test as he stood there and announced to everyone that we were there because I was a cheater. I felt totally humiliated.

For four years, I was strangled by the fears of failure and loneliness. The result was an embarrassing effort that had me ranked near the bottom of my class at the end of my junior year. That's when reality kicked in. Before my senior year started, my dad sat me down and asked me what my plans were when I finished high school. I remember telling him that I didn't have any and he replied that I had three choices. I could enlist in the military, join the priesthood or attend college. The choice was simple but the implementation would require a miracle. I had not yet taken the SAT but I sucked at standardized tests. To make the task harder, I was ranked 211 out of 212 in my class. So much to do and so little time! Fear gripped my body as I realized that life was staring me in the face and I was unprepared. A dramatically new approach was needed and the only one I wanted was to study. And that's what I did. By studying every night, and attending sessions offered by the faculty to help seniors gain acceptance into college, I scored reasonably well on the SAT test. My grades for the first half of the year qualified me for admittance into a local Christian Brothers university.

College was a life changer. Pure and simple. While grade school and high school were all about imposed structure and discipline, college was the exact opposite. College was freedom and self responsibility. It was 1972 when I arrived and the war in Viet Nam was winding down; streakers came to most events; keg parties; the sexual revolution; psychedelic drugs; anti-government movement; and most importantly females. I forgot to tell you that I attended an all-boys high school but God was gracious and stopped that foolishness when I started college. I'd sit in the quad day after day and watch the girls walk by and loved every minute of it. It was especially nice during springtime when the girls would shed all those heavy winter outfits and start wearing shorts and tee shirts. All I could say was, "God is good!"

But, better than all of that, I felt connected. For the first time in my life, I enjoyed being where I was and who I was surrounded by. The faculty and administration had a genuine concern for the students and took time to learn about us on a personal level. I felt that someone cared about me and wanted to see me grow as a person. For example, my academic advisor spent time asking me about my personal interests and hobbies. He helped me select courses that I could relate to and, for the first time ever, I enjoyed going to class. However, despite the positives, I was still unable to make a lot of friends. To cover the tuition, I had to schedule classes so that I could work about twenty-five hours a week. Plus, I worked every Saturday so I had very little time for a social life. As a result, the only friends that I had on campus were the guys that I went to high school with and by sophomore year they had moved on to the frat life and the bonds of our relationship weakened.

But something happened very early in college. The proverbial light bulb went on and, when I studied the material this time, it made sense. At first, I was still very reserved about my class participation but, as the first semester rolled on; I gained some confidence and volunteered to participate in the classroom. It was an unexpected feeling and every day, I was scared that I would revert back to the way I was in grade school and high school. But, when I received my first report card, it contained four "A's" and one "B." Thereafter, the more I studied, the better I performed.

Before I knew it, I was ranked fifth in my class. That produced some unexpected benefits. First, for the first time in my life, I had succeeded at something and there was a feeling of accomplishment that I never felt before. Truthfully, I didn't know where it came from but it enhanced my self confidence and spurred me on to greater academic success. I also started to groom myself a little better and improved my appearance by buying new clothes when I could afford them. I was still a total nerd and a loner but, for the first time in over nineteen years, I had succeeded at something. Second, I was invited to join all the academic clubs on campus. It was not much more than a title but at least I belonged to something even if the members were bigger nerds than me. I never attended the club meetings but being able to claim that I belonged to the Accounting Honors Society and the Academic All-American Club was something that I could boast about. Third, there is little more beautiful in life than a female who needs your help to prevent flunking a class that you excel in. No, I wasn't a slime ball but the fact that I could spend time with a pretty girl was a new and refreshing experience. Over the four years I tutored about ten females so I became very popular. My friends nicknamed them "Dan's Angels." However, since I had never been close to a girl before, I didn't know how to act or what to say. Despite my academic success, when it came to females, I was "developmentally challenged." So, to avoid saying something stupid, I stayed "on topic."

I wanted the four years of college to last forever but sadly they didn't. I was forced to graduate and earn an honest living as the accountant that I had studied to be. I was employed by an international accounting firm and quickly hated my chosen profession. Sitting there day after day preparing work papers and related documents was too slow and impersonal for my taste and the more I did it, the less I liked it. Within two years of college graduation, I decided to abandon the accounting profession and become a lawyer. I ended up being accepted into a small law school and entered the "evening" program so that I could work during the day to pay the tuition. While the experiment was successful in the long term, it was a short term nightmare. On a typical day, I woke up at six o'clock and was at my desk by eight. Then I worked until five when I drove for an hour to school where I attended classes till nine-thirty and then drove home. I'd study until I was too tired to keep my mind active and then started all over the next day at six. That was five days a week and then on the weekends, I'd attend study group where I'd share study materials with other classmates in order to keep up with the work load.

My social life, never to be described as "on fire," was worse than ever and the biggest problem I had was that a large percentage of the other classmates thought they were playing Paper Chase (remember that movie). They took the shit way too seriously and I couldn't tolerate them. Sure, our common dream was that we'd end up as attorneys in major law firms or with *Fortune 500* companies but the reality was that we would be graduated from a small law school that had recently been accredited. Our chances of being general counsel at Microsoft were less than slim. Get a life, asshole!

The law school experience proved two things to me. First, it reinforced my belief that I was good enough academically to compete with the top students in my class. While I was not as successful as I was in college, I was in the upper twenty percent of my class and, given the rigors of the schedule, I was fine with that. Second, I had started talking to a really pretty secretary at the firm where I was a law clerk; but, I was scared because she seemed to like me. Over the course of a few months, we became friends and I wanted to ask her out but couldn't muster the courage or find the right words. Finally, one Friday, I stuttered them out and we began dating. I learned that I wasn't a total nerd and there was some hope for me. To impress the young lady, I started buying nicer clothes and having my hair cut by a stylist instead of Joe the barber (where fruit in season and golf balls were also sold). Our romance quickly flourished and within a year of our first date we were engaged. Looking back, it was a tragic mistake. While we would have been good for each other, we both carried a lot of baggage into the relationship which would eventually crush our marriage.

We were married just before I commenced my last year in school. Money was tight and our schedules prohibited us from spending much time together. When we did catch up, it was either happy talk or beer talk. We never discussed what was going on in our marriage or what factors were influencing us. More tragically, we never discussed what happened in our respective lives before we dated. It was as if we both hoped that our marriage would destroy the skeletons that we carried to the altar. In any event, at that moment, we were young and in love – the last year of school and the future was bright. I was going to be a lawyer. What was there to be unhappy about?

The next few years were crazy good. I started a job with a law firm and my accounting degree came in handy. Mostly, I worked on drafting tax opinions for public offerings. I loved both the technical side of the income tax implications of the offerings and the interaction with other professionals that was required to properly draft the documents. I began to see where the law was heading and I could design IPOs and offerings that anticipated trends others did not see.

Soon, my reputation grew and I was making speeches before other lawyers and writing articles for professional publications. The time pressures were enormous but the compensation package more than rewarded me for the effort.

For the first time in my life, personal possessions meant something to me and things like vacations, new cars, hand-made suits, fancy dinners, concerts and theatre were part of my world. I loved bringing home unexpected gifts to my wife. Then, our first child was born and we carried him home to our first new house. I was on cloud nine. I had a beautiful wife whom I adored and a baby boy who I was certain was going to be the President someday. Who'd a-thunk that a kid that started from a world that consisted of two city blocks could have all this?

Things were very good and improved rapidly. I started my own practice which expanded quickly. Soon, I would have associates, partners, secretaries and my name on the door. The hard work paid dividends financially as my wife and I bought whatever we wanted. There was no such thing as a budget for us. We paid cash for everything and it looked like it would never end. More enjoyably, people treated me differently than I was accustomed to. I had shaken my past and overcome my beginnings as a lonely nerd who was scared of his own shadow. I was recognized everywhere I traveled in the small community where my family lived. Everyone was asking me to join this golf club or that business organization. People seemed to want to associate with me and that was a new experience for me. Up to then, I was the intelligent, nerdy type. But, believe me, having people respect and admire me was a thrill unto itself. Life was a lark at Palisades Park.

But life, and especially relationships, require work. While I went to work every day and put in long hours, there was no balance to my life. It was all work, and while the money would smooth the bumps over for a time, eventually I had to face the fact that my wife and I were drifting apart. The baggage that we carried into our marriage was slowly but surely eroding our relationship. Then, I realized that I was working seven days a week to avoid the realization that my marriage was failing. As I considered my alternatives, I concluded that I was so hung up on "being somebody" that I failed to work on our relationship in order to make it thrive. Then, the practice began to suffer as the economy slowed down and, to maintain the elaborate lifestyle that we enjoyed, I stole funds from my clients' escrow accounts.

At first, I lied to myself by rationalizing that I was "borrowing" the money. To repay the initial "borrowings," I stole more money by offering shares in "sham" corporations that I created. Before I knew it, I was forging documents to funnel client funds into my personal bank accounts. My depravity reached its nadir when I forged a Federal Judge's signature to steal funds from a probate estate.

I was constantly robbing Peter to partially repay Paul. The public was at risk and they didn't know it. In reality, they didn't stand a chance when I was on the phone. On a daily basis, my professional life was spinning further out of control. The worse part was that, to a logical person, everything I did was totally illogical but to me, given my "scrambled egg" mindset, it was all part of the perfect "end game" where everything would fall into place and work out. As I gyrated from scam to scam, partners and clients abandoned me as I wallowed in an ever mounting pile of debt. Before I knew it, I had stolen over 1.2 million dollars. Accounting for where it went was useless. It simply wasn't there anymore. I figured the only way to repay that amount was to work the phones for more money; a perverse game of dialing for dollars.

On a personal level, my home life was ruined as my wife suspected that something was terribly wrong despite my protestations to the contrary. She confronted me by saying that my personality had changed and that I was upset and nervous all the time. Once she started receiving telephone calls at home from irate victims, she insisted that I straighten out the mess. That resulted in a constant, full-blown screaming match between us. Our home had become a war zone where hatred and loathing replaced love and nurturing. Our children were traumatized over the tension and bickering between mommy and daddy. All the happy sounds of childhood were silenced as our children waited stiltedly for mommy and daddy to start arguing again. I wanted so badly to be a good parent and create a home environment that would enable them to thrive and grow properly. Sadly, my hopes and dreams were all crumbling before my eyes. I felt trapped in a deceitful web of my own making and didn't know where to go; what to do or whom to talk to. How could I explain the train wreck that my life had become?

And suddenly, it came to a crashing halt when my secretary handed me a target letter from the FBI. My heart throbbed, as my pulse pounded within me, when I realized that the government knew all my dirt. Soon, the world would.

This is my story. I hope you enjoy it. More importantly, I pray you learn from it.

Dan Holmes

1

A Not So Typical Day

So...
　　long...
　　　　ago...

I was in a rush, as usual. It was the story of my life. I had to file a Motion with a District Court Judge by the end of the day and I was only half done. Another day doomed to overload.

I had been awake since five o'clock and had arrived at the office before six. My skull was throbbing from the consumption of too much alcohol the night before. Despite the pain, I considered the headache a small price to pay for my success. Here I was, at age thirty-eight, a respected lawyer; in fact, I was the managing partner of a three partner law firm. Ten years ago, the office was headquartered in a spare bedroom of my marital residence. Now, I had partners, chair rails, diplomas and secretaries scurrying about.

I was highly thought of in the community but no one knew the real me. Success had changed, better make that destroyed, me. I morphed into a sarcastic asshole who thought he was better, and knew more, than everyone else. On top of that, I was a drunk. I told myself that my constant drinking was a necessary part of the wining and dining that was required to generate business. In reality, it was a way to self medicate the pain from a broken marriage and the hatred of what I had become.

It was about eleven o'clock. I was standing behind my desk staring at the telephone messages Annie had placed on my chair. I had just left Charlie Crawford crying in the small conference room that adjoined my office. Charlie was a golfing buddy, a banker, and a pillar of the community. Oh,—and Charlie had a big problem.

According to the FBI, Charlie had conspired to defraud his employer, a federally insured bank. The purported scheme involved Charlie and an electrical contractor, a customer of the bank for over twenty years. Two years ago, Amp-It-Up, Inc., choking on its fixed debt that accrued interest at credit card rates, wanted to consolidate the obligation into a lower rate commercial bank loan. Amp-It-Up's owner asked Charlie to review his loan request and tweak it to assure approval by the loan committee. Charlie, the conservative church-going banker that he was, sought and received many verbal assurances that the loan would be paid on time and in full.

Amp-It-Up received approval for a loan in an amount near the bank's single customer legal lending limit. The bank would be financially impaired if the loan was not repaid.

For a while payments were prompt, but with new construction in a slump, due dates were missed and double payments had to be made to catch up. Eventually, the loan fell ninety days delinquent. After a number of ever more urgent collection calls, a check was received.

When that check bounced, the federal examiners, who happened to be conducting a routine examination of the bank's loan files, started reviewing the Amp-It-Up files.

Six months later, and the day before a court hearing on a motion to enter judgment in the bank's favor, Amp-It-Up filed a Petition in Bankruptcy.

The examiners started interviewing bank personnel.

Vice President Charles D. Crawford cooperated.

Charlie admitted quite freely that he'd advised Amp-It-Up on how to prepare the loan request and that he had failed to disclose his participation during the loan committee presentation. Charlie headed the retail division, not commercial lending. By the time the U.S. Attorney's Office leaked the story to the press, it sounded as if Charlie had prepared the loan request in return for unspecified consideration, and then had supported the loan in committee without disclosing his prior involvement.

For more than a year, a storm brewed as the bank struggled to stay solvent. Charlie lived with an ever-darkening cloud over his head and the burden affected him. At the country club's lounge, where our small circle of friends often congregated, his wife Becky mentioned out-loud the concern she had about his weight loss, which was evident. They'd been married eighteen years.

"He's edgy," she'd say when Charlie was out of earshot. "And he's in his own little world most of the time. Daydreaming. Don't you see it? It's hard to get his attention sometimes. He needs to see a doctor. You're his buddies. Convince him to go see the doctor."

So we'd ask him what was going on.

"Oh, I'm just under a lot of stress at work," Charlie would say casually with a worried expression on his face.

Charlie's uncertain fear had turned into harsh reality about three hours ago when the FBI showed up at the bank and met with the bank's president. Technically, the agents didn't have an appointment, but their business cards and physical presence secured an audience. They were behind closed doors for about an hour before the president came out and motioned for Charlie to come in.

The agents were standing when Charlie entered. The president said he would be "just outside" and closed the door as he left.

"Are you Charles D. Crawford?" said the smaller of the two agents.

"Yes."

"This is Special Agent Barkley, and I'm Special Agent Franks."

No one held out a hand.

"Okay," said Charlie after a moment.

"Why don't we have a seat?"

The agent motioned toward the conference room table.

Despite being in familiar surroundings, Charlie felt strangely uncomfortable.

When they were settled, agents on one side, Charlie on the other, Special Agent Franks started, "Well, Mr. Crawford, you no doubt know why we are here. Now, please let me advise you that you don't have to answer any questions, but you can help yourself if you cooperate voluntarily…"

Charlie was so relieved that the ordeal was finally coming to a head, and he could explain once and for all what happened and get everything off his chest. He rattled along answering questions for about ten minutes when he was asked, "Did you receive any consideration from Amp-it-Up to prepare the loan request?"

Then he realized where the conversation was headed.

"Hey," asked Charlie in a surprised tone of voice. "Am I a suspect? Do I need an attorney?"

"Well," Special Agent Franks explained. "You can have an attorney if you want. Anybody can have an attorney any time they want, as we know from TV. But right now it would be better if you stayed and continued to cooperate as you've been doing. This is routine as I said." He looked at Special Agent Barkley for a moment. "You're really helping yourself so far."

To his credit, Charlie didn't buy it.

"I want an attorney."

"You can do that if you want. It'd be a shame to stop the progress we've been making."

"I want my attorney," repeated Charlie, semi-demanding; semi-scared shitless.

"Okay."

Special Agent Franks nodded to his partner.

Special Agent Barkley opened a file and handed a single typed sheet to Charlie.

"Then I am obligated to see that you receive this document," he said handing the paper to Charlie.

Charlie read the letter. Then read it again, mouthing the words a little as he proceeded line by line.

"I think I'll excuse myself now," said Charlie standing up; now totally scared shitless.

He walked out of the bank; proceeded to his car and drove straight to my office.

I was in a meeting with clients in one of the large conference rooms when he arrived. The receptionist sent a runner around the floor to locate me.

"He's here?" I inquired after I'd read his name on the folded paper I'd been handed.

"Yes, sir."

This was out of character for Charlie. He didn't make business or social calls without an appointment. He was a banker, very proper.

"Now would be a good time to see him if you could, sir."

This was office code-speak for an emergency; one of those unavoidable interruptions lawyers hate.

"There's a golfing pal of mine out in the lobby," I fibbed to the group around the table. "I'll just be a few minutes. He probably scored two holes in one and wants to show me his balls."

I smiled and received smiles in return as I left.

I hurried around the work cubicles to the lobby door and passed through it ready to shake Charlie's hand. At first I didn't see him. Mine was a modest firm with a large reception space that contained three sitting areas sufficiently apart to facilitate private conversations and to project an air of grandeur beyond the firm's true stature. A perception and reality thing. One sitting area had a group of clients chuckling over some joke. The second one by the kitchen was empty. Then I saw Charlie bent over in a leather wing chair with his head and shoulders on his knees as if he were on an airplane headed for a water landing.

The smile dropped from my face. "Charlie?"

He picked up his head and appeared close to tears. My level of concern increased. "What's wrong?"

"Dan," he choked off my name in a whisper. "Oh, Dan."

He stood up as if he were a stiff old man struggling through arthritis.

Come with me," I said taking one of his hands in mine and putting my other hand on his shoulder to steer him across the lobby.

"That's it, Charlie. It's all right. Let's go where we can have some privacy and you can tell me what's happened. It'll be okay. Right this way, Charlie. Through here to the right."

I kept up the chatter until I could seat him in the little conference room next to my office. I told Beth, one of my two administrative assistants, to make excuses to the clients in the other meeting. I would return to them as soon as I could.

Beth asked, "What should I tell them?"

I was way too busy mentally at that moment to provide her with a convenient lie so I threw her under the bus with, "Beth, that's why you make the big bucks. Tell them whatever you think will work. Just go for it and smile a lot. You'll be fine."

Then, in front of Charlie, I set out a bottle of Coke, poured some over a crystal glass of ice, and opened a couple of Captain Morgan Spiced Rum minis. I could supply him with any type of alcohol he wanted from my office bar but I knew from the golf club that the good Captain was his drink of choice.

Given copious amount of alcohol and sufficient patience, honest clients will reveal all. Charlie complied. He poured out everything. I asked a lot of questions to comprehend the events as I took appropriate notes. Created a time-line. I knew Charlie to be a forthright person. After all, a golfer knows if his partner plays according to the rules.

Charlie seemed much better after unloading the entire story and having consumed two more minis to finish the bottle of Coke. He seemed relieved; the burden shared; his catharsis complete.

From what I could see, Charlie had gotten involved in a series of events that the feds could manipulate and make him look bad even if Charlie's only benefit was heartburn. Amp-It-Up had blown a fuse (pardon the pun) and someone's head had to roll. Maybe Charlie had made a mistake. Maybe he hadn't.

"What's gonna happen next?" he asked.

I had the response memorized. I'd been in litigation for more than eleven years and I knew the investigative process. I told Charlie that he'd received a target letter that the feds issue when they were about to convene a grand jury and seek an indictment against someone for the charges outlined in the letter.

"Do you think I'll get indicted?"

"Charlie. When the government sends out a target letter, it is a near-certainty that they will secure an indictment. You know the old joke. They can indict a ham sandwich."

That stopped his breathing for a few seconds.

"Am I going to jail?"

That's the killer question because the percentages favor the feds who have unlimited resources, manpower, and time. Prosecution is the name of their business. The cold hard fact is that the government obtains a conviction in over ninety-eight percent of the cases they pursue.

Hence my answer so as not to be accused of sugar-coating anything later.

"Charlie. The target letter means they've already done their home-work. The grand jury will indict you. Once you're indicted, we can try to plea it down. From what I know right now, you might end up having to do a bit of time."

He put his head on his forearms on top of the table and cried like the saddest person the world had ever seen. I removed a box of tissues from the credenza and nudged his hand with the corner of the box so he'd take it. He didn't look up.

"Here, Charlie," I said in the bedside manner voice I saved for such occasions. I pulled a tissue and placed it in his hand. "It's a long process. They have to do every step just right. I'll be watching and talking to them to see what evidence they have. It might not be as bad as you think it is. I won't lie to you. When the feds come after some-body, they get something from them. Now that you have a target letter, you better prepare yourself for a few harsh months, even years. And you have to keep your head on straight all the time."

This was so unusual for me. None of that good-hearted comic-sarcasm I entertained Charlie with on the golf course.

I said, "As soon as an indictment is handed down, the case will be published in the newspapers and on television. The media have report-ers hanging around grand juries to review new indictments. That'll be in about a month or so. Everything is supposed to be secret until then. That's why you're so surprised right now—it's been a secret. You're going to have to be strong from here on out. You'll have to adjust to that feeling of helplessness you have right now. There's nothing you can do to make it go away."

Such is the fate of the accused.

I kept talking, trying to soothe without being too hopeful. Until I saw what evidence the feds had, it would be better to impart the worst.

I turned the discussion to finances and I informed him that he should start looking for new employment since he soon would be an ex-bank vice-president. Be sure the life and health insurance is up to date. Put available cash in an out-of-state bank account in Becky's maiden name in case there was a restraining order on assets. Pay eve-rything with credit cards. Hoard cash. Let the utilities go unpaid for a while since they are hard to shut off; babies might freeze. Might have to sell the house. Becky might have to get a job. I didn't mention the near certainty of divorce.

Talking about how to protect himself seemed to help him gather his wits.

"Let me check on the meeting I was in when you arrived, Charlie," I said when he was strong enough to be left alone. "I need to see how they're doing. I'll be back in a few minutes."

"How do I tell Becky?" he asked wiping his eyes.

Normally I would have said something like, "When she doesn't have a knife in her hand," but instead I stalled for time.

"Let me think about which words to pick. Meanwhile, I'll have someone get you something to eat."

I left the door open and went out to my two administrative assistants' desks. Beth was there.

"Please get Charlie a bagel with cream cheese. He likes that. He's a friend of mine so sit with him and chit-chat until I get back."

The firm hadn't had a client throw himself through the window of our thirty-seventh floor office and I wanted that record to stay intact.

I walked around a chair-railed wall through the door to my office.

I stood behind my desk and took a deep, relaxing breath. My head was still pounding from a night out with my friend, Jack Daniels. A collection of papers, mail, books, folders, and documents stared back at me. I was the height of disorganization and never put anything into its proper place. Annie, my legal administrative assistant, first employee, and "right arm" had placed a stack of telephone messages on my chair seat as was her habit. They would be lost on the desk. I stared at them. There were usually about ten for the amount of time I'd been away at the other meeting and with Charlie. There must have been fifty messages this time. They would have to wait. They were other people's headaches, anyway.

Annie came in.

"Open a file for *U.S. v. Charlie Crawford.* Start the billing when he came in and asked for me."

"The U.S. Attorney's Office faxed over a target letter," she said as she ignored my request.

I looked at her.

She had the fax in her hand. She held it out.

I smiled.

This was good news and meant another new client for the firm. I knew about the problems of cash flow. Practices the size of mine required a constant flow of new clients to satisfy financial obligations. I had to make it rain in the desert every day to keep the associates busy. A target letter was a good thing.

"Who is it?" I asked as I mentally scanned the list of clients who were awaiting such a communication.

Annie's face took on a mixed expression of anger and disappointment. I didn't know what to make of it.

"You!"

"Me?!"

"Yes, Dan. You!" This was her end-of-the-world look. "It references the conspiracy and RICO statutes."

Oh, no!

My legs buckled as I plopped down in my chair.

Oh my God, no!

Somebody compared the signatures!

2

Attorney Meeting

One hundred and twenty-three months ago…

I stood on the Center City sidewalk in front of *One Liberty Place* waiting for my attorney. This would be the last meeting we would have before the press swarmed. I was wearing a double-breasted gray pin stripe suit with a blue silk tie and matching handkerchief. My French-cuff shirt was pale blue with gold cufflinks on the doubled sleeves. I appeared as prosperous as ever, but was a bit rag-tag from not having dry cleaned my suits in more than two months. I previously had them laundered after every wearing. I glanced down at my Italian-made Testoni shoes, the last one's I'd bought before I drifted into a life based on thrift. I wondered for a moment if I could sell them for half the twelve hundred dollars I'd paid. They were nearly new. I decided I might get fifty bucks for them. Ah, the price of failure.

"How are you, Dan?" asked my lawyer Steve Kaufman by way of greeting as he approached. Steve was one of the most sophisticated attorneys in the area. He was highly respected by his criminal law practicing peers for his intelligence, insight and integrity. Now in his mid-fifties, he had that air of confidence that originates from having a track record loaded with success. He was a big-ticket item from a big-name downtown firm. At one time, my goal was to be as highly re-spected in the legal community as Steve was.

We shook hands. "I'm okay," I replied without much thought.

"You ready?"

"As ready as ever for my execution."

"It's not going to be like that." He was doing a bad job of acting now. I'd worked cases with him long enough to recognize it. "Some-times you are so morbid." He smiled.

"Well, sometimes I feel like I'm already dead."

"Oh, you're not dead. Far from it."

This was the same sort of encouragement I would offer my clients before a pressure-packed meeting like the one we were about to attend. I didn't want my client to suffer unnecessarily, and Steve didn't want that to happen to me.

I patted myself on the back.

"Buckle-up, Danny boy. This shall be your red badge of courage for all to see."

"That's the spirit."

I didn't think he heard me.

He headed to the brass lined revolving glass doors of the building. I followed him and stared at the way he held his briefcase.

"This too shall pass," I whispered to myself. "This too shall pass." Once inside, the security station upset the building's elegant lobby of polished stone, wood, and brass and brought the rich entryway down to reality. We emptied our pockets into plastic baskets and Steve put his briefcase on the rollers to be scanned. He walked through the arch. I did the same. After we'd gathered our effects, he led me aside and whispered a final piece of legal advice.

"Remember, don't say anything. This is a reverse proffer and all we have to do is listen. Let's hear the evidence, at least the evidence they tell us about."

I insisted, thinking I still had Constitutional rights, "They have to let us see the evidence they have. It's the law."

That was the attorney in me defending an idiotic client.

"Your license is in abeyance, Dan. You have to rely on mine. Just be quiet no matter what happens."

I nodded.

This was the third such session. I knew the drill. Steve didn't trust the feds to tell him the correct day of the week.

"Take notes if you must to stay busy. Try not to blink your eyes a lot. Don't look guilty."

I had those instructions memorized. I was adding them to my arsenal of things to say to my clients when this was over. We headed to the elevator. Steve pressed the call button. While we waited, he repeated the wisdom that he imparted at the first two proffers.

"Assume the elevator and the lobby are bugged. Don't say anything."

We stepped into the elevator and Steve pushed the button for the seventh floor. The ride lasted less than a minute even with someone getting on at four and off at five. Couldn't use the stairways in this high-security building.

When the doors opened, we faced the lobby of the U.S. Attorney's Office. I'd been here dozens of times before in Steve's role, but the last two trips here had been different. My swagger and passion as an advocate were gone. It's easy to project a certain swash-swash buckle-buckle attitude when the client has the risk.

Steve approached the glass-protected reception window and looked around for a person to receive us. I saw his fingernails were shiny from a manicure as he tapped on the glass.

"Hello?" he announced in a conversational tone.

We waited.

I wasn't eager to proceed.

A young woman walked by in the background and saw us. She motioned to someone she could see but we could not.

A man in a motorized wheelchair drove up to the window, put the brake on his chair, and pressed a button that raised the floor so his head was at window height.

"May I help you?" he asked.

"We have an appointment to see Greg Marshall, please. Dan Holmes and Steve Kaufman."

Greg Marshall was the Assistant U.S. Attorney assigned to my case. Greg Marshall and I, well, we didn't mix. Not since I'd beat him a few years before in the Gurrelle case. Marshall had an elephant's memory now that my skin was on the line.

"I will let him know that you are here."

The man put an earwig in his ear and punched numbers on a telephone console.

We took a seat.

The truth was Marshall thought I was a scumbag, and I thought Marshall was Darth Vader; lording over everyone who Marshall proclaimed was "unworthy."

Marshall opened a door to the reception area beside the glass wall and motioned for us to follow. He escorted us down a short hallway into a meeting room where three other government attorneys were waiting. Marshall turned around and shook hands with Steve and then introduced him to everyone else.

"This is Dan Holmes," Steve said on my behalf. I felt like a leper because I received simple "nods" but certainly no handshakes. They didn't want to touch me.

We sat down.

The session lasted about a half-hour.

For me it seemed like three hours. This was business as usual for them; what they did for a living. They were calmly and coldly talking about the evil events in my life. I wanted to die. Hearing the gruesome details of my mistakes was difficult.

I was referred to in such endearing terms as "him," "the perp," "the offender," and "the supposed accused." I was way more than "a person of interest."

True to instructions, I stayed silent, watching the wheels of justice turn. Since I'd refused to plea, the arraignment date was scheduled and the last minutes of the meeting were devoted to housekeeping items. When would evidence and witness lists be exchanged? Let's make sure our calendars agree. Were my income tax filings current? Was there any activity I'd like to make them aware of? What would be the asked-for bond amount? Steve answered everything for me.

Just before we adjourned Steve said, "Dan is going to accompany me to the arraignment. I will assure you and the Court of his appearance. Is that all right with you?"

This seemed to present an unidentified problem. They already had my passport. Only severe flight risks are taken into custody before arraignment. I wasn't running. I had nowhere to go and nothing to go there with.

The other side of the table rolled their chairs into a circle and consulted with each other in professional whispers. I could see facial expressions take on a serious demeanor, but I could not hear a word. After a minute and a half, they broke up and rolled their chairs back under the table.

Without looking at me, Marshall said to Steve, "If I concede this point, I'll have to redo some paperwork and it may be too late to reverse what's in process."

I knew that he was telling me, through Steve, that he had ordered the U.S. Marshals to pick me up and have me "locked up" so that I couldn't continue playing "dialing for dollars."

Suddenly, my level of hopelessness increased as I realized my freedom was now subject to the whims of the U.S. Attorney's office. In a few days, the U.S. Marshals would be knocking on my door and the person known as Dan Holmes the attorney would be gone and soon forgotten.

3

Capture

One hundred eight months, and six days ago…

Back then, there were a few dregs left of my life. I worked out early in the morning before hitting rush hour. I wanted to be in the office by seven, so the coffeemaker went off at four-twenty, and the alarm clock at four-thirty. That provided me an hour for weight lifting or running before the long commute. I hated working out, really hated it, but it did relieve stress and I was under a lot of stress.

"How soon?" I would ask Steve.

"Any day now," he would reply.

At least he was right on that one.

I needed to know "when" since the thought of "when" was consuming my life. Friends called and asked me how I was doing. They were looking to see if I were still here. A perverse death watch.

That particular October morning was like most others at four thirty-one. I was sitting up and technically a free man, not quite caught as I soon would be, but not free either. I put on my glasses, wobbled into the kitchen, poured a cup of black coffee and carried it with me as I did the usual duties upon first awaking. I was wearing the same T-shirt and boxers I'd slept in. I wandered into an empty bedroom to stretch. Today was weight lifting. Tomorrow, if I were still here tomorrow, I would run.

I was living in what previously was one massive beach house that was converted into eight condo units. An eighth of the former beach house was now my primary residence. I moved here about three months ago. The tension at home was unbearable. My soon-to-be-ex-wife and I only spoke when we argued and we argued constantly. We weren't trying to cover up our mutual disdain and, day by day, the degree of erosion in our relationship worsened. We tried counseling but that was a waste of money. Neither one of us listened to what the doctor advised. We were cemented in our positions and determined not to give in. The impact on our children was obvious. Instead of living in a home encased with love, they were subjected to the open hatred exhibited by their parents. The emotions of the children were fragile and their need for peace was palpable. To defuse the situation, I relocated to the beach house. It would be a temporary move at best.

While I was limbering hamstrings and calves in the darkness, I heard a clattering sound overhead like small animals scurrying across a roof.

Then I heard muffled voices coming through the window screens. I gagged on a sickening realization.

Could *this* be it?

Panic overtook me. My head was spinning and I was having trouble keeping my thoughts straight. Right until this point, I deluded myself into believing that the problem would go away. Somehow, I would be able to explain what happened and that would be the end of the matter. I would resume my legal practice and start over. But the sound resonating from the roof changed that. I swallowed hard and tried to calm myself. It didn't work. Reality told me that my descent into the abyss would continue with no end in sight.

Steve promised me that I could self-surrender before the Indictment. The Assistant U.S. Attorney had said so. I heard him myself. What happened to the deal!? What was going on? Why hadn't Steve called and told me that the plans had changed? Why was the U.S. Attorney's office fucking with me?

I pushed myself up from the floor and walked to the window overlooking the central courtyard. I couldn't see anyone in the moonlight. I went to the sliding glass door, opened it without much noise and peeked over the rail.

I didn't breathe as I listened. A clattering equipment sound below my unit made me pull my head back. Then came a clunking sound like a piece of metal hitting wood. I peeked over the rail again. Couldn't see anything. The decorative outside lights around the courtyard were turned off. That was strange and contrary to the Condo Association guidelines. A radio voice from below said, "Back door secure."

"Front door ready for breach." This was a voice from below.

"Anyone not set?"

A pause followed, then a loud barking, "Go! Go! Go!"

Four men rushed the door across the courtyard holding a log-shaped object between them. They rammed it headlong into a solid wood door that cracked vertically with the grain. Once the door splintered, the men dropped the battering ram and wrestled with the pieces of the door, its hinges and security chains. The door never had a chance, but the security chains held the wood to the jamb and the door's cross-members wouldn't surrender.

"Crowbars. Get the crowbars on it!" commanded the voice from below.

I thought to myself, "Wow! What did Ms. Kroposky do?" I started clinging to the hope that they were here to arrest her.

A radio voice cracked, "Back bedroom clear."

Another voice said, "Laundry room clear."

The men at the front door were battling the security chains. They wore body armor and a lot of equipment making them appear like robots. The door had caved in but remained sufficiently intact to prevent their entry. Plus, a Johnny Bar buttressed the door on the inside. The helmeted men were prying the jamb away from the sides of the door and pushing it inside. Ms. Kroposky was afraid of "daughter-rapers." She had about six locks, chains and a Johnny Bar bolted to the floor on the inside.

I watched, fascinated.

This was some sort of sanctioned raid stymied for the moment by the defenses of Ms. Kroposky.

"Three seconds!" screamed the voice below me. "The front door is *supposed* to take three seconds, you piss-ants! I count sixteen… seventeen… eighteen… nineteen… Push it in, Reynolds! No, no, no! You fuck-ups!"

At last they were in. The man below me walked out far enough for me to see him. He had a clipboard and a gun.

Sounds of thumping blows and objects falling came from inside. No lights were lit. Voices shouted orders too indistinct to discern. Women screamed back and forth.

The man below me barked into his lapel mike, "Go off night vision. Turn on the lights."

The windows lit up from inside, not like a flashlight, but much brighter, closer to a blinding white light.

More voices.

"Bring out Bogie One," commanded the man below me. He threw a beam of light like a Klieg on the courtyard below me.

Ms. Kroposky came through the bashed-in front door in her nightgown followed by a team member with a no nonsense face. He held a Taser at her back and pushed her forward with it. He instructed her to lie on the ground.

"Bogie Two is a teenage girl," someone said over the radio.

"Bring out Bogie Two," ordered the commander.

"Got a Bogie under the bed," said the radio.

"That's gotta be Holmes," said the commander with a hint of satisfaction in his voice. "Piece of shit like him hiding under the bed like a scared bitch."

My stomach shot to my throat.

Oh my God! They're here for me!

My world stopped at that moment. All I could do was stare at Ms. Kroposky; unable to move my eyes from the look of fear on her face.

Another helmeted man, a brawny one with a menacing machine gun, pushed Sandy, Ms. Kroposky's middle daughter, out of the unit. The man held her by her long blonde hair. He instructed her to lie down next to her mother, and then he shoved her. Sandy was rolling as she hit the lawn. Her nightshirt twisted up in a mess and tangled around her waist. Her long blonde hair was a spider's web. A college sophomore, she was near tears and wide-eyed.

"Bogie Three coming out."

Jessica, Ms. Kroposky's eldest, came out in a T-shirt and panties followed by another helmeted man pushing her by the neck. When they were next to her mother and sister, the man dropped her to the ground with a sweep of his leg.

"Ow!" she screamed. "That hurt!"

"Bogie Four is a little girl," the radio said.

"Damn!" said the commander. Then he said into his mike, "Bring her out and clear the unit."

I gulped air for the first time since I'd heard my name, unaware that I'd been holding my breath. I made enough noise to be heard down below, but no one noticed. I tried to keep myself together and not panic, but it was too late for that. My heart was ready to jump out of my chest.

Nevaeh, the third child, a middle-schooler, came out followed by another man, this one wearing goggles. He guided the little girl over to the other three.

I swayed away from the rail and crawled into my unit. I felt close to throwing up. I crept to an open window and listened as Jessica, Sandy, Nevaeh and Ms. Kroposky were identified and told to stand.

"Saddle up for upstairs," ordered the commander sounding frustrated.

This was surreal, in America of all places, land of the free, home of the brave. Seeing Jessica taken down at the knees made me wonder what they would do to me, because *they were coming after me!* The other six units in the complex were vacant, this being the off-season, and a weekday.

"It's the other unit," I heard the commander say. "Let's move."

They pounded up the wooden stairs.

I was trapped. I could hear the men on the roof repositioning themselves so they could point their guns at me from the opposite roof.

I had to think fast. When I was "doing my thing," that came easy but this was different. There'd be no conversation here. No bullshit flowing. Whatever I came up with here would have to be more visual than verbal. The right thing to do would be to surrender but I didn't have the "balls" to do that.

I tiptoed into the bathroom, stepped into the tub, pulled the shower curtain across the rod, and turned on the shower. The cold spray bit into my skin through my T-shirt and shorts. I grabbed the soap and kneeled down soaking my hair. By the time the water was warm, I had a head full of soap.

Through the bottom of the tub I could feel the vibration of heavy boots. It seemed as if the men were all around me. I let the water run down part of my face and pulled the shower curtain back about a foot.

The bathroom door burst open.

In my best little kid's voice I called out, "I thought you went to work, Ma." I closed my eyes and had soap and water running down my face. My head was about two feet over the edge of the tub. I opened one eye and saw a U.S. Marshal six feet away. I reclosed my eye.

"Ma? Is that you, Ma?"

I heard the man leave. I cracked an eye. No one was there. The door was left open.

On my hands and knees, I bowed my head forward to rinse off the soap. I was a goner. I stood up and stripped off my shirt and shorts. I then washed, shaved, shampooed, and conditioned. I prayed that the shower would last forever. As a consolation, at least I would be clean for the Indictment.

I peered around the shower curtain resigned and beaten, expecting to see a gun barrel.

Nothing.

I toweled off and walked to the bedroom, my heart pounding hard, knowing that at any moment I would be ordered to freeze.

I crept from room to room to see if anyone was in the unit. I was alone and in awe. Nobody!

How could they have fucked up?

I poured some coffee. I wasn't shaking now. Dare I go outside? Sure.

My door had burst open from the thrust of the battering ram, the striker pushing out the wood from the jamb. I didn't have extra locks, chains and Johnny Bars on my door.

Downstairs, the building super was examining the remains of Ms. Kroposky's broken door.

"What's going on, Nick?"

He didn't look at me.

"Police raid of some kind." I walked over to him as he talked. "They done left. The lady called me. Wants a new door." He examined the splintered wood. He held up a piece of paper. I saw, "221 Westwick Unit B," written in block letters.

Nick was the condo association's maintenance man but had no clue as to any tenant's name. Ms. Kroposky had called him and given him her address. He bent over and examined the broken wood until he found the letter "B." He was verifying the address.

I added, "I need a new jamb on mine in unit 'F' upstairs. They got me too."

He looked at me for the first time—no recognition of who I might be. He lifted a pencil from his pocket and wrote "F" on his paper next to the "B."

I asked him, "Do you know who did this?"

"They give me a card to send the bill." He pulled it from his pocket and handed it to me.

Federal Bureau of Investigation, Special Agent Todd Burns.

They'd come for me, all right.

There was nothing else I could do with Nick. I handed the card back to him and climbed the stairs back to my unit.

Standing in the kitchen, sipping coffee, I surveyed my few remaining possessions. What a long fall! From eight million dollars on paper six months ago to a few well-used appliances, some pine furniture, clothes and a few personal items in this one dinky over-mortgaged condo. And soon, all too soon, this would be gone.

I stood there and looked around the room. A rush of memories from happier times flooded over me. My mind drifted back and I fought to return to the present.

No doubt the FBI would be waiting for me at my office.

I wondered why they hadn't come back into the bathroom to have a closer look at the little kid behind the shower curtain. There were no kid toys here or any women's clothes. Maybe they thought mother and son were time-sharing.

I left a message on Steve's voice mail. At least he'd know to be at the courthouse.

There was nothing else I could do. I headed for my last day of work. Usually, you receive a gold watch on such occasions. Lucky me, by the end of the day, the press would be recording my being walked out of the office in handcuffs so they could air the story on the nightly news. I could hear the anchor say, "And in our other top story, Dan Holmes, a highly respected attorney, was arrested today and charged with stealing over two million dollars from the estate of one of his clients."

This was it.

The beginning of the end.

4

Mind Games

Present day...

When the alarm goes off, I lean over and hit the snooze button. Then I lie under the covers and thank God the nightmare isn't real. By my count it's been nine months and two days; long enough to bring a baby to full term, yet the nightmares persist. Maybe there were some clean afternoon naps after a big lunch, but at night, especially the Rapid Eye Movement period from four to six is when the nightmares return. Each is different, though I'm always in the same place.

I'm back *there*.

The sights, the smells, the noises, the feelings, the touch of things are so real. Everything is so real that I may as well be back there.

I *am there*.

I'm there as if my waking hours are the dream and the nightmare is the reality. Each dream recalls another part of the prison experience. Sometimes, I'm at my "Good-Bye & Good-Luck" party; other times I'm at the clerk's desk in the Power House or some other place like the dining hall, the law library, or the main office. The list could go on and on. But, regardless of the place, the images are so powerful that I wake up and think that I'm back in jail. All the pain returns. I faced the nights with dread. As each hour passed after waking, I would become more nervous. By sundown I'd have built up a manic anxiety. At bedtime, I'd watch movies, read books, or do puzzles to keep my mind off being in jail. My goal was to fall asleep with my mind on something other than my prior existence.

I needed help. I was an emotional mess.

I tried everything I could think of to remedy this continuing stream of nightmares.

So, I took the plunge and visited a psychiatrist reputedly well practiced in the dark arts of head-shrinkery.

He called the nightmares dreams.

I expressed how disturbed I was about being free but not feeling free. As I talked, the Doctor stared at the top of my head. I suddenly was self-conscious about my tattered appearance especially since my eyeglasses were courtesy of the BOP and not exactly designer by any stretch of the imagination. As the session progressed, he occasionally glanced at the top of my head increasing my level of discomfort.

Eventually, he advised me to exorcise the dreams from my consciousness by writing them down in little vignettes using the most descriptive language I could craft. While I was doing this, I was to imagine the emotions being transferred from my spirit or self or ego onto the paper. After completing, signing and dating each story, I was to store it in an expandable file. If I dreamed the same experience again, I was to edit the story based on the more recent version. Then I was to burn the story to ashes in a ritual designed to expunge the experience in a physical sense.

"Do I start from the last dream?" I asked.

"Not necessarily. Start anywhere you like. The goal is to eradicate from your subconscious that entire segment of your life. You might start with the most common dream first, to make it a habit, and then monitor your progress. Keep me informed."

"Burn the stories?" I repeated. My inner voice was speaking out loud now. "Sounds like Voodoo. Do you guarantee this will work? My electrician guarantees his work."

"There are no guarantees," replied the doctor. "That's why they call what I do a 'practice'." He stood up from his chair. "I'm afraid that's all the time we have for today. Please pay my assistant before you leave."

I stood up to leave and noticed that there was a wall clock hung on the wall behind where I was sitting. It read ten of two. Nine months after I'm released and I'm still stressing every little thing.

That was it—the fast food equivalent of psychiatry in a fifty minute session. I couldn't afford the never-ending fifty-two week plan.

I paid cash and left.

5

The Scaffold

Arrival...

My cousin Emily's green Taurus had passed through a series of near-abandoned mining towns. From the research I'd done, coal mining, once the dominant industry here, was long dead. Our destination had replaced the mines as the primary employer. I was in the back seat as I stared at the emptiness in silence. I felt like the dead man in a funeral procession, unable to speak or move.

As we crawled along, I reviewed the highlights of my first forty years on God's green earth, decent—except for that one series of events. I'd worked hard through college and law school. Then I'd worked harder for my wife and children as I climbed the ladder of success. I started my own practice and, as the office expanded, I'd lost control. Personal issues took a backseat to business. My life had come crashing down. Now, as I'd done so often lately, I struggled with the pain and humiliation I'd brought upon those closest to me. Sometimes I contemplated suicide to end my pain, but I never advanced past the 'idea' stage.

I had few friends left. My cousin Emily was one. My mother, Mary, sat in the front passenger's seat. Both stared ahead. Emily watched the road and drove carefully; mom traveled as if comatose. The radio seemed not to matter.

I wondered what would happen over the next ninety-six months. Eight years seemed like an eternity to live in a world that I knew nothing about except what I'd seen in movies or read in books.

So often these days my thoughts turned religious to seek comfort and guidance. I pondered the workings of God a lot. Where did I go wrong? Why didn't God stop me? Then I realized that I'd lived without God until I faced this tragedy and then I prayed for Him to rescue me.

It seemed hypocritical and natural at the same time.

I saw a clock on the side of a bank. I was worried about arriving on time. Check-in was noon and "not a minute later" I'd been told on the phone, in writing, and again when I'd called to confirm my arrival earlier that morning. It was just after eleven. Emily was a careful driver, though slow. I wondered how much longer it would take to get there. Where were we anyway? I wasn't certain we were on the right road. What if we weren't? What if there was a tie-up? What would happen if I arrived there late? The smallest abnormalities wrecked me emotionally. I hadn't slept well the past few nights. Right then, fear gripped me, twisting my insides. Maybe we should stop and call? A panic attack was on the horizon.

By quarter past eleven we were at the intersection of US Routes Twenty and Seventy. Now we were close, and I felt better. We crossed Route Seventy and then slowed down as we searched for the entrance, the ladies in front whispering opinions to each other in soft voices. An obscure turn-off appeared that led to a pitted gravel road up a mountain. Was this the entrance? It was unmarked and nondescript, avoiding public attention.

A two-lane road twisted up a mountain through a grove of thick trees. At the top the road turned right and changed to lined blacktop. The trees on either side overlapped, forming a canopy. Despite the midday hour and a bright sun, the way was dark and foreboding. On the right, a driveway appeared that led to a parking lot. Two buildings were on each side of the lot. A few cars were present, but otherwise it was deserted. No signs identified buildings, no directional arrows, no handicap parking. Anyone who needed a sign to tell them where they were didn't belong here. No birds. No squirrels.

We went further up the mountain and then down the other side to find a building on the right along a flat stretch. This resembled the facility described in the letter. A parking lot for about fifty cars contained ten. One was a dented "K" car. Most were in need of paint and trim. All of them showed rust. The only apparent time they were washed was when God rained on them. The pick-up trucks had gun racks inside the back windows. Despite being deep in the coalmining country of Pennsylvania, two cars had Confederate flag stickers on the bumpers.

Emily parked the car and turned off the radio before shutting down the engine. An uncomfortable silence followed. Until the last half-hour, the ladies had been silent or chit-chatted about deceased relatives. Now that we'd arrived, they stared at the block building and the crumbling asphalt in silence.

Signs in the lot reserved spaces for "Official Visitor," "Administrator," "Staff Only," and "Officer of the Month." Emily parked with the nose of the Taurus facing the building's entrance. The walls were cinderblock and were painted tan. A small patio was on the right and windows were on the left. The single entry door was black metal. With no flowers, bushes, or trees, it resembled a blockhouse. No litter. The area looked sucked bare by a giant vacuum.

My thoughts returned to the metaphysical. In an analogy to the question of life after death, I wondered what life was like on the other side of the black door.

To the right of the main building, up a slope, sat two, four-story block buildings. As we watched, a horde of men dressed in khaki raced down the hill toward the building we were facing, the fastest dozen or so in front. One man tripped and knocked down three or four of those behind him. It looked like a stampede run amok. The second four-story building was further up the hill and farther away. A khaki mass poured from it as well and swarmed down the hill. At the main building confusion reigned. It reminded me of South American soccer fans crushing themselves to death.

After a minute or so, everyone turned around and trudged back up the hill. The two groups had been eager to bolt to the main building. Their body language, and the resentment they showed, indicated that they were ordered to return.

I sat in the car with my *Life after Death* thoughts. Hell must be on the other side of that black door just waiting to swallow me up. I was terrified and I felt I was being sucked toward that door.

Suddenly, the door burst opened with a loud crack as if the hinges were out of alignment. I jumped a little in the seat.

A woman walked out. She was wearing black slacks, a white pull over sweater, and loafers. She was of medium height and build. Her sandy blonde hair was combed, though not well. A metal chain wrapped around her waist held a large number of keys on a clip. My skin tingled.

She stared off into the woods and lit a cigarette. I wondered if she knew we were sitting in the car.

Mom said, "Well, Danny. I guess this is it." She struggled to maintain her composure. *It's not every day that a mother sees her child off to federal prison.*

"I—uh—I guess I better get going," I offered weakly.

Mom, Emily, and I got out of the car. I hugged mom. She was eighty-one years old, and was about to cry. I could see it. She'd lived a quiet, simple, and humble life. And then I had go and do this to her. Eighty-one years of being a God-fearing person destroyed by my greed and stupidity. She'd stopped attending Church and senior citizen activities. She'd become a recluse because she was ashamed to hear, "Mary, is that your boy who's in all that trouble?"

I held her close to me. On my shoulders her arms felt frail, no strength at all. This might be the last time I would ever see her.

After what seemed like the shortest minute of my life, I let her go, and she put her hands to her face. I turned and hugged Emily, all of us near tears.

If only I could go back and correct those terrible mistakes. I'd follow the straight and narrow. But, it was too late for that.

"I'd better go," I conceded.

"I know you'll be all right," Emily said, ever the optimist. Her sunny disposition was the reason I wanted her here. She was in her mid-fifties and had recently retired from a bond trading company. She was single, wealthy, and sophisticated. Most important, she always knew what to say and what not to say, a talent I never acquired. She'd support mom on the drive back to New Jersey and stay with her tonight. "No matter what, we'll be here to pick you up," she declared. "That's a promise. You got that?"

I wouldn't collect on that promise for ninety-six months. By then, Mom would be almost ninety, if she lived that long…

God Almighty.

This was awful.

"I'll count the days," I said controlling the quiver in my voice. I told myself not to think about how long ninety-six months was. I looked at Mom, who'd lowered her hands to her cheeks. I said to Emily, "Take care of the boss here 'til I get back." I smiled as best I could.

"You got it, Danny," Emily said. "We'll go up to the summer cottage in Newport and laugh about this one day. Don't worry about us. We'll be fine."

"Call me, and let me know that you're all right," Mom said. Then both hands covered her eyes, and she fell sobbing onto my chest. I placed my hands on her shoulders and felt her shudder. I couldn't stand myself. I was a total fucking loser.

I said, "As soon as I can… I will…. But it may take a while…"

I'd been told it would take a few days to activate telephone privileges.

With that last cautious promise, I kissed the top of her head and leaned her shoulders back. Then I kissed her forehead.

"I love you, Mom," I said in earnest. "You take care of yourself. I'm a big boy. I can take care of myself. None of this is your fault. I did it to myself." I was surprised I could say all that without a break in my voice.

Emily took Mom from me. I glanced at my watch. Quarter to twelve. Fifteen minutes to spare. I took it off and handed it to Emily. I turned away and walked toward the black door of the main building.

6

Buckles

Going through the black door—a recurring dream. Beyond that door is a place of confinement.

During my last physical, my doctor told me that most people were in prison, whether they admit it or not. Their prisons were drugs, alcohol, work, religion, economics, hatred or an all-consuming feeling of helplessness. Their prisons enslave them. It took me a long time to realize that he was right.

The first time I went through that black door was the hardest. That's why this dream is so regular.

The woman was still there smoking her cigarette. She appeared to be about forty. Same age as I, different career path.

"Hi," she inquired politely. "Who are you?"

"I'm Dan Holmes. I'm…" I didn't know how to finish. Was I "checking in" like at a hotel? Was I "reporting as ordered?" Was I "rendering myself?" What *was* the correct term?

"I'm…"

This last stammer hung in the air since I was hoping she would complete the sentence for me.

"I'm Miz Buckles," she said, heavy emphasis on the "Miz." She exhaled smoke onto my chest. It rose to sting my eyes. "I'm the Camp Administrative Assistant," she said establishing hierarchy. She sized me up for a few seconds, and then she volunteered in a friendly voice, "You still have time to go get something to eat, you know. You're not due 'til thirteen hundred hours."

"The letter said the deadline was noon. I confirmed it by phone."

"Not on my schedule sheet," she replied. "You have about an hour to go. My sheet says ETA is thirteen hundred hours." She glanced over toward Mom and Emily. I peeked, too. They were standing together beside the car watching me. Emily was probably waiting until I'd gone through the door to get back in the car. "Why don't you go into town and grab a burger? There's a first class McDonald's not far from here." The words "first class McDonald's" seemed ironic to me. I had been wondering where on the social scale the people who worked here would be. I wasn't expecting "blue bloods" but who deems any McDonald's to be "first class?"

I turned away from the gazes of Mom and Emily. I could feel their sadness in that one small glance. And while I wanted to spend more time with them, I couldn't endure another good-bye session. My nerves were shot. Mom's had to be worse. I wouldn't, couldn't, put her through that again no matter how much extra time I had—not an hour, not a day, not a week.

I turned to Miz Buckles. She exhaled on my chest again.

"I better not," I told her.

She said, "Hey, pal. I read your jacket. You'll be here a long time. I'd go get a last supper if I were you. The food here tastes like shit." She stated this in an everyday tone, as if it were an undisputed fact. "Go get yourself a couple double Big Macs and some fries for real. We got nothing' like that here."

The *Last Supper* reference stung me. I knew very well what happened to "The Big Guy" after His *Last Supper*. Panic was swallowing me whole.

Then it occurred to me that this might be some sort of trick.

I'd been told in writing and on the phone to arrive by noon sharp with dire, though unspecified, consequences if I were late. I didn't know this woman and didn't know if I should trust her.

"I better not," was all I could say.

I waited as she smoked.

She'd said her name was Miz Buckles as if she were someone whose first name was "Miz." She didn't look like a Jessica, a Kimberly, or an Ashley. Through the rising smoke I imagined her mother laying eyes on her new daughter and declaring, "I shall name her 'Miz' and she shall be great!"

Miz Buckles finished her cigarette and dropped the butt onto the concrete slab beside the trash can. She didn't bother to step on it. She turned toward the black metal door, and I saw the metal chain and the keys she wore around her waist. The wide black belt had leather pouches that contained handcuffs, a flashlight, a whistle, and, poking out of one of the pouches, latex gloves. The sight of the gloves sent a shiver through me. I'd had a prostate exam a few years ago and the thought of having a gloved finger inserted into a very private area again made me wince. Then, I wondered if Miz Buckles was the anal prober.

She looked over her shoulder and snapped, "Let's go."

She pulled open the black door. It wasn't hinged plumb, and the door emitted a shrill metal-against-metal "Skreeeee!" like a dungeon door. The sound gave me goose bumps.

I turned and waved good-bye to Mom and Emily. They returned my wave, neither saying a word. Mom was sobbing and leaning on Emily. I smiled at them one last time and followed Miz Buckles through the door.

7

Wilkinson

From light to darkness. That's what it was like going through that door. Now I was cut off from all I knew. At least I wouldn't see that "Shame on you!" expression on the faces of people any more.

I didn't know a soul here. And I didn't have many friends out in the Free World any more. Maybe I had five of them left. Enough to count on one hand. Five stalwart souls. By the time I was released, that number would be closer to zero.

The door opened onto a long corridor. A glassed-in bulletin board was on the left with typed announcements and snapshot photos under pushpins. The floor was linoleum. The cinderblock walls were painted powder blue.

Miz Buckles opened a glass door that led into an office area. She ordered, "Stay here. Someone will process you. We're pretty busy to-day. There are three of you due. At least that's what the schedule says, but it's usually fucked up. You may have to wait, or," she laughed out loud, "maybe you won't."

Miz Buckles' voice had changed. Now it had a military ring as she gave me orders and reeled off a jailhouse joke. Inside this building she was in charge and she knew it. More importantly, she wanted me to know it. Outside we'd been in the Free World. Now we were in Her World. Point made.

"Stand right here until he says you can come in," she told me pointing to a man sitting behind a dull, gray metal desk. Miz Buckles opened the glass door to the office and left me standing in the hall.

I could see most of the room. Offices surrounded an open central area. A man stood at the center desk with his back to me. Miz Buckles disappeared into one of the side offices.

This was the first time I heard the background noise of a federal prison. It sounded like it did in the movies, constant talking, laughing, yelling, objects clicking and clacking and banging together; nothing soft anywhere to baffle the sound. It was a noise I learned to ignore.

Down the corridor a half-dozen men milled around. They wore sweat pants and sweat shirts. They appeared swarthy, perhaps Italian or Sicilian. I heard one of them say, "Id dat him, Ace? I didn't see no limo."

No one answered.

One of the men began walking toward me down the incline of the hallway. He'd about halved the distance when he stopped, stared hard at me, and turned back.

I recognized him, though I couldn't put a name on his face. I was a diced and shredded wreck; my mind racing everywhere at once. How bad was this place going to be? Would Mom be all right? How hard would it be to live here? What were my children doing? My head was so full of thoughts I was near paralysis, or oblivion.

"Nah. Dat ain't him," I heard the man say as he rejoined his little group. "Dat some other stupit mudda-fucka."

Great, I'm here five minutes and I'm classified as a "stupit mudda-fucka." Welcome to the club!

Once back together, they loitered about as if they were on watch. They presented like Mafia types trying to be inconspicuous but drawing attention to themselves by being overtly idle. Another chill ran through me. They were waiting for someone coming in a limousine. Were they out to whack him?

I turned back to the glass door and the office area. The seated man was dressed in a white shirt with a red clip-on tie. The shirt was well worn with ink stains at the bottom of the left pocket. The tie had yellow spots at the bottom. Looked like mustard. His tie was affixed to his shirt by a pin designed as handcuffs. Funny. He had short gray hair combed down the middle. He wore aviator glasses held together on one side with a wire, or a piece of a paper clip. His face was gaunt with pasty loose skin and a mustache. His expression was blank, as if he'd been worn down over the years and he couldn't expend the energy necessary to give his face a personality. As I watched, he lifted a piece of paper from a stack on his desk, reviewed it, tapped on a computer keyboard with his right index finger, examined the screen, re-reviewed the paper, looked at the screen again, and fed the paper into a shredder beside him.

The standing man was dressed in khaki and spoke to the seated man who did not acknowledge him, and in fact, appeared to ignore whatever was being said to him. After a minute or so, the man behind the desk peered over the top of his glasses and with minimal effort muttered something. The man standing before him slouched as he listened.

A huge bald black man strutted down the corridor and stood next to me. He folded his arms across his chest, stoic and silent, like a cigar store Indian. He wore wrap-around sunglasses that prohibited me from seeing where his eyes were looking. His muscled neck, arms, and legs bulged through worn-out khaki. His face was chiseled and taut. He looked dangerous. I stepped away from him.

The man standing walked out of the office. As he passed by me, I heard him say, "Fuckin' son of a bitch."

The seated man picked up the top paper from a stack and squinted at it. The black giant unfolded his arms and stepped to the door, his nose almost touching the glass. The man behind the desk ignored him as he examined the paper. The black giant stood silently as he stared through the glass. A minute or so passed. It was a staring contest with the black giant as the only contestant. The seated man shredded the paper and looked over the top of his glasses at the imposing black figure. Then he glanced back at his stack of papers. He raised a hand and flexed his index finger in a "come hither" motion. The black giant opened the door and walked to the desk leaving the door ajar. The seated man turned from the desk to take a paper off a printer on a table beside him. The black giant stood motionless. The seated man turned and looked at the computer screen, then at the paper from the printer.

I realized that I'd just lost my place in line to a professional. At that moment, I'd been more concerned about the black giant beating me to death than any protocols he was showing me.

"What is you doin' here, Washin'ton?" asked the seated man.

In a slow and deliberate voice the black giant said, "Don't you play you mime game wid me, Hickle. You knows I be Wilkinson. You be my Counselor in da medium down de hill in 91."

"Well," Hickle answered in a heavy southern accent. "You is in my camp now, an' it's my camp, so you better be keer-ful or I'll ship you right back to da medium down the hill."

"Man," said Wilkinson neither impressed nor intimidated, "Who do you thinks you is bullshittin'?" This was said in a normal tone, no bitterness or edge. "I'm a short time motha-fucka. I only got a minute up here in dis joint, for real, man. I'm gonna lay it down. I already did twenny. I know wha's-up."

Black giant had served twenty years and I was worried about a mere ninety-six months.

Hickle said, "You been doin' them stereos to git that big?"

"What the fuck you talkin' 'bout?" The edge in his voice told me the black giant was annoyed at answering a stupid question.

"Down the hill. You been doin' stereos to bulk up? To git them big muscles?" Hickle leaned back in his chair and examined Wilkinson. He continued, "I don't needs no road rage up here in my camp. An' it's *my* camp." Hickle leaned forward in his chair. "I thinks I'm gonna call up and have you provide a yer-rine sample to see if you gots any ster-ee-os in youse." He picked up the phone on his desk. "Go on aroun' to R & D and gits processed. You can do the paperwork later."

Wilkinson said nothing to Hickle as he left. As he brushed past me I heard him say, "Waste o' money, pissin' me."

I made a mental note. In my first ten minutes, I'd made no progress checking in and I was waiting to be granted an audience with a man who didn't know the difference between steroids and "stereos." Let the games begin.

8

Luka

My ex-wife was so angry at me for all the lies and deceptions that she swore I'd never speak to my children as long as I was in prison.

For them, it would be like I'd died. Their mother would destroy any letters I sent them and wouldn't let me talk to them on the telephone. At best, I would be gone and probably forgotten. At worst, she'd bad-mouth me with no end. The mental anguish was like a giant screw boring into my stomach one-quarter-turn at a time. I can feel it now just thinking about it. No other emotion hits me so strongly and persistently.

A man turned the corner by the idle Italians and limped toward me. Damn! I recognized the bastard right away. He was five-seven with a slight build, more bird-like than human. He had graying brown hair combed straight back.

Luka Slobodo, an inconvenience from my past. He was a client I'd represented in tax matters that were part of his criminal prosecution. From the first day that I met him, he was a series of misrepresentations and exaggerations. For Luka Slobodo, truth was irrelevant.

Luka grew up in Texas where he supposedly graduated from Texas Christian University with a degree in Comparative Religion. He always called it "Competitive Religion." He wanted to be a Buddhist Monk but changed his mind when he realized that women were prohibited from joining and monks, with their vows of poverty, had no money for him to mooch. He eventually graduated from Southern Law School and joined, in his words, the "U.S. Division" of the international law firm of *Slobodo & Slobodo*. This paragon of "The Law" was based in Luka's brother's condo in Virginia Beach. He chased ambulances. This lasted three years until the judges on the local benches dismissed Slobodo's filings as frivolous as a matter of routine. Virginia

Beach's loss of a village idiot became Philadelphia's gain when Luka relocated there to sell health insurance.

Luka, now about forty-five, unwisely decided to go to trial despite my urgings to plead out. His company sold health insurance to poor minorities, except there was no insurance. All the premiums went to "administrative expenses" which usually meant "to Luka." The company grew fast and presented itself as profitable due, as the court records showed, to multiple entries of the same income and a shameful failure to record expenses. For five years Luka was the pride of Affirmative Action initiatives, reaching out to minorities no one insured because they had little money and high rates of substance abuse, disease, and poor health care. He displayed his photograph on his business cards and in his ads like a realtor—or a preacher. He was a difficult person to like, and as his company and ego grew, he became intolerable, dismissive, and a master of promising lies. Only beautiful women were exempt from his wrath. In the sixth year, the company's cash flow hemorrhaged from court-pursued medical claims. Slobodo had spent the cash on a lavish lifestyle. At trial he claimed that both the prosecution and the District Court Judge misunderstood his case. He insisted the company was self-insured. The jury didn't buy that lie and he was sentenced to eight years.

"Dan!" Luka said flashing a wide smile at me. "It's good to see you in jail!"

I couldn't help but grimace a little at that.

"Luka," I said. "I'm pleased you're glad to see me in jail."

"I know what you mean!"

I certainly did. This was one of his meaningless, fill-in-the-gap phrases. Best to ignore it.

The man called Ace had walked down the incline toward us. Arrivng, he said, "Eh—'scuse me." He talked to me and pointed at Slobodo. "Do youse know dis piece of shit?"

"Ace," said Slobodo. "Why do you Sicilians hate me so much? It was the Romans who killed Jesus. Not the Jews. Romans are Sicilians, right? An' you are Sicilian, right?"

"Snowblow.... Sloblow... Whatever youse fuckin' name is. I don't even know what the fuck you is talkin' about," admitted Ace, shaking his head in confusion. "I hate youse 'cause youse a soft mudda-fucka. Youse didn't fight da mudda-fuckas like I did. Plus, youse a rat 'cause youse always down here talkin' to da hacks. I hate rats. When I sees a rat, I wants ta break his bones. Dat's what I'm programmed ta do." He tapped the side of his head with his forefinger for emphasis. His speech was slow and deliberate, the words coming out as if he had to concentrate on forming each one. "Doan fuck with me. I kill youse, and youse knows it."

Clearly Slobodo had the same effect on people inside prison as he had on people on the street. Almost everyone wanted to strangle him.

Slobodo pleaded, "Would you please leave me alone so I can talk to my lawyer?"

Ace's expression changed instantly.

"Youse looks familiar. Youse his law-yah?"

"I unfortunately represented him once upon a time."

"I'm Ace Baldini. I'm sorry for da way I acted jus' now. Please egg-cept my 'pology." He bowed politely. He was a little fellow, about five-four, maybe a hundred and thirty pounds with deep olive skin heavily crinkled with age. His eyes were dark brown under bushy brows speckled with gray like his hair. "I can see youse is a genna-min. But dis mudda-fucka here make me crazy."

"I'm Dan Holmes, and I've met you before." The connection came to me. "I represented your co-defendant, Nicky Buonaviri."

I was feeling more comfortable now as I realized I knew a couple of guys here. They weren't all murderers and rapists.

Ace was hard core criminal, though. He was now sixty and had spent about half his adult life in federal penitentiaries. Born and raised in Palermo, he and his parents immigrated to America when he was thirteen. He never attended school. Instead, he worked on the docks. His education was learned from hanging out with the boys on the corner and it became a lesson in the drug trade. His current crime involved trying to rob a drug supplier of his drugs. The dealer turned out to be an undercover DEA agent and instead of buying "dime bags," Ace was convicted of conspiracy to possess an illegal substance and was sentenced to a "dime."

"I knowed dat I recognize youse." Ace contorted his face into what he thought was a room-winning smile. He had large horse-like teeth and smelled of garlic. Ace Baldini need never buy a Halloween mask. "Youse a stand-up guy, I recall. Youse did all right by Nicky."

"Where is he now? Do you know?"

"Fed pen, Terre Haute. He shanked sum piece of shit what was starin' at his lady da wrong way in da Visita Room, know whadda mean?"

"Is he still hearing voices?"

"Yeah, I guess. Fugget-abou-dit. Whadda youse doin' here? Maybe youse can help summa da boys wid their cases."

"I doubt it. This is where the Bureau of Prisons assigned me."

"Oh…" Realization crept across Ace's face. What passed as a smile left and was replaced by open-faced sincerity. I could almost see his thought process evolve. "Soze youse is one of us? Youse not here ta gets sum-buddy out?"

"Nope. I'm a guest for the next ninety-six months."

"Wow," said Ace drawing back from me a little. "Nine-dee-six." He drawled it out as he looked me up and down. "Not as good as my one-twenny, but das a respectable stretch." I assumed that he meant that as a compliment. "Youse musta gone hard."

I sighed at his comment.

"I've never quite heard it put that way," I admitted.

"Fugget-abou-dit." Ace pointed up the hall at the welcoming party still milling about. "I'm just waitin' with da boys for Frankie Bananas to show up. Youse know him?"

"I don't think so."

"Well, Danny, Frankie Bananas izza a made member of da New York Gambino family. He's a *capo*, youse know whadda mean? He's da head of da egg-tortion business for da East Coast. When he was 'rested, id took five cops to knock him down so dey could get da cuffs on him. Ta get him ta stops fightin' and put him inna cruiser, dey hit him with da stun gun, da Tay-zah. He's a bad mudda-fucka, Frankie Bananas. Know whadda mean?"

I wondered why a capo like Frankie Bananas would be coming to a minimum-security facility. The pre-sentencing process was supposed to assign someone that dangerous to a more secure facility. The story didn't add up. It was the first of many.

"When he gets here, we just wanna make him feel welcome an' show some respeck. We made a party for him for tonight. Why doan youse stop by an' I'll introduce youse-self 'round, too." His Halloween mask was back. Ace must have never looked at himself in a mirror. His eyes darted over my shoulder into the office beyond. "I godda go see wad dis mudda-fucka want." Ace pointed at Slobodo. "An' stay away from dis piece o' shit." He opened the door, went in, and stood in front of the gray metal desk.

The man at the desk peered up and spoke a few sentences as Slobodo and I watched from the corridor. As far as I could tell, Ace never said anything. Then the man at the desk looked at his computer and Ace came back outside.

"Wha's-up with Hinkel, Ace?" one of the men up the corridor yelled at him.

Ace shouted back, "Mudda-fucka sez he's gonna write me up for being outta uniform an' not bein' at my woik detail."

"Wad jouse say?"

"I tol' da stupit mudda-fucka dis *is* my uniform and dat I'm done workin' in da Rec Centa at ten in the mornin'." I said ta him, 'How you like dem apples, Hinkel, you dumb-ass crackah? Go 'head and write me up. I doan give a shit.'" He gasped a couple of breaths going up the corridor. "He doan scare me none. Who da he think he's talkin' to? I'm Ace Baldini. That's wha's-up. I ain't scared o' him. Stupit mudda-fucka." He rejoined his group; pats on the back ensued.

Slobodo and I stood in front of the glass door.

"So," Slobodo said. "How are you?" He didn't wait for an answer. "I was reading about your case in the paper. The judge stuck it to you. Can you get relief on appeal?"

I was wondering how the Bureau of Prisons could assign Luka and me in the same camp. Slobodo was someone with whom I'd had a prior business relationship and these connections were supposed to be severed. The goal was to reduce future criminal acts by the same prior partnered felons.

"No," I told him. "I'm guilty so I pled out my case as best as I could."

I'd assumed responsibility for my criminality, a prospect alien to him. But my admitted guilt was a fleeting thought as he placed a hand on my shoulder and leaned up to whisper in my ear.

"I *am* glad to see you, Dan." This was the voice of conspiracy. A scam was in transit. "I've been waiting for you. I put together a plan so we can make some money."

"Luka," I resorted to my let-the-client-down-easy tone. "I'm not scheduled to be released for ninety-six months. By then someone else may have perfected your plan."

"No. No. We can make thousands right here. Thousands! Are you with me?"

I said, "In the physical sense, I'm right here with you. Otherwise, I just want to keep my nose clean and get out of here when I'm supposed to. I fought the law and the law won. I don't want to fight them any more."

"But you've never been scared."

Whatever that meant?

"Luka. You were a deviant out on the street. I can't imagine how much lower you've sunk since I last saw you. How long has it been? Three years?"

"Will you just listen?"

I might as well listen since he would refuse to stop yapping until I heard his speech.

"I know this is a mistake." I closed my eyes to prepare for something ridiculous. "If you must, go ahead."

He'd missed every tell-tail to stop I was launching at him.

"Every day inmates arrive here." He reached into his back pocket and extracted several folded papers and held them out to me. "We contact 'em before they arrive and charge them ten thousand dollars to set them up and help them get established in jail."

"What do you mean, 'set them up?'"

He ignored the question. He was rolling now; in his element.

"I've worked hard to establish my credibility here. Between you and me, I pretty much run the place. Best part is, everyone knows it, and when they want something done, they come to me. Someone wants to live on a different range? They come to me. Someone wants a better job? They come to me. There's nothing I can't handle. That's how I devised the idea for my venture. Here, read the business plan." He unfolded the papers and pawed through them. He looked at each page, taking longer than I thought necessary to recognize his own writings. He handed the crinkled fourth page to me.

Typed words, ink and pencil printing, whited-out spots, some veiled attempts at cursive, erasures, and exed out lines covered the page. It was designed like a five year-old's attempt at a business plan. Before I could examine it further, Slobodo snatched it back.

"Lemme 'splaine. We'll contact guys who were just sentenced and send them a package telling them about our services and instruct them to send *me*—I mean us—ten thousand dollars, and we'll set them up with a good job and bunk assignment. Plus, if they send us their clothing and shoe sizes, we'll have them waiting here. And they'll fit! He'll walk right in and be ready to go."

The stupidity of the idea stunned me.

Not sensing any feedback, he plunged on. "Now, you like the whole idea don't you? But wait! Wait until you hear the best part. We *franchise!* We'll have a franchise at every prison. We'll set up guys with our idea and charge them a franchise fee. We'll corner the market and be a monopoly. You gotta love it, don't you? I can tell! You're speechless!" He was fired up now. Cruising in overdrive. More selling the idea than explaining it. This was when he was at his best, and most dangerous.

I was speechless. Here I was in federal prison for less than fifteen minutes, not even processed yet, and Slobodo was arranging for me to do more time. Why bother making enemies when I had friends like him?

"Luka," I said, patience wearing thin. "You've got to be kidding me. We're in prison. We're not supposed to be doing business of any kind here. It's one of the rules. If the cops find out, you'll do more time. Besides, how will you know who the new arrivals will be before they get here? There's no way to do that. Finally, nobody is going to send ten thousand dollars for stupid promises like that. This is one of the dumbest ideas I've ever heard."

For a natural salesman, or a con man, rejection was a hurdle to overcome and he required but a few seconds to regain momentum.

"You're a little cranky today, aren't you, Dan? First day in jail, and all. You look tired. All we're doing is assisting our fellow inmates to adjust. And I got case law that allows us to do business."

"What case is that?" I asked with unveiled sarcasm. Although he had been a lawyer, Slobodo had never read a case in his life. He was a McLawyer, with, at best, a degree from some correspondence law school. No telling who sat for the bar exams for him in Virginia and Pennsylvania.

"Supreme Court. *Brown versus Board of Education.*"

He had to be kidding.

"You're an idiot, Luka. *Brown* deals with school desegregation. How are you going to argue that *Brown* allows you to franchise a business from prison?"

"The hacks don't know that. They can't hardly read."

"Well, since you didn't read the case, how do you know what it says?"

"Somebody told me about it. I quoted it to desegregate the GED classes. I argued that since only blacks and Hispanics were forced to attend, it was discriminatory. No white guys in there at all. Nobody for the blacks and Hispanics to cheat off of. It wasn't fair."

How could people like Luka Slobodo ever survive in the real world? Well—they didn't. That was why Luka and those like him ended up in prison. They could concoct the dumbest ideas, and then be stupid enough to try them.

"Listen. I want to go home some day. Leave me out of it."

"Okay," he relented. "But I'm gonna work on this some more. There has to be a case that allows us to do this. I'll find it. But hey! At least let me pave the way for you with the 'Man.' He's a real 'Heckle and Jive' if you know what I mean."

I didn't know what he meant. Wilkinson had called the man behind the desk "Hickle." Maybe Heckle and Jive referred to Heckle and Jeckle, the old cartoon show.

"Lemme go in and make sure he knows you're a personal friend of mine. Then you'll see the 'Jive' side of his personality."

Oh... it was a Dr. Jekyll and Mr. Hyde reference.

"I need to do this myself, Luka. First impressions. You know what I mean. And I've practiced before Federal District Court Judges. I can probably handle a cop in Catskill County."

"That's the mistake everybody makes, see? This is why you need my help. He's not a hack like you think. That's Mister Hinkel. He's a Counselor." A pause followed. "He's *The* Counselor, and he thinks he *owns* this camp. He's scary."

"His name is Hinkel, like the German airplane?" I turned and studied the man through the door glass. I summed up my first impression of him. "He's scary in a pasty, ghost-like sort of way. And he's slow-witted. See how long he takes with each of those papers. Plus he's a one-fingered typist."

"He's a hater," interjected Slobodo. "He hates everybody."

"So he's not prejudiced. At least give him that."

"Lemme go in and make sure he treats you good. I would consider it proof of my business plan."

Slobodo placed himself in front of the door just like Wilkinson had done.

"Stand straight," he instructed. "Make sure your shirttail is in. Don't button the top button of your shirt. If you do, he'll accuse you of being in a gang. Try to look good. See, this is the procedure. You wouldn't know how to do this 'cept for me telling you. I can write a whole book of how things work in here. We can make a ton of money."

Hinkel studied one paper at a time, typed a dozen or so letters on the keyboard, checked the computer screen, reviewed the paper, read the computer screen, and then fed the paper into a shredder.

Ever the con man, Luka rambled on about his business plan. He still hadn't learned to stop "selling."

I looked at Hinkel's glasses and decided it was a paper clip that held the frames together. He opened a brown paper bag and removed an apple and a sandwich wrapped in Saran Wrap. He laid them on his desk in front of the keyboard. He glared over the top of his glasses at us. He curled his index finger twice to indicate we could enter.

9

Hinkel

My first impression of Counselor Hinkel was that he was a worn out and worn down cog in the BOP machine. I figured this was the only job he'd ever had and he was now well beyond "burned out." I wondered how old he really was, how long he'd actually been with the BOP and how badly it had aged him. Then I wondered how I'd look in eight years.

Slobodo opened the door and limped up to Hinkel's desk.

"Counselor. This is my lawyer."

I went through the door, and stood next to Slobodo.

Hinkel's face turned beet red as he screamed, "Slowblow! Gits outta my office! I done told you never to come back here agin!"

Slobodo spoke to me in a stage-whisper, as if Hinkel were not present. "The Counselor is upset because I wrote him up when he refused to allow me to practice my religion."

"I done told you to go to the Jew services any time you wants to."

"I'm not Jewish anymore," Slobodo informed me. "I'm a Norse God. For religious purposes, I'm known as Vultran, King of Sleet and Rain."

"Aw… Tell yer lawyer the truth," clarified Hinkel. "The Jews excommunicated you, and the Nurse thing is an attempt to gits a meal delivered from the street oncet-a-week."

After all he'd been through, Slobodo hadn't changed a bit; he was still scamming. Why wasn't I surprised? I quipped, "Your rehabilitation doesn't seem to be going well, Luka. Why don't you quote *Brown v. Board of Education?*"

Slobodo continued talking as if Hinkel couldn't hear him. "My religion requires a red meat feast at least once a week, and pursuant to Bureau of Prison regulations, I'm entitled to practice my religion as if

I were on the street."

Hinkel glared at Slobodo and said, "Cleeta! Do Slowblow here have a 'legal' scheduled for today?"

Miz Buckles' voice arose from one of the offices.

"It's not on the schedule. I hate it when lawyers show up unannounced and expect us to drop everything and kiss their ass."

Her first name was Cleeta? Forty years on earth and she's the first Cleeta I've encountered. Must be a Catskill County name.

Miz Cleeta Buckles.

Unbelievable.

Miz Buckles walked out of her office with a *7-Eleven* cup in hand. The telephone on Hinkel's desk rang.

"Counselor Hinkel," he answered.

He listened a moment and hung up.

"Cleeta. Close the main line. Shut it down."

Miz Buckles strolled around the corner beyond a neck-high partition. An ear-piercing crack, like thunder, exploded across the room. I flinched, almost ducking for cover.

"That's the PA system," Slobodo informed me.

Miz Buckles' voice announced, "Attention inmates. Main line is closed. Main line is now closed."

Luka smiled at me. "Now you know. That's how they close down the chow line. You would have known that before you got here if you were in my program."

Another peal of thunder as she switched off the mike.

"It's the feedback from the speaker," said Slobodo still selling his con. "It sounds okay out in the camp, though."

Miz Buckles came back from around the corner and pointed at me. She fumed, "He's no lawyer! He's a self-report! Slobodo's playing a scam. I'm gonna write him a shot."

"No! No!" protested Slobodo. "Dan *is* my lawyer."

Hinkel looked at me. "Is you his lawyer?" The tone was menacing in its monotony. "Or is you a self-report?"

I was getting nervous; I didn't like all this attention. "I'm a self-report. I used to be his lawyer but I surrendered my license."

Hinkel eyed me with a steely glare. "You off ta a bad start, boy.

You already on my bad side an' I think you is stupid. Knows why?"

I was curious as to the source of my stupidity so I decided to let him to explain it to me.

I ended the pause that followed by saying, "Why?"

"Three reasons. First, 'cuz you admits that youz knows Slowblow here. Second, 'cuz you admits you is his lawyer. Third, 'cuz you admits you *is* a lawyer. I hates lawyers."

Slobodo begged, "Please, Counselor Hinkel. There's no reason for this. I'm just trying to introduce you to a good person and make sure he gets off to a good start. Plus, and this is important, he's going to be part of my Law Library staff."

Hinkel glared at me and spoke as if Luka weren't present.

"See. He don't understan'. He thinks I just does what he says." Hinkel spoke to Luka next. "I forgots to tell you, Slowblow. You doesn't work in the Law Lie-berry no more."

"Why not? I'm the perfect person to be the Head Clerk. I'm a lawyer and I've improved the quality of the Law Library a thousand percent."

Hinkel grinned with satisfaction, "You is fired after I walks by the Law Lie-berry at ten this mornin' and you warrant there."

"I went to the bathroom," Slobodo shot back.

"Then I wents to your unit." Hinkel then spoke as if he were telling the tale of the *Three Little Bears*. "And guess who was sleepin' in youz little bed?"

"I wasn't sleepin'. I was reachin' for something under the bed and I got a cramp. I'm gonna write you up for being out-of-bounds, Counselor. Like a citizen arrest. You know Warden Bonnevie don't want you outside the Admin Building. You meddle too much."

"This is my *whole camp*." He swept his arm in a wide arc for emphasis. "Warden Bonny-vee so new here he don't know the difference 'tween the FCI and the FPC. 'Sides, he usually too drunk to know where he's at anyway."

I was thinking how ludicrous the conversation had become. I became aware I wasn't so nervous any more, at least for my physical well being. The environment couldn't be too bad if Luka could survive.

"Where did you transfer my job to?"

Hinkel smiled and showed teeth the color of his gray desk. He was proud of his decision and exhibited his pleasure by saying, "Overnight cleanin' detail in da medium security facility down the hill. You be workin' all night 'long with Corrections Officer Judith Tork. I done tol' her special to have you clean the same spot all night long. I done tol' her its punishment. She's likes punishment. Cleeta? Assigns Slowblow here to CCS-1 startin' tonight at ten."

"That's not fair," Slobodo whined.

"Was it fair when you cheated them peoples outs of their insurances?"

"I didn't cheat them, Counselor Hinkel. The judge misunderstood the case. Dan!" He turned to me. "Explain it to him."

"Oh," Hinkel feigned astonishment. "You 'spect me ta believe this here convict instead of a United State federal judge?"

"My company was self-insured, and I'm happy my lawyer is here to verify what I say. Tell the Counselor what happened, Dan."

Hinkel turned to me for a reply. I closed my eyes and shook my head to let Hinkel know I preferred to sign in rather than defend Luka. I'd lost once before trying to defend him. I saw no reason to try again.

When I opened my eyes, I saw Hinkel pick up a piece of paper from his stack. He said, "You know whats I thinks of you story?" Without looking at the paper, he fed it into the shredder.

"Counselor," protested Slobodo. "You didn't look at that paper. It might have been important."

"It ain't important now, is it? See, when I doesn't like somebody, this is what I does to their paperwork. Now, do you wants to leave this office? Or do you wants me to see if I can find any paperwork here that is important to you?"

I realized there were two rules that would dictate the next ninety-six months of my life. No matter what level of intelligence the staff had, or lacked, *they* were in charge. They had positional authority and I would lose every argument no matter how right I was. Next, I was in *their* house, playing under *their* rules. No inmate was going to beat them at their game, so the path of least resistance was the way to go. Pull in the oars and let the boat float downstream wherever the currents pushed it.

"But, Counselor—"

"Gits out of here soze I can process yer lawyer," ordered Hinkel cutting him off. "Then the two of you can do whatever you wants to."

Hinkel took a bite of his sandwich and looked at the stack of papers.

"Luka," I said with as much sarcasm as I could muster. "This was worth every cent of ten thousand dollars."

Hinkel looked at me. "He done told you 'bout his inmate set-up scheme, huh?"

Slobodo was surprised Hinkel knew about his proposed venture.

Hinkel said, "I knows everything, Slowblow. I may be a hillbilly from Wes' Virginny, but I knows everything that goes on here in my camp."

This was my first inkling that being a rat was a pastime in prison.

"Be at the front door by nine-forty-five tonight to go down the hill. Don't be late or you go to the hole. Now gits outta my office."

Slobodo walked from the room.

Hinkel explained, "The hole is solitary confinement down the hill in da medium-security. You don't want to go there."

"I agree, Counselor."

He had the unfeeling eyes of a snake, or a shark.

"Cleeta?" he called from his chair. "Where's Slowblow's lawyer's intake form? I knows that I has them here someplace." Hinkel pawed through the papers on his desk.

Miz Buckles appeared from her office, file in hand.

"Here they are. I kept them so you wouldn't lose them."

Hinkel laid the file beside the computer. He opened it and read the top sheet.

"Hole-meese," he said, long and slow. Hooked on phonics.

"It's 'homes.'" I corrected. "The 'L' is silent.

He glared at me as if I'd insulted him. Correcting an officer—I wouldn't make that mistake again.

"These here are intake papers. Sits over there and reads them. Signs them as you go along. There's three things you needs ta 'member 'bout here. First, four o'clock is the Four O'clock Mandatory Stand

Up Count. Make sure you is on you feet in you cube at four o'clock. Second, if in you tries to egg-scape, I won't chase you down. The FBI will. After you is caught, you comes back here and gits five more years added to you sentence down the hill. Third, the bear in the woods is mine. You don't do nuthin' to my bear. You got that? He's mine."

"Yes, sir. I got that."

The bear in the woods? What's up with that?

"Does you require any medicines?"

"No, sir. I'm not taking any medication."

"You can keep you glasses you is wearin', but there ain't no contact lens in my camp. Gives me you watch. Can't have no jew-ree. No rings. Empty you pockets. You gots enny money for the commissary?"

"Yes, sir. Here's three hundred in cash. The instruction letter said cash would be processed faster than a check."

I gave him fifteen twenty-dollar bills.

"I didn't bring a watch or any personal items except my driver's license." I handed it over. "The letter said I have to prove I'm Dan Holmes."

"Don't matter to me none unless they is somebody out there willin' to do ninety-six months for you."

Well. I hadn't thought of that. I wondered how much it would cost for somebody to serve my sentence. Didn't matter; I didn't have it anyway.

"Sez here, you gotta fake tooth."

"Yes sir." I'd forgotten about my prosthetic front tooth.

"Hand it over. Nothin' like that allowed."

I removed the tooth and the palate piece and dropped them into the manila envelope he held out.

Hinkel wrote out and handed me a receipt for the cash. Except for his signature, which he printed, the date and the monetary amount were written with digits. I guess he had issues with spelling.

I pocketed the receipt and sat on a metal folding chair to complete the forms. Hinkel mumbled something under his breath about providing the best possible service to inmates, especially those that didn't tell him how to do his job or hide teeth from him. I got the hint.

Miz Buckles walked out of her office.

"I'm going for a cigarette."

Without looking up from his computer Hinkel said, "If it wasn't for smokin', you wouldn't have much to do, Cleeta. By the way, when is you takin' my *Stop Smokin'* class?"

"As soon as I stop being pissed off about taking your *Anger Management* class."

Still not looking up, Hinkel inquired, "Why is you mad about that?"

"You compared everyone's personality to an animal."

"What's wrong with that? I always does that."

She turned on him at the door and spat, "In front of thirty inmates, who haven't had sex in God-only-knows-how-long, you compared me to a beaver! That's why I'm mad, goddammit. And I'm going to stay good and mad until I get over it." She sneered at me and said, "He just doesn't get it."

The door slammed closed behind her. Hinkel smiled as he looked at a stack of papers. "Yes I does," he said. After a short pause, he continued, "I gots to have some fun, doesn't I?"

Silence fell in the office as Hinkel worked, ate, typed, and shredded at the pace of cold syrup. I flipped through the package Hinkel had given me. There was a main form with name, address, nearest relative, date of self-report, height, weight, etc. Then a couple of pages of rules and regulations that outlined the policies and procedures under which the camp operated. Next was a list for close relatives and attorneys for the staff to approve before I could call them on the camp telephones. Then a list for the individuals that the staff would check out before allowing them to visit me.

Miz Buckles walked back into the office holding the stub of her lit cigarette.

"Wait 'til you see what just stepped out of a limo," she giggled. She noticed her cigarette and held it out in front of her. She said to Hinkel, "He looks like one of those flamingo things you have on your lawn."

Through the glass in the office door, an obese man in a pink shirt walked past. Seconds later he came back and looked in. He was white, with graying hair slicked back on his skull. He opened the door and walked up to Counselor Hinkel's desk. He had plucked eyebrows and black eyeliner on his upper and lower lids. A pink muumuu shirt, bright purple pants, and yellow flip-flops completed his ensemble. His distended stomach challenged the buttons of his shirt. "No gut, no glory," I said without thinking.

"What is you and why is youz here?" asked Hinkel.

Fashion statement surveyed the room. He said, "I'm lookin' for Stooper. Know where he's at?"

"I'm Counselor Hinkel."

"Glad to hear it," said fashion statement. "Can you tell me where Stooper is?" His eyes were glazed. He was high on something. "'What kinda dumb-ass name is that, anyway? Stooper. It's like a coma. Good thing my parents didn't name me Stooper. Can you imagine the beatings you'd take in school if your name was Stooper?" The man shivered like a wet dog, gut flopping like shaken warm aspic.

"I'm Counselor Spooter Alvin Hinkel," Hinkel said in a soft voice. He stood up and roared, *"S-P-O-O-T-E-R. It's my birff name! It's on my driver license! I am proud I has it. My Mama give it to me. Now, who is you?"*

"Frankie Bananas."

Oh my God!

This was the guy Ace Baldini was talking about?—the head of extortion for the Gambino crime family? I wanted to take back that, "No gut, no glory" comment.

"My lawyer told me to come here, but it's a mistake. I'm supposed to be back in court this afternoon. That's why I got Candy with me."

Hinkel said, "Cleeta. Is we egg-pectin' a flit today?"

She grabbed a clipboard hanging from a screw on the wall.

"We have Wilkinson who's already at R&D. Holmes is here. We're expecting a Paulo Ciriello."

Hinkel asked, "Is you Cereal?"

"I'm Paulo Giovanni Ciriello, but my friends call me Frankie Bananas. Nice ta meet youse." He stretched out a hand to Counselor Hinkel.

Hinkel ignored it.

"Cleeta? Brings me the paperwork on Cereal!"

She went into her office still holding the cigarette butt in her hand so the ash wouldn't fall off. She returned with a file, and dropped it on Hinkel's desk as he extended his hand to take it.

Frankie Bananas picked up the telephone from Hinkel's desk. Hinkel snatched it back with a quick stroke.

"Gimme that!" he snapped. "What does you think you is doing?"

"Callin' my lawyer."

"This is for staff only."

"So how do I call my lawyer?"

"'I-T-S-.'"

"I-T-S-?" said Frankie with a puzzled expression on his face. "It's a phone. What do I look like? Some kinda moron? I know it's a phone. I just wanna use it, that's all."

Hinkel said, "'I-T-S-' is the inmate system. It's all egg-splained here in you paperwork. Sits over there an' reads it."

"What about Candy? She's supposed to take me to Philly."

Hinkel opened the file Miz Buckles had dropped on his desk. He moved his finger around the page before stopping on the line he was searching for.

"'Cordin' ta this," he said with some satisfaction, "she'll be waitin' seventy-eight months."

Miz Buckles interjected, "If she's out in the limo, you have to tell her to leave. She's not allowed to be in the parking lot after dropping you off."

A bleached blond mounted on stiletto heels wearing a white halter-top and a black leather mini-skirt swished her way into the office taking everyone by surprise. She was bouncy except for her hair, which was heavily sprayed and brittle. Her makeup was thick and appeared to be applied by trowel. She had huge hips and large breasts, no doubt augmented by surgery.

"Frang-kee," she slanged. "Let's get outta he-ah. I'm bored. There ain't nothin' 'cept trees. Let's go back ta Philly. Nuffa da country."

Frankie introduced her proudly, "This is Miss LaVonda Pinciaro." He smiled as if showing off a trophy. "Her stage name is Candy Bahr, a tasty morsel. Know whatta mean?"

"You has to go," Hinkel told her pointing a thin pale arm toward

54

the parking lot.

Pinciaro glared at Hinkel as if he were a cockroach.

"Believe me, Mista, I wanna leave. I doan wanna stay he-ah. Let's go, Frang-kee. I been trone outta woi-sah places dan dis one."

Hinkel looked at Ciriello.

"You sits there an' reads." He pointed at Pinciaro. "You have one minute to gits in that car and leaves my camp 'fore I calls the police and charges you with trespassin'. You ain't even supposed to be in this here office."

The woman turned to Frankie.

"Poochie? Youse comin' or ain't cha?"

Ciriello suffered a rush of doubt. Hearing seventy-eight months stung, or at least sobered, him.

"I wanna call my lawyer. It's his fault." He looked at me. "Am I right or wrong? I'm not supposed to be here."

"Call me, Poochie." Pinciaro turned and followed her breasts toward the door. "I'll miss you, baby."

She closed the door behind her.

How fleeting is love.

Hinkel said to me, "Finish up you paperwork." He turned to Ciriello. "Sits next to him and fills out these forms." Hinkel handed Ciriello the papers from his file.

Miz Buckles went into her office holding the burned-out stub of her cigarette. Frankie Bananas sat next to me and began thumbing through the pages of his packet. With a whisper he learned in a steel mill he observed, "He's mean. I don't like him."

I thought Hinkel would snap at him. He didn't.

"Here." Frankie offered me his forms. "Help me do these, will ya?"

"Sez here," piped-up Counselor Hinkel, "that Mr. Bandana here never bothered to learn to read. You bein' a lawyer and all, Hole-meese, you can help him finishes his paperwork."

Frankie Bananas dropped his packet on my lap.

I watched Hinkel shred another paper from his pile without reviewing it. He mumbled to himself in the same steel mill whisper Frankie had used.

"Universal free education an' his'n cain't read a-lick. What is we commin' to in this world?"

Candy strode back into the office.

"The driver don't got my money, Frang-kee. He sez you ain't give it to him yet."

Miz Buckles came out of her office to referee the encounter.

Frankie looked at me and then at Counselor Hinkel, then at Miz Buckles, and groaned. He stood up, reached into his pocket, and pulled out a wad of bills folded in half. He peeled off four one hundred-dollar bills and handed them to Candy.

"This is for you and the driver," he said.

Candy snatched the money and counted it bill-by-bill, her lips mouthing the numbers from one to four.

"Four hunnert." She looked at Frankie. "The driver's on salary, Frang-kee. The rest is mine."

"Whatever," said Frankie waving a dismissive hand.

"Gits out!" ordered Hinkel remembering who was in charge. "Gits out now!" He put his hand on the telephone.

Candy ignored him, still looking at Frankie.

"Youse gonna give me no more tip than this?"

"No way, baby." Frankie said this with a flick of his wrist. "Get lost."

She gripped the bills around their middle so that they stuck out of her fist at the top and bottom. She shook them. "If that's the way youse wannit," she shouted. She went for the door. "You can't get it up, anyway. Too stubby and fat." With that parting shot, she left.

So this was Ace Baldini's Mafia big shot. Frankie Bananas—head of the Gambino crime family's extortion ring. Someone somewhere had played an elaborate joke on Ace Baldini and his boys. I smiled to myself.

"They ain't real boobs," Frankie counterattacked.

"You boys. Back to them papers," Hinkel ordered.

10

Fitted Out

I dream about forms, rules, and regulations. That's what this place is about. Rules, rules and more rules. There is a rule or a regulation for every situation. It seems like there is somebody in Washington whose job is to write rules to create paperwork. The paperwork has to be right or there is big trouble. No matter what the rule, you cover it over with enough paperwork and then the problem goes away.

In ten minutes, I completed Frankie Bananas' forms; asking him the questions and writing his answers in the blanks. When I finished, I told Frankie to sign on the bottom line.

"Do you think this is okay?" he asked.

I leaned over to Frankie's ear. "I put down what you said. I didn't add anything or make any suggestions. I've never given better legal advice."

"Yeah, okay." Frankie signed, and we each handed our papers to Hinkel, who, without surveying them, hole-punched them, and fastened them into two files.

Hinkel relieved Frankie of his personal items—a driver's license, a pocketknife, a small pot pipe, and a piece of folded aluminum foil. Hinkel gave him a receipt for his commissary deposit of twelve one hundred-dollar bills.

"You takin' any medicine we should know about, Bandana?"

"No."

Frankie was deflated by the process. Or maybe the drugs were wearing off.

Hinkel leaned back in his chair, hands clasped behind his head.

"You both is now official-entitle' inmates. Con-grat-chew-lay-shuns." His smile gave us a look at his gray teeth. "You belongs to me now. There's just three rules I cares about. First, four o'clock is the

Four O'clock Mandatory Stand Up Count. Make sure you is on you feet by you bunk at four o'clock. Second, don't goes outta bounds. The FBI will come after you, not me. You then gits five more years. Third, don't mess with the bear in the woods. The bear in the woods is mine. Now, gits up to R&D and gits processed." He pointed to the glass door. "Goes out the door to the left. Gits with the pro-grim and wel-come to Cass-kill County."

Frankie said, "Going left out the door puts us in the parking lot, you dumb–"

"We'll find it, Counselor Hinkel," I interrupted.

Frankie and I took a right turn out of the office and headed up the linoleum-tile hallway. A bulletin board displayed photographs of the current GED class and the winner of the Distinguished Inmate Award. Both pictures were surrounded by lick-and-stick gold stars. Next came a door with drawn blinds and a plastic sign underneath them that read R&D. No one else was in the fifteen-foot wide corridor, not even Ace Baldini and his welcoming committee.

"Here it is," said Frankie reaching for the knob.

"Knock first," I said rapping my knuckles on the door.

A voice inside yelled, "Yo!"

I opened the door and we walked in.

An officer was sitting behind a gray metal desk with his feet crossed on top of it. He was wearing a white dress shirt with gray pants, black boots, and white socks. The lenses of his glasses were badly scratched. His mustache, pork-chop sideburns, and hair were dyed jet black like Elvis, but unlike Elvis, they appeared to have been combed with his fingers. A cigarette hung from his mouth. Wilkinson sat to his left on a folding chair.

The room was large. Filing cabinets lined the wall behind and to the right of the desk. Fingerprint equipment lay on a table to the left. Next to that was a photo area with a camera, backdrop screen, and metal chair.

"Okay, inmates. Now that we're all here, let's step into the chang-ing room and outfit you in some new duds."

The officer pointed to a room behind him. The four of us walked into a clothing storage room. It was a large, though narrow, walk-in closet. Both sides were lined with wire shelves that held shirts, pants, shoes, socks, boxers, and T-shirts. It smelled like a military surplus store. And, like those stores, the clothes were jumbled together and picked through. The three of us stood shoulder-to-shoulder with me in the middle and the officer facing us. It was a tight squeeze.

"All right, inmates," said the officer. "Get naked while I find you some of the government's finest." He picked through the clothes, a collection of well worn tee shirts and khakis, as he eyed Wilkinson for size.

Wilkinson began peeling off his clothes as if stripping were an everyday chore. I turned away from him to see Frankie doing a strip tease to music only he could hear. He gyrated as if he'd disrobed professionally before, though in a different venue than a federal prison. Frankie was so fat that his flab touched the racks in front and in back of him as he undressed. I eased away from him and almost slid into Wilkinson who was completely naked except for his sunglasses.

"Let's go in the middle," rushed the guard. "No need to be shy."

That was easy for him to say.

Shame from my Catholic school upbringing had twisted my insides and shriveled a part of my outside. I was transformed back to 1960 and Sister Danielle Marie's warning that we should never be seen naked (ex- cept by our mothers, of course) or we'd be doomed to hell!

I unbuttoned my shirt, nervously and cautiously, and tried not to bump into the other two as I removed my pants. I didn't want anyone staring at me. I was self-conscious about my pigeon chest and the pimple that acted like my penis. I folded my clothes and held them in front of me to cover myself. Frankie seemed to enjoy the proceeding. When he finished removing his clothes, he leaned over and stared at Wilkinson.

"Goddamn!" he yelped. "Look at that Zulu's third leg. No wonder he got so many muscles—he has to tote that monster around all day."

Despite Sister's warning, I glanced at Wilkinson's "thang." It was longer than my arm and in better shape. He wasn't well-endowed, he was blessed by God.

Wilkinson stood expressionless in his wrap-around sunglasses.

Frankie peeked behind my clothes by pulling on a corner. I twisted away.

"I bet you ain't got no tripod like him. You prob'ly got just a little two-inch turtle all shriveled up in its shell."

Frankie was correct. I was embarrassed.

"I bet I can tickle it and make it come out," he smiled with glee.

"No," I stammered looking straight ahead. "That's okay."

The officer distributing the clothing said, "'Bout alls I got is one size fits nobody. Not nobody that ever come through here, anyway. Nope. Not ever."

I didn't care if anything fit. I was putting on whatever he handed me damn quick.

The boxers stayed up as long as I held them on both sides. They were big, but were in good condition.

The officer handed Frankie a handful of boxers. "Here you go, fat boy."

Frankie pulled them up one by one, each being too small. One large pair had a brown spot.

"Somebody crayoned on this one," he observed.

"That's not crayon," the officer told him. "Somebody drew mud." He laughed at his own joke. "We call that a 'skidder.'"

Frankie dropped those shorts on top of his pink shirt and purple pants.

The next pair fit, but they had a hole in the back.

"Looks like the last man wore those was a catcher," noted the officer.

Frankie put them on. He asked the officer, "How do you know he played baseball?"

I didn't know the punch line but knew one was coming.

The officer answered, "Get with the program, fat boy. He got nailed leaning over with his shorts still on." He cackled to himself. Sophomoronic humor at its best. Welcome to the middle of nowhere, Dan.

Frankie Bananas was dumbfounded. Then he smiled. "I'll take 'em," he said. He earned his nickname honestly.

None of the clothes fit Wilkinson. Muscles were popping out of the worn khaki. The clothing was closer to tearing apart than staying on his back.

Frankie couldn't button his shirt because of his gut. My arms and legs were inches too long for the shirt and pants which had enough material to cover a heavier person than I. The belt saved me.

"Not bad," the officer said as he observed the finished product. "Take one of these cardboard boxes, fold your old clothes in it, and address the box to where you want your stuff sent." The officer pointed at some folded-up U.S. Postal Service boxes. "We don't keep nothin' of urine past the first day." He laughed again. None of us smiled.

When we'd finished packing our clothes, the officer taped each box shut and stacked them on the floor beside the door. Then he said, "Fingerprinting is next." He went out to the main room. "The camera is broke today, so you'll have to come back to get your photo ID tomorrow, if it's fixed. I hope you got the time to wait."

Very cute one-liners, Elvis. Then I realized something strange. I'd be leaving in eight years; he'd probably be here for the rest of his life. Sucked to be him.

We returned to the main room and sat down. The officer called Wilkinson to be fingerprinted first. For Wilkinson, this was a routine process. He rolled his fingers by himself across the inkpad and onto the appropriate boxes on the fingerprint grid with the dexterity of a pro. I was next and the officer guided my fingers so as not to smudge the impressions. The officer repeated the process with Frankie.

Then, the telephone rang and the officer went to his desk to answer it. Frankie pressed both his hands onto the inkpad and massaged them together.

"What are you doing?" I asked.

Frankie slid his blackened hands down the front of his pants and smiled.

"Gettin' myself some of dat ol' black magic."

I was awestruck.

"Are you out of your mind?"

Frankie theorized, "Look at what it did for the Zulu Warrior over there. It turned his dick into a python. What can it hurt? Am I right or wrong?"

The officer was still on the phone with his back to us.

"I think it's working." Frankie shook his belly, smiling like a Buddha. "Candy will love me now." He pulled his pants away from his stomach and peeked down. "I can't see!" He stared at me. "Hey! Tell me, tall guy. How big is it?"

"I'm not going to look," I said. "Besides, Candy already opined on your size."

Frankie smiled at me with his plucked brows and lined eyes.

"Hey now. This gut cost me a lotta money," he said proudly. He examined his hand. "Any time you wanna look, just lemme know."

I'd be in no hurry to accept that offer.

The officer put down the phone and turned to us. "Wash the ink off your fingers at the slop-sink with those wipes." He pointed to a wash-up area. "When you're done, pick up a bedroll and sheets, and go back and see Counselor Hinkel so he can assign you a bunk. It's quittin' time for me. I'm headin' home to fire me up some brewskies."

His dried, wrinkled skin showed me that firing up brewskies was part of his daily routine.

'Hey, fat boy," said the guard now back at his desk. "From the looks of your hands, you'd better get a key to the wack-off room from Counselor Hinkel before you get yourself into any trouble. Best to ask him for it up front a-fore you get caught with your pants down."

The wipes proved useless against the indelible ink. We removed as much as we could rub off.

We picked up the bedding from another set of bins. The mattresses were well-worn gray-striped twins. Flat as a pancake. I'd slept on one previously in summer camp. Even the musty smell was the same. It had been uncomfortable then, and wouldn't be better now. There were only about eight from which to pick, all in about the same condition. We had our choice from among six pillows. The officer handed us sheets from a stack of twelve. Lastly, the officer handed us a plastic bag that contained a towel, a small soap, a pad of paper, and two pencils. That completed the R&D phase.

We walked out of the office and back into the powder-blue corridor. The officer locked the door to R&D and, without saying a word, jetted toward the building's main entry. Somewhere brewskies prepared to die.

Thus far in my visit, I was surprised at the lack of concern or per-sonalization exhibited to us. Then I understood why Wilkinson was immune to the treatment. I decided I'd better become accustomed to it. The treatment wasn't going to improve. At that point, I wanted to pull myself together before I presented myself to El Supremo unto himself, Counselor Hinkel again. Wilkinson walked down to the office where I'd encountered Hinkel and I followed him; more to be with someone who knew what to do. Frankie Bananas, hands completely black, trailed behind me.

Wilkinson and I stood in front of the office door waiting for Coun-selor Hinkel to motion us in. I watched Frankie approach us as he mumbled to himself, "They have a room just to jerk off? This place ain't so bad."

I gulped and braced for another encounter with the powers that be in my New World. I had ninety-six months less one hour to go, and I was already counting. I decided that was a bad thing. I looked at Wil-kinson standing there in his wrap-arounds. He was a man in his mid to late thirties who'd been in jail for twenty years. He was hardened to the process. I wondered if in the next eight years that I'd reach that plateau. Frankie Bananas shuffled up and the three of us waited for Counselor Hinkel as he slowly picked the top paper off of a stack of documents. Apparently, he wasn't in a hurry.

And I prayed that God would bless us all—for no one else would.

11

Worst and Best

Can I survive? I have no idea *of what is going to happen over the next eight years. Can I live through the years of confinement without contact with the three people in the world that I care about the most? How sad to think I would have to wait more than ninety-six months to see my children. Joe was seven, Shannon was five and Brendan was three. They'd be fifteen, thirteen and eleven when I'm released. Every time this cold, hard fact rose out of the depths, I felt the screw turn a bit more, splintering the wood in the wall behind me. My legs would buckle.*

And my mom would be dead...

I spent the next few days wandering around Federal Prison Camp (FPC) Catskill in a fog unable to analyze, much less stabilize, my mental condition. I expended the strength I had reconciling the emotional and financial losses I had sustained. I couldn't make sense out of the quagmire. I was stuck and unable to move forward. I was cemented into the past—longing to reclaim it.

I reacted to everything with just enough energy to survive to the next moment. Eating and sleeping were tedious. The food was tasteless, and the snoring and night noises kept me awake. When I took in a second notch on my belt, I made a conscious effort to eat more. Otherwise, all I did was watch life pass me by.

I was depressed. I was in a place I didn't know and didn't want to know. I don't recall much of those first days other than the despair I felt at how low I'd descended and helplessness at not being able to do anything about it. How much further down was the bottom? I plumbed the depths locating it.

I thought a great deal about my children. They were with their mother in Arizona with some guy named Brad. My ex-wife would never bring them to visit me, that much was quite clear. She'd enjoyed the good times, but resented my presence once I achieved "felon" status. I guess she hadn't married for "better or worse." She'd married for "better" and when it didn't work out, she'd abandoned me.

So, while I was in jail, I would miss the most formative years in my children's lives. Brendan told me he loved me the last time I saw him. He wouldn't remember that. He'd said it the way little children say they love grown-ups, by rote, not really comprehending the meaning of the word. I wouldn't have a relationship with them after being out of sight and out of mind for eight years. They'd never be eating dinner and have their mother say, "Hey, I know what let's do. Let's reminisce about what a great guy Dad was before he got his sorry ass hauled off to jail."

I'd be a stranger to them; someone little kids weren't supposed to talk to. What if they moved and I couldn't find them? Eight years from now, I wouldn't even *recognize* them.

The first positive feeling I had, which I dredged up from God knows where, was when I realized that everything bad that could happen to me already did. The worst was over. They'd thrown the book at me, and I was still standing. I could start over and remake myself into something new, someone different. I'd already earned and been stripped of a legal degree and a CPA license. I'd never get them back, but so what? I'd achieved a fair level of success before I earned them. And there were other things I could do. I wasn't sure what they were but I had eight years to discover what they were.

In the interim, I'd own nothing of any physical value other than my glasses and what the BOP had issued me. Nothing. The government, my ex-spouse, and Steve, my attorney, divided my assets among them right down to my cufflinks. Three houses, two cars, a legal practice, and over three million dollars in cash and marketable securities—gone.

My once beloved wife took half my legally earned net worth, and then ignored me as if I were a criminal. Well, I was a criminal, and not a successful one considering my circumstances. Steve bled away a half-million dollars in legal fees before the Department of Justice filed a forfeiture action that Steve charged me to contest. To pay Steve, I had to borrow money.

At sentencing, the government seized my remaining assets to compensate victims and the Judge ordered restitution of one million eight hundred and eighty-four thousand dollars.

Opposite a period of incarceration with no houses, no cars, no bills, no job, and no family, there was the reality that I'd never own anything again.

But I wasn't just stuck on financial losses. The loss of freedom haunted me. The longer I was incarcerated, the more I longed for my freedom; my individuality.

The feeling of doom started during the FBI investigation as I struggled to accept my certain incarceration. To help me deal with that, Steve told me to divide the legal process into three phases.

"The entire matter will be easier to understand and more logical for you," he reasoned from behind his desk.

I was eager to know how my dire situation could be improved.

"The first phase is pre-trial. That covers indictment, retaining counsel, meeting with the FBI, the IRS, and the DOJ, and trying to provide a non-criminal explanation for the case."

Phase one lasted eleven months.

Steve continued, "Phase two is when trial starts, and it lasts through sentencing."

"Good," I remember thinking as trial was about to start, "I'm a third of the way through."

Phase two was easy because I ended up pleading guilty. If I lost trial, I'd get thirty years and there was no way I could win at trial.

"Phase three is serving the sentence," said Steve as if serving the sentence was a snap.

At sentencing I told myself, "Now I'm two-thirds of the way through. I'll be done before I know it."

I was glad to be so close to finishing.

It wasn't until I reported to camp that the reality of phase three set in. During the first two phases, you can delude yourself into believing that the mess will somehow be resolved. Steve's third phase, reporting to serve the sentence, ended the delusion. Steve's little gimmick was a trick to calm me down.

Given the circumstances, the healthy thing was for me to learn to deal with the eight year sentence. That much I knew.

"The game isn't over until *I* say it's over!! Ain't no fat lady singing here!" I would tell myself out-loud. "If I never give up, the game's never over. And that's all it is, a *game*. A simple and easy game. Just keep breathing, eating, and staying warm in winter."

Sometimes it felt like "Game Over" though.

When I arrived, my initial bunkie was Jack Cass. Jack was in his late twenties and was doing ten years for drug distribution. He was a good-looking white kid born and raised in the "river wards" of Philadelphia, where, as Johnny Cash sang, "His fists got hard and his wits got keen."

He was the oldest child of divorced parents. He didn't know where his father was. He'd studied to become an electrician right out of high school. But an apprentice didn't earn enough to support a mother and a sister, and then, despite the precautions against unprotected sexual intercourse, his girlfriend became pregnant. So Jack went into the drug trade for the same reason as John DeLorean—he needed the money. He told me he'd been in camp for thirty-one months so he knew the ropes. But getting him to guide me on a tour of the camp was next to impossible.

"I'll miss my pre-dinner nap," he whined.

In the nicest tone I could muster I pleaded, "Well, I don't know a thing about this place."

He didn't move.

"Aw, come on, Jack," I whimpered at him. "You know where everything is."

That got a response.

"Awww, shit!"

He stood up and we started a slow walk. Jack didn't talk much. He pointed and grunted.

"Range," he said motioning vaguely at the floor of cubicles and bunk beds. "Activity room," he said as we passed by its door going down the stairs. "Laundry." He pointed at a doorway.

I had questions.

"Wait a second, Jack. Let me look at it."

I ducked inside and saw four washers and dryers with no coin slots. There were no laundry soap dispensers hanging on the wall like a laundromat.

"How do you pay for these?" I asked.

Not hearing an answer, I turned to see that Jack had not followed me into the room. I went out into the hall to where he was standing.

I had to drag information out of him like it was a state secret. Laundry room rules, TV room rules. He would have rather been anywhere else than with me. His resistance arose because I'd broken the pattern of how he did time. His routine called for his daily nap. Breaking in an "FNG" was not on, and conflicted with, his agenda.

We continued to the garden, the nature trail, and the track where any inmate could walk off the property. His first voluntary comment was at the nature trail where he smirked, "You can guess what goes on in 'Homo Heaven.'"

Great, as I wondered how prevalent homosexuality was.

Everywhere we went there was a lack of inmate activity. Apathy was abundant. This was so different from my legal and business experience where constant movement and multiple deadlines were commonplace.

"What are they doing?" I asked, pointing at a group of twenty guys leaning on rakes and shovels.

"Landscaping."

I kept asking questions, trying to drag information out of him. He would have been a great spy.

Out by the weight pile Jack called out to about five guys working out. "Hey! Mr. Norton! How 'bout showing this FNG around? I don't feel so good. Need to get back to my cube and lie down."

"Afraid you'll miss your beauty sleep, jackass?" said one of the men.

Then one of the men said, "Keep the faith, prisoners," and waved as he headed in our direction.

I thought Jack might be offended by being called "jackass," but he ignored it.

A white guy about a head shorter than me walked over. He had the type of face show-biz people called even-featured—a good-looking guy. He had long, straight, brown hair tied in pigtails running down his back. He was too young to be a sixties hippie. Maybe he was in his late thirties.

"Welcome to merry Camp Catskill," he said. "I'm Arlen Norton." He held out his hand.

"I'm Dan Holmes." He had a moderate grip. "Nice to meet you."

Jack turned to leave.

"Hey, jackass!" an inmate yelled from a handball court. "You owe me two packs, you asshole."

"Yeah, yeah. Come see me Friday." Jack waved a dismissive hand.

"You ain't playin' cards here again 'til you pay up, fucking asshole."

Jack kept going.

Only then did I realize his parents had tagged him from birth as Jack Cass, and he'd grown up being called "Jackass." Some people never have a chance.

Arlen Norton was delighted to show me around. He chatted away about anything and everything as we walked. He escorted me to the Admin Building and showed me the locked commissary door, the weight room, and the infirmary. He pointed out the camp-information bulletin boards and the forms rack. The dining hall I had already seen as I'd walked by with my mattress and linen, then he led me through the kitchen, pantry, loading dock, and freezer.

"What's for dinner tonight?" he asked an inmate who was opening boxes in the freezer.

"Dead beef."

"How long's it been dead?"

"The date is what?" The inmate flipped up the cardboard flap and examined the label. "'Bout seven years." He glanced up at us. "Just over seven years, Mr. Norton. Probably went out and back with the Navy a few times."

Norton reached in and pulled out a clear plastic bag with a crystalline yellow mass inside. Extreme freezer burn.

"Clearly corn-fed beef," deadpanned Norton dropping the bag like a bad habit.

I searched for some of the other dates. Most were between two and four years old.

"How tasty is this going to be?" was the obvious question.

"Depends on how long you've been here," Norton snickered.

The statement was sad but true.

As we resumed the tour, everybody greeted Norton as, "Mr. Norton," when he would stop and introduce me to an inmate or hack. Everyone was happy to see him. I was ignored. FNGs usually are.

"The Recreation Center is called the 'Wreck Center.'"

The wall beside the door had a plastic sign printed with exactly that. We investigated the equipment and discovered that it was worn and broken from the lack of a maintenance program. Norton filled me in. "As the budget shrinks, something here goes without." Then he showed me the phone banks and reviewed the phone rules.

"There are six television rooms."

He told me about each one, first pointing out the two rooms in the housing units where our black and Latino brothers determined the viewing schedule.

"It's wise not to go in there and change channels," he advised properly.

"What passes itself off as intelligentsia communes in the Admin Building where the main TV is always tuned to Fox News or CNN. The other TV is in the Visiting Room and is more or less potluck if it's not broken."

The two remaining TV's were in the exercise room and were tuned to Sports Center, BET, or a Spanish station depending on who was working out.

"If you want to see a special show, go to the TVs in the Admin Building a couple of hours ahead of time and tape a note to the TV with the show's name and the time it starts. Most of the time it works. Sometimes you're SOL."

Along the way, he was greeted with "Hola, Senor Norton," or "Yo, Mr. Norton!" or "Whas-sup, Mr. Norton?" He was a gentle, kind man who always personalized his greetings. He acknowledged everyone with a smile and a wave and said the other person's name. He was one of the few inmates who could cross racial barriers. That intrigued me.

No matter where we went, he knew everything about everybody.

He would relay to me the details of cases he thought were interesting.

"Do you work in the office?" I wondered if he had access to inmate files.

"Nope. Just passed through there once on Opening Day."

"How long is your sentence?"

"Six months."

"What'd you do?"

"I crossed a *No Civilians Past Here* sign at Ft. Benning where the U.S. Army trains foreign civilians in military tactics so they can topple governments the U.S. doesn't like. It was during a tour of the fort. I hit a helicopter with a Styrofoam hammer."

"What type of crime is that?"

"Civil Disobedience."

I vaguely remembered watching the nightly news and seeing a tape from a security camera that showed a man swinging a mallet at the front glass of a helicopter. It was one of those unique moments newscasts show because the act was insanely quirky.

"The most important rule here, besides not walking *Out of Bounds,* is not to mess up the Four O'clock Count. That's the one the hacks send to the BOP in Washington, D.C. every day. Heads roll if it doesn't add."

We passed by the softball field bleachers.

"To survive here, you need a decent job, especially if your people don't send money to you. The cops'll assign you one. You'll probably start at twelve cents an hour. Pay is deposited into your Commissary Account from which is deducted the cost of your Commissary purchases. You can also use your prison ID in the soda and candy machines. The card has a magnetic strip on the back like a credit card.

And, remember, if you have restitution, the hacks will expect you to make a monthly payment to pay off victims."

"Even if I have to make it on twelve cents an hour?" I asked.

Norton shook his head slowly and sadly. "They want you to start a restitution plan while you're here."

I hadn't figured on that possibility. My existence just got skimpier.

"You being a lawyer, the guys here'll want you to write motions or do other legal work for them. Get paid for it. Charge 'em stamps, cigarettes, cokes, candy, whatever. Anything on the Commissary list is fair game. Make 'em do chores for you. Just be sure you get paid. Read the little green handbook Hinkel gave you. That sets out most of the rules. This is federal prison and you gotta know the rules. You got your good clothes yet?"

"I didn't know how to get them. Nobody tells you how to do anything around here. Besides, R&D didn't have much."

"That's because the bozos in R&D just do a temporary fit-out so they can mail out the clothes you wore in here. They issue the stuff Laundry would burn." He studied his watch. "You're lucky 'cuz Laundry is only open thirty-minutes a day and it's open now."

We hurried to Laundry in the Admin Building; Norton continued my orientation along the way. He was great; lots of tips on how to survive.

"Hey, Stinky," Norton said slapping his palm on the half-door cap. "I gotta FNG here named Dan Holmes who needs a set. All he's got is the hospital scrubs they gave him in R&D."

A short bald black man appeared. He had a twinkle in his eyes, which had an uneven and odd yellowish color. He said, "Always a pleasure to see you, Mr. Norton." He held up his fist and tapped it against Norton's fist as a greeting and a sign of respect.

Stinky stuck his head over the half-door and gave me the onceover.

I wondered why Stinky was called "Stinky." Nicknames in jail are usually easy to connect, like a bald guy named "Moon." He didn't have BO. I wondered what was Stinky about him?

"Poor boy," he said.

Oh man! I learned the hard way. His nickname was well earned.

He had the worst case of bad breath in the world. He spit out two words and the bacteria flew from his mouth like birds escaping a cage. I was knocked back a step.

Despite his oral issues, Stinky was dressed immaculately, not a spot or wrinkle, sharp creases on his khaki shirt and pants.

"He's such a FNG he doesn't have his ID yet," Norton told him. He held out both arms as if I were a blank puzzle being presented by Vanna White.

Stinky beamed a jumbled set of yellow teeth at me. He said,

"Hasn't been no civilians ever done come straight off'n da street lookin' fo' prison clothes so's theys can wears them to theys church every Sundee. I git the boy all fixed up for you good, Mr. Norton." He could have been an extra in *Gone With the Wind* with that accent.

Stinky turned to the rear of his realm.

"Yo, Juice! Gimme one full set skinny tall to six-four up here."

Stinky looked back at Norton and grinned. He pulled a piece of paper from his top shirt pocket and held it tightly against his chest.

"Ah's gots one fo' you, Mr. Norton. Is you ready?"

"Slap it to me."

Stinky pulled the paper off his chest like it was a hole card in a poker game and held it up to his eyes so only he could see it.

"What is the square root of sixty-six thousand, oh-forty-nine?

His accent had disappeared. Norton answered quickly, "Two hundred and fifty-seven."

Stinky looked crestfallen. He handed me the paper.

Both numbers were neatly drawn around the square root sign.

"Never fails," Stinky shook his head in disbelief. "Most amazin' thing I've ever seen. If you can get Mr. Norton here to answer, he's never wrong. Sometimes he won't answer if it's a stupid question. He doesn't say he doesn't know, he just says it's a stupid question."

"And Stinky won't tell anyone what he did to get in here," said Norton. "It's some big secret not even I know. So, as punishment, I only answer one question from *him* per month."

In the next three minutes Stinky assembled for me five sets of briefs, T-shirts, and socks, three pairs of khaki pants and shirts, towels, a belt, work boots, a winter coat, and a pair of shower shoes.

Norton carried half the clothing back to Camp Two for me. He stopped at the second floor door.

"I'm in Camp One. We're not allowed to go on each other's ranges, so I'll let you take it from here." He handed the clothing to me.

I said, "I guess it's best to be a stickler for rules."

"Amen to that, brother."

"Would you mind if I asked *you* a question?"

He stared at me like he was reading my soul.

After a moment I said, "Can you tell me the answer before I ask the question? I'd be blown away if you did that."

"No. You have to ask the question so there's no confusion about what the answer is."

He kept staring at me, flicking his eyes back and forth from one of my eyes to the other.

"Okay," he said. "I'll let you ask one question. Anything at all. Are there flying saucers? When will the world end? Anything you want."

"All right."

There was no way he could know this.

"What are the names of my children?"

I didn't even tell him how many there were.

"Joseph, Shannon, and Brendan."

Oh, my God! There was no way he could know that!

He smiled, turned and trotted down the stairs.

Sadly, that was the last time I ever saw him.

12

Camp

Spooter seys "Bees careful of whose toes youse steps on 'cause they may be attached to an ass youse ones days has to kiss."

Norton was released that week. After he left, I pieced together what I could learn about him. He was an engineer from MIT who started his own firm in New York City; accumulated a lot of money and at the same time tired of the rat race. He sold everything and moved to Vietnam to "ease the suffering" of its unfortunate people. He stayed about ten years, building bridges, roads, railways, schools, hospitals, offices, and reclaiming swampland. He garnered a reputation as a clone of Mother Theresa, but in the building and engineering fields. He'd been nominated for the Nobel Peace Prize but had his name withdrawn from consideration. He'd described himself as a "Nation Builder."

When he came back to the U.S., he began writing and lecturing about the evils of the American military machine. He developed quite a following among university students and Vietnam-era peaceniks with an organization he called, "The Future as One."

About a year ago, he'd organized a protest at the School of the Americas at Fort Benning, Georgia where the U.S. Army trained foreign nationals in military tactics. He'd claimed the U.S. was creating terrorists to overthrow foreign governments, people he called, "nation destroyers." During the demonstration he'd crossed a "No civilians beyond this point" barrier and struck a helicopter with a Styrofoam hammer. That symbolic trespass resulted in a six-month federal sentence.

At Camp Catskill, Mr. Norton was the person who had answers for everything; a human form of the Internet. He was outgoing and friendly. As a job, he tutored the GED students, but he was always uplifting the other inmates by writing letters for them or counseling them through personal tangles. Since he lectured around the country preaching Brotherhood and Peace, his visitors list included members of different religious orders. But above all, he didn't sermonize a message but walked his talk. Everyone liked and respected Mr. Norton. He received the highest compliment of all; he was "the anti-Slobodo."

For my part, his willingness to treat everyone like a brother caused me to reflect. Norton's presence made our secluded world a more peaceful place. It was a unique and welcome change.

I was now into my second week. Jail had become a game of hurry-up and wait. The pace was one hundred and eighty degrees from what I was used to but I was adapting to the rules, regulations and operating procedures. Also, I was constantly worried about everything that happened in the outside world as if I were able to do anything to solve the problem. Consequently, anything and everything stressed me out. I needed a way to calm down. I'd noticed that a lot of inmates walked every day. I decided to try it myself. I wore the boots out to the track to break them in. They were black, had steel toes and were broken-in by someone else's feet. Blisters formed after twenty minutes of walking. That was fine because by then I was exhausted.

I went back up to my cube and took off the boots. I sat at the desk thinking about the differences between my three houses and their contents and the upper bunk and the possessions in my locker. I could stuff my belongings into a single pillowcase. It would be tight, but I could do it. And everything in the pillowcase belonged to the BOP.

That was a memorable low point.

"Attention in the Camp. Attention in the Camp. Inmate Hole-meese. Report to R&D. Inmate Hole-meese. Report to R&D."

That was Counselor Hinkel. He murdered everyone's name that wasn't Smith or Jones.

I knew where R&D was, so I put on my blue sneakers and walked down to the Admin Building.

Someone had fixed the camera. I was issued my inmate ID, which was a plastic DOJ/BOP card with a magnetic strip, a photo, and my U.S. Marshal's number. This replaced my credit cards. The only other ID I had was my Pennsylvania Driver's License. In one picture I had a power suit and tie—in the other, an open-buttoned khaki shirt.

Norton's message rang in my ears, "Your starting wage will be twelve cents per hour, whether you earn it or not."

The thought of paying taxes was suddenly appealing.

"Don't ever get caught without your ID," Norton warned. "If you don't have it with you, you're considered an escapee. That's five more years if they want to stick it to you. You have to learn the rules."

I put my driver's license in my locker.

I wouldn't need it for a while.

My biggest challenge early on was sleeping. The daytime was murder. Adjusting to living with three hundred men of different colors, races and creeds was difficult enough. Add in the fact that most of the guys were total loud assholes and it was no wonder that I longed for the solace of night. Then I discovered that the nights weren't much better. I sorely missed my Sealy Posturepedic and the quiet suburban darkness. At home, the worst that would happen was my wife would wake me up and "want some." I'd stick her with both inches and go back to sleep. This was different. I felt like a referee in a snoring contest. I'd be lying on my bunk staring at the ceiling four feet above my head as I listened to the snorers attack each other on the range. There were fifty guys on the floor. Bare block walls, a concrete ceiling, and a linoleum floor—and every sound echoed, especially the snoring.

I was able to group the snorers. Some guys produced staccato snorts without any tempo. Others had an even cadence. One fellow about three cubes away snored in waves that, at their peak, resembled a locomotive. He woke up the inmates around him. I could hear them groan at the start of one of his cycles. I couldn't understand why he didn't wake himself up. Sometimes six or more guys would snore at the same time.

But snoring wasn't the only overnight noise. Someone would always be walking to the bathroom. I could tell whether or not he'd washed his hands. Lord, I could tell what every inmate *did* in the bathroom because my bunk was on the other side of the cinderblock wall. Inmates made no attempt to conceal body noises. The louder the prouder.

Finally, there were the overnight counts. It was kind of like a young child leaving their bedroom and climbing into Mommy and Daddy's bed. There you were, fast asleep, and magically, your two year old was your new bed partner "because I'm scared, Daddy." It was always okay with me as long as they slept away from the wet spot.

At two-thirty there was a count during which one hack carried a clipboard and counted while another shined his flashlight at every bunk to be sure the inmates were present. The hack had to see a face in every bunk. This meant we were spotlighted with a high-intensity flashlight. Since the hack had to see flesh, he pulled down the blanket or sheet if skin was not showing. It's very disconcerting at first.

After the flashlight count was cleared, until about five o'clock, it was as quiet as it got. At five, the count process was repeated, and then wristwatch alarms started going off and inmates began snorting and grunting themselves awake. Some had to go to the kitchen to prepare breakfast. Others woke up to exercise. Regardless of the activity, they were a loud bunch.

Due to the noise, sleep time was over and you might as well start your day. The opening event was breakfast from six to seven. Many inmates skipped it and just slept until a few minutes before eight when the hacks conducted their daily sanitation inspection. Inmates can be written up if shoes were out of place, if dust was under the bunk, if a bed was not properly made, or if the trash can wasn't empty. When the hacks left, inmates not otherwise engaged in a work detail or GED class could go back to sleep. One inmate down the range seemed intent on sleeping away his entire bit. He was classified "idle," meaning not eligible for work. Sitting in his upper bunk he boasted his goal was to sleep sixteen out of every twenty-four hours. His theory was he was only doing a third of his sentence.

Hey, at least he had a plan.

Most didn't.

By the tenth day, I had acquired better shower shoes, a toothbrush, and a small tube of toothpaste, two more towels, a pencil and another pad of paper. Oh—and for the occasional emergency—one Band-Aid. These extra items were issued by the range orderlies after a serious amount of begging. As I put them away, I realized that I was getting comfortable. That scared me.

13

NFL Reorganization

One of the ten thousand guys I stumbled across in my "journey" enlightened me by saying, "I'd rather be hated for what I am than loved for what I'm not."

Those first days I watched inmates to observe what they did to kill time. My career had been a continuous whirlwind from the start of law school until the day I reported to FPC Catskill. By day five, I was already bored. I wanted to do *something* worthwhile to keep my active mind occupied and sharp.

A few cubes down the range from me the black giant, Wilkinson, bunked with a Korean-American named Lee Kim Wong. Wilkinson was called "Big Jim" and Wong was tagged "Ping-Pong" because he was the table tennis champ. There weren't many Asians in camp, but they were all named Wong. Hinkel thought it was a conspiracy.

Anyway, Ping videotaped an opening-day movie from his theater seat. The authorities secured a warrant and searched his house to discover DVD copying equipment and hundreds of bootlegged DVDs. He was sentenced to thirty months for violating the FBI's warning about unauthorized reproduction of DVDs.

Before dark one evening when I was bored stiff, Ping announced excitedly in gook speak, "I have completed my mission!"

"What'd you do?" someone asked.

"I reorganized the NFL."

He held up a pad of paper with most of the sheets turned over the back.

"Oh, yeah?" This was from the cube next to me. "How'd you change it?"

"I didn't know it needed changing," came a sarcastic voice on Ping's side of the aisle.

"Do you have a permit to do that?" someone else joked.

Laughter followed.

"You got no permit, sum-buddy gotta go to jail."

More laughter.

"Do Spooter know?"

Chatter along the range was like that. Guys busting on each other; breaking balls. It was a constant.

"I did 'em *all*," smiled Ping, showing pride of paternity.

He flipped the pad to the first page.

"First I did it by region to make it the most efficient travel-wise. That eliminated a lot of rivalries, but reduced travel costs for the owners. Then I did it by rivalries like the Cowboys and Redskins, the Bears and the Packers. But there aren't enough good rivalries to make it work. Then..."

He flipped back a few pages.

"I put the most recent Super Bowl winners in the same division."

Ping flipped another few pages.

"Then I put the birds together."

He read from his sheet.

"Cardinals, Ravens, Eagles, Seahawks, and Falcons. Then the cats. Jaguars, Lions, Bengals, and Panthers. There are two divisions of humans. Cowboys, Redskins, Saints, Packers, Patriots, and Buccaneers in one. Chiefs, Vikings, Raiders, Steelers, and Texans in the other. Then one for the other animals like the Bears, Broncos, Dolphins, Rams and Colts. Then last, the ones nobody knows for sure what they are like the Browns, Bills, Jets, and Chargers. The two wild cards are the Giants and Titans." He looked at the bottom of a page. "That's five birds, four cats, five other animals, six nobody knows what they are, and twelve humans."

Ping looked up from his list as if he expected a standing ovation.

Everyone ignored him. They returned to their monotony when he started reading.

Ping looked at his bunkie Big Jim.

Big Jim never talked much. When asked what he was doing he would always say, "Chillin'." He was a loner who spent most of his time watching sports in "his" TV room wearing his wrap-arounds, even at night. He loved football, and while he knew little about its details, no one ever corrected him since he was, as they said, "the biggest, meanest dog in the pound."

Ping looked at his bunkie. In a quiet voice he asked, "What do you think, Big Jim? Which do you think is better?"

Big Jim took about seven seconds to say, "Dat's some bull shit."

I wondered why Ping would bother reorganizing the NFL. There was no chance the league's Commissioner would ever see it. Some office flunky at NFL headquarters would trash it after they saw the return address was a Federal Prison Camp. Ping had to be smart enough to realize that.

Someone said, "All the divisions have to have the same number of teams. Not some four, some five and some six."

As if he had an audience, Ping said, "I moved some of the teams around. The final divisions are four cats, four birds, four animals, four nobody knows what they are, and four divisions of four humans each plus the wild cards. The Dolphins I moved to humans because they're mammals and the Cardinals I moved because they're the most sissy of the birds." He held up the pad showing eight neatly drawn boxes with the team names inside each.

"So that's the final structure?" I asked, my curiosity becoming more morbid at the futility of the task. "Is that utopia for the NFL?"

"No, it's not." He flipped to the next page. "The best way is align it by regions so it's more travel-efficient combined with keeping the rivalries in the same divisions." He held up the sheet so I could see it. "For instance, the Jaguars go to the NFC South and the Panthers to the AFC South."

I slid off my bunk. Ping walked toward me and handed me the pad.

Here was someone who'd taken most of the day to tear to pieces something that wasn't broken and who'd put it back together again six different ways. Neat penmanship on every page. The rival teams were matched together. He'd identified eighteen teams that had long-standing feuds. Boxes were drawn with sub-categories precise in their page positions. It was art. Useless, but it looked pretty.

"I'm going to send this to the Commissioner, the owners and the players' union," he said. "I'll give them mileage figures. The NFL is relatively stable right now, but they need to make these changes for efficiency."

Ping was immersed in his task.

"You have no hope in getting anyone to even look at it," I told him trying to bring sanity to the situation.

"Doesn't matter," he said, still smiling. "I know it's the best and it's mine. It'll get wrecked when they add the first international teams. Say London, Moscow, Seoul and Tokyo come in. That makes thirty-six teams in two divisions of eighteen. That's the maximum number of teams. After the first ones go international the marginal teams like Detroit and Jacksonville will be relocated to Rio and Singapore. It'll become a planetary league."

I wondered if Ping could figure a way to make the United Nations functional. He certainly had enough time.

Then it hit me.

It didn't matter much what a person did whittling away at a sentence day by day. It mattered that you could find something that was of interest to you and indulge it, no matter how futile it was in reality. It didn't have to be important, viable, or realistic. All it had to be was a time killer. When I got my feet on the ground, I would find something that interested me as much as reorganizing the NFL interested Ping. The BOP could control my body, but they couldn't control my mind. I refused to allow that to happen.

14

Les Artistes

Frankie Bananas was assigned to the kitchen detail and was caught stealing ten oranges. The kitchen hack asked him, "Why are you stealing?" Frankie responded sheepishly, "Because my rehabilitation is not going well."

I've been here for a couple of weeks. I realize that if I don't bother anyone, no one will bother me. My physical safety was no longer a primary concern. I split my time between my job at the Power House and the Law Library where I prepared exotic Motions for guys in the slim chance that they may succeed.

Based on my vantage point in the Law Library, I divided the inmates into two groups—drug dealers and white collars.

The drug dealers had either been judged non-violent during presentencing or had worked themselves down from higher security facilities to minimum security based on good behavior. They appeared to have come from a segment of society where formal education was frowned upon. Alcohol, drugs, violence, and incarceration had played a role in the lives of their parents and that pattern of life had perpetuated itself into the current generation. Instead of following the advice of their high school teachers and counselors, the "old heads" in their neighborhoods introduced them to "the game" where money brought status. Unfortunately, it led to jail.

The other group was white collar and non-violent. Many were physicians who'd abused the Medicare/Medicaid system. Their numbers surprised me as I listened to their conversations and heard their crimes. Billing for non-performed services was commonplace. Others were accountants and attorneys who'd dipped into client escrows. None of them would admit their guilt. There were always extenuating circumstances to justify their actions, always "a story."

Most of the other white collar types were game-fully unemployed Robin Hood types who tried to create the perfect scam. Out on the street, they planned their crimes instead of stooping to work for a living. They were the *artistes* of their trade. Or, at least they thought they were. Regardless, the stories were interesting.

Seymour Turner was a self-proclaimed *artiste*. His moneymaker was to fabricate invoices on his computer and remit them to Fortune Five Hundred companies. The invoices requested payment between two and eight thousand dollars for materials and supplies relating to the company's business operations. He provided detailed explanations that sounded plausible, like wood trusses supplied to a residential apartment builder. No two invoices were alike.

"At the peak," Turner told me, "about a third of the invoices got no response. A third called the number on the invoice and reached a recorder I'd set up for that purpose. I never returned those calls. The rest paid in full, no questions asked. I refined the process as time progressed. I knew who would pay if I worded the invoices right. The key was not to get greedy."

Not to get greedy.

I'd have to remember that.

"So how'd you get caught?" I asked.

He sighed.

"My wife turned me in." His chin fell toward his chest. "We had a fight about where to put the boom-box in the house. I told her to fuck off and she ran to the FBI about what we were doing. She got immunity. Fucking bitch."

He looked up and smiled.

"Don't worry though. I figured out how to do it next time. When I get out, I'll do it right and they'll never catch me."

I thought Seymour Turner was a bold dude to try such a scheme. Of course, like most other inmates, he could justify his actions, albeit with a twist.

"I did the same thing big companies always do with government contracts. It's like building fighter planes or providing community relief when there's a flood or a hurricane. Some company is awarded a contract with the government to do something that costs them three hundred thousand dollars and then they bill ten times that much, plus all the cost overruns they can justify. All government contractors do it. It's a rule. If they get caught, they say, 'Oops. We must have made a mistake. Government paperwork is *so* complicated. Give us back that stack of invoices so we can double-check 'em all.' Remember, most government contractors can't be replaced. Government people are too dumb to assemble fighter planes, build roads or anything else that takes brains. Sometimes I wonder if it's a question as to who needs who more. From the prices paid by Uncle Sam for some of the stuff they buy, I think the government needs the contractors more. What's the government's alternative? Go into the jet-making business? Imagine a jet fighter designed and manufactured by the government?"

"Yeah, that's true. Only private industry could build a jet or put a satellite into orbit."

"Government doesn't build anything," Turner said. "Contractors build the roads. All the government does is regulate. That's why nobody went to jail for the four thousand dollar toilet seat you hear about occasionally."

Seymour ran his finger across his moustache.

"I thought it was a four thousand dollar screwdriver."

"Could be," he said. "Anyway, it doesn't really count as fraud as long as I spend the money and you know, put it back into the economy. It's the buying and spending that keeps things going."

Interesting approach to self-justification, I thought.

"How long before you're unleashed on corporate America?"

"Sixteen months."

"Don't get married next time," I told him.

"Don't worry, Danny Boy. I ain't never going to marry again. She wanted the boom-box in the bedroom. Imagine that, the dumb bitch. Boom-box goes in the den or living room."

Another *artiste* was Joe Nichols who was doing forty-seven months for duping Newport News, Virginia salvage contractors into depositing funds to dismantle the retired aircraft carrier *USS Intrepid*, permanently on display in New York Harbor.

Nichols met each contractor dressed as a Rear Admiral.

"The Navy has decided to scrap *Intrepid* for its steel and metal.

The carrier will be towed to Newport News after dark. The hull has to be broken into three sections within hours of arrival. The Navy requires this to be done on low radar because the veterans of that ship would cause a stink if they found out before it happened. The Navy doesn't want the scrapping to be public knowledge until it's too late to do anything about it. The winning company has to be large, capable of doing the work on time and on budget, and be willing to handle the negative press. For that, there would be a premium in price."

"What kind of documentation did you give them?" I asked.

We had this conversation while walking around the track. A lot of ideas for future criminality were passed back and forth as guys walked around that track. Prison is a breeding ground for refining future scams.

"I gave them a standard off-the-web GSA RFP plus request specifications, time frame, cost estimate range, basic ship specs from old books. It took some work."

"Were you ever in the Navy?"

"Yeah. I was deployed in the shipyards in Newport News. That's how I knew the ins and outs of how salvage worked."

Rear Admiral Nichols required a quarter million-dollar refundable deposit payable to some U.S. Navy subsidiary created for the purpose of scrapping the *Intrepid*. The deposit was to assure the Navy of the company's financial strength, pledge of silence, *and* willingness to take the heat from the veterans. All of this was max hush-hush. Good ol' Rear Admiral Nichols told them that the ship specifications showed *Intrepid* contained tons of asbestos that had to be removed and disposed of in an environmentally safe way. The Navy would disclose the existence of this toxic fact to justify the scrapping. Disposing of the asbestos would command an additional premium. All documents and the RFP were to be returned to Rear Admiral Nichols via courier if the salvager decided not to bid on the contract. It was so secret, Rear Admiral Nichols told them, that the names of his superior officers in Washington, D.C. could not be disclosed.

"I got the idea from a scheme by a French con who sold the Eiffel Tower for scrap in the 1920s. Not once. Twice."

"He sold the Eiffel Tower?" I asked. I did not know that. We live and learn….even in jail.

"Yeah. The tower was a temporary symbol for the World's Fair built in 1889. It was supposed to be taken down after the fair. Secrecy was the key for the con. People liked seeing the tower on the skyline. The steel scrappers knew the tower was supposed to come down, they just didn't know when. The guy collected deposits by claiming he was in charge of the take down but he got caught somehow."

"I would think you'd want to know how he got caught."

"Yeah, maybe…"

He took a moment to think about that.

"Anyway, he got caught. But the beauty of it was, none of the contractors would press charges against him as long as they got their money back. They didn't want it known that they'd been conspiring to take down one of France's national monuments in secret. The police had to let him go."

"How could he do the same thing a second time?"

"He refined it and went to different contractors. Three the first time. Three the second time. He scammed the six steel scrappers in Paris."

"How'd he do the second time?"

"Got caught again." He shrugged his shoulders. "Don't know how then either. People talk, I guess. What can I say?"

Joe Nichols was a well educated fifty to sixty year-old. He presented well, somewhat regimented like military types, and quite clean. He looked good in prison khaki. How could he not realize that the odds of the scheme working were in the range of astronomical to none?

Oh, but then there was my case. To other people's eyes, my case was probably just as dumb.

One question remained and I had to know.

"How'd you get caught?"

I recognized the "Oh, shit!" look inmates give you just before they disclosed how fate and circumstance conspired to bring them down. He confessed, "Well, I made up my ID, stationery, and business cards based on the *real* Rear Admiral Nichols who really *is* in the Navy. That way they could see I was in the records if they looked me up. I had it all scoped. A no-fail plan. The Admiral's name was the same as mine, Joe Nichols. When the feds picked me up, I already had two deposits, five hundred thousand dollars."

"How many deposits did you hope to get?"

"Six."

That would be one and a half million dollars and Joe Nichols in a non-extradition paradise like Iran.

"The FBI was waiting for me in the third contractor's reception area when I arrived to pick up his check."

Just then he took a few seconds to compose himself.

"That third guy had contacts in the Navy. They all did, but he telephoned the contacts. Turns out Admiral Joe E. Nichols is Josephine E. Nichols. Dammit!"

He held out his hands.

"I had it all right here."

He stared at the palms of his hands.

This was typical of how scams ended for white collar criminals. "But for a nail, the kingdom was lost," I said by way of condolences.

Many missing nails led to many sad tales.

15

Pat O'Donnell

I didn't want to be a "brother." Everyone is a "brother" in prison. I just wanted to serve my sentence and go home. Go back to the way things were before I absorbed myself in money, position and power. I would rather be homeless and happy with my kids than live alone and be sad in a Fifth Avenue penthouse.

This was far from being a penthouse.

This was the outhouse.

The first meal I recall was a combination of meatless potpie and a plain lettuce salad. No salad dressing. In jail, there is an acute absence of everything. I imagined the potpies must have been produced without meat by mistake. The manufacturer's post-production options were few, lucky me. Some corporate bean-counter was planning our meals based on production errors and income tax deductions.

Another possibility was that the BOP bought large lots that were close to expiration. This saved the corporation from throwing them out, and they probably negotiated a lucrative price for the goods with the government, contracting with our federal friends being so profitable for everyone but the taxpayers.

But the potpie wasn't the issue. My main problem was that I had way too much time on my hands and was pondering problems that I couldn't possibly resolve. How could I affect the purchase of a flawed batch of potpies? What power or influence did I have? The answer was none. Inmates have no power or influence. However, that didn't stop me from thinking about the problem.

The seasoned brothers told me to stay busy to pass the time. It sounded good, but I was not yet assigned a job so I had nothing to do but hang around.

Doing nothing was boring. I decided to get my endorphins moving by starting a workout program.

I walked the track. I explored the camp some more. I had no interest in weightlifting or handball. Basketball and softball were sports I played when I was younger, but the black brothers didn't need an older slow white boy except as a whipping post. I don't play a musical instrument. But I did go to church, attending all the religious services I could.

Based on my early findings, this was going to be a *long, slow ninety-six* months.

One day, before I was assigned a job, I was walking the track and an inmate wandered over from the weight pile. He was white, about six feet tall with an average build. He had salt and pepper hair tied in a ponytail with a rubber band. And he had the rattiest set of sweats I'd yet seen.

"Hi. I'm Pat O'Donnell. You the new guy?"

He seemed like a decent fellow, overly familiar maybe. I recognized him from somewhere but I couldn't recall.

"Yeah. I'm Dan Holmes."

"Doing a long stretch, right?"

"Yeah." I wondered how come everyone knew that I had a long sentence. Bad news travels fast, I guess.

"Well, may God bless. We still have our obligations to the Shepherd."

Now I remembered him.

He was the guy who'd assisted Father Baker at Mass on Saturday night. O'Donnell set up the altar, did the first two readings, and put everything away once Mass ended. I'd gotten to Church early and seen this guy and Father Baker watching television. I thought it was an evangelical show.

I smiled. "I'm still trying to find my way around. Get used to the place."

"You Catholic?"

I wasn't sure how to answer that question. I'd attended church with my children more for appearance than for salvation. I'd contributed a good bit of my illegal income into the collection basket, but to claim that I was Catholic would beg the question of why I had swindled people out of their money. I decided to tell the truth. "My mother would say I'm Catholic."

He looked at me, put a hand on my shoulder, and said with a flat-line voice, "The Word says that when you adopt Jesus Christ as your Lord and Savior you are a new creation. Your sins are forgiven, and you are washed clean by the blood of the Lamb." He smiled—one of abject belief.

"Wow."

That dazed me.

He said, "If you're not doing anything tonight, how about if I stop by your hut about six and go over some things with you?"

"Uh—Okay."

He turned to walk away, and then turned back.

"Do you mind if I tell you something?"

"Go ahead."

He cleared his throat.

"You're risking your most valuable possession, good buddy. You're putting your eternal soul at risk."

I didn't like being called "good buddy" by someone that I didn't know.

"How am I doing that?" My cynical side added, "Friend."

"By hanging out with Abe Nagel."

Abe was an avuncular CPA from Duchess County, New York doing forty eight months for conspiracy to commit bank fraud. His crime had occurred when a client supplied Abe with false information for a financial statement and then presented the statement, issued on Abe's letterhead, to a federally insured bank to borrow money. The client split with the funds and left Abe holding the bag since he'd prepared the financial statement. As Abe told it, the Feds never believed that he hadn't inserted the fraudulent figures. The Feds alleged that Abe was sophisticated enough to have recognized the figures were bogus which then qualified as a conspiracy. Abe went to trial. The prosecutor asked him on cross, "Did you get paid to prepare the financial statement in question?"

The government had already entered the cancelled check as evidence. Abe testified, "Yes."

Saying "Yes" means he received consideration for the act of supplying a false financial statement. Such consideration was akin to splitting the illegally gotten gains and constituted tacit, if not overt, conspiracy under the law.

As Abe told it, he never had a chance.

"The jury got ridiculous instructions. They had no choice but to convict."

Despite his circumstances, Abe had a positive attitude and never exhibited anger or bitterness. He accepted what life gave him and kept going. He encouraged everyone to do likewise.

Here at Camp Catskill, Abe was the "inmate rabbi." He formed a loose inter-denominational congregation of Jewish inmates and inmates of other religious beliefs. The purpose of the group was to promote religious tolerance. He was more than a good person. He was an advisor, teacher, mentor, and advocate. Everybody in camp liked Abe.

I thought Pat O'Donnell might be the Catholic version of Abe Nagel. I said, "You don't like Abe?"

"He's a Jew!"

Ouch!

He was serious; I was shocked.

"Oh. That's just an accident of birth." I smiled trying to take the edge off him. "Besides, what other kind of accountant is there? The good ones, I mean?"

O'Donnell didn't laugh. He preached, "Jews are doomed to hellfire and can't be saved. They don't accept Jesus Christ as their Lord and Savior. Plus, the Jews killed Christ, good buddy. The Jews killed our Savior. They're doomed. You may think that little Jew is being nice and helping you out of the kindness of his heart, but he's stealing your soul. That's why the Jews are so miserable. They know they're doomed. Be careful, good buddy. Be careful he doesn't steal your soul."

I was speechless. Pat O'Donnell was no Abe Nagel, that was certain.

"Is that in the Bible?"

"Father Baker told me."

Father Alva Baker was the Catholic priest I'd met when I attended

Mass.

I hoped O'Donnell was kidding. He wasn't.

I'd been to one of Abe's meetings by that time. It ended up being a good way to kill a couple of hours and have an intelligent conversation, a rare and cherished event.

"Oh, come on. Abe and his group seem like nice guys," I said. "They made me feel like a regular. They shared their grape juice and bread like I'd always been in their group. We talked about the trials of Job. It was nice."

"There you go, good buddy. You said it yourself. You're being sucked into being a Jew. Father Baker says you are that which you surround yourself with."

O'Donnell had an unlined face. No worry lines. I wondered what was going on behind those eyes. Why all the hatred? Where did that come from?

"So, following that thought, if I attended a bunch of Harlem Globetrotters' games, I'll become a black basketball player?"

He pondered the statement, as absurd as it was, and then said, "I'll have to ask Father Baker about that."

"Are you at war with everything non-Catholic?"

His face lit up as if he had received a revelation.

"I never thought of it that way, but, yes. Good versus evil, in a holy war."

"Sort of like a jihad?"

"What's a jihad?"

That sufficed as an answer.

"Never mind."

"Anyway, Danny. We don't live in the Old Testament. We live in the New Testament. The New Testament has better covenants and promises than the Jews received in the Old Testament. The Jews have a covenant, but it isn't as good as ours."

Now would be a good time to leave. My feet were chafed from re-breaking-in my used boots. And trying to debate Pat O'Donnell on religious questions would give me a headache.

"Well, my friend," I said. "I better go back to my cube. You've given me a lot to think about."

"And I'll have a lot more to tell you tonight when we meet," he promised as I headed for Camp Two.

Can't wait for that, I thought.

The backs of my heels rubbed against the boot leather as I walked. Now, both my head and feet hurt.

The hacks showed up to do the Four O'clock Count.

After they left Jack Cass snickered, "I saw you got ordained today."

I was at the desk and I looked over at him as he sat on his bunk.

"Try English?"

"Father Pat recruited you into the Catholic army. I saw you talking on the track."

"Oh, yeah. He wants to come over here tonight."

"No. He wants to suck you into his gang. He tried to ordain me when I arrived. Pat O'Donnell is the *Onward Christian Soldier* recruiter for Father Baker."

"I thought they were close. I saw them watching some evangelist on television before Mass Saturday night."

Jack started laughing "My man, you gotta lot to learn. They weren't watching any kind of God show. They was watching a horse race."

"You're kidding?"

"Father Baker ain't no priest. What priest do you know whose three favorite past times are horses, gambling junkets, and drinking?"

I was about to say that priests were human beings too when Jack said, "Do you know why Father Baker is here?"

"No."

Jack stood up and opened his locker. He fished around until he located a folder. He handed me a newspaper article. The headline read, "Priest Accused of Stealing Bingo Proceeds."

The article said that the Cardinal for the Archdioceses had reassigned Father Alva Baker to the mission field of "prison chaplaincy" after accusations were proven that the Good Father had helped himself to the proceeds of the weekly bingo game. Supposedly, Father Baker paid off gambling debts with the money. He was assigned to the camp as punishment.

An inmate poked his head into the cube and said, "Hey, jackass. You got a file on me?" He was intimating that my bunkie was a rat.

"You're not worth blowing up," Cass replied.

I read the article again. All I could do was shake my head and think, "It gets better by the minute around here. At least it's not dull." I decided I'd had enough fun for the time being and went to chow.

16

Zolton

Society terms us scum, worthless and a scourge on humanity. Soon, because you are inundated with the negativity, you begin to believe it. One night, when I thought about the cruelty of my actions and realized their impact, I cried. Then I knew I had a soul.

I always walked down the hill to chow. Half the inmates ran when their camp was called, but I never felt like running to eat an unattractive, tasteless, cold, or burned meal. And if the meal *was* good—like hamburgers or pizza—twenty or thirty guys would cut in line if the cops weren't monitoring. Respect and decency were irrelevant.

Standing at the end of the line, I felt a tap on my shoulder.

I turned to face a tall, well-tanned, white guy in his mid-fifties. I'd seen him around. He had a casual gait and a charming smile with wavy salt and pepper hair. He stood up straight, shoulders back. He was dressed in khaki pants and shirt instead of the usual sweat pants and T-shirt. He had an air of laid-back formality.

"I don't think I've had the pleasure. I'm Zolton Krechevski," he said with an engaging grin as he held out his hand.

"Dan Holmes." I shook his hand.

"I know," he said. "The guys in the Law Library tell me good things about you. They say you're helping 'em out."

This was sort of true. I'd spent some time in the Law Library. When inmates heard I was an attorney on the street they'd pepper me with questions that related to their cases. I even assisted a couple of guys with the appeals they were drafting.

Besides, I had nothing better to do.

Maybe Zolton Krechevski wanted an attorney.

"Do you need legal help?"

Instead of answering, he said, "How long are you here?"

"Ninety-six months."

He cocked his head and assumed, "Drugs?"

"No. I was a lawyer. I dipped into client accounts."

The smile left his face.

"Those bastards," he said in disgust. "Why ninety-six months? The taxpayers would have been better off if you were sentenced to community service—or to provide free legal services to the poor. Or serve in the Peace Corps. Or Vista…"

I heard this skewed logic hundreds of times from inmates. It goes something like: *The sentences are too long, prisons are overcrowded, and society would be better off if we were sentenced to volunteer in a charitable endeavor. Contribute something. Pay back in some way. Being here is a waste of tax dollars.*

Debating the merits of incarceration with Zolton was painful. I argued the point with the Honorable Emil N. Smert at sentencing and lost by ninety-six months.

To move the conversation off this topic, I played a game I had invented and called "Name that Crime." From listening to my fellow inmates talking about their schemes, I devised a game that was divided into three parts. The first part, if I could convince Zolton to play, was a brief description of the criminal activity with appropriate non-criminal excuses.

"If you don't mind," I asked. "What did you do?"

The smile widening on to his face told me "Batter Up." First pitch, "I was arrested on the high seas because of the inability of the government of Mazitland to process my 'IDCC.'"

I needed a couple of explanations.

"Where's Mazitland? I've never heard of it."

"Mexico. Pacific side."

"You mean Mazatlan, the resort town."

"Whatever."

That was one question answered. One to go.

"What's an "IDCC?"

"An 'International Drug Registration Certificate.'"

He broke into the broadest smile yet.

"Wouldn't that be an 'IDRC?'"

Zolton wasn't tripped up by technicalities.

"It's the document that the International Drug Certification Board issues when they approve a drug for human consumption. The Certificate is better than the approval you're granted from the FDA. The standards are higher. We spent years pulling this off and we finally did!"

Part one was completed. In a nutshell, Zolton used the promise of an unissued certificate to rip people off. But it wasn't a crime, in his mind, since he was in international waters and not on U.S. soil.

Next was part two where Zolton would expand on his explanation of the crime while continuing to assert that his actions were non- criminal.

"To celebrate the IDCC approval, I booked a cruise to Bermuda on the QE2 with my girlfriend. Well, being an openhearted philanthropist, I told the ladies at dinner about the IDCC and they decided to help me end world hunger."

The line moved up about four feet.

"So, *you're* the one who solved the world hunger problem?" I said this with the least amount of sarcasm I could muster. "I've always wanted to meet you."

Zolton was unflappable; didn't hear a word.

"I worked on it in Bora-Bora for years. That's where my charity is located. The scientists and I developed a pill that would stop hunger."

Sounded as real as turning water into gasoline.

I inquired, "It's not a pill that you put a drop of water on and it turns into a steak, is it? It must be a diet pill or a food substitute."

"It works both ways. It stops you from feeling hungry and it provides nutrition. If we give it to all the starving people in Africa, they wouldn't go to sleep hungry every night."

I almost laughed in his face.

"After spending millions on equipment and research, and not a little bit of despair wasted on untold trial and error, we did it. Success! Yes, sweet success! And how grand it tasted. We were going to end world hunger. We filed the papers for the IDCC at the Mazitland office. It would take six to twelve weeks to process the certificate, so I cruised to Bermuda with Margaret. There I was on a British vessel in international waters, and I'm arrested for crimes in the United States."

We shuffled up a few more feet.

"How can that be, Dan? I ask you. How can that be? I'm in international waters—not U.S. soil. Plus, for God's sake, I'm a philanthropist, not a crook. All I did was share my good fortune with the ladies on the QE2. By God, I don't need the money. I'm a millionaire several times over. I *allowed* them, after much urging by them, I might add, to buy into the betterment of humanity. It provided meaning and purpose to their lives, for God's sake. Since when is that a crime?"

Zolton finished part two. His scam was a version of the old Certificate of Deposit trick where the huckster sells a Certificate of Deposit backed and secured by a foreign country that promised a high rate of interest. His twist was that the victims were saving humanity as opposed to the old "come on" of earning high interest rates. And, to make it easy, his "marks" were feeble, old widows who would be swayed by his charm. His MO was his engaging personality and the tale of his noble humanitarian acts. He charmed his victims-wined and dined them, danced with them, made the rich, lonely, old, biddies love him. A few of the ladies he'd mesmerized must have thrust money at him, and when they'd informed their not so ditzy friends, the authorities were contacted.

Part three was next and Zolton would explain why incarceration was, in effect, his choice.

We moved up the line another few feet. Someone up ahead said the main course was lamb chops. How pale compared to the fare served on the QE2.

Zolton said, "How could I prove my case when the FBI turned everyone against me? Those bastards! And you know who's really behind my incarceration? Who's doing the big cover-up? The drug companies, that's who. They don't want me to market my pills because it would cause an instant decline in their stock value," he snapped his fingers, "just like that. The boards of directors would lose their cushy offices and their big fees and the shareholders would revolt. So, in this dog-eat-dog world, it came down to big business against a well-meaning philanthropist."

Zolton had this speech memorized. He was smooth and convincing. Polished. His voice inflected at the right times and places.

"I threatened to fight the bastards. And I would have beaten them. They'd be like putty in my hands, just wash it off. One trip to Bora-Bora, and I'd come back with the documents proving my claim. I'd have demanded an apology from the Attorney General. That's what those lovely ladies begged me to do. They would have given me the money to retain Johnny Cochran and expose the plague being cast upon the world by the drug companies."

The pulpit missed not having Zolton, especially as an evangelist on some Sunday morning television show.

"But, I told the ladies that the far greater victory would be to accept this petty form of punishment and, once I'm released, go back to Bora-Bora and oversee the manufacture and distribution of my pill. And, by God, that's what I'm going to do! I can't wait to pick up the *Wall Street Journal* and watch their stock prices tumble."

He held his hands together in a prayer mode and mimed a slow dive to reflect the decline in pharmaceutical stock prices. He was smiling his widest. With his tan, he was glowing.

Zolton declared, "Victory shall be mine!"

I heard an inmate shout from the front, "Meat's dry. Get lotsa gravy."

Up ahead someone said, "Let's nuke pasta on the range. I done had this shit and it sucks."

Four inmates dropped out of the line.

I moved up.

"'Scuse me, Dan. I think I'll eat on the range, too."

I smiled watching him go. He hadn't disappointed me with his excuse. In part three, he wrapped up the matter by claiming that he was the victim due to the blunders at the office in Mazitland where his "IDCC" wasn't processed. It made sense to me that he choose jail over the trip to Bora-Bora to vindicate himself; well, not really.

As he walked out the door of the Admin Building, I wondered if he thought that I swallowed his word salad scam like the old biddies on the QE2.

17

Charity

I've attended religious services for the various denominations of the world and I've concluded that we are different peoples separated by the same God.

Back on the range, Pat O'Donnell was waiting in my cube. When he saw me, he slid a laundry bag to the side of the cube with his foot. I said hello and put the cube's two plastic chairs together so we didn't sit on Jack's bunk. You don't disrespect your bunkie.

We sat facing each other, my back to the window.

I thought I'd allocate O'Donnell fifteen minutes, walk the track, and watch the news. I assumed O'Donnell would proselytize and then wash his laundry. I was wrong.

"Is that your escape pack?" I asked pointing at the bag.

He ignored the question. So much for levity.

"How are you feeling?" he asked. "You settled in?"

For some reason I didn't tell him, "I'm fine." Instead, I told him the truth. My bad.

"I'm depressed."

His face grew taught and he stared at me as if he were about to hear a confession. He said bitterly; his tone sharp, "Don't say that! You just *spoke* your depression into existence. The Bible says the tongue has the power of life and death. You have to be careful what you say. You'll cause your own depression."

I felt a creeping nausea. Sixteen years of Catholic school and I now learn that I can speak things into existence when I'm in jail, probably from a drug dealer. How strange is that?

I looked at my watch. Just past quarter to five. A long road to the nine o'clock count.

"Dan. When the Bible says, 'The tongue has the power of life and death,' it means that we can speak things into existence. That's what the Bible says. Once we *say* it—*it is.*"

I decided to have some fun with this idiot. I had nothing better to do.

"Can I speak my immediate release into existence?"

I planted my tongue in my cheek, but, for a split second, I was hoping it was true. Sure, it was the waste of a few brain impulses but the fleeting thought of not being here for another ninety-six months provided me a sudden shot of elation—like the fleeting pleasure that buying a lottery ticket with seventy-million-to-one- odds provides.

O'Donnell's face never changed. A couple of inmates passed by my cube; saw who I was talking to and rolled their eyes. Lucky me!

I inquired, "How come you haven't spoken your release into existence?"

"Because I accept my punishment as a gift from God." He smiled benevolently.

"So, God would rather have you waste away in prison? That makes sense to you?" I had to ask.

O'Donnell smiled, "I view this period of my journey as a blessing from the Almighty."

All I could think was "sick mother fucker."

Suddenly I couldn't stand any more religious conversation. I'd seen it too often already. Go to jail; God up. Everyone is a scriptural scholar and they're not in jail but are on a Christian journey. I'd have to change the subject or risk a murder charge.

"Maybe you can help me with this," I picked up a paper from my desk. "Can you look at this commissary sheet and make sure it's filled out right? I need about everything in the toiletry department."

O'Donnell took the sheet.

I continued, "I've been seven days with no deodorant or shaving cream. I'm starting to bark."

He looked at the sheet for a second or two. He seemed distracted.

"Looks good to me. Be sure to hand it in before noon tomorrow or you won't get to shop 'til next week."

That sparked another problem.

"How long does it take the cash I deposited to be posted to my account? It's been a week already. I have no money and no way to use the phone. Is there something I can do to speed things up?"

"Don't you understand? You're in jail. The hacks think they're doing you a favor when they do their job. They're not in any hurry to help you."

"So I'm fucked?"

He thought a moment; unaffected by my cursing.

"Did you try Miz Buckles or Counselor Hinkel? On occasion, if they like you, they'll try to help."

I'd already tried to see Counselor Hinkel in the Admin Office during "open house," a period during chow time when inmates can discuss issues with the staff. Hinkel was eating a sandwich from a paper bag. About twenty inmates milled around outside his glass door, one or two standing at attention. After fifteen minutes of watching Spooter eat a baloney and mustard sandwich on white, I left. I hadn't thought of trying Miz Buckles. That might be a possibility.

I said, "I'll ask her if I see her."

"Well, maybe this'll help you out some."

He picked up the laundry bag, put it on the desk and opened it.

He smiled as he did this. He said, "We're all in a bad way here, so I've started a little Welcome Wagon to help our new Christian soldiers. I collect things from the Catholic guys who have moved on so that when a new guy arrives, I can share our bounty to help him out. Christian charity, so to speak."

I was thrilled in the same way I'd been before my sentencing when Steve comforted me, "Sentencing won't be too bad." Steve meant not "too bad" for him.

A stained drinking mug with a broken handle fell out first, then two mismatched shower shoes, three toothbrushes, one arm and the lenses of a pair of sunglasses. Last was a threadbare winter coat he had to wrestle out. I picked up the mug and looked inside. In the bottom was a three-cent stamp.

Now I was as thrilled as I had been *after* sentencing.

O'Donnell was delighted with these treasures.

"Father Baker says we should give thanks when we share His bounty. Let us give thanks."

He knelt down facing Jack's bunk, his hands in prayer position. His head bowed.

Norton had told me, "In prison, you can be anyone you want. If you aren't careful, you will be tagged as something you don't want to be. Remember, once you establish a reputation, it's impossible to change it."

I wasn't about to pray with O'Donnell and be labeled as a religious nutcase.

"No thanks, Pat. I think I'll take a closer look at this old stamp."

I reached into the mug; pulled the stamp out and held it up on my finger.

"That's mine," snapped O'Donnell snatching it.

Shamefully, he slid the stamp into his pocket. Then he asked, "Do you want me to put these in your locker?"

The truth would have been "No" but that would have been cruel. I should have been cruel. I relented.

"Sure, go ahead."

I spun the combination and opened the door. Inside were neatly stacked pants, shirts, T-shirts, boxers, socks, a new sweatshirt, a good pair of sneakers, and a winter coat.

"I thought you were having trouble getting commissary? How'd you get the sweats and the coat?"

"Abe Nagel *gave* me the sweats and sneakers as a retainer for legal work. Jewish charity. Stinky gave me the coat from Laundry."

O'Donnell turned from the locker to me.

"You have to give them back. Abe killed our Savior. You can't have anything to do with him, or your soul will be damned. Father Baker says so."

I wanted to tell both O'Donnell and Father Baker to go directly to hell. Only in jail is there so much intolerance. Instead I said, "I thought it was a nice Christian gesture on Abe's part. The sweats are in good condition. Not like this stuff." I gestured to the junk on the desk.

Pat's face was pale, almost ashen. He said, "I'll have to talk to Father Baker about this. You may not be permitted to receive Communion. The Vatican doesn't permit us to accept gifts from Jews."

He was out of his fucking mind and I wanted nothing more to do with him.

"Put all this stuff back in the bag. Give it to somebody else." I insisted. It was a more polite way of saying, "Take your shit and get out of here."

O'Donnell picked up one of the shower shoes.

"Where are you going to get shower shoes before you go to commissary?"

"I'll cut a deal with the Muslims for legal work."

"Don't associate with the Muslims. They're worse than the Jews. We've been at war with the Muslims since the Crusades. You look at them and your soul is going straight to hell." I was close to losing it; he didn't know how to stop.

I was still sitting when Jack Cass came into the cube. He looked at O'Donnell and backed away.

"I'm not interested, Pat. I appreciate what you're trying to do but this won't work. I understand that God is very important to you, but whoever and whatever your God is, He's not the God of Love that I know.

"I'm going to do my time and get along with everyone I can here, regardless of religion. And I didn't come to jail to be told what to do and what to believe."

I handed O'Donnell the pillowcase.

"Now, if you'll excuse me, I'm going to attend a Buddhist service."

"But you'll doom yourself to the hellfire" prophesied O'Donnell.

I paused for a second. Then I realized if I'm not doomed after stealing two million dollars, then attending a Buddhist service couldn't push me much deeper into the flames.

18

Confrontation

Waiting for the mail to be distributed is a dream I can't shake. Mail is love—true and absolute love. What would it take for my friends to drop me a line? Nothing special, just a chatty letter to keep me informed and connected. Inmates said that when you went to prison your friends forgot you. I was living proof of the truth of that statement.

After dinner on my first Wednesday in camp, I remember it well because the meal was called "sewer trout," I went to the track to exercise and think. I was falling into a pattern. Watching the morning news, eat breakfast, clock time at the Power House, eat lunch, clock more time at the Power House, be present for the Four O'clock Stand Up Count, eat dinner, walk the track, watch the evening news, hang out in the Law Library until the Nine O'clock Count. That was my day—that was every day. A way to kill time that wasn't unpleasant. No more nights out with Jack Daniels or Bud Weiser, but I didn't miss them much. Then I realized it—the beginning of Institutionalization.

The outside facilities sounded better than they appeared. The track was a quarter mile oval with an inside border of rotting railroad ties. The asphalt base had been crushed into dust from inmate boots. Two basketball courts had one unbent rim between them and no nets. The weight pile was under a carport type roof. The weights showed wear-and-tear from being dropped on the concrete when the "rep" was completed. The softball field was a combination of grass, weeds, and dirt with a backstop of bent and rusted chain-link. The package resembled a well-used inner-city playground in a poor neighborhood.

Track rules provided that the joggers had the inside lane along the railroad ties and the walkers were on the outside. I was walking the track as I communed with nature and the low station into which I had fallen.

"Yo!" a voice. "You be Holmes?"

When I spotted the source, I stopped walking. He was short, wide, black and muscular. My gut told me to run. A few weeks ago, I would have presumed that a robbery was in progress. My white, suburban lifestyle did not expose me to any but the most cultured minorities. African-Americans, outside of business, were professional athletes or an undignified "them." Now, to best handle the encounter, I tried not to look as scared as I was. I was prepared to tell him that I was shaking because I was epileptic and not because I was petrified.

"I am." I forced myself to start walking again. He fell in step beside me.

"Yo! Phone Sex need you right now. You know."

He'd made a statement, not asked a question. But that was the litigator in me. Anyway, I didn't know who Phone Sex was.

"I don't know who you're talking about."

"Yo! Mack Mackenzie. Phone Sex. He want you now. Yo!"

Now he was 0 for 2. I didn't know who Mack Mackenzie was either.

"Okay. Where is he?"

"Yo. He be cleaning de Visitin' Room. Yo! He want you now."

I was afraid that this guy would beat me to death, but I refused to be ordered around by an inmate.

Besides, my first name wasn't, "Yo."

"I'll go see him when I'm done walking."

He hesitated and then skipped a step; apparently expecting immediate compliance.

"Yo! Why don't you go see him now and walk after, you know?"

Now we were negotiating. This was good.

"I have a regular schedule going. Walk after dinner before watching the news."

"Yo! Phone Sex got to talk to you."

Just then I realized who Phone Sex might be. While I was waiting in line for one of the phones, I noticed one of the guys was swallowing the receiver. His eyes were scrunched and his right hand was down the front of his pants playing with himself. He was moaning words like, "I can feel me in you, baby... Heaven on earth... That's it... All wet..."

I was absolutely disgusted. I turned away; closed my eyes and emitted an, "Ugh," sort of noise.

"I'm not using *that* phone," I groaned to no one in particular.

I looked up after a moment as the inmate in front of me moved up.

There were four telephones here so I had a one-in-four chance. Unfortunately I had too much time to think. At one time or another, that pig had talked on every phone in the camp. I had an immediate need for hand sanitizer, latex gloves, and a surgical mask. I almost left the line I was so repulsed. But I didn't. It was my first call to my Mom and I needed to talk to her no matter what.

"Why don't you have him come out here and talk?"

The guy breathed a heavy sigh. He was flustered now. He'd expected me to roll over and obey without question. He sputtered around for a few seconds and then said, "Yo! He workin,' you know. He cain' leaves there."

"Well, I'm busy, too. Like I said, I have a schedule."

"Yo! Phone Sex be waxin' de floo' in de Visitin' Room. Yo! He cain' leave."

"Waxing sounds like important work," I deadpanned.

I could tell he was annoyed now and I wanted to avoid his beating me to death. I decided to end the back and forth and meet Phone Sex, lucky guy that I was.

"His name's Mack Mackenzie?"

"Yo."

"And he's in the Visiting Room in the Admin Building?"

"Yo."

I stopped and turned to face him. The guy stopped and faced me. I said, "Okay. Go back and tell Mackenzie I'll finish this lap and do one more. Then I'll go to the Visiting Room and ask for him."

He stared harshly, and then gave a quick quarter-inch nod. "Yo!" he said as he walked off.

I finished my laps and then walked toward the Admin Building.

19

Mack McKenzie

Seeing "Out of Bounds" *signs has become a constant nightmare. In jail, almost everything was* "Out of Bounds." *Kissing your children good night, helping them with homework, comforting them when they're scared—all that was* "Out of Bounds." *Lots of sympathy from the hacks. They always said,* "Holmes, you did it to yourself." *The reality was that I did it to my children.*

The Visiting Room was alive with activity. One inmate was buffing the floor while another squirted wax from a plastic bottle. Five others supervised. Typical.

Although I was still new, I wondered why there would be activity in the Visiting Room at midweek. It was only utilized on weekends and holidays. Maybe this was a punishment detail.

I looked around.

No hacks in sight.

"If you ever find yourself alone, you're in the wrong place," Norton had warned me. "Go find some people and be with them. If you ever find a work detail and there's no hack, you don't want to be there either. Go someplace where there's a bunch of guys or a hack."

Well, there was no hack here. I followed Norton's advice and made myself scarce. I turned to leave and nearly collided with someone rushing through the door.

"Hey, man," he said in astonishment as he pulled up short.

I recognized him as the disgusting Phone Sex guy. I'd almost touched him.

"Oh, you're Holmes. Hey, thanks for coming. Gimme a minute. I need to make sure these guys are doin' this right."

Clipboard under one arm, Mackenzie squatted down in front of the buffing machine and examined the floor as if he were a boot camp sergeant inspecting the work of recruits. He pointed at a tile. The man operating the buffer nodded. The waxer squirted the tile. Mackenzie stood up and turned back to me.

"Kid's doing a good job," he complimented.

Since I'd never waxed a floor, I had nothing with which to compare.

"If you say so."

"I'm Mack Mackenzie. I need to talk to you 'bout something. Let's go over here."

I later learned that Mack Mackenzie, aka Phone Sex, had been a major player in the cocaine trade in the City of Brotherly Love. He started supplying in high school and graduated to the street where his customer base expanded. By age twenty-four, Mackenzie had regular customers who often brought their cars in for repairs at his automotive repair shop. Phone Sex liked the money and the toys that the "trade" allowed him to acquire. He loved that babes adored him and that bling adorned his arms and neck. It stopped when the DEA started its investigation and, to beat a twenty year sentence, he dug up a tube in his backyard that contained over one and a half million dollars. The "buyout" reduced his sentence to ten years.

Anyway, this was our first meeting and he led me out of the Admin Building through the squeaking black metal door. This area was "Out of Bounds."

"Aren't we 'Out of Bounds?'" I asked, with grave concern.

"Not when you're with me. We're okay."

I didn't believe that for a second. My nerves started to unravel. I could hear Hinkel saying, "You is here not a week and you is Outta Bounds! You is goin' to the bucket."

I wanted back "In Bounds" as quickly as possible. Following rules was something I learned to do the hard way and I was determined to make the Honorable Judge Smirt proud of me. At the same time, Mackenzie might not be someone to offend.

"What can I do for you?" I asked in order to get back In Bounds as soon as possible.

"Call me Mack." He was an affable sort, not apparently concerned with the "Out of Bounds" rule.

I just wanted to end this; whatever "this" was.

"You was a lawyer on the street, right?"

"Yeah. I practiced law for a living."

"What type of lawyer was you?"

"Mostly tax law and real estate syndications."

I didn't like answering questions without knowing the purpose of the conversation, especially if the person asking the questions was the scumbag I'd seen at the phone bank.

"Did you do marriages?"

"I was there for mine," I answered stupidly. "My wife took care of the divorce by herself."

He missed the joke.

"No, no, no. Did you do them things that you sign before you get married? I saw it in a magazine with Pamela Anderson on the cover. A pre-natal agreement. Ever done one of those?"

This was an interesting request. Stupid, but interesting.

"No one's ever done one," I informed him.

Because I didn't know who he was, I didn't add, "you moron," to the end of the sentence. It's not polite to insult stupid people in prison.

"But I thought all the Hollywood stars got 'em? The magazine said, like, they don't get married without one."

"Let me try to help you." I didn't add, "You fucking idiot," but I wanted to but—Oops I was in prison.

"Pre-natal means before birth. Babies aren't allowed to sign legal documents before they're born. It's a Canon of English law and, on a more basic level, they have difficulty writing. You're talking about a pre-nuptial agreement, which means an agreement before marriage for the division of assets if the marriage ends in divorce."

"Whatever—"

Mackenzie must not concern himself with minor syllabic distinctions.

"Can you do one for me?"

I was incredulous. But wait—Why would anyone in federal prison need a pre-nup drawn? I could understand interpreting or reading one, but not drafting one.

"I need one of them pre-natal things," Mackenzie continued.

"What would you charge me to do one?"

I needed to back this up and start over.

"When do you get out, Mack?" I would refuse whatever he offered. I wanted to be fully settled in before I made any enemies.

"In a hunnert-and-seven months if I get twelve months off for the drug program."

He was referring to the five hundred hour program available to qualified drug and alcohol abusers that potentially entitled them to a sentence reduction of up to one year.

"You need a document tonight that's not going to be executed for over nine years."

He didn't seem to grasp that.

I continued, after a pause. "And how many assets are you going to have in nine years when you're released?"

"You don't understand."

"True that."

I was baffled at this point.

"I'm getting married tomorrow at twelve-thirty."

I thought he was kidding. I guess it showed. He looked at me as if I were an explosive device he had to disarm. He couldn't be getting married in federal prison, could he? Was that why the Visiting Room was being waxed on a Wednesday? More wondrous still, could there be some loonette out there willing to marry an inmate who had nine years left on his sentence? The questions stunned me into silence.

"Well? How much it gonna cost me?"

I could not have moved from that spot if Counselor Hinkel burst through the door to declare me "Out of Bounds."

"Well, Mack—let's see—let me just think out loud for a minute." I forced myself into legal mode. I figured that if I explained to him the amount of work involved and the impossibility of the deadline, he'd drop the request. So I started. "A pre-nuptial agreement will take hours, even days to draft. Both parties have to list, and have verified, their assets. It's a document to be signed by both parties who are represented by separate counsel. Even if I could draft a document tonight, when would your spouse-to-be have a chance to have her lawyer review it?"

"She'll just sign it."

I tried again.

"She'll have to have her lawyer review it. Under Pennsylvania law, it's not legal if it's not reviewed by her counsel."

"If she asks, I'll tell her it's okay to sign."

"That would be lying to her after I informed you she had to have her lawyer review it. You're going to lie to your intended wife on the day of her marriage?"

"Look," Mackenzie insisted. "All I want to do is protect what I got, you know?"

"What do you mean by 'protect?' Why do you need to protect something from your wife?"

"I don't want her to know what I got. That's what the document does, don't it? It says she can't spend any of my shit if she finds it. Ain't that right?"

Well, here's a stand up guy. He wants some girl to marry and be faithful to him for nine years, but he doesn't want her to spend his illegally gotten gains if she uncovers them. And I wasn't supposed to worry that he escorted me "Out of Bounds?" Like I thought, what a guy!

I decided to burst his bubble. It was time to kill the conversation and walk away from him.

"No. In a pre-nup, both parties have to disclose their assets. Usually appraisals and tax returns are required. It's a *full* disclosure of your assets. Sounds like that's the *last* thing you want. You're trying to hide your assets until you're released. Right?"

"Yeah. Somethin' like that," he admitted.

"A pre-nup won't work for you, Mack. Any lawyer could have the agreement declared null and void if your spouse wasn't represented and the document didn't disclose your assets."

"It don't work?"

The muscular black man from the track joined us. Now he was "Out of Bounds," too.

Mackenzie said to him, "Don't work, Jimmy. I'd have to tell her what I got, ya know. If she knows where all my shit is, I'll be broke before I get out."

The black guy looked at Mackenzie, then me, then back to Mac-

113

kenzie. He summarized the conversation briefly but accurately, "Yo." Mackenzie concluded, "Thanks, Dan. I appreciate your time."

The black man turned out to be Jimmy Green, Mack's lackey.

Green was serving a sixty month sentence for being a mule in drug deals. He was five-ten and weighed two-ten. He was a rat who squealed on six guys to beat a ten-year sentence (called a "dime").

I shook his hand and felt a steel grip between a palm and callused fingers.

Mack said, "Hey, why don't you come to the wedding tomorrah?" He leaned forward and laughed, "You gotta give me a present, though."

What could I possibly have to do tomorrow better than attend a prison wedding? I'd ignore the repulsion I felt for Mack Mackenzie just for the entertainment value.

"Let me check my palm pilots." I glanced at the insides of both hands. "Looks like I have a clean schedule." I put my hands down. "I'll be there."

"You can be the legal witness."

"As opposed to an illegal witness" I replied kiddingly.

Mackenzie took the clipboard from under his arm and stared at it as if it solved his pre-nuptial problem. I walked through the squeaking metal door and moved myself back "In Bounds."

I looked at Phone Sex and Jimmy Green a final time before the squeaking metal door closed as I headed to the TV room and the evening news.

20

Stan Gillette

I always enjoyed skimming the paper for oddball stories that were too dumb to be true, but they were. Like women with stomachaches who visit the doctor to learn they were pregnant. Or the guy who robbed a bank using a holdup note written on the back of his checking account statement. Or the guy who ran into the woods at night to escape the police wearing those sneakers with blinking lights.

People like that were all around me waiting to be released so they could "do it right" next time. I wanted to abandon them and reunite with my children. Without me, my kids might grow up to be like these idiots. I didn't know how they were doing, and it was eating me alive.

If you're out in the real world with a medical condition or a disease that would bankrupt you if you paid for treatment, you can solve the problem by throwing a brick at the window of any federal building. It doesn't have to break the glass. Just make sure you throw it in front of the video cameras.

Once processed through the justice department, you become a federal inmate and are eligible for free medical treatment like a member of Congress, with a few differences.

One problem about not being a Congressman is that not all physicians graduate in the bottom five percent of their class. Those who achieve that distinction devolve into the least desirable and lowest paying positions in the medical profession, which include employment in the BOP. On the good side, if an inmate receives a correct diagnosis and was assigned the proper treatment, the therapy would sustain itself without interruption. The same rule applies for medications, even expensive ones. Once prescribed, meds are dispensed pursuant to the physician's orders. Valium is popular. So is Prozac. There are even medical facilities designated for inmates who are terminally ill or in need of surgery. Sometimes, however, illness proves fatal.

So much happened on the day of Mack Mackenzie's wedding that the events transformed me from an FNG into someone with peach-fuzz.

To start, there had been an early morning incident that had carried over from the night before.

Stanley Gillette was an inmate in his early sixties from Burlington, Vermont serving a twenty-four month sentence for failing to disclose financial obligations and making false statements on an application for a bank loan. The loan proceeds funded his financially distressed auto repair business. After the business defaulted on the loan, the bank officer learned of the undisclosed debts and contacted the FBI. Another John DeLorean case.

Gillette was a hard-nosed, hard-working, formerly hard-drinking Marine. His prison job was in the welding and fabrication shop next to the Power House. That Wednesday evening, while he played Texas Hold 'Em, he complained about pain and numbness in his left arm. He had a heart condition and took pills to regulate his heartbeat.

I'd been watching them play since after dinner. I enjoyed the loud, card-slapping, cursing players and I could see who was who and what the social order might be.

As he played, Gillette became visibly distressed.

One of the players told him, "Fuckin Rushdi's still at pill line. Move your lazy fuckin'fat ass and go see her."

"Nah. I've felt worser than this before. It'll pass. Besides, I'm not moving til I got all your money."

"Bitch ain't gonna be there in half an hour. Then what you gonna do?" the same player persisted.

"Fuck her," Gillette responded. "I ain't leavin' til I'm done torturing you mother fuckers, so eat shit and die."

Rushdi was Dr. Rushdi, either Indian or Pakistani, I was never sure. Regardless, once she was finished dispensing meds, she'd be gone for the day and there would be no one in Camp to examine Gillette until the next morning.

Suddenly, Gillette had trouble holding the cards with his left hand.

"Fuck it," he griped after losing a hand. "Maybe I better go see the bitch. Fuckin arm is killing me."

Twenty minutes later, he returned and was holding his left arm with his right hand like a sling.

"What'd she say?" someone wanted to know.

"Best fuckin' medical advice I ever got. She said, 'Go drink water and take walk. That make you feel better.' She didn't even bother to pull my folder."

Gillette resumed playing and beat two guys for a pot of cigarettes and stamps.

Just after six the next morning, I was walking the endless oval. I'd awoken early and been unable to fall back to sleep. I got dressed and went to the track for a few pre-breakfast laps. The day was pleasant with no wind and a light dawn chill. The sun was an orange ball rising in the haze over the mountains. Perfect wedding weather, if you asked me.

As I came around the curve near the handball courts, I saw a pile of khaki crumpled in a fetal position. The visual resembled a passed out wino.

I ran over.

It was Stan Gillette.

"Are you okay?" I asked. "What are you doing out here?"

He barely opened his eyes. His skin was gray.

He shook his head "No." Too weak to speak.

"You need to get inside. Can you walk?"

I lifted him to his feet, a struggle pure and simple. He was too weak to stand. I could leave him, or I could walk him in. I remember thinking, if he passed out he might never regain consciousness and that if I were he, I would want someone to be with me in my final moments.

I held him under his arm and around his back. It took us twice as long to stumble to the Admin Building than if I had walked alone. When we arrived, his facial features were badly distorted.

Just inside the door, I sat him on the floor and leaned him against a window near the phone banks. He could barely sit up.

I ran down to the pill line where Dr. Rushdi was dispensing pills in little paper cups.

"Doctor!" I said cutting to the front of the three person line.
"An inmate's down. It's an emergency. You need to examine him
now. He's up by the phones. He's not conscious."

"Go away," snipped Dr. Rushdi. "It Thursday. No sick call today.
He have to come back tomorrow."

I'd seen this attitude several times already in inmate-staff encounters. Technical correctness; moral bankruptcy.

"Oh, come on!!!! He's so weak that he can't stand up. I think he's
had a heart attack," I pleaded. "He has no color in his face. He might
die."

"I see him tomorrow on sick call day. Tell him drink water and
take walk. That make him feel better."

"What if he dies?" I yelled.

"You no shout at me!!! You inmate. I write you up and send you to
bucket."

Dr. Rushdi resumed issuing pills as if I weren't there. She'd me-
thodically check the inmate's photo ID against her sheet, then hand the
inmate one paper cup containing the pill and another cup filled with
water. She watched each inmate swallow the pill.

I ran back down the main corridor toward Counselor Hinkel's office and saw the Compound Cop coming out of the rest room.

"Officer! Come quick. Man down."

Together we trotted to the phone bank where Gillette lay motionless on the floor with a group of inmates milling around, including Ace
Baldini. The Compound Cop knelt down, picked up Gillette's wrist
and felt for a pulse.

Other inmates were now coming into the building for breakfast.
One of them was Milo Cohen. Those on both sides of the BOP badge
called him "Doc" because he'd been a physician on the street. He'd
become bored with dentistry, his original profession. Facial recon-
structive surgery was not exciting enough for him so he'd turned businessman. He moonlighted as a financial advisor and, over fifteen
years, developed an investment banking firm and a mortgage broker-
age company. The two enterprises boasted over fifteen hundred clients.
Unfortunately, for most of them, he sucked at financial matters. By the
time the SEC had completed its investigation and issued a "Cease and

Desist" Order, he'd bilked investors to the tune of thirty-six million dollars that supported investment losses, charitable endeavors, and personal expenses.

Doc's defense was that the risk of the marketplace caused the losses. The government asserted that Doc made false and misleading statements to hide the true state of his operations. The Jury agreed with the prosecution and the judge sentenced Doc to ninety-seven months.

But in this medical emergency, Doc instinctively knelt and pressed his hand on Gillette's neck. The Compound Cop knew him and moved aside.

"Is that as good as you can breathe?" Doc asked Stan looking him frank in the face. Cohen's voice was calm and reassuring, like a physician's bedside manner should be, or a con man's would be. "What's your name?"

Stan's eyes weren't focused. He offered no response.

"Shallow breathing," Doc reported. "Pulse faint and thready."

"He don't look like he gonna make it," someone said.

"He's having a heart attack," Doc announced. "I need a bag and a defib kit." He instructed the Compound Cop, "Keep his windpipe open like this. It will help him breathe."

Doc flew down the hall double-time.

"Da guy needs an ass-sprin," Ace Baldini said. "I geddim one."

Ace opened the door and headed for Camp One. He must have seen a television commercial that claimed aspirin was good for heart attacks. Ace would likely be sidetracked before he could return with the pill.

"Dat woan woik." This was from one of Ace's Sicilian sidekicks. "He suffa-katin'. Sumbuddy gotta gib him mouth-to-mouth restitution."

The Compound Cop said, "Look-kit, guys. He's dying. Couple of you carry him down to pill line."

I crossed Stan's hands on his chest and grabbed one leg. Another inmate took the other leg. We dragged him down the linoleum as the crowd dispersed and wandered into breakfast.

The Compound Cop ran ahead of us. He showed something I hadn't seen a staff member exhibit so far—compassion.

As we pulled him down the hall, Stan's shirt was pulled up his back to his shoulders. His mottled chest was gray with a few red splotches on hairy parchment. His skin seemingly would tear at the touch and he had a long scar from a prior heart surgery.

The Compound Cop had the door open when we arrived, and we dragged Stan into the office. Dr. Rushdi stood there unaffected. Four of us lifted him onto a gurney. As I looked at him, either Stan was dead or very close to it. Dr. Rushdi was oblivious to our presence as she packed her medical equipment into a black bag.

"This inmate is in cardiac distress," Doc told her. "The initial diagnosis is a heart attack. He needs a defib kit and a heart trauma bag, statim."

"You not doctor," Rushdi sneered. "You inmate."

An inmate said, "Doctor Cohen knows more about medicine than you ever will, Wog." An English accent; I was going to ask why he was here but now was not the time.

"This what I think of that," said Rushdi. She spat on the floor in Doc's direction. "You not doctor. You inmate. Get out. I write you up. He not sick. He malingerer."

Rushdi's favorite word. *Ma-lin-ger-er.* Four syllables. Biggest word she knew.

"Dr. Rushdi!" snapped the Compound Cop.

"I come back later," she said. "I go to pill line down hill now. I can no be late." She pointed at Stan. "He do this all the time. Complain about chest and arm. Have him drink water and take walk. He feel better."

"Listen to me!" shouted the Compound Cop. "This guy is dying! I'll write *you* up!"

"Oh, so you doctor, too." She snapped. "You know what wrong with him. You treat him!"

The Compound Cop took a reactional step toward her. I thought he was going to smash Rushdi's nose into the back of her skull.

Gillette, lying face-up on the gurney, emitted a loud, pitiful groan that wheezed into a death rattle.

That awful sound drew everyone's attention, including Dr. Rushdi's.

She went to the gurney and pried open Stan's eyes with her fingers. Whatever she observed, she went back to her medical bag and started unpacking it, taking her time in the process. I had the idea she was gathering her wits and plotting treatment alternatives. She lifted her lab coat off the wall hook, put it on, smoothed it out, and then went to the examining table.

She turned to us.

"Get out!" she shouted. "You not allow here. You disrupt my concentration."

All of us left the room.

We stood outside the door looking at each other.

"Nothing you can do for him now, guys," said the Compound Cop. "He's getting the only care we can give him. I'm going to call 911."

The Compound Cop headed to his post.

Doc, concerned for Stan's wellbeing, sat on the floor by the door and said, "I'm staying until she comes out or an ambulance arrives."

We shuffled off to the chow hall, heads down, shoulders slouched, pondering Gillette's fate.

Breakfast conversation revolved around whether or not delivering Gillette into Dr Rushdi's hands was a death sentence. I thought we'd heard him die.

After the morning sanitation inspection, I was walking down the main corridor of the Admin Building on the way to the Power House when I saw an ambulance pull up to the back door. I stopped as a paramedic team went into the building. They rolled a gurney toward the pill line. One of the paramedics stood outside the office. Other inmates milled about, drifting up and down the hallway, trying to learn Stan's fate without attracting the attention of the all-seeing, all-knowing Counselor Hinkel.

I approached the paramedic.

"How's he doing?" I asked.

He looked at me.

"He died."

He dropped his head and stared at the floor. "Any chance he had was gone when Rushdi took over. She ain't no doctor unless it's for some third world country like Camden."

Stan Gillette was dead!

"That's terrible," I said.

"Yep. Coulda been different from what I was told."

His family would receive a notice from the BOP that the patriarch of their clan had died on the way to the hospital. That's the way it's written. According to BOP protocols, nobody ever died in jail. You always died on the way to the hospital.

Stan's death was the main topic among the inmates that morning. I didn't hear much of it because I was at the Power House. At lunch, I noticed a few inmates sitting quietly, mostly older men. No one else seemed to be affected. Halfway through the meal, the public address system came to life.

"Attention in the camp. Attention in the camp." The unmistakable drawl of Counselor Hinkel created silence among the lunch crowd. "This mornin' Stan Gillette pass' away on the way to the hos-pit-tal. Enjoy yore meal."

Silence hung in the air as if the slightest word would shatter this moment of respect for Stanley Gillette. A few "Amens" could be heard, and then the natural noise level of the chow hall resumed.

Poor Stan had passed from this world to the next via medical indifference. He'd seen Dr. Rushdi with clear symptoms the night before. He was still alive when he arrived at Rushdi's office. Now he was gone.

Sic transit gloria mundi...

After lunch, I saw Counselor Hinkel standing in the corridor outside the entrance to pill line. He appeared older and more frail than usual. Stan's death must have affected him.

"Counselor Hinkel," I said, "What did you think of Stan Gillette dying?"

He looked at me, his expression neutral. He whispered in a voice barely audible. "It made me sad."

I hadn't expected this. To me, Hinkel was an unfeeling cog in a system designed solely to incarcerate and humiliate. Why should he be sad?

"I'm sorry to hear that, Counselor."

He didn't seem to have anything further to say.

"Did you like him?" I asked.

"Nope." Hinkel looked toward the Visiting Room where Mackenzie would be married. He had a faraway expression. "I'm sad 'cause I was gonna write him up for not making his bunk and having dust balls under his bed. That would have been his second write up this month, and I would have cancelled his furlough scheduled for this Saturday. He don't know how lucky he is that he died 'cause I can't cancel his furlough now." He glanced down at the floor and pawed the tile with his toe. "Makes me sad."

"But he's dead."

"Still ell-gible for furlough though. I can'ts cancel it. That's policy and I has to follow policy."

I was stunned. Man's dead and he's worried about policy.

He looked up with a faraway expression on his pasty face.

"That furlough gonna stay on his record unfulfill until per-pet-choo-it-ty."

Hinkel's eyebrows furrowed as he focused on the increasing amount of activity near the Visiting Room.

"Sad day. Sad day." He sighed heavily. "I hates loose ends."

He turned away slowly and walked toward his office.

21

Prison Wedding

I feel a tap on my shoulder and shudder. There's a hack wanting a urine sample. My body freezes up due to my shy bladder.

I have this dream all the time. I can be talking to the hostess at a restaurant and I feel a tap on my shoulder. Sometimes it's Spooter, sometimes Skorzeny, always someone I know. Always the same message, "Piss test." No respect. No privacy. Even in dreams, I'm subject to the pauperization of it all. I hate it.

I have to improve my attitude or I will trap my mind in a prison of my own creation.

By eleven forty-five, chow line was closed and the assigned inmates were cleaning up. I walked down to the Visiting Room to see how the wedding preparations were proceeding. A group of inmates were gathered around the bathroom on the far side of the Visiting Room with Officer Ratner. He wore latex gloves and carried a stack of forms, plastic Baggies, and vials. The bathroom door was propped open by a trash can.

Officer Ratner was collecting urine specimens or, in prison parlance, a piss-test.

Ratner was in his mid- to late-twenties, stood five-five, and had a medium build. He was a Bureau of Prisons lifer. "BOP All the Way" could be his motto, or the words of his tattoo. Since he was always enforcing Regulations, the inmates thought he had small man's disease. He was akin to a traffic cop who would write a ticket for driving forty in a thirty-five mile an hour zone.

Ratner was telling the inmates to drink water and walk.

"It'll help you pee."

The phrase reminded me of Dr. Rushdi's medical advice to the dying Stan Gillette, except Ratner threatened to throw any inmate who failed to produce in the bucket. Regulations allowed an inmate two hours from command to produce.

"Hurry up and pee."

There were three inmates present and I had met them all. They were Roland Shifflett, Paul Wright, and an Old Russian everyone called Dostoyevsky.

Roland Shifflett was a New Yorker in his early fifties. He bragged that he had been a minor league hockey star and a champion softball player. But his spastic efforts in the Camp Softball League would never support that claim. He also asserted he was a VP for Toshiba, but another inmate who knew him on the street revealed that he'd actually been a Tobisha deliveryman. When you encounter the Shifflett's of the world, the age-old expression comes to mind "some guys don't know when to stop the bullshit." His crime was conspiracy to distribute drugs and occurred when he came to the aid of his ex-wife who'd been threatened when she didn't deliver the drugs she had been paid to supply. Shifflett threatened to beat up the purported buyer who turned out to be an undercover DEA agent.

Paul Wright was in his late twenties and came from Boston. Tattoos of intimate female body parts covered the visible parts of his body except his head. He was known as "Animal." He had long, brown hair that stretched down to the middle of his back. At best, it was dirty, oily and scraggly. He had a goatee that looked like pubic hair. Belching, burping and farting augmented his persona. He was aptly described. Also, he was an ex-Marine and an ex-Hell's Angel. He said the Marines taught him to ignore pain, so he was always attempting to lift an insane amount of weight. The Hell's Angels taught him how to ignore personal hygiene so he rarely bathed, flossed, or brushed his teeth. He was doing ten years for his part in a biker gang sponsored drug deal. He developed a friendship with Shifflett based on their common inability to play guitar or any card game, especially the prison favorite, "Spades." Birds of a feather, so to speak.

Little was known about the Old Russian except that he was old and Russian and he refused to speak English. Dostoyevsky was substituted for his otherwise unpronounceable name, although he never responded to it.

"Okay," Ratner said to no one in particular. "Who's ready?" Wright emitted a wet belch. He'd eatin' a bowlful of hard-boiled eggs for breakfast. The protein helped his weightlifting.

"Yum..." he grinned. "That was tasty."

Wright walked to Ratner in a slow prison punk walk. "I'll give it a try." Wright handed Ratner his prison ID.

Ratner filled his name on one of the forms, handed Wright an empty vial, and followed him into the bathroom to ensure the accuracy of the piss-test.

After a few seconds Wright yelled, "Fire in the hole!" A loud and messy fart echoed from inside. Ratner came out squinting and holding his nose. Wright followed him with a smile as he held a vial of amber fluid.

"I had to bear down a little to get going," Wright explained. Then he warned Shifflett, "I wouldn't go in there. I fuckin' blew the room up with them hard-boiled eggs. Fuckin' Ratner almost suffocated. Look at him. He's white as a sheet."

That was a true statement.

"Me," said Dostoyevsky to Ratner.

I saw Mack Mackenzie and Jimmy Green pass by the door inside the Visiting Room, and I left the Old Russian and Ratner to their business. On the other side of the room, inmates were setting up guitars, amps, keyboards, and drums. The equipment was well worn but serviceable. Nothing much else was happening.

Through the open door I could see Ratner standing outside the bathroom. Dostoyevsky was inside. Counselor Hinkel watched the corridor and the Visiting Room through the door of the Admin Office. He seemed irritated and peevish. Hinkel didn't appreciate inmates having fun in *his* camp. To Hinkel, prison meant punishment. From the expression on his face, he was plotting an attack.

Frankie Bananas came stumbling down the hallway with his belly rolling in waves. Unlike most other inmates, he'd certainly not lost any weight since his arrival. But his face was pale without the eye makeup and khaki washed the color out of him.

This where the yer-rhin test is?" he asked Ratner.

"You Ciriello?" Ratner responded.

Frankie nodded.

"You're late, fat boy. I'm gonna write you up."

"Awww… Why can't we be friends?"

Ratner barked at Shifflett, "Go see what's up with Dostoyevsky. He's been in there long enough. Go make sure he ain't stroked out or nuthin'."

Shifflett stepped back. He said, "That's *your* job, Ratner."

"Do it or go to the hole."

Ratner called his bluff. Now I'd see if the big shot Toshiba executive had any balls.

Shifflett harrumphed; he was debating whether going to the bucket for two weeks was worth being bitched out by a cop. He looked at Ratner, shook his head, and sighed. He was ball-less. He crept like a thief to the bathroom's threshold and leaned around the jamb for a quick look. He pulled back with a jerk and turned to Ratner. "I don't think he understands it's piss you want," he said with a look of disgust on his face.

"Youse is mean," whined Frankie to Shifflett. "Maybe he shy. Did youse ever think of that? I think not! All youse do is think about you-self and you-self only."

"Get lost, Daisy," Shifflett snarled back.

Just then the Old Russian walked out of the bathroom with the front of his pants soaked from his waist to his knees.

"Look," said Wright laughing at him. "The old man pissed himself."

Shifflett, Wright and about twenty inmates cracked up, clapping their hands and whooping. Ratner's expression beseeched, "Why me, Lord?"

The Old Russian mimed washing his hands in the sink and drying them on the front of his pants. He mumbled something indecipherable. The vial he carried was half full.

I pulled away from the Visiting Room door as more inmates came in. A prison wedding is not an everyday occurrence and the chance to scope out new "bitches" would surely draw a crowd and Spooter's wrath. The band was set up and the equipment boxes were stacked in a corner. A few tables and chairs were available. Most would have to stand. The floor had a bright shine without being slick. I remember thinking how loud it was. There must have been forty or fifty inmates in the room whooping and hollering. More were out in the corridor where sound rebounded hard. The musicians practiced a few songs. None had a wedding motif. Counselor Hinkel stood motionless at his glass door staring at the crowd like a lion watching lemmings gather at a watering hole.

"All right guys," said Mackenzie going out into the corridor. "Break it up. Break it up. It's just a piss test. Happens here every day. Get inside. We gotta get going." He motioned for everyone to come inside. He seemed naked without his clipboard. "Let's get more chairs set up. Come on!"

Hinkel opened the glass door, walked up to Mackenzie, and struck. "Whut is you doin'?"

Mackenzie held up his hands as if hoping he had a clipboard. Not seeing anything there, he put his hands back down and looked at Hinkel.

"Settin' up for my weddin'."

"What is they doin'?" He pointed to the musicians.

"They're doin' the music for the weddin'."

Hinkel said, "Who gaves you the permission for thems to play an' why is them instruments out of the Wreck Room?"

"Mr. Stark."

"Well, Mr. Stark ain't here today and it's not okay with me. So put them instruments back and have all these here inmates reports back to their work details 'fore I write 'em up for stealing gub-mint property or being outta bounds."

"But Counselor," Mackenzie whined, "Mr. Stark approved my request to have the band play at my wedding."

Hinkel leaned back on his heels and lowered his chin to look at Mackenzie over the top of his glasses. That paperclip holding the one arm of his glasses to the frame jiggled to a stop. He asked in a low voice, "Did he writes it in the log book?"

"Jeeze!" Mackenzie groaned. "He didn't give me no notarized permit for it, Counselor. He jus' told me I could do it."

"Well, you shouldda had him tell me 'cause I'm the one who needs to hear it. Back theys go. Youz gots no permission for this, boy."

This was a battle Mackenzie knew he would lose. He informed the band members to return their instruments to the Wreck Office and report to their work details. The musicians groaned their displeasure.

"Counselor Hinkel's orders," Mackenzie huffed.

Like magic, at the mention of Hinkel's name, Mackenzie was off the hook. The inmates knew the power and capriciousness of Counselor Hinkel.

Mackenzie fussed about not having music while the band members packed up and cleared out. He said it loud enough for Hinkel to hear him. He'd promised his bride a live band. Now he wouldn't have it.

"It's hard enough to be an inmate without this kinda shit," he grumped. "With all the other crap that goes on in here, why does a simple wedding have to get fucked up?"

"You should have thought of that 'fore youse committed theys crime," Hinkel retorted. Shifflett walked out of the men's room, vile in hand. He handed it to Ratner who wrote on the label and dropped it into a plastic bag.

Mackenzie called out to Shifflett, "Hey, Roland. I need you."

"Yo, Mack," Shifflett said. "Whas-sup?"

"Fuckin' Hinkel just screwed me by not lettin' the band play at my fuckin' wedding."

"Really?" Shifflett looked around the room and realized that the band was no longer there. "I was supposed to sing 'Mustang Sally.' My best song."

I've heard Shifflett's version of "Mustang Sally." Hinkel did the wedding party a favor.

Hinkel announced that everyone had to report back to their work details, or he would write them up for being Out of Bounds. No one had permission to attend the wedding except those in the wedding party. This, in his words, was "a work camp and not Soul Trail."

Mackenzie said to Shifflett, "Go get a bunch of radios and have them tuned to the same station so that we can listen to some kinda music. It's important. Round up some radios and headsets. Get Green to help you with the brothers." He pulled Jimmy Green out of the crowd, which was now slinking through the door away from Hinkel's wrath.

"Sure, Mack. No problem." Shifflett and Green left.

The wedding was falling apart bit by bit. I stood near Mackenzie and intended to claim I was in the wedding party. I had a verbal invitation from the day before and I was dying to learn what type of person could have awoken this morning and decided to marry a Federal prison inmate. To me, this was the most fun I'd had since my sentencing. I'd already conjured up mental images, and I wanted to see which one, if any, was accurate.

Ratner said to Frankie Bananas, "You ready to piss, yet?"

Frankie said, "Don't rush me. I'm delicate. I'll have it for you tomorrow."

"If you don't piss in the next twenty minutes, I'm taking your delicate ass to the bucket 'cause your two hours will be up."

"I just got here," Frankie protested.

"The two hours started when I called your name."

"But I had to finish my make-up."

"Hurry up, Frankie," Mackenzie shouted from the Visiting Room. "I got a weddin' scheduled here at twelve-thirty. I don't want you standing there trying to piss every thirty seconds when Clarissa gets here."

A limousine pulled into the parking lot and stopped at the entrance to the Admin Building. As word of the arrival spread, those in the Visiting Room crowded around the windows. Three white women bounced out and jiggled their way around to the trunk. The black-suited driver opened it and handed out garment bags and make-up cases. If I'd been down for a couple of years, like most of these guys, the ladies would have qualified as hot. Being in prison only a few weeks, they rated as slightly better than slutty. They wore tank or halter tops with short leather or jean skirts and six inch spikes. They seemed giddy. They walked to the front door of the Admin Building strutting their stuff —they were the main attraction and they knew it. The crowd of inmates shifted to the corridor door to watch them enter the building.

"You ready to piss yet, Ciriello?" Ratner was browbeating Frankie.

"Okay, okay." Frankie held up his hands in defeat. "But I gotta problem."

"You can't piss."

"No," said Frankie. "My gut's too big to see what I'm doin.' I can't see the vial or my dick. An' I'm not that coordinated." He paused and looked at Ratner. "Youse gonna have to hold one or the other."

Ratner handed Frankie an empty vial. He yelled into his ear, "Ciriello! Either you fill that vial yourself or you're going to the bucket!"

Frankie took the vial and slumped into the bathroom. Ratner followed.

Officer Tracie Lumpkin came down the corridor from the staff lounge to prepare for the GED class that was scheduled to begin at one o'clock in the Visiting Room. Lumpkin was liked by the inmates. She was calm and easy going. She wasn't a stickler for the rules. She was in her early thirties, divorced, with one daughter. She'd graduated from Catskill Rock College (a bastion of higher education in Catskill County), and hated working for the BOP. Unfortunately, it was the only employment she could secure when she was desperate for money after her ex-husband failed to pay child support.

Officer Lumpkin was surprised to see so many people walking toward her. Then she saw Hinkel near his office shooing them along. She walked up beside me and stopped, apparently hoping someone would inform her what was going on.

The limo driver opened the squeaking metal door and the three women stepped in. All eyes turned their way. There was a moment of silence as the hotties gazed around the inside of a federal prison. The inmates ogled them and fantasized. Then, coming from the bathroom, I heard what sounded like stall doors slamming, yelling, thumping, and a heavy thud as if someone fell. Hinkel's bear, trapped in the bathroom, couldn't have generated more noise. Then, a shrieking scream. Everyone turned toward the bathroom door, including the women. Slipping, sliding and yelping noises. Seconds passed, and then Ratner burst out, ducking and dodging through the doorway, arms flailing wildly, a yellow stain painted across his chest. His gray pants spotted black. The image of a runaway fire hose crossed my mind. He slipped on the yellow stream flowing from the bathroom and spun to the tile floor taking Officer Lumpkin's legs out from under her. She fell on top of him, knees and elbows first.

"Glwalk!" she yelped not too loudly considering the circumstances.

The three women were just a few yards from where Officer Lumpkin lay sprawled on the floor. Ratner rolled out from under Lumpkin with an abrupt push that sent her flying. He jumped to his feet; amber droplets dripping from an eyebrow.

"You're in the bucket, Ciriello!" he screamed. "You're in the fuckin' bucket right now!" His body shook and his face turned red then purple. Officer Lumpkin flipped over so her hands and knees were on the floor. "Don't you come out of there until you clean up that mess. You fuckin' hear me?" Ratner removed handcuffs from his Sam Brown belt. His back had a wet streak. He shook his head like a dog. Drops flew. "You gonna be an old man by the time you git outta the bucket, Ciriello!"

Ratner huffed and puffed as he glared at the door. Officer Lumpkin rose to her feet, unaffected by having been tackled. Counselor Hinkel, for the moment, was speechless.

Inmates burst into unrestrained laughter that Counselor Hinkel could not tolerate. He stepped forward, held up his hand like a cop stopping traffic, and blew his whistle for a full breath. That drowned out the noise. He shouted, "Quiet! Alla ya'll! Quiet! We will have order in this here camp!" He thrust his chin up, and shot his hand down, a finger pointing at his foot.

Silence returned after a few more guffaws. One of the women oblivious to all of the commotion went straight to Mackenzie. She dropped her make-up bag and handed her garment bag to a bystander.

"Hey, baby!" She smiled, giggled, and then hugged Mackenzie. "I'm so glad to see you. I miss you so much. You've made me the happiest girl in the whole world!"

22

The Ceremony, Part 1

I received a letter with an Arizona postmark. My ex-spouse's address.

At last!

She's relented.

I opened the envelope and withdrew a single sheet. It said, "You will never speak to them while you're in prison. I told you that and it is a promise I will keep."

I thought that time and distance were supposed to heal all wounds. I guess the person who said that never met my ex-wife.

Counselor Hinkel awoke from his stupor.

"Who is all these peoples?" he yelled at Mackenzie. Hinkel's cheeks were now red, his eyes on fire. Everyone looked at him. Silence ensued. The paperclip holding his glasses together swung to a stop.

Mackenzie's whispered in a sheepish voice, "My bride and the girls in my wedding party."

"Not iffin they ain't on you Visitin' List. Now, what is they names?"

Mackenzie was losing confidence now. "This is my fee-an-see, Clarissa Powell, and her bridesmaids, Stella Preston and Princess."

"Stay rights here," said Hinkel. He popped into his office and grabbed a folder. He came back out and opened the folder; the paper clip jiggling.

"Po-well an' Pressed-on can stay. But Princess here, she gots to go. She ain't on you Approved Visitor List. You only got three on the list. T'other's a boy's name. This Princess here hasta leave this facility immediate. The sooner is better."

Clarissa was horrified.

"Mack!" she demanded. "Do something! Princess took the day off from the strip club to be my bridesmaid. She s'posed to be a surprise for you! That's why she ain't on the list." She poked a finger at Mack, but didn't touch him. "Don't let him push you 'round like this."

For the first time, I had an unencumbered view of Clarissa. Five feet tall max, thin, with brown hair freshly sprayed in place. Looked maybe late-twenties, early thirties. Heavy on the "make up." Thin lips, round face, large plump breasts supported by a structural bra in defiance of gravity. She was hard bodied and out for fun. Her wiggle expressed her "atty-tude." She was hot and she knew it. The expression "rode hard and put away wet" came to mind.

The entire adventure begged the question, why was she here?

Could it be love?

The cynic in me said "NFW."

There had to be something else. Why do you marry a guy who will be in prison for another nine years?

Hinkel said, "An' you better hurry up with you little say-yance here 'cause you gots to be out of the Visitin' Room by thirteen hunnert hours so's Officer Lumpkin can teach her GED class."

The unfortunate Officer Lumpkin had comported herself nicely and appeared as if nothing had happened to her.

Hands on her hips, Clarissa stared hard at Mackenzie. Then she pointed at Hinkel. "What's up with you, Mack? You said you were gonna kick his ass if he gave you any shit. So what's the story? How much more of his shit are you gonna take?"

Miz Buckles came out of the Admin Office to watch.

Hinkel smiled. "Twelve minutes you gots, Mackenzie, and then I's gots me a terl-lit that needs scrubbin'." He drew a toothbrush out of his pen pocket pouch and handed it to Mackenzie. "Take that." Mackenzie grabbed it by the bristle end.

"Wuss-sat?"

"Scrubbin' brush." Hinkel looked at his watch. "Eleven minute for-ty-five second, Mackenzie. You is wasting time."

Clarissa was upset with Mackenzie for not kicking Hinkel's ass. She was mad at Hinkel for telling Princess to leave. I watched as the realization dawned in her face that Hinkel was in charge and there was nothing she, or anyone else, could do about it.

She hugged Princess. "I'm sorry, baby. I'll make this up to you. I'll call ya when you can come back in the limo."

Mackenzie looked around. "Where's Waterbug?"

"I tol' him twelve-thirty sharp," someone said. "Last time I saw him he was in the shower jerkin—" He clipped this short.

Clarissa and Stella went into the Visiting Room bathroom to change clothes and fix, or maybe add to, their make-up.

"Where's the goddamned preacher?" Mackenzie huffed to no one in particular.

He turned to me. "Dan, can you watch the parking lot and tell me when he fucking arrives?"

An old junker rolled into the parking lot and pulled up to the front of the Admin Building. It looked like a Chevy Malibu, but different colored panels and rust made its heritage difficult to pin down. The motor continued turning over a few seconds after the engine was shut down. The driver was old and wore a charcoal-gray suit. His white shirt was closer to tan. His tie extended halfway down his shirt and was bright red with a faded design of a Christmas tree. Brown Hush-Puppy shoes and white socks adorned his feet. Hair was slicked back and wavy. He carried a thin black book.

Mackenzie was rushing around placing everyone where he thought they should be. Hinkel was standing at the Visiting Room door examining his watch every half minute.

The elderly man came through the Visiting Room door. Mackenzie went to him.

"Are you the minister?"

"I am the Right Reverend Billy Westover," proclaimed the newcomer with high solemnity. "Where is the deceased?"

"What?"

"Do you know where the deceased is? A certain Mister Mackenzie Mackenzie is being buried today."

"No, no. I'm Mack Mackenzie. I'm getting *married* today. It was some guy named Gillette who died. He ain't here. They took him away. You *are* the minister for the wedding, right?"

The Right Reverend Westover seemed taken aback. Alarm showed on his face as he sputtered. "My… My… calendar… It said… Mackenzie… Mackenzie Ceremony at twelve-thirty. It was booked two weeks ago. I thought it was a buryin' ceremony."

What did he think the corpse had been doing for two weeks since the appointment was scheduled?

He sighed, "I done brought the wrong book. I thought this was a burial." He raised his eyes toward the ceiling, or at God, and pondered. "Golly gee. What am I going to do?"

His eyes dropped to Mackenzie.

"It don't matter none. You're in prison. You got no choice. If you got the money, I'll make it up as we go along!"

Frankie Bananas came out of the bathroom. His pants and shirt were soaked as if he'd been running a marathon.

Officer Ratner shouted, "Ciriello! Assume the position!!"

"Huh?"

One would think that Frankie Bananas had never been arrested before.

"Put your hands on the wall and spread you legs."

Ratner flipped him around, walked him to the cinderblock wall and put one of his hands on the wall. Then he went around him and put the other hand on the wall, and spread Frankie's fat legs with his foot. Ratner snapped a handcuff on his left hand.

"Ow!" Frankie cried. "That hurt."

"I don't care if it cuts you to the bone fat boy."

Ratner jerked the arm behind Frankie's back.

"Hey!" Frankie's voice had urgency to it now. "What are you doing?"

Ratner held Frankie's left hand as he walked around to secure Frankie's right hand.

Staring curiously at Banana's still inked hands, Ratner asked, "You got some birth defect, Ciriello?"

"What?"

Ratner jerked Frankie's right hand from the wall causing Frankie to fall forward and hit his head on the cinderblock. Sounded like a melon hitting concrete.

"Oww!" he howled taking a step forward to gather his legs back under him. "My head. You're killing me. Stop! I'm delicate."

"Watch me."

"Am I bleeding?"

"I hope you bleed to death!"

"Ahh!" said Frankie as Ratner snapped on the cuff.

Ratner had to force Frankie's two wrists closer together in order to lock both cuffs.

"I didn't do nothing."

"Like hell you didn't."

Ratner held the back of Frankie's shirt with one hand and the cuffed hands in the other as he turned him toward the Admin Office.

"You're gonna weigh about one-thirty when you come back to this compound, fat boy," Ratner promised as he led him into Hinkel's office.

Meanwhile, back at the wedding.

"Okay, I'm marrying Clarissa," said Mackenzie to the Reverend not missing a beat. "She's in the ladies room gettin' changed."

Waterbug came strutting down the corridor with a camera in his hand. He was a black man in his early thirties from Washington, D.C. He'd spent time in several of Virginia's penal institutions, and was now doing a long stretch for a drug charge. Waterbug was respected by the inmates because prison policy was meaningless to him. He was hardened to the system and constantly pushed the envelope. Consequences were inconsequential. He earned his nickname by being hard to cover on the basketball court. He'd made a big deal out of being the wedding photographer because he was hoping to bang a white chick.

Mackenzie hugged Waterbug and shook hands brother-style, a sign of respect. "Peace, my man. Fuckin' Hinkel won't let the band play, and he threw out one of the bridesmaids. But you're okay to take pictures, right?"

"Jive-ass mother fucker," said Waterbug referring to Hinkel. "Why he always hatin' on us? He just *wrong,* man."

"Listen. We gotta hurry. Officer Lumpkin is here to start the GED class. Hinkel's countin' down the time."

Shifflett and Green came charging down the hall, radios and headsets in tow.

"Here you go, Mack," Shifflett said. "Best we could do."

Mackenzie said, "Hand 'em out and tell everybody to put them on and play the same station."

"Where's the bitches?" asked Waterbug holding up the camera.

Mackenzie ran around arranging everyone in their place.

"Come on out girls," he kept calling. "We gotta get movin.' Come on out now or we're gonna run out of time."

The chairs were placed randomly around the room. There were about eight of us standing there including Counselor Hinkel and Officer Lumpkin.

Clarissa and Stella emerged from the bathroom. Clarissa was wearing a white mini-skirt with white stockings and six-inch-high clogs. Stella was wearing a pink sundress with matching pink high heels. She looked ready for the beach.

The Right Reverend Billy Westover stood in front of the podium.

Some black guy said, "You fight dey's men. I fuck dey's women."

Someone else muttered, "Dey's is so fine."

23

The Ceremony, Part 2

It was refreshing to hear my mother's voice. I called at least once a week. I ran out of new things to say since my days were all the same. She can't call me. No one can call me. My ex-spouse refused to allow me to speak to my babies. She was filled with hate. She was too angry to realize that she was not only hurting me but she was hurting the children as well. All I wanted to do was stop their pain and start communicating with them. But her anger was in the way.

Thank God, Mom was still there, connecting me to my children. She was doing the best she could, even at eighty-one.

"Mack," Clarissa asked as she scanned the room. "Where's the band? You promised me a band!!! 'The Deaf Tones?' Wasn't that their name?"

Mackenzie whimpered an apology.

"I'm sorry, honey. That asshole Hinkel threw them out. The paperwork was fucked up."

Clarissa started to cry. "And I fucked up Princess's paperwork by not sending it in." Tears started to clot her eyeliner. A drop rolled down her cheek trailing a dark track.

Mackenzie hugged her and copped a feel. "Don't worry, baby. It's gonna get better." He wiped her tear away with his thumb as his other hand continued to fondle the side of her breast. He didn't seem to care that we were watching him grope his wife-to-be. What a guy!? "Here. Put these headphones on. We'll listen to a great song and rock this joint."

Cheeks wet, mouth in a pout, Clarissa put on the headset. Waterbug aimed the camera at her and clicked a picture.

"Yo, man!" snapped Mackenzie. "What the fuck you doing? Show some respect here!"

"Chill, man," said Waterbug. "I got you back. Ain't no film in dis here."

"No film! Where's the fucking film?" Mackenzie was angry now. "Where's the fuckin' film, you dumb shit?"

"Wreck got de camera, but Hinkel got de film. An' he say he ain't got the key to the film cad-net right now."

Mackenzie looked at Hinkel who was standing beside the door and allowing only GED students to enter.

"That no good mother fucker—"

Hinkel held up both hands showing two fingers with each. "Three minutes!" he announced.

Clarissa tore off her headphones and threw them to the floor. She started to cry again.

"I hate this fuckin' country bullshit," she whined to Mackenzie. "It ain't even fuckin' music. Some fuckin' jerk-off cryin' 'bout whiskey. What kinda weddin' music is that?"

Mackenzie said, "Fuck it, baby, let's go. Let's get married and show these hillbillies how to do it in style."

Clarissa brightened at hearing this. She'd needed a rallying cheer and Mackenzie supplied her with one. "Let's do it, baby."

Clarissa and Mackenzie turned to face the Right Reverend Billy Westover. Green, Shifflett and I stood on Mackenzie's right. Stella stood on Clarissa's left.

Just then, the biggest queer in camp walked in, Liberace. He was in for drug distribution and was always on the edge of getting his ticket punched by the homophobes. I never understood why he was assigned into a general population like ours. Budget cuts most likely.

"Miz Buckles lent me her make up kit. She's such a doll. We girls have to stick together." He brightened up as he recognized that the wedding was taking place for real.

"Yo! Can I be a bride maid?" Liberace asked Mack. "I always wanted to be a bride maid." He clasped his hands together in front of his chest. "An' oh, Clarissa! You look fab-u-low-so, girlfriend. And Stella! Why, I could just eat you alive, girlfriend. Wonderful! Wonderful! Wonderful. Can I? Can I be a bride maid?"

Mack shook his head as if saying, "What else can go wrong?"

"Sure, Liberace," he surrendered. "You be a bride's maid. Just hurry up."

"Hell, no, he can't be a bride's maid," Clarissa countered. "He's a fuckin' guy!"

Their first fight. How cute. Phone Sex was speechless.

"Well," he stammered. "Technically, he is a guy. But what harm can it do? We don't have much time, honey. Let's just go with it."

Clarissa digested that. Maybe she was wondering if Liberace played a role in Mack's life when the lights went out. No telling what she was thinking.

"All right. He can be a bride's maid. But he can't be in any of the pictures."

"It's a deal, baby," Mack promised. "Hurry up, Reverend. Hinkel is counting down the seconds."

"Oh, Mack," she said. "Can we have a picture of just the two of us standin' here?"

Mackenzie looked at the mascara and make-up already smeared by Clarissa's tears and his thumb.

The Right Reverend Westover interjected, "I thought the camera didn't have any film?"

"What do you mean? No film?" Clarissa cried. "No band! No Princess! I gotta queer for a brides maid! An' no pictures! I fuckin' hate you, Mack Mackenzie! My Pa was right. You *are* a total fuckin' loser!"

"Oh, come on, Clarissa. I'm doing the best I can. Let's just get married and then none of this will matter."

Counselor Hinkel walked up.

"Two minutes, Mackenzie. Or to put it in terms you'll understand, two times fifty seconds."

I bit the inside of my lip to keep from laughing. Hinkel was translating minutes into seconds—evil genius that he was. Judges do the same thing at sentencing. The sentence is pronounced in months as opposed to years. Too bad he couldn't add.

"What do you want me to do?" asked the Right Reverend.

"Get us married quick," Mackenzie told him.

"I'll give you the Catskill County Special. They're big in this here area when people gits married. They almost ta-skip the ceremony so they can gits down to the makin' babies part, if you know what I mean."

The Right Reverend straightened to his full height. He looked at Clarissa.

"Does you loves him?"

"Yes."

He looked at Mackenzie.

"Does you loves her?"

"You betcha."

"Then 'cordin' to the oh-thor-ah-tee passed down to me by my cousin and brother in spirit, Elmer Westover, Jr., first Minister of the Peace on Earth Evangelical Church of Our Almighty God Jesus Christ the Savior of these here parts, I say you're married." He paused. "As soon as you pay my fee, a' course."

At that, everyone broke out in smiles except Counselor Hinkel. Inmates congratulated Clarissa and Mackenzie. Hugs and kisses abounded. Waterbug snapped scads of pictures with his filmless camera.

Mackenzie smirked at Green. "Got me, Jimmy?"

Green whispered back, trying not to be noticed, "Be quick. They gonna start this class inna minute."

Mackenzie opened the storage room door, where the Catholic priest stored the religious items needed to celebrate Mass, and shoved Clarissa inside. The Right Reverend collected an envelope from Stella. He counted the contents, stuffed the envelope into his pants pocket, and began signing documents.

Inmates were dribbling into the room like cows coming in from the field. There was no reason to rush since they knew Officer Lumpkin never wrote them up regardless of how late they were.

Lumpkin stood in front of the chalkboard and asked the inmates to arrange the chairs. Hinkel observed it all, noted the time on his watch and matched it with the time on the wall clock. More inmates wandered through the door.

"Where's Mackenzie?" Hinkel asked Waterbug.

Waterbug shot back a standard jailhouse line.

"I wanna mouthpiece! Lawyer me up, man."

"Just tell me where's Mackenzie!"

Spooter was red in the face.

"Why… why…" Waterbug's face brightened into a smile revealing the gold edges of his teeth. "He be on he hunny-moon, mass'sah." Then he snapped Spooter's picture.

"Give me that there camera!" Spooter bellowed. "It's agin regulations to take any pictures of staff."

Waterbug gave the camera to Spooter and ricocheted down the concourse like his nickname suggested.

"Where's Mackenzie?" Spooter repeated to no one in particular. His voice demanding an answer. He surveyed the room.

The Right Reverend headed out of the building. The wedding party ambled toward the door. The student inmates were sitting in front of the podium. Officer Lumpkin turned to the chalkboard.

No chalk, as usual. She went to the storage closet. Jimmy Green was guarding the door.

"Why are you here, Green? You're not in this class."

"Could you repeat the question? I'm not sure I knows whats you is astin me."

"Answer the question!"

He didn't know what to do. "Yo. I'm waitin'." He was stalling for time. "I'm waitin' to—to—eh—you know—."

A thump came from the closet. "What's that?" she quizzed.

Like most inmates, Green was a defender of the cause. Lie, deny, or make counter accusations—it's the inmate creed. This time, Green played the lie card, "I didn't hear nuthin'."

There was no mistaking the thumping sound now. A deer could be loose in there.

"Step aside," she demanded. An inquisitive look crossed her face but Green respected the authority of a direct order. He reluctantly complied with the speed of someone mounting the gallows. More stalling.

Officer Lumpkin grasped the handle and opened the door. The sight stopped her cold.

Clarissa and Mackenzie were making marital atop the Catholic al-

143

tar.

Officer Lumpkin closed the door as calmly as could be, apparently not embarrassed or shocked. Mackenzie's wedding motivation was now exposed.

Lumpkin turned away from the door and was face-to-face with Hinkel.

"You see Mackenzie anywhere?" he asked.

"I believe he's in that storage closet helping his wife dress. You may want to give him a minute."

"I already done gone past give him a minute."

Hinkel opened the door.

A full two heartbeats passed.

"Macken-Zie!"

24

Release

People were released all the time. I was always glad when they left because that's how I marked time. I knew who would be transferred just before me and I couldn't wait because I knew that I was next. Every time someone got out, I told myself that I was one person closer. How fucking sad was that?

I'd been at FPC Catskill for a few weeks before the first holiday weekend arrived. Through simple interaction, I'd realized that there were some decent guys in the federal prison system, and most of the hacks were okay as long as they were left alone. The goal of almost everyone was to survive each day with as little drama as possible. Even better, I'd been to the commissary and I now had deodorant, shaving equipment, a radio with earphones, and an alarm-clock wristwatch. Small things taken for granted and then lost became obsessions. Now that I didn't smell, didn't have an itchy face and could drown out the range noise with earphones, I felt better. The slow creep toward hell halted—little comforts meant so much and stabilized me.

Labor Day weekend was approaching. This particular holiday began early because one of the nicer guys was being transferred to a halfway house the Friday before.

Everybody liked Brian Armstrong. He was pleasant to be around and carried more than his share on work details. A high school graduate, he'd married his tenth grade sweetheart, Gwen. They both had good jobs, a home, two pre-teen boys named Derek and Dennis, and in general, a good life. During visiting hours, the Armstrongs taught us how a family pulled together in a time of crisis.

The day before any transfer was unique. By nine in the morning the primary means of inmate communication, the telephone, was shut off, and the inmate's debit card was cancelled so his telephone and commissary funds could be calculated and distributed to him the next day. Thursday morning Brian was on the phone with Gwen, tears in his eyes, promising nothing would ever separate them again.

Brian's crime? Publicly urinating in a Federal Park Reserve. It never made any sense to me. There had to be more to the story.

His sentence? A year and a day. The sentence was important because a sentence of a year and a day qualifies an inmate for time off that is known as "good time."

Brian went to trial and it cost him seventy-five thousand dollars in legal fees. I would have charged him a lot less and probably could have lost just as well.

To raise the money for legal fees, the Armstrongs refinanced their house and wiped away fourteen years of accumulated equity. To pay the refinanced mortgage, their siblings and cousins chipped in each month. The loss of Brian's paycheck for a year meant that Christmas was less merry, certainly less opulent, and pitching a tent in the back yard substituted for a National Park visit during summer vacation. It is true that, when someone goes to prison, the quality of life changes for the entire family, not just the inmate. Wives and children also do time. Everybody's impacted. But, as Brian sobbed to Gwen during that last call, "It's all over now."

Thursday night after the nine o'clock count cleared, C Range in Camp Two morphed into a "7-Eleven." Chips, dips, pretzels, sodas, juices, crackers, salami, baloney, ham, turkey, condiments of all sorts, rolls, buns, pizza, and a cake appeared on tables borrowed from the activity room. Trash cans were full of iced sodas. Inmates gathered around and waited for Armstrong who was being brought over from Camp One under some pretext.

Brian was like a little kid at Christmas when he saw the tables and realized the celebration was for him. Inmates hugged him and wished him well, a look of disbelief and joy on his face. The number of inmates attending grew since word of free food and soda attracted them like money draws legislators. Soon the party was no longer for Brian and his closest friends. A few of the late arrivals wished Brian well, but most were there for the feast and didn't know, or could care less, about the occasion.

Brian talked and laughed with the inmates he had been friendly with. He said he would pray for them and stay in touch. Several wrote their names and ID numbers on napkins or pieces of paper. Brian folded them up and put them in his pocket for later transfer to his address book. Brian was the type of guy who would follow up if he promised to.

In thirty minutes everything was eaten and the party ended. Inmates rearranged and policed the room. Brian thanked everyone who'd provided and prepared this "feast" and had thus put themselves at risk by either stealing from the kitchen or preparing the stolen food.

Just before he left, Brian told us that his only regret was not being able to say goodnight to Gwen and the boys for the first time since he'd received I-T-S rights.

The next morning at six fifteen Brian climbed down from his bunk and took his toiletries with him for his last shower. He came back and dressed in the going-home-sweats he'd bought from the commissary. No more khaki for him, ever. No more jobs designed to kill time. No more USDA Grade D food. It was all over. He asked his wife to be in the parking lot by eight. Brian would be at R&D in time to meet them when they arrived.

I envied him. My ex-wife and three children were gone from my life out in Arizona. I had another ninety-four months before I would be released. Right now, my plan was to have Cousin Emily pick me up. We'd probably visit my mom's grave first. My eyes welled up at that prospect.

Ten of eight.

Brian idled away the minutes by fidgeting around the range or sitting in the TV room not watching TV. His mind was jumping from subject to subject and his stomach was full of butterflies. He'd already stripped his bed and returned his sheets and towels to the camp laundry. Nervous energy abounded. All that was left was to report to R&D and collect his commissary account money. Then he'd be released.

On the last trip by his cube he noticed that his mattress, a thin cloth affair better suited as a floor mat, had been taken by another inmate to "double-up" on his bunk. Feeling ripped-off at first, he realized that it wasn't his problem any longer and chuckled. He'd given away his oth-

147

er stuff, most of it to an FNG who had nothing. All Brian had now was a shoebox that contained the letters he'd received from his wife and children that reminded him that he was loved and needed.

Five of eight.

Brian looked around the range one last time. His emotions were churning too fast to be remembered. In a few minutes he would be hugging Gwen and his sons as a free man. The ordeal would be over. Life would start anew. He glanced at the other inmates, some sleeping, and some going through the motions of cleaning. A sense of relief settled on him.

He walked from Camp Two to the Admin Building. He saw Gwen's SUV in the lot. Then he spied Gwen and the boys. She stood at the front bumper looking up the hill for him. As soon as she recognized him, she blew him a kiss. Derek and Dennis stopped running around the lot and began yelling, "Daddy! Daddy!" Tears rose in Brian's eyes. Gwen had told him that Derek was bringing a picture he drew of the four of them eating together at IHOP and Dennis was bringing a football so they could play catch. All this love but Brian still had anxiety churning throughout his body. A million thoughts raced through his mind. He struggled to remain calm. His pace quickened.

Along the Admin Building's main concourse a couple of inmates stopped to shake his hand. Brian couldn't keep the smile off his face. By the time he arrived at R&D, he could see Gwen, Derek, and Dennis at the front door.

Brian's case manager was Mr. Eggars, a middle-aged Hitler Youth. His daily attire never varied. Starched white shirt, polished jackboots, crisp creases in his pants, tie and shirt metal perfectly aligned. He believed himself upwardly mobile within the BOP. He was hardnosed and devoid of humor. He knew the regulations and applied them fastidiously. He had an air of superiority about him. He often mocked and derided inmates.

Eggars came out of R&D holding a folder.

He saw Armstrong.

"Return to your unit," he ordered.

"But—" he stuttered. "I'm—I'm supposed to report for release. It's on the callout sheet."

"Return to your unit, Armstrong. You will be paged when I'm ready for you."

Armstrong couldn't move. He was confused. He looked from Eggars to Gwen and the boys not forty feet away, then back at Eggars. He almost dropped the shoebox.

"Start stepping, Armstrong or you'll go to the bucket."

Brian tried during his tenure to befriend Eggars but with limited success.

"Do it now," ordered Eggars.

Brian knew that he had to obey the order. He was still on BOP soil.

He turned and walked back toward Camp Two. He wanted to sneak a peek at Gwen and the boys, but was afraid Eggars might send him to the bucket. Until he was out the door, cops dominated his life.

Outside, out of Eggars's view, he turned to the parking lot to see Gwen and the boys beside the SUV. He thought of the picture and the football that his sons had brought with them. He was trying to imagine their emotions and he started to cry.

"What's wrong?" she shouted to him. "They told us to leave!"

Brian's chest clenched when he heard that. He muttered, "I don't know." He didn't think he said it loud enough for her to hear. All the life was squeezed out of him.

Miz Buckles walked out of the Admin Building toward Gwen. They spoke briefly, and then Miz Buckles climbed the hill toward Brian. He waited for her hoping for good news.

"Listen," she said from a few feet away. "There's a problem." She stopped in front of him. "Eggars fucked up your computation. He realized it this morning and called Regional." She was referring to the Regional Office of the BOP. "Your release date has been changed. You won't be leaving for another fifteen days."

Brian felt close to panic. He forced himself to be calm and think.

"Gwen's gonna have to leave with the boys and come back in two weeks?"

"I'm afraid so."

Two more weeks. It seemed like forever.

"What am I supposed to do?" Freedom was gone—again. The captive had been freed, and then captured again. What would this do emotionally to Gwen and their sons? How much more could he expect them to endure? And he was in a bind himself. "I gave away all my shit. My phone's off. I don't have any money."

Miz Buckles knew all this.

"Look. Let me work on that. I should be able to have your phone turned back on today, and you can have visits this weekend." She paused. "Your wife is really upset. She and the children don't understand what happened. I told them to go to the Visiting Room where you can explain it to them, but you've only got five minutes. Hear that? Five minutes. Eggars is acting Camp Administrator, and if he comes out of the kitchen after breakfast and he sees your wife and kids still here, he'll have them arrested or something. You better move and make it quick just in case he finds out they ain't got no bacon or there ain't no more eggs except the powder ones he don't like."

Brian ran to the Visiting Room. This was supposed to be his Big Day. The kids didn't go to school. They were going to have breakfast at the IHOP to celebrate his transfer to a halfway house.

They met with hugs and kisses, short and tearful. Brian explained that his release date had been calculated incorrectly. And sure, Eggars was an ass, but what could be done about it? The only reasonable answer was to persevere for two more weeks.

The rest of the morning Brian explained to everyone what happened. After lunch, he reclaimed his mattress and lay on his bunk staring at the ceiling. His composure had been stretched and broken, his disappointment extreme. He cried himself into a nap.

After the Four O'clock Count cleared, Brian was still struggling with the morning's disaster. He thought that if he could talk to Gwen and the boys he would feel better. Miz Buckles had told him before lunch that she had already contacted the commissary and telephone people at the Medium Security facility and she assured him that the telephone would be operational. Plus, his seven dollars and nineteen cents would be put back into his telephone account. He raced to the phone banks as soon as the count cleared. After waiting in the telephone line for forty minutes, his fingers punched the keys. He thought only of hearing Gwen answer, "Hello?" He waited as he heard clicking through the receiver. A recorded voice said, "The PIN number you have entered is not active. Please check the PIN number and try again later."

PIN numbers activate a list of pre-approved telephone numbers that an inmate can access.

Brian had dialed the number daily for almost a year. He hadn't made a mistake. He tried again.

"The PIN number you have entered is not active. Please check the PIN number and try again later."

If the telephone account was not set up by now, it wouldn't be operational until Tuesday because of the Monday holiday. Brian looked up in frustration. An expression of "How much more, Lord, how much more do I have to endure?" crossed his face. Tears welled in his eyes. Instead of pancakes with his family, it was a walk to a meal that he did not expect to eat. That's life with the BOP. You learn to expect the unexpected.

25

Labor Day

Major holidays were depressing because there was nothing to do. On the street, I hated them because I visited with my in-laws who celebrated with lots of alcohol and arguments.
Oh God. How I missed those days.

Facing my first holiday away from my children, I worried about how they were handling the tragedy that had befallen their lives. They were way too young to understand what happened and many years away from learning how to process it. Life in the BOP churned along heedless of an inmate's family problems. The only solution was to love and support them by sending letters. Plus, I had to deal with my first holiday in my new surroundings and the surprises it would bring.

It seemed that there were two areas most directly impacted by a holiday. The first was Food Service, or, as it was known, Food Circus, where an outside bar-b-cue would be prepared in addition to a special lunch. The big question was: *What would the main course be?* Everybody was talking about it. I was told chicken had been served on Memorial Day and again on the Fourth of July, so roast beef or steak was expected. Breaking the weekly cycle of repeating meals for a chance at roast beef or steak was something to anticipate, even celebrate. Inmates assigned to food service and warehouse details were questioned but could not answer. Some claimed fried chicken, others said prime rib, and others said filet mignon. One goofball said lunch would be catered directly from Outback Steakhouse. The most reliable sources, those who made a living stealing food from the kitchen, didn't know.

The holiday camp schedule was posted on the bulletin boards. Like a weekend, breakfast was pushed back an hour and served from seven to eight. Starting after the special weekend and holiday Ten AM Count cleared, the principle meal of the day was served in two seatings—one camp at a time. To prevent inmates from going through the line multiple times, Meal Tickets were distributed to each inmate. After the main meal was completed, hot dogs and hamburgers were served until three PM when Food Circus closed for the day. Dinner was not served on holidays. You were issued a brown bag and could eat in your cube.

The Recreation Department, known more accurately as "Wreck," was also impacted on holidays. Wreck ran card games, board games, softball tournaments, handball, bocce, horseshoes, and more. The winner of any tournament won a six pack of soda, a prized commodity in the camp's bartering system.

I knew the Wreck Officer by chatting with him in his air-conditioned office. He was Mr. Crowder, a local—born, raised, and educated in Catskill County. Mr. Crowder was five-eight and stocky. A former jock, his specialty was baseball. Drafted by the Dodgers, he'd had enough talent to be promoted to Double-A ball where a lack of height and speed ended his career. Eventually he gave up the life to join the Real World and, with his professional sports background and dearth of an education; he was a natural for the position of a Wreck Supervisor. His face was round with a close-shaved head, ears that stuck out like sails, and no chin. A feral face if I ever saw one. He loved his office and recovered there from the pressures of his marriage. The office contained the three most important things in his life: a television, a telephone, and an air conditioner. Mr. Crowder let Wreck run itself. The only time he left his sanctuary was to filch food from Food Circus.

I asked Mr. Crowder about the holiday tournaments. He directed me to Luka Slobodo. When I said Slobodo didn't work for Wreck, Mr. Crowder replied that Slobodo didn't work anywhere, but that didn't stop him from knowing everything that was going on.

At about six fifty-five AM on a crisp, clear, and beautiful Monday in the mountains, my first holiday as a felon began. Weather forecasters had predicted a gorgeous day. Bingo.

About two dozen inmates lined up at the Food Circus door for breakfast. At seven, Spooter unlocked the door and the inmates rushed inside. For Labor Day, Food Circus offered a choice of Cheerios, Bran Flakes, Sugar Frosted Flakes, honey buns, coffee, tea, milk, and orange juice. For an inmate, this was living large. The rest of the inmates did not go to breakfast on holidays. A few paid underlings to sneak food to them in their cubes, the prison equivalent of breakfast in bed.

By this time, I'd been assigned as clerk-in-training at the Power House. Hot water for both the Medium- and Minimum-Security facilities was heated, monitored and pumped from there. My job reminded me of an episode of *The Simpsons* where Homer sat at his desk at a nuclear power plant sorting Skittles into piles of the same color. Most prison jobs are like that; time-killers at best. I was going to be around for the next ninety-four months, and this job was as close to office work as I could get.

My job consisted of writing the temperature and pressure for each water pump on a designated form every hour. This was the sum total of my job. For this I was paid twelve cents an hour. Depending on performance, I could increase my compensation package to forty cents per hour. A tad short of the four hundred dollars per hour that I was accustomed to billing as an attorney. Then again, I had no overhead.

I was one of the unfortunates who had to work on Labor Day because the regular clerk had been excused for a scheduled visit. I arrived to see Mr. Bass, a cop at the Power House, fidgeting outside the building. Mr. Bass was in his early forties, but his receding and graying hairline aged him. He was a reformed alcoholic who'd put down the bottle, picked up the Bible, and adopted Jesus as his Savior. The revelation changed his life.

"How are you this morning, Mr. Bass?" I said walking up to him.

He looked sleepish since his shift started at midnight. He said, "I'll be better as soon as Skorzeny gets here."

I suddenly felt ill.

"Corrections Officer Skorzeny is your relief?"

"I feel bad for you, Dan," he empathized. "I really do. But I'm outta here as soon as he shows."

This was going to be unpleasant. I'd been warned about *Corrections Officer Skorzeny* from the other Power House cops, and I'd sat one shift with him already. No first name or at least no one knew his first name. Of all the hacks in camp, Skorzeny was the only one who insisted on being called "Corrections Officer." He was the cop from hell. And, to be honest about it, he deserved every bit of the disrespect heaped on him. On my first day at the Power House he told me that Mr. Bass was a closet drunk who used religion as a crutch. Skorzeny's insults were free flowing and offensive. He humiliated inmates by ordering them to clean spit he'd just spat off of the sidewalk and to scrape tarnish off of the water pipes with miniscule pieces of sandpaper. Inmates who weren't terrified of him just didn't know him well enough.

The sound of a motorcycle approached from the bottom of the hill. We turned to look. None of the cops had a motorcycle. Must be a lost soul. Wrong place to be lost.

From behind a row of trees that lined the institution's entrance road, the sound of a Harley became louder. We watched the cycle pull into the CO's parking lot. The rider wore a black leather jacket. As if he were going through a checklist, he put the bike up on the kick stand, turned off the engine, and inserted the key in his jacket pocket.

Mr. Bass would have to tell this person to leave the property. No unauthorized civilians were allowed on prison grounds.

The man stepped off the bike. He started working the fingers of his gloves off his hands.

"What's this asshole think he's doing?" Mr. Bass muttered under his breath.

The man took off his helmet.

Skorzeny!

Mr. Bass and I stared at him in open-mouthed astonishment. He fastened his helmet to a piece of metal at the back of the bike and unstrapped a backpack. His gray uniform was under the leather jacket. He tossed the backpack over his shoulder and walked toward us.

26

Skorzeny

Victims.
My children.
Victims of my greed and foolishness. If only I could turn back time,
I'd stay on the straight and narrow.
Innocent little kids just starting out and their father is snatched
away for eight of the most formative years of their lives.
I may as well be dead.
No big deal for Counselor Hinkel—he said, "If you can't do the
time, don't do the crime."

"You clean my shitter, yet?"

Skorzeny was talking to me.

"No sir. I just arrived."

"Don't make excuses, Holmes. Gitter done." He farted. "I need it."

He looked at Mr. Bass who was "catching flies."

"Mike, I know you're ready for me, but I can't use a blowjob right now. So, close your mouth. Take the rest of the day off." He looked over at me. "Is my shitter cleaned yet?"

Corrections Officer Skorzeny marched into the Power House leaving us outside.

Skorzeny was in his early thirties, stood five-eleven and had a medium build. He had a crew cut and wore Ben Franklin-type glasses—Heinrich Himmler glasses would be more accurate, but unkind. He was from Catskill County and had returned after a ten year stint in the Army. He lived in a trailer park near his parents but, the only time he visited them, was to wash his laundry.

He told me that twelve years ago, when he was stationed in Texas, he'd fathered a baby by a woman he had not seen since. He loved his "little angel" so much that he sent her one hundred dollars per month for support. Otherwise, he had no contact with either his little angel or her mother, "the slut" as he referred to her. I wondered what that made Skorzeny.

Mr. Bass said, "Good luck, Dan. He's done gone and got hisself a chopper. He'll be fired-up t'day."

We followed Corrections Officer Skorzeny into the Power House. I walked to the clerk's desk, inserted my earplugs, and checked for messages from the prior shift. Mr. Bass entered the CO's office, handed Skorzeny the key-set for the Power House, picked up his lunch box, and split. I went into the CO's office to grab the chemical supplies and clean the officer's toilet.

Skorzeny looked up from a newspaper.

"What you want? I'm busy."

The paper was open to the comics.

"The chemical supplies, sir."

"You finished my shitter yet?"

"Not yet, sir." I picked up a toilet brush, a bucket, and two spray bottles. "That's where I'm headed now."

Skorzeny lifted a cheek from his chair.

"Hurry up. I gotta 'splow-shun comin.'"

I cleaned the officer's toilet double-time. No sooner was I finished than Skorzeny bolted in, closed the door, and locked it. I thought the lock unnecessary. We were the only two people in the Power House and there was no way I was going into the officer's bathroom any time soon.

On holidays and weekends, a special Ten O'clock Count was held. Idle inmates were required to stand in their cubes, beside their bunks, until two range cops completed the count. At the Power House, the CO reported the number of inmates by telephone and filled out a Count Slip. The Outside Patrol Cop would then stop by, pick up the Count Slip, and take it to the Admin Building.

Just before ten o'clock, Skorzeny walked out of his office and up to the clerk's desk. With one hand, he signaled me to stand. I complied. In a voice I could hear through the ear plugs, he announced, "Ten AM Mandatory Stand-Up Count; Federal Prison Camp Catskill in process." He paused to take a breath. "Commencing count." Another breath. "One." Short pause. "The Ten AM Mandatory Stand-Up Count FPC Catskill is now complete. Inmates will resume normal functions. Thank you."

He turned toward his office.

Just as I started to smile at how ludicrous that was, he jerked his head back toward me.

"Inmate Holmes."

He came back to my desk. I was still standing, my hint of a smile faded. "Since you're an FNG, recite the Inmate Creed."

He had me there.

"I've never heard of the Inmate Creed, sir."

"Well, it's time you learned. It goes like this:

'Every day is a holiday.
Every meal is a feast.
And God bless the BOP.'

"Can you handle that?"

I was a head taller than he was and I kept my eyes straight ahead.

"Did you want me to write that down, sir?"

"No. Just say it back to me."

I started off, "Quisque dies est festivus—"

"What the fuck is that?"

"It's the Inmate Creed in Latin, Sir. I dressed it up so you'd be proud of me."

I was fucking with him and he wouldn't like it. Before he had enough time to realize that fact, I recited,

'Every day is a holiday.
Every meal is a feast.
And God bless the BOP.
Can you handle that?'

That seemed to satisfy him. He walked away.

I sat down and resumed doing nothing.

He was nuts; I wasn't sure of the limit.

Not two minutes later he was back at my desk.

"You're in charge while I go to the shitter again. If anything happens while I'm there, it's on you. Got it?"

"Yes, Corrections Officer Skorzeny. I got it."

Skorzeny returned to the officer's bathroom. A few minutes later, the Outside Patrol Cop came by to pick up the count slip. Not seeing a hack in the office, or in the plant, he walked over to my desk.

"Who's on?"

I didn't recognize him.

"Corrections Officer Skorzeny."

He spun around in a quick about-face, entered the office, picked up the Count Slip, and scrambled out of the plant. Apparently, Skorzeny was feared by cops as well.

Just then, Mr. Carter, a cop in his early thirties, who supervised inmates at the Outside Warehouse, arrived. He wore sneakers, jeans, and a flannel shirt, and looked as if he'd just rolled out of bed. An intimidating mountain of a man, he was quite gentle. He told me his life's story in the first five minutes of my meeting him. He'd been married and divorced. His wife had conducted an informal intervention on him and had him committed to a mental hospital for a thirty-day observation. She'd claimed he was a danger to himself since he was so huge and such a moron. Admittedly, Carter was a bit on the dim side but he was too big to confront or insult. On the plus side, he was a part-time volunteer fireman and served on the church vestry. Best of all, he didn't give a damn about anything. His favorite expression was, "I don't give a fuck." If he saw an inmate stealing, Carter would warn him, "Hey! I saw that. You gotta do better than that or you'll end up in the bucket." I'd been told he'd never written up an inmate, which made him popular.

"Hey, Holmes! Who's on duty?" He had to scream from the door to be heard over the din of the machinery.

"Corrections Officer Skorzeny."

"Dad-gummit!" He was startled, like a surprised Kramer from *Seinfeld.* "Boy, it sucks to be you." He leaned his head forward like a bird dog and did a slow three-sixty around the room.

When he didn't see Skorzeny anywhere, he asked, "Did you whack him?"

"No. He's in the bathroom."

"Let him stay there. Hey! Ask him what his first name is when he comes out."

Mr. Carter, like most of the cops, was a practical joker. I learned that every day could be April Fools.

"Hey. You got the keys to the van? I gotta get propane for the camp. Food Circus is holding a cookout today for twenty-two hunnert inmates and nobody thought to check the propane. Bunch of geniuses runnin' this place. So fucked up."

"They called you at home for that?"

"Naw," said Carter. "They called the head of the department who called my boss who called me."

"It looks like you just got out of bed."

"Woke me the fuck up. I don't give a shit. I'm getting eight hours at time-and-a-half for a two-hour gig."

Skorzeny exited the officer's bathroom and marched into his office without saying a word. Mr. Carter followed him inside and came out a couple of seconds later with the van keys and took off. Skorzeny came out of his office and motioned for me to come into his office. I closed the door behind me.

"Holmes. Do I look tired today?" With the door closed, the office was insulated from the pump and boiler noise. I took out my earplugs.

"You look fine to me, Corrections Officer Skorzeny."

"I was at a weddin' reception last night an' I met this forty-three year-old wench, an' I rocked her world, know what I mean? I used my Polish charm to lure her in, and then I took her back to my trailer an' I fed her my ten-inch Genoa. What do you think of that, Holmes?"

"I didn't know Genoa was Polish, sir."

Skorzeny's eyes narrowed. I wondered if he was thinking that a lowly inmate would dare to make fun of him.

"See. You learn somethin' every time you pay attention." He rubbed his shoulder. "Know why my shoulder hurts?"

"Foreign Legion wound?"

Another dirty look passed in a moment.

"I got that bitch with my right arm, an' I hoisted her onto my dick, an' I rotated her back an' forth like a fucking yo-yo for 'bout two hours until she couldn't take it no more, know what I mean?"

"You're a beast, Corrections Officer Skorzeny."

Or at least a hopeful liar.

He looked around the top of his desk.

"Hey! Did you steal the Count Slip? It was right here before I went to the shitter."

"The Outside Patrol Cop came by and picked it up."

"Did he give you a Meal Ticket? You can't eat without one."

"No, sir. He just came in, picked up the Count Slip, and left."

"Well—the count cleared. You can leave at eleven thirty."

How generous. Usually I left for lunch at eleven. I'd have to wait an hour and a half, and then have fifteen minutes to hustle up to the dining hall before the chow line was closed.

"An' you'll have to see whatever staff member is on duty up there to get a Meal Ticket."

I'd have to *run* to the Admin Office.

"Yes, sir. Thank you, Corrections Officer Skorzeny."

He looked at me as if he were contemplating a dark secret. He said, "Recite for me the Inmate Creed."

Even this early in my sentence I knew I was there purely for Skorzeny's listening and dancing pleasure. It was a no win situation. The system would back him if I wrote him up. It was easier to play along.

"The Inmate Creed, sir:

'Every day is a holiday.
Every meal is a feast.
And God bless the BOP.
Can you handle that?'

He returned to the comics.

"Okay. You can go back to your desk."

I wanted to ask about his motorcycle but thought better of it, and left.

27

The Meal Ticket

At mail call today, I'm surprised that I received a package. I opened it and all the daily letters I'd sent to my children were there. Unopened.

I'm pissed that my ex won't let me communicate with my children. I think to myself "How much more of this can I endure?" My ex was just hurting the children but she'd never see it that way. She'd argue that I was a bad influence, and they shouldn't be exposed to me. In spite of the pain and anger, I forced myself to stay calm. If I said or did the wrong thing, I'd be shipped to the Medium Security facility, and I don't want to take a step backwards.

Back at my desk, I decided to scope out Skorzeny's first name. It must be Murgatroyd or Aloysius or Dweezil or Mars Unit or some other embarrassing name. Or something easy to mispronounce, him being a monster Polish Genoa sausage and all.

At eleven thirty, I slinked to the office.

"Is it all right if I leave now, Corrections Officer Skorzeny?"

"Yeah," he said not looking up from a magazine. "Get outta here."

"Thank you, Corrections Officer Skorzeny. Have a good day, sir."

I didn't have much time, so I left on the double. I trotted to the Admin Building. The route was In Bounds if you had a reason to be here. Up ahead, dense forestation surrounded both housing units. The FCI was down the hill on the right, its razor wire shining bright in the sunlight. I never saw rust on that wire during my stay at Camp Catskill. Outbuildings for grounds keeping and storage were on the left. If they cut down the trees around the grounds, there'd be room for more housing units, and there would be a need for more unendingly until the justice department changed its philosophy from "lock them up and throw away the key" to something more efficient.

As I passed the rear loading dock of Food Circus, hamburger and hot dog thievery was under way. Inmates pilfered uncooked patties and dogs in plastic bowels like kids in an Easter egg hunt. The food would be taken back to the range when the coast was clear. Watching the quantity of food being stolen, I guessed that food sales on the range that night would be at discounted prices. I didn't dwell on it though. I had to get my Meal Ticket.

Inside the Admin Building I noticed the food line was short. I saw Ace Baldini strolling my way.

"Is this the end of the line for the second serving?" I asked.

Ace was half-asleep.

"Yeah, I guess," he said looking around. "That mudda-fuckah Hinkel gonna close it down dough."

Hinkel was supposed to be off today. I was hoping to get my Meal Ticket without being hassled.

"Hinkel's here?"

"Mudda-fuckah's in a bad mood," Ace reported.

"He's always in a bad mood."

"He's worser today. At da ten o'clock count he make Lupo take off his box-ahs."

This was a non-sequitur. Lupo was a baby-faced Italian kid in his early twenties from New York City who bunked on the same range as I did. He was the orderly who cleaned the range bathroom, not an easy task considering its near constant use and the personal habits of the users. As a side gig, he washed inmate laundry in exchange for commissary items.

Ace must have thought that I was telepathic.

"What did Lupo do to deserve that?" I followed up.

Ace took a moment to recapture the thought.

"Aw—when Hinkel come on da range to do da count, Lupo was wearin' dose boxers dat he drawed his Yankees emblem on. Hinkel saw dat an' dat cracker say, 'We in Philly country, boy. Dem shorts is contraban',' an' he make Lupo take 'em off an' han' dem over. You know how stupid Hinkel sound when he talk, dat cracker."

"In front of everyone?"

"He always talk da same."

"No. I mean did Lupo have to take off his boxers in front of everyone on the range?"

"In fronta everyone includin' dat lady cop Lopez. Da kid was real embarrass 'cuz he ain't got nothin' to brag about, know whuddah mean? I thought he wuz gonna cry."

"Hinkel kept his shorts?"

"He held dem boxers out on his finger an' finish da count wid Lopez standin' there facin' Lupo's lil' dick. Last time I saw dem boxers, Hinkel wuz walkin' off da range wid dem."

"I need to get my Meal Ticket from Hinkel."

Ace's smile evaporated and was replaced by a combination of shock and surprise. With eyes wide open he said, "Why din't you ged one when Spires hand dem out?"

"I wasn't on the range. I was at the Power House. Skorzeny didn't have mine."

"Aw, dat's no surprise. If Skorzeny hadda jus' drunken a twelve-pack he wooden piss on your foot if id was on fie-yah."

"He's got a motorcycle though. A chopper. And a leather jacket. I saw the whole rig this morning. Any idea what his first name is? What Skorzeny's first name is?"

"Motorcycle?"

Ace ignored my question and looked as if he didn't know what a motorcycle was. Then he advised, "You better hurry, Danny. Da line gettin' short."

He was right.

I hurried to the Admin Office where Counselor Hinkel was sitting at his gray metal desk. I stood in front of the glass door so he could wave me in. He didn't look happy. After an appropriate passage of time, he nodded for me to enter.

"What does you wants?" His voice registered his agitation.

"Counselor Hinkel. I need a Meal Ticket."

"Why didn't you gits one when they wuz handed out on the ranges? Where wuz you?"

"I was working at the Power House."

"Oh…" moaned Hinkel leaning back in his chair. "So you is the *one!* I droves over to there special to brings you a ticket, but you was cleanin' the Officer's ter-lit. I gives it to Corrections Officer Skor-sneezy."

Damn! Skorzeny didn't give me the Meal Ticket on purpose, and then he held me late. Next time I see him, I bet he asks how I liked the Labor Day Dinner, with my Meal Ticket in his pocket the whole time. Jerk-off!

"He didn't tell me that, Counselor. He told me I'd have to get it from you. Do you want me to go back and get the ticket from him?"

"I'd hafta write you up for bein' outta bounds." I could almost see the wheels clicking inside his head. "If the Outside Patrol truck sees you, they'll prolly shoot you, since they'll assume you is tryin' to egg-scape. Now…" He tipped his head down to peer at me over his glasses. "We don'ts wants that, does we?"

"Not really, Counselor."

Hinkel's train of thought delivered more potentially bad news. "Besides. I'd hafta contact yore next o' kin an' ruin they's pic-nicky day by telling them that you bin kilt trying to egg-scape, and we doesn'ts wants that does we?"

"No, Counselor Hinkel. We should try to avoid that outcome if possible. I wouldn't want that to happen." I sighed audibly so he could hear my pain. "So, how do I eat?"

"I guess you don't, bein's that yore ticket is back to the Power House an' you cain gits there an' back alive 'fore I hafta close down the chow line."

Things were not going well at the moment.

"Doesn't 'pear much I can do for you, Hole-meese."

I decided to beg for mercy.

"Well, would you happen to have an extra Meal Ticket, please Counselor?"

That annoyed him.

"We is real strick about our Meal Ticket count, here, Hole-meese. 'Sides, what does I looks like? A tickee-taker at a rolly-coaster?"

I doubted Hinkel had the brains to make change. Considering my plight, I surrendered.

"Aw, all right, Counselor," I said. "I guess I'd rather eat a hot dog than get shot. Thank you for giving me such good advice on this issue."

"That's why I bees the *whole* Camp Counselor over all t'other Counselors," he said with a smile of satisfaction. He waved me away from his presence.

I left and headed for the chow line on the double. I hoped Hinkel didn't know how to use the PA system without Miz Buckles' assistance.

At that moment, I prayed the special Labor Day meal would be lobster. I know that's insane, but that's what I was thinking. Everything else in my life was gone. The children; my friends; my law degree; the houses; the assets; all gone. The only connection to my former reality was a decent meal.

"Please let it be lobster. Please let it be lobster." I said to myself. When was the last time I'd had a decent meal, let alone a good lobster?

It had been a few months ago at the Green Room, a four-star restaurant in the Hotel Dupont. I'd made a point to eat well before I reported. I ate prime rib, veal, and salmon steak. I cherished those feasts. Now I was rabid for lobster.

I had to have a Meal Ticket. Passions arose in me. My last connection to an existence I knew and cherished. I refused to let go.

The Kitchen Cop, guarding the door and collecting Meal Tickets, was Mr. Cobb, a pudgy dwarf with brown, curly hair, and John Lennon glasses. He resembled Doc from Snow White.

"Hi, Mr. Cobb," I said running up to him. "I have a problem."

"Whass-at?" He wasn't even looking at me. He was counting Meal Tickets.

"I was at the Power House this morning and didn't get a Meal Ticket."

"Who was the CO?" More counting.

"Corrections Officer Skorzeny."

Now he looked at me straight in the face.

"Guy's a Nazi," he said quietly. "You're lucky you're still not down there. You try Spooter? He's in his office."

"He said he went to the Power House this morning and handed my ticket to Corrections Officer Skorzeny. He said he's not a tickee-taker at a rolly-coaster. He told me I might get shot if I went back to the

Power House to get it. I told him I preferred not to get shot."

Mr. Cobb shook his head.

"'Rolly-coaster?' What a dumb-ass. He thinks those tall wood things in the parking lot with wires on top is telegram poles."

I nodded my head in agreement. "I don't think correcting him would have improved my chances."

"He got a twin brother, you know. Xerox copy of him."

Holy Shit! There were two Hinkels?

Mr. Cobb said, "The name on his brother's birff-certificate is 'Scooter.'"

"Ha!" I belly-laughed. "No, no. Say it ain't so. Spooter *and* Scooter?"

"Swear to God." He held up his hand in confirmation.

"Well," I said. "God certainly has a sense of humor. Which one's older?"

"Spooter says he ain't never gonna tell nobody. Made a big point 'bout it couple years ago. Got pissed 'bout it." Cobb smiled. "That would make Spooter the younger brother in my book."

I decided I liked Mr. Cobb. I smiled back. "What does Scooter do?"

"Don't know. Gub-mint job. Prol'ly way up in FEMA somewhere."

This conversation was almost worth missing whatever *cordon-bleu* lobster tail was being served in the dining hall. I imagined Scooter and Spooter side by side in a roller coaster car with cotton candy streaming from their hair. Then I caught a whiff of sizzling meat and decided I had the time to talk to Mr. Cobb during the next ninety-four months.

Cobb said, "It sounds like Skorzeny to have your Meal Ticket and not give it to you." He harrumphed. "Go on ahead an' eat. Least I can do knowing what Skorzeny and Hinkel musta put you through."

"Say, Mr. Cobb. Do you know what Skorzeny's first name is?"

"Nope. Far as I know, nobody does. He's been asked an' he always invites the asker to go straight to hell."

"Okay. Thanks. I appreciate this."

I grabbed a tray and was served a hamburger and a hot dog from serving pans, and a piece of dripping meat from a big vat. Salivating with anticipation, I looked at the steak, covered with a brown sauce that disguised the texture, and pretended I was in a Chicago steakhouse. I ladled string beans and mashed potatoes from the hot bar and filled a glass with iced tea. I was determined to enjoy this meal. I'd just learned every meal was a feast. I tried to find a quiet table for one but the dining room was crowded. I sat at a table with three elderly black men.

"'Sup." I said. The universal prison greeting.

"'Sup," they mumbled. The universal response.

I stuck the piece of meat with my fork and examined it

"What's this?" I asked, pretending I'd been in jail too long to recognize a steak.

"That be yo' Lay-ba Day meat."

I put it down, cut a narrow slice and then cut the slice into bite-sized servings. Brown throughout, with a thick sauce. Despite being over cooked, it cut well. I had to swallow the saliva rushing into my mouth. I lifted a bite. Civilization at last.

"I wooden do that," the man on my right warned.

I stopped mid-air.

"Why not?"

"Slobodo."

"What about him?"

The man across from me explained, "He mar-in-ated the steak and now the meat tastes like the Great Salt Lake. Looka 'roun.' Ain't nobody eatin' it. Taste like you eatin' salt."

I looked at their plates and the plates on the other tables. No one had eaten the Labor Day Special.

My head slumped forward. It was going to be a long ninety-four months.

I put my fork down in disgust. Boos and catcalls arose from around the room. I looked for the reason.

Slobodo had walked out from the kitchen. Word of his involvement traveled fast, but Luka, accustomed to being the object of ridicule, seemed oblivious.

He walked to my table. Lucky me.

28

The Games

Some guys restart their illegality as soon as they were on the street again. Unbelievable.

I hated this place and would do whatever I had to do to be released as soon as possible.

What were they thinking?

Don't they have families? Don't they care about them?

At least they had visitors and pictures that they could cherish. I didn't. In my world, Joe, Shannon, and Brendan were locked at the ages of seven, five and three.

That was the only image I had to carry forward.

"Need you to sign somethin'," Slobodo said to me.

"You dumb fuck!" burst an inmate at another table. "How'd you fuck up this steak so bad?"

"I didn't do it. Somebody sabotaged it. They put soy sauce or Tabasco into the vat when I wasn't looking. I'm just sick about this."

"So somebuddy fuckin' wid jew, huh?" said the inmate on my right.

"I won't mention names, but I think that Muslim fucker did it. I've been having a problem with him since I started baking the bread for the Jews. I think he did it."

"You sure you didn't piss in it? Thas what everybody sayin'." This was from another table.

"I didn't piss in it!" He objected with conviction.

I interjected, "Is that the Arab kid you've been trying to convert to Judaism?"

"Yeah. He says I got an unclean spirit an' I need to be killed. You know, them Muslims, they think all Jews are devils."

"You *are* a devil," the man across from me opined.

I said, "I thought you were a Norse God?"

"I said that to have meals brought in from the outside. It didn't work. Anyway, I gotta tell you, this Muslim kid's a real problem, and I'm gonna have to resort to my Torah trainin' to kick his ass."

"So," I said. "It's some mad Muslim's fault that the steaks taste like the Dead Sea, and you're going to employ your deeply entrenched scriptural training to smite him?"

"Yeah, that's right. Now let's get on to important matters." From a pants pocket, he took out two pieces of paper. They were sports pairing brackets—the type seen in the NCAA basketball tournament. The brackets were filled in. "Here, sign the two lines where your name is."

I examined one of the sheets. I'd been around Slobodo long enough to know not to comply with his requests without thought.

"This says I'm playing Sid Clayman in backgammon."

"And congratulations to you," he said. "You won." He pointed at the paper trying to hustle me along. "Sign the form. You lose to me in the championship."

"I don't know how to play backgammon," I said. "I've never played it in my life."

"Don't get technical. Crowder told me to run some board games. I'm makin' him look good." This was another of Slobodo's favorite tricks. Your reward is the verbal credit while he captures the financial gain.

I looked closer at the pairings.

"Except for me, there's only Jewish names here. There's more Jewish names here than there are Jews in the camp. Don't you know any gentile names? I don't want to get jammed-up in one of your scams."

"Tell de man de troof, Slobodo," said the inmate to my right. "You be hustlin' six packs o' soda. Yo! That be what this about, for real."

Slobodo's body posture collapsed.

"Okay," he conceded. He leaned to my ear. "How many sodas do you want? The winner gets a six pack an' second place gets three, so that's nine. How 'bout we split it down the middle? I'll take seven and you can have the rest?"

I shook my head. "You're a grifter, Luka. Everything you do is a scam. And you always hog the biggest piece of the pie."

"Attention in the camp!" barked the public address system. "Attention in the camp. The main line is now closed. The main line is closed." The microphone thumped against something. "An' for the afternoon's entertainment, let's see..." Paper shuffling sounds. "We got, lessee... *Risk, Pair-cheesy, Chess, Checkies, Monogomy, Backpackin* and *Ole Yeller* tour-knee-mints that will begin shortly in the large classroom."

Slobodo pointed at the papers in my hand.

"Look. Just sign. I'll get you the sodas later."

I reached for the pen in my shirt pocket. Slobodo had fabricated all the names on the list but mine, so I was an accomplice. I wondered how much longer Judge Emil N. Smert would extend my sentence if he heard about this. I held my breath, scratched out my printed name, and scrawled an illegible signature. Slobodo snatched the sheet from under the pen.

"Good," he said, businesslike. "Now here. Sign this." The next paper was a similar grid. "This is the *Parcheesi* tournament."

I laughed.

"What?" said Slobodo.

"This says I beat Mike Carr in the first round."

"Muscle-tof," smiled Slobodo. "You beat him solid."

"You nit-wit. He was your Bunkie and he went home a couple of days ago, Luka. He's been released."

Slobodo did a double take on the bracketed name. He looked at me and said with a fallen voice, "You're right." He inhaled. Exhaled. "I was wonderin' where he went. There's an FNG in his bunk. Now give me that back."

He grabbed the paper, erased Carr's name with a pencil, and wrote in a new one. He handed it back.

"Great," I said. "This doesn't pass any kind of smell test."

"Why not?"

"Not unless John Gotti was transferred here from his cell at Leavenworth because you said I beat him in *Parcheesi*."

"Are you sure, Dan? I thought I saw him this morning." He looked around the Chow Hall searching for him.

"I'd love to meet him," I said. "Introduce me when you can. How many sodas do I win for coming in second in Parcheesi?"

"You didn't want any more Jewish names." He was distracting me.

"Answer the question. How many sodas?"

"After I get my seven, you can have the rest."

"Luka. Have you thought about what the winners of the *Parcheesi* and *Backgammon* tournaments will do to you? Do you think they're going to want their sodas?"

"I'm gonna tell 'em that Corrections Officer Skorzeny has 'em and they hafta get 'em from him."

I shook my head and repeated another scratched-out, illegible signature on his sheet. I said, "It's tough being you all the time, isn't it, Luka?"

"You don't know the half of it," he admitted as he handed me a third paper. "Do you wanna play croquet? Game starts at two."

"No, thanks. I can't be in three places at once. I might get arrested for cloning myself. Who's going to win croquet? You?"

"No, no. Croquet's not fixed. You think I'm stupid?"

Two of my tablemates groaned. The inmate to my right nodded his head and said, "Yeah. I do. You is a major league fuck up, Slobodo."

Someone at another table said something colorful about Slobodo's mother. Then, a piece of marinated meat bounced off Slobodo's chest and settled on the table. It had been hand flicked with a high arc so the hacks couldn't be sure who tossed it. The assault left a medium-sized brown stain on Luka's shirt, not a dripping splat that would have resulted if it had been drilled at him full force.

Slobodo sensed it was time to leave. He said, "I have to set up croquet." He began folding his papers.

I said, "Put the wickets six feet apart. The strumpets go on top. Red is positive. Black is ground. Keep all the extra croutons and sconces in reserve until someone asks for them. Have fun."

Slobodo took in everything I said without any sign of understanding. He pocketed his papers and left.

I ate the hamburger and the hot dog and chatted with the three guys. They had their own stories to tell about their lives on the street. When I was done, each of us rapped twice with our knuckles on the tabletop as a sign of respect, picked up our trays, and headed to the drop off area. I dumped my steak into an already overflowing barrel. Maybe Spooter's bear in the woods would devour his annual ration of salt, soy, and Tabasco while foraging through the garbage tonight.

Then, to celebrate the Labor Day weekend, I went to my cube for a nap.

29

Croquet

I decided to attend a Sunday morning Protestant service. It was totally disorganized. It started forty-five minutes late and the Chaplain forgot the songbooks. Eventually, we began by singing songs that were in the "Hymnals of our minds." I was glad that I had nothing better to do. Then the Chaplain began to preach about Jesus in the Garden and His disciples not being able to "keep watch for one hour." I figured the point would be "did someone keep watch" with me in my hour of need. I was wrong. The Chaplain paused and questioned calmly, "Was there anyone that I had not kept watch with in their hour of need?" I suddenly was staring at myself in the proverbial ego mirror and didn't like the reflection. The Chaplain was jump-starting my rehabilitation.

I set my wristwatch alarm for two o'clock, put on my headphones, and crashed.

When the alarm went off, I put on my shoes and went to the outside grill to get a burger, some salad, and a couple of hot dogs for dinner. About fifty inmates were lined up holding plastic bowls that they intended to fill with hamburgers, hot dogs, macaroni salad, potato salad, potato chips, and lettuce. The tomato supply was limited and, by this time, there were none left. Each inmate took enough food to feed a family of four. I waited in line and grabbed a burger and some chips and took them back to my cube.

With nothing better to do, I went to the athletic fields.

As I walked up the small incline, seven middle-aged members of the Jewish community were playing croquet. I assumed Slobodo had scammed them into participating. Looking at them, they seemed allergic to the sun. Over ninety degrees with no breeze, they were covered from head to foot in hats, sunglasses, long-sleeved shirts, gloves, and sweatpants with sunscreen on any skin still exposed. The sight of former lawyers, doctors, and stock jocks sweating profusely was comical. They resembled a chain gang cutting weeds with a sickle.

The playing field was on the side of a hill in ankle-deep grass. Only the top of the ball was visible. The bickering over the conditions and the rules of play was the icing on the cake. Everyone was cursing Slobodo as if he were Moses leading the Israelites for forty years in the desert. They hated him with good reason but they kept playing.

Luka limped by studying the grid for one of his rigged tournaments.

One of the croquet players said, "Hey, Slobodo! Why is the damn grass so high? Why didn't you get it cut if you were going to have us play here?"

"It's that cocksucker Crowder's fault. He forgot to call the Landscape Cop and tell him to cut it. No! Excuse me. Crowder *refused* to call the Landscape Cop."

"Iz bloody 'ot ou' 'ere, Wanker," said an inmate with an English accent. "Oi'm drippin' sweat for a six pa' o' cola. Oi feel like tossin' it in, nackered ou', Oi am. Oi didn't come 'ere to ge' a sunburn."

"Go ahead and quit," Slobodo told him.

Two of the men started toward Slobodo, mallets in hand, one tapping the peen on his palm.

Slobodo said, "I'm gonna give Crowder a shot right now 'cuz he fucked up the game by not cuttin' the field."

That stopped the march of the two men.

"It's called a match, Wanker! An' it's played on a pitch, a flat pitch. No' the side of a 'ill. Buggerin' stupid sod you are."

"Whatever."

Slobodo limped down the side of the hill toward the Admin Building under the glaring eyes of the croquet players. The stares were hotter than the temperature.

I had to know.

"What did he promise you guys?"

"We finish the game and he'll have us transferred from the garden to the kitchen detail," admitted one inmate who, with a short haircut and thick glasses, resembled a CPA.

I asked him, "If you are in the garden detail, why didn't you cut the grass here?"

"We're not allowed to run the tractors. The Hispanic's do that and they won't let us drive. So, we do all the grunt work to grow the corn and tomatoes."

"So now you're going to prepare the meals?"

"Hell no. We're going to steal anything that's decent before it's served at main line."

I looked at Slobodo as he limped into the Admin Building.

"Good luck with those transfers. Remember, you're dealing with Luka and you know who generally wins those battles."

30

Mr. Crowder

I asked Mom to send me a picture of my children. She said she talked to my ex about once a month. Mom called her. At eighty-one, she was too frail to travel to Arizona so she didn't plan on visiting them. She didn't know when they might come east, if ever. She told me the kids were doing well in school and other activities.

"The children are fine, Danny," she said. "Can't keep them in shoes, I'm told. Their toes pop out of the end a month after they're fitted."

I wondered if she was lying just to keep me from being upset.

I did the same thing to her when I told her I was doing fine.

I went up the hill to the basketball courts. Blacks in their twenties bulked up from lifting weights and ingesting massive quantities of protein were playing hoops. They looked like they were in a sauna, sweat free flowing. The game appeared more like a turf war between the Rucker League of Harlem running ball with the "DC" Boyz. The play was rough and inconsistent. In fact, it more closely resembled a rugby scrum. Fouls were liberally applied but none called. Without tee shirts, the scars on their bodies from stabbings and bullets, the cost of the drug trade, were evident. Also, tattoo's adorned their arms, legs, necks, and torsos. I glanced around and noticed that there were no cops present and that I was the only white guy there. I decided to change the statistics and walk the track-just in case.

On the way, Luka Slobodo limped by.

"Sounds like you were having a hard time on the croquet hill," I said from twenty feet.

"You know—what the fuck do they want? I set up the game for them, and that's how I get thanked. Complain, complain, complain. Typical Jews."

"Did you complain to Crowder about not getting the grass cut?"

"I'm going to see Crowder 'bout the case of sodas I won. Four six-packs. You help me carry 'em and I'll give you one." He clipped short, in mid-limp. "You know, with all the money I paid you to defend me, you should carry the sodas for nothing.' You lost my case."

I laughed. "Okay, Luka. I'll come with you. The entertainment value of watching you work is worth a soda. You can keep all but one. I don't want the real winners putting a bulls-eye on me."

"Hey, do you know what a wanker is?"

"Do you like the word?"

"Yeah, I like it. It's unusual. What's it mean?"

"It's British for masturbater."

We approached the door of the Admin Building.

"You mean like a real good fisherman?"

I didn't follow his logic. He was always doing this. "What are you talking about?"

"Somebody who baits hooks real good? A master baiter?"

Without skipping a beat, I said, "Exactly."

He showed a big smile.

"He's the early bird who always gets the worm," he said with some pride.

I wondered how far I could make this go.

"That's you, a master baiter, a man of mysterious skills, and a true wanker!

"Say, what's your favorite kind of fish?"

"McNuggets."

Luka's ship sailed on, oblivious to details.

"McNuggets are chicken."

"You know what I mean."

I was close to hysterics by now. I'd told him the absolute truth and he didn't have enough brainpower to understand that the Brit was insulting him.

I decided to push the envelope. "He's telling you that you're a master at baiting hooks that catch McNuggets. It's a *Chicken of the Sea* sort of thing."

"Well." Luka thought that over for a moment. "Why does he think

I can bait hooks? I've never baited a hook in my life. I get seasick easy."

"If I were you, I'd start telling people your nickname is Wanker. Use it all the time. Write it on your tee shirts and shorts. It sounds good. "Wang-kah." Say it like the Brit. "Wang-kah." It's a soft 'R' at the end."

"Yeah! That's how the Englisher said it. 'Wang-kah.' He said it like that! I alluz liked the sound of the way he talks. Wang-kah!" He smiled. "Wang-kah! I'm a big Wang-kah." We got to the door of the Admin Building with Slobodo saying over and over, "I'm a Master-Baiter. I'm a big fucking Wanker."

"You should call yourself "Big Wanker," Luka. It sounds better and it fits you to a "Tee"."

"I like that even better."

We went inside.

In the Wreck Office, Officer Crowder sat with his feet on the desk spitting tobacco juice into a Styrofoam cup. He wore his Eagles cap instead of the required BOP hat. He was watching a twelve-inch black and white TV.

"Not now, Slobodo. I'm busy."

"How do you know what I'm here for ain't more important than you watchin' TV?"

Crowder said, "Nuthin's more important than me watchin' TV. I wouldn't even help you escape right now. I'm watchin' the finals of the Catskill County Labor Day Demolition Derby. My cousin's favored to win."

"You're kiddin'." Slobodo moved around so he could see the screen.

"Fuck you. Look at this." Crowder pointed to the screen. "There's my cousin Willy Ray in number GJ-73." The car gunned its way across the dirt and Crowder screamed wildly at the TV as if Willy Ray could hear him. "Go ahead, Willy Ray! Smash that mother fucker's ass!" We watched GJ-73 smash into the side of a red car, and then GJ-73 was hit by another car on the driver's side door. Inertia slammed Willy Ray against the driver's door, and then bounced him across the flat front seat into the passenger door. Willy Ray wasn't wearing a seat belt in a demolition derby. He slid back behind the wheel, reversed out, and drove off.

"That ol' Willy Ray is one crazy motherfucker," Crowder howled as he clapped his hands.

"Hey, Mr. Crowder," said Slobodo. "Why is your cousin's car number GJ-73? Is he a bingo freak?"

"It's complicated but let me try to explain it to you. The '73' is his IQ, and the 'GJ' means he got a gub-mint job. Best trash collector in Cartoon County. I'm prouda tha' boy. Loves his mamma, too."

Slobodo was speechless. Rednecks still surprised him.

During a commercial, Crowder looked up and said, "Slobodo, you're bothering me. Go away."

"I came to collect my prizes. You owe me a case of soda."

"What tournaments did you win?"

"Croquet. Backgammon. Cannylan'. An' crazy-eights."

Crowder sighed. "The croquet game started ten minutes ago. I can see them playing out the window. An' we ain't got no cards to play crazy-eights with." He smirked at Slobodo. "An' Cannylan' is not an approved tournament game. You didn't win nothing. Now, get lost, jerk-off."

"All the guys showed up late for croquet. I won by default and we used a pinochle deck for crazy-eights."

I laughed at that. Pinochle decks have no cards below a nine.

"An' we gotta Cannylan' game," Slobodo insisted. "I win Cannylan' every time we play. I never lose at Cannylan'."

Crowder wasn't in the mood to argue. He just wanted Slobodo gone.

"Okay. Go get Pill Line an' have him fetch you the sodas."

"Why not me, Crowder?" Slobodo asked him. "Give me the key. I'll get 'em."

"Not likely. Pill Line is signed up to be one of the counters for to-night's race, an' I need to be sure he can count."

"But he don't know English," said Slobodo. "He can't count at all. Why don't you get some white guys?"

"Warden's new directive. All racial groups are to share equally in the educational, social, and athletic aspects of this here institution."

Crowder looked at the trash can beside him. "There's the memo if you wanna read it. Be careful, though. I dumped a cuppa juice on it."

Slobodo said, "Are you gonna have someone help him count?"

"Bronco."

"Bronco? You gotta be kiddin' me. He can't count to two."

Crowder replied, "Well, that's one more than I trust you to count."

The day's last event was a five-mile race and was Crowder's brainchild. It was the first of its kind at the camp and it created a lot of trash talk among inmates. Also, the bookies were covering bets at a record pace. By the day of the big event, the betting line was down to Animal and Quackenbush. Quackenbush was a twenty year-old punk of a wise ass who was doing eighteen months for selling pills at a local club in central Pennsylvania.

When the race was first announced, several inmates trained. Soon after, the realization grew that this event would be too strenuous for most of the loud mouths, and, eventually, the amount of trash talk exceeded the amount of training. Somehow, that seemed typical of inmate activities. Since the oval to nowhere was a quarter mile lap, it took twenty laps to complete the event. That was about eighteen more than most could finish. There were fifteen inmates entered for the race. From appearances, only about five could be expected to last beyond the fifth lap.

"You want sodas? Go get Pill Line," ordered Crowder. "We'll let him practice counting to twenty-four. He only has to count to twenty for the race.

"I'll make him hand each soda to you one at a time and count them out loud. Right now he should be sitting on the back loading dock counting the inmates who're stealing more than one hot dog and one hamburger."

Slobodo stood still with a look of disbelief. He didn't know what to do. He countered with a weak, "You're shittin' me, right?"

Crowder shot back, "Slobodo. When it comes to following the Warden's directives, I don't shit anybody. Go get Pill Line and Bronco."

Slobodo walked out of Crowder's office shaking his head.

I watched the demolition derby as Crowder urged on his cousin.

A few minutes later Slobodo returned, Pill Line and Bronco in tow. Crowder exclaimed, "Hola! My two amigos. How goes the food stealing?"

Pill Line and Bronco looked at each other and spoke in a Spangloricano dialect.

Pill Line was a Puerto Rican in his mid-thirties. He was tall, lanky and spoke next to no English. He was always happy and had animated body language, especially on the softball field. He was called Pill Line because every morning, noon and evening, he went to pill line where he was handed meds that chilled him out. Plus, no one could pronounce his long multi-syllabic Puerto Rican name that sounded like Ed-dil-hum-ber-to.

Bronco was in his mid-forties and was also Puerto Rican. He loved baseball and was supposedly a boxer in his native land. His face seemed to affirm the rumor. He was best known for his announcements when he ran onto the softball field as he shouted the only English he seemed to know, "One, two, three out, gentlemang! One, two, three out!" This had become a camp chant that the inmates repeated when Bronco took the field. No one knew Bronco's real name either.

Crowder said, "How many guys did you count? How many guys were stealing food?"

Pill Line smiled and looked at Bronco. More Spangloricano. Crowder started a rallying cry, "Come on, hombres. Numbers. I'm depending on you. I need you to count tonight. Numbers. Don't let me down."

Pill Line and Bronco looked at each other again. More Spangloricano. Then Bronco said, "One, two, three, out, gentlemang. One, two three, out."

Crowder stood up and high-fived a smiling Bronco. Then he high-fived Pill Line. "Way to go! I knew you could do it. I knew I had the right guys to help with this race." He paused. "All right. Here's another test." He looked at Bronco. "Go get Slobodo a case of soda. Got that? Twenty-four cans of soda." He held up two fingers on one hand and four on the other. "A case of soda." He handed Pill Line a key. "Any questions?"

Pill Line and Bronco spewed more Spangloricano at each other.

The amigos finished jibbering, looked at Crowder, smiled, nodded their heads, and left.

Slobodo said, "I don't believe this, Crowder. They won't come back."

"I don't care," said Crowder. "I'm following the Warden's directive."

"I don't want to wait here all day."

"Got someplace better to go?" Crowder countered. "Go there."

Crowder returned to the demolition derby. Nothing else was said. The wait droned on and on, interrupted by the occasional coaching commands Crowder yelled at Willy Ray. I wondered how anyone could watch a demolition derby for more than two minutes. Crowder had bragged during commercials that his cousin was favored. Was there a betting line? After twenty minutes of similar mundane thoughts, Pill Line returned with a box balanced on his head large enough to hold a case of soda. Bronco walked beside him.

"Here they are," announced Slobodo standing at the door.

Crowder's rapture at the fate of the three remaining cars faded. He said, "See, I told ya. Give 'em a chance, I always say. They came through. They're *sleepers*. They do the unexpected. Surprise the hell out of us."

Pill Line and Bronco came in the office.

Crowder stood up as they entered. "Way to go, amigos. Apply yourselves. Think about what you're doing. Practice, practice, practice. I knew you could do it."

Pill Line took the box off his head and dropped it on Crowder's desk. There were seven Diet Cokes, a chalk board eraser, and some magic markers.

"This is just *terrible*," Crowder mocked. "They got a case of soda an' somebody ripped 'em off on the way back here. You can't trust anyone these days. The neighborhood is goin' straight to hell. That's what happens when minorities move in. The crime rate goes up."

"Or, in the alternative," I suggested, "maybe these two gene- splicers negotiated a swap of seventeen sodas for an eraser and these pretty colored markers they liked better."

"Yeah, right." Slobodo mimicked Crowder in a high, whiny voice.

"All they need is a little more work, Slobodo. They'll be fine." He dropped into his own voice. "You turned the prizes into a joke, Crowder. Why even bother offering prizes?"

Crowder was angry. "Shut the fuck up, Slobodo. How long 'til it's six o'clock?"

Slobodo looked at me with an expression of helplessness. He said, "Mr. Crowder. Why don't you teach your boys here how to count? I'll come back and get the rest of my sodas later."

"Slobodo," snapped Crowder. He took a soda from the box. "That's all the fuckin' sodas you get. Now get the fuck out of my office, or I'll throw you in the bucket!"

Crowder opened the top drawer of his desk and started throwing ping-pong balls at Slobodo who ducked out the door into the hall.

"What you gonna charge me with?" Slobodo yelled as he retreated. "I didn't do nuthin'."

"Where do you think you are? This is the BOP! All I gotta do is plant somethin' in your cube an' you'll be in the Medium in ten minutes. You don't like it, don't come to prison."

"Aw, Mr. Crowder. You wouldn't do that."

"If I wasn't so goddamn lazy, I'd have done it already," screamed Crowder. "Now get lost 'fore I find some motivation to lift my ass off this chair an' go plant a shank in your cube."

"Okay, okay!" yelled Slobodo. "Pick up the sodas, Dan."

I picked up the six remaining sodas and handed two to each of the Hispanics and one to Mr. Crowder. I popped the top on one for myself. The four of us left the Wreck Office. Bronco opened the door to the corridor for Pill Line, Slobodo, and me.

As Slobodo passed him, Bronco screamed, "One, two, three, out, Slobodo! One, two, three, out!"

31

Five Mile Race

The only person I called was Mom. I prayed that she didn't get a cold because she took a long time to recover. She had friends that brought groceries for her and drove her to the doctor. I used to do those things. She had to rely on other people now.
Every time I thought about this, I was sick to my stomach.

Slobodo and I went to our respective cubes.

Once the Four O'clock Count cleared, the inmates milled around until ten of six when they assembled near the athletic field for the five-mile race. Crowder was nowhere in sight.

Finally, the much anticipated and talked about race was to begin. I was approaching the track trying to avoid the bookmaking that was taking place. Standing proud and tall near the Start/Finish line was Crowder's answer to the Warden's Equal Opportunity Employment Program. Pill Line and Bronco were drunk with power, a blur of activity, pointing everywhere, and instructing others in their Spangloricano dialect. It was complete mayhem. Betting was more important than lining up the racers. Trash-talk flowed. Mr. Crowder came out of the Admin Building and walked toward the track sipping a Diet Coke.

More time passed before Crowder finished some paperwork. Then he matched each runner with a lap counter and had the runners line up on a crooked line of lime at the midpoint of the oval's straightaway.

Twelve inmates were at the starting line. Crowder crossed off three no-shows from his list. Each runner wore a number taped to his chest and had a designated lap-counter to ensure the accuracy of the lap count.

Crowder announced more than asked, "Bronco. We're ready to go."

Bronco smiled at Crowder.

"Okay. Start 'em up."

Bronco said, "One, two, three, out, gentlemang."

No one moved.

"One, two, three, out, gentlemang."

Still no one moved.

"Go!" Crowder roared.

The runners took off.

Crowder headed back to the Wreck Office. Slobodo heckled him, "Why don't you stay and watch?"

"It's too fuckin' hot out here," Crowder said. "I'm going back to my office."

All eyes were on the race. Animal sprinted from the line but could not maintain the pace past the second turn. A pack formed and overtook him near the end of the first lap. This incensed him so he sprinted past them and then stopped fifty yards further down the track. Sprint-and-die appeared to be Animal's strategy. The pack continued at a steady pace for the first nine or ten laps with an occasional runner dropping out.

As the runners passed the Start/Finish line they grabbed cups of water handed out by their supporters. Some poured the water over their heads; some tried to drink it while running and slopped it on the track. During the first two-thirds of the race, heat and humidity took a toll on the runners and eight dropped out. The four remaining contestants were on the same lap, stretched over fifty yards. Bronco and Pill Line consulted in Spangloricano and Pill Line made notes on his clipboard. The race continued round-and-round. Some of the inmates cheered favorites. Others cheered in general. Some booed everything.

Animal was in the lead. As he passed the start-finish line, he gasped to his lap counter, "How many?"

"Nineteen," came the reply.

Animal picked up the pace to full-bore. The other three inmates didn't break their stride. Quackenbush, an early betting line favorite, stopped running, turned around, and walked in the opposite direction. His face was twisted and contorted. Red splotches covered his cheeks and neck. The heat and humidity had exacted a heavy toll. The people most concerned were those who'd wagered on him. Animal was in a balls-out run. He rounded the last turn in a huff, all elbows and knees, and crossed the finish line. He ran another five feet, bent over at the waist, and collapsed onto the ground. Foam trickled from his mouth onto his goatee. Nasal emissions flowed onto his mustache. Snitters pocked his face. His long brown hair was strewn about his face, back and the ground. He was an ugly sight. Then, he began to dry heave. A crowd gathered around him aware of the pending bad news but not wanting to get too close in case he hurled an organ.

His lap-counter ran up to him. "Animal! Why'd you stop? You got one more lap!"

Animal blurted out as he was panting, "You—(breath)—told—(breath)—me—(breath)—nine—(pause)—teen—(heave)."

"You were starting your nineteenth lap. You got one more to go!"

The first of the remaining two runners passed.

With difficulty, Animal stood up. His legs buckled and he was wobbly. By the time his lap-counter pointed him in the right direction, he was a quarter of a lap behind. Quackenbush was still walking the track backwards oblivious to what was going on or where he was. Apparently, his brain farted. He appeared to be having conversation with someone none of us could see. Animal burst into a gallop with whatever gas he had left, which, though not much, allowed him to make up ground. The two lead inmates saw him closing the gap, and their facial expressions signified they were digging for additional speed but without an apparent result.

The crowd anticipated a close finish as the three inmates cleared the backstretch and headed for the finish line. Inmates screamed as if it were the Kentucky Derby. The first guy crossed the finish line, and then Animal edged over the line just ahead of the third man. The first and third place inmates hugged and congratulated each other. Animal walked in circles, hands on hips, eyes searching for his lap-counter who was nowhere to be seen. Quackenbush continued walking the track in the wrong direction; no one seemed to care about his disparate mental state. A few inmates cried, "Fixed!" to avoid paying up on a bet.

Bronco and Pill Line walked over to a Puerto Rican who had quit the race early on. He was Bronco's bunkie. Bronco and Pill Line raised the inmate's hands in a sign of victory.

"One, two, three, winner, gentlemang," declared Bronco. "One, two, three, winner!"

Inmates, realizing how bogus the two Hispanics were, tossed water at Pill Line, Bronco, and Bronco's bunkie.

As I walked to my cube, I imagined Crowder sitting in his air-conditioned office, filling out paperwork and being pleased that he had complied with the Warden's directive. Another feather in his cap.

32

Happy Baby Pose

I wondered how much I'd aged since I arrived here. I had my BOP ID card and from looking at the photo from my second day, I didn't think I'd changed that much.

My children had changed though. Now they were playing sports in school. My mom told me Joe was chosen as an all-star on his cross-country team. I've never seen him race. Mom let it slip there was a "bring your Dad to school" day. He refused to go to school that day with Brad. His mother had told everyone that we were divorced and I was on business in the Middle East for the next eight years. She didn't want anyone to know that I was in jail. Joe didn't want to lie.

Some inmates couldn't tell the truth if it bit them in the ass. A classic example was Herb Nagle who claimed he was a rhythm guitarist for *Pink Floyd*. His story was that he took the hit on a drug bust so the creative minds of the band could stay free. He had an American accent. After he got out of prison, he said he rejoined the band and sacrificed himself again by getting busted so the band could record *Dark Side of the Moon*. As Herb told it, he'd written the song. *Pink Floyd* music is noted for other-world words and hard driving guitars. Herb played standards he arranged alphabetically in a three ringed binder.

Every Thursday after the Four O'clock Count, Herb went to the music room, picked up an electric guitar, tuned it, turned on the mike, and did an impromptu concert for anyone who cared to listen. Since he penciled his name on the schedule, everyone was required to allow him to do this.

The first time I listened, I couldn't believe anyone could be so bad. No sense of rhythm, and a weak voice. However, he did know most of the words and the chords were somewhat correct because I recognized the songs.

Week after week, Herb would sit there, playing and singing, mostly to an audience of none.

I heard Herb twice. The first time lasted about ten minutes. After that I decided I needed to go to my cube to get ready for breakfast the next day. The second time was when I learned about the Happy Baby Pose, a real-life yoga position.

I was lying on my bunk reading the remains of a two-week-old "USA Today" when Animal and Shifflet invited me to the music room. I asked the purpose behind the invitation and Animal said that he and Shifflet were sick of hearing Nagle, who they claimed "was horrible" and interrupted their group, *The Deaf Tones'* practice. I thought that was a little like the kettle calling the pot "black" but what did I know. At any rate, they had devised a scheme to stop Nagle from playing and wanted as many participants as possible.

When I arrived, the Music Room was packed with inmates; there was an energy and excitement in the air. Something momentous was about to happen.

What's going on?" I inquired of Animal.

"We're gonna to do a *Carrie* on Nagle."

Like most of Animal's comments, I didn't know what that meant. I asked for enlightenment.

"In the movie *Carrie,* they have a fake vote and elect Carrie the high school prom queen. Then they drop a bucket of blood on her."

"So, you're setting him up to shame him off the music room schedule?" I asked.

Animal smiled and said, "Just watch."

He turned to the front and chanted, "Herb Nagle! Herb Nagle! Herb Nagle!"

Others picked up the chant and soon the room resounded with his name. Mick Jagger would have been proud. I looked for buckets of blood hanging from the ceiling.

Counselor Hinkel must have been strolling the hall because he came in to see what the commotion was about. True to his character, he said nothing, only watched, a foreboding presence, his thin eyes scanning the room.

Through the side door came Herb Nagle. The crowd stunned him into motionlessness. He recovered; started waving his hands over his head to acknowledge the crowd and smiled as if he were accepting an Oscar. He was pleasantly surprised. His smile told me that he thought he was "back on stage."

He crossed the room, picked up a guitar, and motioned for quiet. He strapped the guitar over his shoulder and sat on the drum throne. He opened the three ringed binder.

The crowd became silent.

"What would you like me to play?"

Some mumbling in the crowd and then someone said, "Don't play *Hotel California.*"

"And don't play *Hey Jude.*"

Undeterred by these two non-requests, Herb said, "Well… What do you *want* me to play?"

"Why don't you not play *Mustang Sally?*" came a voice from the front.

"An' after that, don't play *Satisfaction.*"

"Don't do anything from *Kiss* or *Springsteen.*"

"Once that's all done, no *Hall and Oates.*"

The "non-requests" came in rapid order fashion that hid the identity of the "non-requestors."

"I got a full book of songs here, guys," Herb noted in a stronger voice so he could be heard.

"I'd just hate it if you played the *Wedding March.*"

This brought a round of laughter.

"Ching!"

This was some chord Herb cranked out to quiet the crowd.

"Come on," Herb pleaded.

Someone said, "Do not insult ze *Funeral March* by playing eet." This was from someone with a French accent.

I was curious. When did he arrive and how did I miss a guy with a French accent?

"Don't play *Yankee Doodle!*" someone shouted from the left.

"If you play *Heartbreak Hotel* again," said a scruffy inmate standing up and pointing for emphasis, "somebody's gonna go to jail!"

This brought gales of laughter. Then, one of the more "weight challenged" inmates, who doubled as the drummer for Animal's band, did a slow rolling somersault across the linoleum in front of the microphone and ended up on his back, feet up, hands on his heels, rocking back and forth like a happy baby laughing wildly.

Next, Animal sat down, rolled onto his back, and did the same thing, his slender frame in stark contrast to the fat man next to him.

Then Shifflet copied them, and then another three followed, all rolling back and forth with their hands on their heels laughing like asylum lunatics.

Hinkel's eyes widened and he lost color. That little paperclip holding his glasses started jiggling as he surveyed the room. I wondered what was going through his mind. There is a prohibition against "organizing" and he could be thinking that we were protesting, a violation of the highest magnitude.

Within a minute or so, every inmate in the room assumed the happy baby pose except Herb Nagle. I looked at him. No change of expression. No anger, embarrassment, or shame. He looked like a physician eyeing a terminal patient.

He took off the guitar, put it down, picked up his book, and went back out the way he'd entered.

Once Herb left, the fun ended, and it should have stopped the future Thursday performances, but it didn't. He didn't get the message.

For as long as he remained in the camp, Herb played the guitar poorly and sang worse every Thursday as if nothing unusual had happened. Every time I walked past the music room and saw him, I wondered what he was thinking. He had to know that the entire camp made a fool of him and we knew that he was a liar. But he kept on playing and insisting that he was a member of "Pink Floyd." I recalled Norton's warning, "When you come to jail, you can be whatever you want to be."

Norton was right. I encountered the situation at least a thousand times. Guys made up all kinds of weird scenarios and then insisted that the story was true. I learned to ignore it. Why? Well, I claimed to be a lawyer and aren't they supposed to be honest? In a way, I was no different than Nagel and there was no sense in being a hypocrite.

33

Peaches

My kids were computer literate by now.
They were growing up and I wasn't there.
Physically or mentally.
I wondered if they knew how much I missed them…

I've been here a while now. It hurts to think about how long I've been here and how much longer I have to serve. On the outside, technology is revolutionizing the world. Gone are beepers, VCRs, and G-strings. Blackberries, plasma TVs, DVDs, and thongs are the rage. I can only marvel and wonder from afar. Go to jail and collect dust as the world evolves without you.

Without sounding bitter, I've concluded that the Bureau of Prisons isn't interested in rehabilitation. Their only goal is to have the correct number of inmates on hand at all times. However, from time to time, an order would be issued that smacked of common sense. One such mandate required that, as a condition of release, each inmate was to attend an "Employability Skills" class. The course objective was to have a résumé prepared as part of the "Pre-Release Program." An idea of the Warden, the résumé was to prepare BOP charges for re-entry into the workplace—or maybe the Warden was stuffing his résumé to climb the BOP ladder.

Despite his lofty aspirations, the Warden didn't figure Luka Slobodo would end up in charge of his initiative.

I was eating Frosted Flakes one March morning when Luka limped up and sat down at my table. He didn't have a tray. He wasn't here for breakfast.

With the lightening legal mind I once had, I said, "No, Luka," as soon as his ass hit the seat.

As usual, he was unshaken at the first, second and then third obstacles I threw at him. When I tired of trying to lose him, he said, "My, my, my, big guy. Aren't we grumpy for six AM."

I wondered what tangled web he'd concocted this time. His smile resembled the expression of a young puppy whose master had just entered the room. So engaging he could be when he wanted.

"I want to go home in seventy-two months. Whatever you want—I'll end up serving more time when you're caught. Thank you very much for your kind consideration, but count me out."

I never escaped Luka's fourth assault. Verbal negotiation for Luka was an extension of war by other means. So far he was untouched by my refusal to listen to him.

"You need to get me off this CCS-1 detail."

"I'm not a cop," was my initial response. Then I realized to whom I was talking and knew that he already had the answer. I was just being set up.

"How am I going to do that?" I asked. The better question would have started with "Why?"

"I'm gonna turn this 'Employability Skills' class into a full time job."

"I'm not going to 'get you off' anything. Everything you touch ends up killing someone. Go find another victim."

He never heard a word I said. He was focused on his mission.

"Since the Warden issued this new order, my employment in the Educational Department would be an institutional need. They'd have to release me from CCS-1."

Luka was at CCS-1 again as a penalty for being snitched on by another inmate. Rumor had it that Luka had formed a close relationship with a toilet down the hill. The visual was almost worth being assigned to the detail. Well, not really.

"Okay, Luka. How do I aid and abet you in this crime?"

"Dan." He looked down at the table top. "Nobody in camp likes me. They hate my guts—so how about you teach the 'Employability Skills' course with me?"

I was nearly finished with my Frosted Flakes, bobbing for the last few with the spoon. A clear-plastic glass held twelve ounces of Joe. At breakfast, I filled a glass to crank me up for the day ahead. When I really wanted to fly along, I doubled the dose. Just then, I realized this might be a thirty-six ounce day.

I said, "What's the relationship between teaching this course and nobody in camp liking you? I don't like you. Why are you always coming to me? What did I do wrong?"

"No, no no. You don't understand!"

He got that one right!

I said, "We already co-teach two ACE courses except you leave as soon as the cop signs you in and he leaves." I'd guessed where he was going with this. A classic Slobodo ploy was to convince somebody else to do the work and then he would take the credit plus any benefits he could negotiate.

"So what you're really saying is that we co-teach this class. That way, you'll be released from CCS-1 and I'll have the honor of doing all the work."

"What do you mean?"

"When you show up, you always say something stupid and I'm left to clean up the mess."

"That's not true and you know it."

"Well, let me give you an example from the two classes that we supposedly co-teach now. In 'Basic Accounting' you told the class that to improve the 'bottom line' all you had to do was inflate accounts receivable or reduce accounts payable. The other course was 'How to Start a Small Business' and you told those guys that the best way to raise equity was to scam bugger the Small Business Administration."

He smiled proudly at his originality and insights.

"I used that expression so the black guys would know what I was talking about."

"And now the black guys want to lynch me."

Not wanting to be sucked into another scam I said, "I need more time to think about this."

It took me about a second to conclude that a résumé was a useful tool for inmates.

"If you agree," he said, "it's a done deal."

He said this with the earnest look of someone pleading for a child's life. He was working hard to be released from the CCS-1 detail.

Counselor Hinkel popped into the Chow Hall and went from table to table examining the pockets of everyone's winter coat for contraband. Some inmates were scared and put back the extra oranges they were trying to sneak out. The rest ignored him.

Hinkel pulled five oranges out of an inmate's coat. He piled the fruit onto the inmate's arms and ordered him to put them back. Hinkel would be at our table in another minute.

Just to fill the time gap, I said, "Okay—"

"Great!"

Luka jumped out of his seat.

I was telling him that we'd continue our conversation once Spooter left. I hadn't agreed to anything. I should have said, "Look—" or "Well—" or "Great Caesar's ghost—"

"Great, great, great," he said allowing no interruption. "I'll see you in the small classroom tonight at six-thirty. We'll get Peaches' résumé together."

Peaches was a drug dealer who was serving a ten year sentence. At least that was the rumor. I'd never spoken to him. All I knew about him was that he was assigned to the kitchen detail (though I never saw him there) and he spoke more Ebonics than English. Oh, one other thing; he lived on B Range where most of the residents were African-American and the area was known as 'the ghetto.'

"What's your scam with Peaches?"

"What do you mean?"

His smile told me that he knew exactly what I meant.

Spooter was at the next table.

Luka got up and scurried out of the Chow Hall, his mission accomplished.

Spooter blinked at me, and then took off after Luka.

Sitting at the table, I felt scam buggered.

I bowed my head and prayed, "Dear Lord, I am a fucking moron. Again."

Six-thirty came and found me alone in the small classroom.

I had formatted a prototype of a résumé so that all I had to do was get the inmate's information and plug it into the various sections. I had broken the document into four parts: Career Objective, Educational Background, Employment History and Personal Data. My goal was to obtain basic information that I could massage into an effective job searching tool. There were problems though. How did you explain in-carceration to a prospective employer? In reality, you didn't and it probably killed any shot at the job. To circumvent that problem, I was going to fill the page with as many employable skills as possible and give the ex-inmate a fighting chance. Realizing that I was probably stood up, I was beginning to feel that my work so far was a waste of time.

While I was standing there, I surveyed my surroundings. It was a sad scene. Gone was my plush office with my cushy carpeting; crown molding; leather high-back chair and cherry wood desk. Now I operat-ed from a classroom cluttered with dirt, trash, broken desks and curses scribbled in foreign languages on a blackboard.

I was pissed off at being stood up and allowing myself to be sucked in again.

At ten of seven, I opened the door and had my hand on the light switch when Luka limped into view.

"You're done already?" he said. "Good. How did it go?"

"Peaches never showed," I said. "It's probably taking him longer than we thought to prepare his list of accomplishments. You did tell him they don't have to be in alphabetical or chronological order."

"Wait here. I'll get him." He limped away. "Stay right there." He repeated, "Stay right there," four or five times in a row like the goons do in Italian mobster movies.

I stared at a metal desk, slowly walked over to it and sat.

I'd give him five minutes.

He was back in two.

"I sent bald Raheem to get him," Luka said coming into the room. "'Nother few minutes."

We sat there as I ignored him chat away about starting a taxi cab company after his release. The company would use solar powered Toyota Priuses painted neon green and driven by hot-looking college chicks dressed in halter tops. The name was the topper; "Hooters for Commuters." I could just see the logo. He was planning on making millions. He had the details on an indecipherable piece of paper that was stuffed in his pocket with several other not-as-yet-mature-enough-to-go-world-wide plans. I made him put them away.

I interrupted him, "When did you get approval to teach this class and prepare these résumés? Did you get it from Counselor Hinkel?"

"Never mind that," he answered "It's taken care of."

"Ending a sentence with a preposition is something up with which I will not put up with."

He missed the joke and droned on about Hooters for Commuters and how we could take advantage of the college-age drivers. Mercifully, Peaches came in before Slobodo could ask me to invest.

Peaches was dark skinned with a wide-stitched scar running from his left ear to the point of his chin. No glasses, nearly bald, a little short, very muscular. He was sweating profusely.

"Peaches!" said Slobodo jumping up, a trace of anger in his voice.

Peaches strutted to a desk next to me. As he sat, Slobodo asked, "Where have you been?"

Peaches said, "Yo! I works-out six to seven, man. Gots to get it in."

Slobodo started off by lying. "We've been waiting here since six o'clock. You could have told us you were going to be late."

With a sigh, Peaches intimated a lack of concern.

We sat silently, each waiting for someone else to start. Condensation rose from Peaches' skull into the lights in the ceiling grid.

Slobodo broke first.

"Did you bring the information I told you?"

"No, man. I didn't bring nuffin'."

Great start.

Slobodo turned to me.

"I asked Peaches to bring me—I mean *us*—a list of his educational certifications and diplomas, along with his employment history. That'll help us do his résumé.

"Well, look," said Slobodo talking to Peaches now. "We gotta get something from you so you can satisfy this résumé requirement. If we don't get a résumé done, you won't be able to go home on your release day."

Peaches didn't care. He knew better. Your release date is when you are released. Period.

"How about if we start and see how this goes?" I had a pad and pen in front of me.

Slobodo started. "What's your name?"

Peaches looked at Slobodo as if he had asked something stupid.

"Yo! Slobodo. You knows my name be Peaches. Why is you askin' a dumb-ass question like that?"

Slobodo clarified.

"No, no, I mean, what name did your mother give you?"

I thought Peaches answered truthfully.

"My Mama done call me Peaches, man. Yo. Who do you think named me Peaches, man?"

"Well, I mean, what is the name on your birth certificate? What name were you given at birth?"

"I ain't never seed no birff-a-kit, man. I doan know."

I decided that the résumé was going to resemble a blank piece of paper and there was no sense in wasting time playing twenty questions. I decided to follow my format and blow through the process. "I'll leave that space blank for now."

"You can put Peaches in there," Peaches offered, pointing at the blank page in front of me.

I wrote *Peaches* at the top of the page and held it up for his approval. He nodded affirmatively.

Slobodo took the pad and pen from me and continued with, "Where do you live?"

Peaches looked at me to see if I thought that was a dumb question. He dripped sweat on the linoleum and the room began to smell like a gym bag.

"Hey, yo!" Slobodo yapped at him. Peaches turned to Slobodo as Luka repeated, with a look of irritation, "Where do you live?"

Slobodo pressed the pen on the paper.

"I lib on B Range with bald Ra-heem, da Rasta Man. Why you ask me a dumb-ass question like that?"

Slobodo raised his head after a few seconds. I wondered if he would lose his temper. In all my dealings with Luka, he never lost his cool. Right now, he looked close.

Slobodo narrowed his eyes and glared at Peaches. He was determined to extract an intelligent answer.

"No. Where were you living when you were arrested?" He asked sternly.

Peaches looked over Slobodo's shoulder at the far wall and said, "Ah-lan-nah."

Slobodo just sat there. We'd be here until the nine-o'clock count at this rate. I decided to end it. I reclaimed the pad and pen from Slobodo.

"I got this," I said.

I wrote.

"Ah-lan-nah," I said, writing as if hooked on phonics. "That would be the home of the Ah-lan-nah Falcons and the Ah-lan-nah Braves, right?"

"Das right," Peaches agreed.

Not wasting time, I relied on my format and rolled on. "What is your career objective?" Since I didn't want to confuse him with that terminology, I clarified. "What do you want to do when you get out?"

He understood. I could tell. He sat back in the chair, took off his sweat drenched headband and twirled it around on his index finger.

"Yo! I'm 'onna' fuck dem bitches, an' drink 'Dom,' man."

I wanted to comment, but the thought 'keep moving' jumped into my head.

"How are you going to pay for that?"

"I doan pay to fuck no bitches," he claimed as if it were a birthright. "I doan pay nothin' to fuck no bitch."

He said it twice so it had to be true.

Slobodo started to say something.

"Hold it," I held up my hand to stop him. "How are you going to get the money to buy a bottle of 'Dom?'"

"I'm gonna open me a men's shoe store 'specializin' in green and orange 'gators so the brothers can look 'tight' when they steppin' out."

Slobodo took in an audible breath. I knew something stupid was coming. "Can I get a pair of white ones?"

"Fo' mo' money. Deys be custom."

I gave up when I heard Slobodo's question. I slid the pad and pen to him.

"Okay, Luka. You do some work. Under Career Objective write, 'Entrepreneur.'"

That was stupid of me. Slobodo could no more spell "entrepreneur" than Peaches could run a shoe store.

"Never mind. I'll write it."

I retrieved the pad and pen from Slobodo.

"Good," said Slobodo. "This way the writing will look like one person wrote it."

He rocked back on the rear two legs of his chair and assumed the role of contented supervisor.

I decided to move to educational background. All I was looking for was high school classes completed, if there were any. I could puff up the curriculum as the résumé was typed. That would be my job, too.

"How far did you go in high school?" I asked.

Slobodo jumped in, "Why don't you say something like this, Dan? 'Peaches has been a victim of the system ever since he was a juvenile delinquent. He went from school to school in an attempt to locate an academic institution that would recognize and accommodate his unique educational talents.'"

I ignored the social commentary. Only Luka knew what it meant, anyway.

"What was the highest grade that you attended?"

"Put down he has a GED," said Slobodo.

"Is that the truth?" I said this as if I were, God forbid, a judge. I hated that tone of voice.

"Put down it's pending," Slobodo conceded. "It's his third try, and he might get lucky if he can bribe someone to take the test for him."

I wrote, "GED, Pending."

It was close to the truth.

The door sprang open and four black inmates walked in.

Slobodo jumped up immediately. "Excuse me!" he announced with an air of authority. "This is an educational activity and takes preference over any other activity."

One of the black men laughed, "Yo! Slobodo. Who you shittin'?

You got nothin' about you that's education. You just running 'nother scam. We's here to play cards. It be time, man. You got to roll out."

One of the men asked Peaches, "He get a book from you?"

Peaches didn't look at the speaker but said, with a taste of anger in his voice, "Slobodo didn't ask for nuthin'. But white boy, here. Yo. He's gots to have a book to make the paper. What a brother to do but pay? You know dey run de game. This here be a whole lotta nothin', man."

I glared at Slobodo. What else could I expect? It was his nature. I got him released from CCS-1 again, and he repaid the kindness by telling Peaches that I wanted a book of stamps to prepare the résumé. I'd straighten that out.

"Card game, hell," Slobodo said. "There is no other activity allowed in here until we finish."

Luka was right. Education had priority. They left reluctantly.

"Come on, Luka," I demanded. "The truth or we're done."

"I got the book from Peaches already and I had every intention of telling you but I forgot." Slobodo looked at Peaches and tried to convince him, "I am doing this for free." Sincerity oozing from every pore. Nobody bought the story.

"Let me try." I turned to Peaches. "Luka here told me he needed my help to get off CCS-1. Instead, he's taking a book of stamps off you and getting me to do all the work. He was keeping the stamps for himself."

In my mind, I was legally, even honorably, off the hook. If Peaches now beat the shit out of Slobodo, that was okay with me.

I decided to plunge into the next section of the résumé and inquired, "Peaches, what jobs have you ever held?"

Silence ensued. Peaches stared at the floor. That was the sad reality.

Slobodo answered quickly as if nothing bad had just happened.

"Put down that he worked for ten years as a maître d'. Say the restaurant seats about four hundred."

"That solves the time gap for the prison sentence," I said to Slobodo.

And would be an outright lie. Puffing was one thing; total outright bullshit was another. Luka didn't know the difference.

I looked at Peaches. "What un-locatable and out-of-business restaurant would that be?"

"He's in charge of the hot bar in the camp's Chow Hall," said Slobodo, grabbing my forearm for effect as he pleaded his case.

"That's not a maitre d' job at a restaurant."

"Poetic license, Dan. You know that as soon as he tells an employer that he spent ten years as an inmate in a federal prison, the interview is over. Is it better to show a ten-year gap in his résumé or boost him up a little?"

I heard him but it didn't register. I was lost in my own realization that I'd have an eight year gap in the Employment History section of my résumé. Somehow, "Clerk in the Power House" would be hard to explain to a prospective employer since it would appear after a job where I was the managing partner of a law firm.

"Put down he worked for the 'U.S. Government – Department of Justice.'" He pointed at the paper in front of me. "Put down his duties included daily managerial and operational control of a facility that serves, maximum capacity, twelve hundred meals a day."

I wrote, "Ten years at the DOJ as a waiter." I figured that the interviewer would discern the truth.

I asked, "What other jobs have you had?"

Slobodo returned to social commentary.

"Victim. He's a victim! Inner city ghetto. Teenage mother. No father. No education. No role-models. Dumbing-down is good. Drugs are good. Drug income is good. Going to jail is a rite of passage. No jobs. No hope. No choice but sell drugs."

I said, "I can't put 'drug dealer' down as a job."

"He was a businessman!" exclaimed Slobodo. "A small business-man, like a lot of people. You and I are lawyers, businessmen dealing in paper. We sell documents and services. Peaches was more like a pharmacist. He sold painkillers to make people *feel* better. Pharmacists are businessmen. Nobody will argue that. He has skills. He had to collect money from the drug buyers, so he was a billing and cash management expert. He also had inventory to control, so he has extensive inventory skills with an expensive product. Demand was high. He had to have a constant supply of drugs to satisfy his customers' needs."

I looked at Luka, "You want me to write that 'drug dealer' was a job?"

Luka clarified, "No, but put down the skills that were part of the trade."

I wrote, "Accounts receivable and inventory control as co- proprietor in a loose pharmaceutical supply consortium."

The quicker I extricated myself the better.

The final section contained personal information.

I dove in.

"How old are you?"

Twenny-eight."

I wrote that down.

"How many children do you have?"

Peaches smiled. "I gots five. Four bitches."

Peaches was winding up a ten year sentence, so he was eighteen when he arrived. Five children from four women before he was eighteen. And he was going back out in the Real World with a life's plan that consisted of, "Yo! I'm 'on' fuck 'dem bitches, an' drink 'Dom,' man."

I wrote, "Single. Five children."

Slobodo rambled on for another two minutes, talking about social reform for inner city youths, and convincing Peaches that his book of stamps was well spent. Finally, he said, "Well, that's it. Dan will have your résumé tomorrow. It's going to make you look terrific, Peaches. I bet you get an offer as soon as you start passing it around."

Slobodo glad-handed Peaches down the hallway. I ripped off the two pages of notes and handed them to Slobodo when he came back.

"I'll give you half the stamps," Slobodo said.

"Not a chance. I'm sick of your bullshit. I'm not having anything to do with this."

Luka reached into his pocket and pulled out the book of stamps. I could see him get ready to speak, but before he could, I snatched the stamps from his hand and stepped back.

"You do the entire résumé, Luka. Get it approved by the staff. Then I might give you half."

"That's not fair!"

"Certainly not to you. But that's the way it's going to be. You're deadline is next Friday."

I left him and told the black guys that the room was available for them to play cards.

I met Peaches the next day after breakfast and gave him back his book of stamps. We talked for about ten minutes. Two days later I gave him a résumé I could defend. I told him not to tell Slobodo. Peaches submitted the document as part of pre-release, and he was transferred to a halfway house three weeks later.

Only after Peaches left the Camp did it dawn on Slobodo that he'd been scammed.

"Very good, Dan," he complimented me. "How long ago did Peaches submit his résumé?"

"Three weeks."

He shook his head, not upset. More in a state of awe. He'd been scammed, and no one else in camp had told him. "Not bad," he conceded. "There's hope for you, yet."

He recovered fast. He'd been had, and he realized it—he accepted it, he forgave it, and he went on about his business. In a matter of seconds, he'd passed through all the phases of grief and had limped out the other side into the next scam.

"Can I have my half-book now?"

"No, you can't have your half-book. The deal was you had to supply an acceptable résumé three weeks ago and you didn't do it."

"That's not fair."

"Certainly not to you," I said. I liked that phrase with Luka. "I gave the book back to Peaches the day after we met."

"You gave it back?"

"Don't worry. Peaches is going to sell them when he gets home and use the money to open his 'gator shoe' business."

34

The Pizza Dance

Connected.
Inmates strived to be connected to the outside world. A telephone call; a visit; a letter; anything that kept us in touch with our family, friends or community was important. Being connected meant you "belonged to something or someone." Without being connected, the inmate was a loner or an outcast.

One thing an inmate can receive that lifts his spirits, other than mail, is a visit. A visit was a chance to spend precious time with a loved one and stay connected to the outside world. It created a sense of belonging. This was especially important when you existed in a place where you felt you didn't belong.

Inmates prepared for a visit with appropriate care. A shave and a haircut were mandatory. Khaki's were washed and ironed. Even if it took all night, inmates "got their shit tight" for a visit.

At Camp Catskill, visits occurred on weekends and federal holidays from 8:30 AM until 3:00 PM.

October of my sixth year was approaching.

Nothing was bothering me at this point. I had my routine memorized, and I was rolling along on *cruise control.*

In other words, I was "Institutionalized."

Acceptance of Institutionalization was startling. I was just doing time until my release, and finishing my sentence was the paramount goal of my existence. My life was relatively good, circumstances considered. I knew the rules, the staff and which inmates to hang with and which inmates not to hang with. After seventy-eight months, there were few mysteries left for me.

The calendar showed Halloween was not far off, and Nature agreed. The leaves had turned different shades of brown and gold, not as vibrant as in past years, and there was a bite in the air. No more T-shirts for the early morning walk—a sweatshirt was required until the sun was higher in the sky.

This Halloween would be different. Milo Cohen, better known as "Doc," had received the approval of the Administrative Staff to allow the inmates to bring the pumpkins he'd grown in the greenhouse to the patio outside the Visiting Room. The idea was to have the children color on the pumpkins and play games on the patio outside of the Visiting Room.

Due to Doc's continuous efforts, the compound had a greenhouse that produced beautiful flowers and healthy vegetables that fed the combined inmate populations of the Camp and the Medium Security facility. The crops included corn, cucumbers, tomatoes, lettuce, snap beans, string beans, and peas.

Being the salesman that he was, Doc convinced the Administrative Staff that there were two benefits to his proposal. First, having the children outside would reduce the overcrowding in the Visiting Room. Second, the parents could have a more meaningful and more relaxed visit. The Administrative Staff missed the liability issue altogether and approved the program as long as inmate volunteers monitored the children.

Most inmates showed the apathy typical of their species, and Doc had to beg for volunteers to mind the children. I was one of them.

As soon as I was cleared through the inmate check-in and check-out point to start my shift, I could see the program was a success. Kids of all ages were drawing on the pumpkins with magic markers, and playing games outside on the lawn. One inmate was carving Jack O'Lanterns. Others were giving piggy-back rides. A kickball game was underway. The sounds of playground laughter, a rare jailhouse commodity, filled the air. Everyone enjoyed the spirit except Counselor Hinkel, who lurked off to one side and scowled as if jealous of their fun.

I walked into the makeshift pumpkin patch. Doc was playing "Simon Says" with two little girls with bright eyes and huge smiles. Doc loved children and, sadly, his crime had driven a wedge between him and his children. The government forfeited their homes and wrecked havoc upon their credit and personal finances. As a consequence, two of his children abandoned him. Doc's second wife had a little more staying power, but over time the strain of loneliness and the stress of sharing household expenses with a boarder became too great. She divorced him two years into his eight year sentence.

Now that I was outside, it was obvious that the children were exuberant at not being confined by the strictness of the Visiting Room. I suppose kids don't like being in jail either.

I recognized one of the girls who was magic markering. She was Stephanie Crane, the youngest daughter of Rodney and Mary Crane. Stephanie, an eleven year old, was a beautiful, thoughtful little girl with long black hair and freckles galore.

"Hi, Steph."

I sat down on the grass next to where she was coloring on a large pumpkin.

"Hi. Mr. Holmes," she said after giving me a quick glance. She seemed more intent on coloring than talking.

Other kids were drawing ghosts, goblins and witches. Stephanie was drawing something far more complex that I couldn't recognize.

"What are you drawing?" I finally asked as I gave up trying to figure out the mystery.

"That's the prosecutor," she answered matter-of-factly. She pointed to a figure in red. "He's a devil. And that's another devil." She pointed to another figure colored in black. "That's the judge."

"The Honorable Judge Flood," I half asked, half guessed. She was doing a good job. He never looked better.

Stephanie said with a huff, "There is nothing Honorable about him. He let the bad people say wrong things about my daddy without stopping them."

Stephanie must have been referring to the half-truths prosecutors sometimes present as hard evidence.

She put down a brown marker with which she had just drawn a long rectangle. She picked up a yellow marker and drew stick people on top of—no, behind— a brown wall.

"Is that the jury?"

"Yeah." Again no emotion. "They're yellow because they're cowards. They were scared of the prosecutor, and they did what he wanted them to." No anger, a simple statement of fact; regurgitating a storyline she had heard in her household for years.

She knew I was there beside her, but she never looked at me. She was absorbed in her courtroom scene, drawn with magic markers on a pumpkin on a prison patio. She was focused on her mission.

What did she ever do to deserve this?

How much had the entire ordeal affected her? I assumed the drawing was therapeutic, a release for whatever demons were bottled up inside her.

How many times had Stephanie drawn this same scene at home or at school? She had a searing hatred of the prosecutor, the judge and the jury in her psyche. Could she ever untangle the mess that had befallen her?

My thoughts turned to my children and I wondered how they were getting along out in Arizona.

I knew better than to mentally transport myself to Arizona. My little babies were six years older than the last time I saw them. Were they better off than little Stephanie who saw her father once, maybe twice a month in prison? To my children, I was out of sight and, if their mother had anything to say about it, I would be out of mind.

I left Stephanie, went to the side of the building and leaned against the wall. I felt weak and needed to support myself. The pain tore at my soul. I turned back to watch Stephanie. She worked carefully, silently, purposefully.

Doc dropped off his two piggy-back riders and came over.

"Ah, Dan," he said. "Beautiful day, isn't it?"

I knew what he meant—I could hear it in his voice. He wasn't discussing the weather.

About this time, one of the pumpkins was cracked open when an overweight Hispanic boy, who'd been jumping on it, fell through the skin. One moment he was king of Pumpkin Mountain, showing off to anyone who would watch, and the next he was knee-deep in pumpkin gore, crying like a baby. More embarrassed than injured, he fussed until Doc rushed over to make sure he was okay. The kid pulled one foot up, gloppy with pumpkin guts and yelled, "Eeewwwwwww."

Doc picked him up by the shoulders and put him on the ground. His legs and feet were a mess.

Doc did a quick visual of the kid and distracted him with, "What's your name?"

"Felipe," the young man answered.

"Okay, Felipe. Let's wipe off this mess." Doc pulled off chunks of pumpkin pulp.

"I'm not touchin' it," screamed Felipe.

"Oh, this is fun. This is how we get pumpkin seeds. Look." He started picking seeds from Felipe's feet. "Get all the seeds you can and we'll cook them in the microwave and eat them. They're good to eat if they're cooked first."

In no time flat Doc had Felipe picking out seeds. Other kids joined them. This started a seed-gathering contest. Someone with a brain, probably not an inmate, brought paper plates from the Visiting Room vending machine area and handed them to the kids. Soon Felipe was cleaned up, and the seeds from the pumpkin were divided up on paper plates. Doc dropped another pumpkin on the concrete, and the kids dove after the seeds.

Doc said, "Pick out the seeds. Whoever gets the most wins—" He paused, "—well, what do they win, Dan?"

All eyes turned to me for the answer.

"A piggy back ride from Uncle Milo."

Doc smiled. The children screamed with delight. The seeds from the second pumpkin were scarfed up in a New York minute. Pumpkin seeds become as valuable as gold nuggets. The kids wanted to crack open another pumpkin. Doc looked around to smash another one. Then, as if he were the Pied Piper, he led a parade of kids to the microwave area in the Admin Building.

After watching that, I felt better. Stephanie finished her pumpkin mural and joined some other girls jumping rope. That made me feel even better. I wanted to tell Doc to smash Stephanie's pumpkin when he came out again.

When my kid-watching vigil ended, I went back through the Visiting Room toward the check-in point where I'd be searched for contraband. I chatted with the inmates and their families, some now familiar, and—oh yes—I looked at the ladies, too—scoping the ladies in the Visiting Room was always good fun.

I glanced over and noticed that Rodney and Mary hadn't moved since I passed through the first time.

Stephanie came by with some pumpkin seeds. Rodney looked over at her and smiled. Rodney lived for his wife and children; they were his pride and joy. Pictures of them were taped all over his cube. He loved visiting day.

"Pumpkin seeds," Stephanie said.

"Not now, Stephanie," Mary told her. "Daddy and I are having grown-up talk."

Their body language translated into bad news.

"Come on Steph," I said "Let's go see if Uncle Milo can break open your pumpkin."

Stephanie and I walked outside, leaving her parents alone to discuss whatever tragedy had occurred amid the privacy of the other inmates and their guests in the Visiting Room.

It didn't take much to convince Doc to break open Stephanie's pumpkin. I was glad to see it shattered. I prayed that the destruction would help eradicate the courtroom scene from her mind.

I looked around at the new team of children-supervising inmates. I could see happiness in their faces, too. They weren't supervising the children really, they were playing with them. For some inmates, including me, there was no better therapy than to play with a child.

I didn't want to bogart into the next shift, and, since Stephanie was occupied now, I left the pumpkin carnage and went back through the Visiting Room. Rodney and Mary were no longer talking. They were sitting across from each other instead of next to each other. Both faces showed abject despair.

Counselor Hinkel walked into the Visiting Room, looked around menacingly and then left.

As soon as Counselor Hinkel was gone, voices raised, laughter increased, activity heightened, sort of a *while the cat's away let's play* thing. I guess wives and children felt the grim aura emanating from Counselor Hinkel, too.

Suddenly, there was a small commotion about three rows over

from me. It centered around Sal Venuto, a first generation Sicilian who had little brain power after fifty-seven years of bumbling through life. He was doing thirty months for bank and mail fraud that arose out of an "auto accident—fake back injury scheme." Sal, pretending to be the mastermind, lined up the medical people and the supposedly injured individuals. The scam unraveled when an insurance company could not verify the credentials of one of Sal's "physicians."

Tony Venuto, Sal's vivacious brother, was here on a visit. I'd met Tony before. Sal introduced him as, "Dony." Considering that Dony was more successful in life than Sal, he more doubled as Sal's guardian than his brother.

Dony appeared to be an outgoing, full of life, fiftyish Sicilian who owned a couple of pizza parlors in Ozone Park. He'd become a local cult celebrity because for years his TV commercials featured "the Pizza Dance." Each night at the restaurants, Dony and his staff would stand in the middle of the floor and perform the "Pizza Dance" for his customers. This routine caught-on like some sort of cult novelty, with newspaper articles and local television stories covering it every few years.

Now that Counselor Hinkel was gone, Dony was being egged into doing the "Pizza Dance" by everyone in the Visiting Room. Dony, ever happy to oblige, needed a dance partner.

Sitting next to the Venuto's was the Irish clan led by Dan O'Flannigan. O'Flannigan was a construction worker in his mid-thirties who was doing eighteen months for selling stolen construction equipment. When Danny arrived at Camp, the average inmate IQ increased dramatically since he was the self-proclaimed world's smartest man. Kind of makes sense if your religious beliefs tell you that the Savior was a carpenter, like O'Flannigan. Built like a typical Irishman, he was five foot ten inches tall with broad shoulders on top of a stocky build. He had close-cropped red hair that he combed straight back, a freckled face, and a square jaw. The pouch in the middle of his anatomy told me that perhaps he enjoyed a malted beverage or two on occasion. He was pure Irish; stubborn as a mule and a two fisted toora-loora- loora.

On this day, Danny's visitors were his two sisters, Moriah and

Carolyn. Moriah, a year older than Danny, was mad at him for his actions and attitude. She had no compassion for his bullshit. In spite of her disdain for him, she felt badly for his wife and children. Their plight was hard to begin with; she rationalized, since he was the breadwinner. She openly said that the only thing his family missed with him locked up was his paycheck.

His younger sister, Carolyn, was more forgiving. She valued deeply the concept of "family" and, despite their differences, Danny was still "blood." To show her support, she was willing to buy him a hoagie and a soda (something that Moriah refused to contribute to since "he wouldn't do it for you") from the vending machines. Carolyn was mad at her brother but knew that her anger was pointless. He was too "rock headed" to get it.

At this point, Dony was scanning the room for a dancing partner. He spotted the pleasantly smiling Carolyn who was sitting there chatting with her sister while Danny ignored them and consumed the vending machine offerings. Dony stared at her for a few seconds and then approached her. He extended his hand, more a friendship offering than an advance.

"Senora, ah, es-cusa. Canna I hava da honor offa dis dance?"

Carolyn smiled politely. She had an expression of confusion, somewhere between "Who me?" and "Why me, Lord?" on her face.

She looked at Moriah for assistance and received a cynical "I wouldn't do it, no way" look. Moriah looked across the room at the inmates, their guests, and the empty food wrappers and soda cans that littered the floor.

"Are you, crazy?" Moriah said.

Carolyn looked at Danny. He was in mid-belch. She looked at Dony, suave and sophisticated (in a Visiting Room sense), as he continued to extend his hand and smile. She tentatively grasped his hand and rose. Moriah was astonished. "You're not going to do this."

Carolyn followed Dony to the center of the room, turned and smiled.

Carolyn passed by a now smiling Sal who took Carolyn's left hand and kissed it gently. Carolyn, not used to this "Italian" style of appreciation, blushed slightly. Sal thanked her by saying humbly: "It'sa very nica you ta dance wit Dony. Dony, hea good singa an' youa dance wit hem. This is a goin' to be very boo-tee-ful."

Carolyn wasn't sure what Sal said. She smiled and said, "Okay."

Now, Carolyn and Dony were in the middle of the Visiting Room.

Sal, in a loud voice intended to attract the attention of the Visiting Room crowd, announced, "Scusa, Scusa, ex-scusa me. Everybody, my broder, Dony, and thisa very nica lady hera, are going to do da Pizza Dance. This is the world famous danca from O-zon-a Park. Thank you very mucha."

Sal then looked at his brother as if to say, "Go ahead."

Dony then leaned next to Carolyn's right ear and whispered: "I'ma gonna danca anna sing and you justa danca wit me iffa you like. No prob-lem. Okay?"

Carolyn appreciated the simplicity of the directions.

Dony stood straight, shoulders back, smiled and began to sing:

"I lova da Pizza Pie
Ita put a smile in my eye,
When I eat a slice
I begin to cry;
Oh yes, I lova da Pizza Pie."

"When you coma to my shop,
I sell you da soda pop,
You drinka it with you slice;
It's all so very nica.
Oh yes, I lova da Pizza Pie."

"You no hava to tip,
Justa watcha you feet so we don't trip,
The floora isa clean so we won't slip,
Oh yes, I lova da pizza pie."

Dony started to sway from side to side in time with the tune. He snapped his fingers and moved his feet in little dance steps. He spun around and then reversed back again. His smile grew wider and, as he hit the second verse, the entire Visiting Room watched, entranced. Carolyn, not a professional dancer, but decent for a white girl, mimicked Dony. Dony had this little dance routine down pat. By the end of the second verse, the visitors had been stunned into silence, staring in awe at a singing and dancing Italian with a girl next to him who was starting to groove.

Someone started clapping to the tune and others joined. It was just like the TV ad. The Pizza Dance was only three verses long so Dony started over, this time the strength of his baritone voice more evident. It was such a silly sight, everyone was smiling, some starting to chair dance. Everyone except Rodney and Mary Crane.

Many of the 'regular' visitors were surprised that there was this much happiness in the Visiting Room. It was highly unusual especially with Spooter on duty. Carolyn became more comfortable as the 'song' played and began to dance with more ease. As Dony repeated the song, Carolyn was back in her "high school" mixer days and she reveled in the action.

Suddenly, like the Wicked Witch of the West brooming down and terrorizing Dorothy and Toto, Spooter opened the door and marched a step or two into the Visiting Room. The sight of singing and dancing, creating a joy in a room usually filled with consolation, angered him. He didn't like it and he sprang into action. As he stood there, his eyes, lifeless like a sociopath's, searched for victims. Carolyn, remembering her "partying" days when the presence of the cops was not a good thing, quickly and quietly slid back to her seat as if she were covertly returning from the ladies room.

Dony wasn't as "street smart" as Carolyn and continued to stand there singing and dancing. Spooter pounced on Dony, who did not appreciate the severity of his dilemma. He shouted angrily, "Who is you and why is you singin' in my Visitin' Room?"

Sal, one of Spooter's favorite whipping boys, stepped forward and said, "Counsela 'Spoot', thisa my broder Dony. He justa doin' da Pizza Dance for dese nica peoples here."

Spooter had no patience for Venuto and said sternly, "Then he can dance his way outta the Visitin' Room because I'm terminating his visit."

A look of confusion came over Sal's face. He couldn't figure out why Counselor Hinkel, one of his favorite people, was mad at him. Spooter turned to face Dony and commanded: "Leaves my Visitin' Room 'fore I charges you with exciting a riot!"

Spooter meant "inciting a riot" but it was close enough. After all, when Spooter was on duty, it was his Visiting Room and his room meant his rules and his main rule was that there would be no happiness in his Visiting Room.

Dony scooted out the door to the corridor and through the black door without a word. I heard it screech shut.

The rest of the visitors and inmates were shocked, hoping this "Hurricane" would not approach them. The clock said two-fifty. Visiting hours ended at three. Some of the guests gathered their belongings and said their good byes. Spooter stood his ground, not saying a word, comparing his watch against the clock on the wall.

At exactly three o'clock, he announced, "Visitin' hours is now over. All visitors must vacate the Visitin' Room ee-mee-dee-it-ly."

His voice indicated there would be harsh consequences for any who did not obey. He hovered over those present for another ten minutes. His presence shortened the good-by hugs and kisses more then usual. I saw Mary Crane leave Rodney without saying a word.

It was now around six-thirty. Dinner was turkey roll served with lumpy mashed potatoes and thick, brown, pasty gravy poured over the top. Desert was a thin slice of pineapple upside down cake baked the way mother never would.

I headed back to the range to check on Rodney Crane. I wanted to know if there was anything I could do to help him. I'd start by telling him how much I enjoyed talking with his daughter.

His cube was in the middle of the range. He was sitting on the lower bunk reading a newspaper.

"Rodney," I said as I put my forearm on top of the cinder block wall at the front of his cube. "What a beautiful little girl you have in Stephanie. I'm sure you're very proud of her. You should be."

He put the paper down near his feet. He sat up straight. Normally chatty, he seemed reserved.

"I got some bad news today," he said in a voice so low that it was difficult to hear. He paused for a few seconds to compose himself. "Mary told me that she filed for divorce. I should be served soon. She's met another guy." He fought off tears.

I sat on the edge of his bed.

I embraced him.

He hugged me.

He sobbed.

In this hellhole of a life, Rodney Crane needed a good cry, and I'd been here long enough to know I could support him. I'd traveled this road. There was no need for discussion, no need for explanation, no need of anything. There was just too much pain for one person to endure alone.

We sat silently hugging for a couple of moments. His chest racked with sobs. Rodney's last anchor to sanity was cut, and he was starting a journey adrift with no wife and alienated children. He was thinking about Mary and the children and whether he would ever see them again. In any future moments of crisis, Rodney would not be available to hold, comfort and advise his children. And Mary would be seeking comfort with someone else. The ultimate slap, and then exile.

He pulled back and wiped his eyes.

"I'm sorry, Dan."

I shook my head.

"That's why I'm here. My wife took my little babies and moved to Arizona before I was sentenced." I could not imagine how I would feel if she'd come to visit every week for a few years and then dumped me. "You want to talk about it?"

He hemmed and hawed, found a towel for his eyes, and straightened himself up.

"I guess the odds are right. You know what they say. If you do more than twenty four months, there is a ninety five percent chance of divorce. I couldn't beat those odds."

He was referring to the well known fact-of-life that the longer the sentence, the greater the chance of divorce. The pressure on a wife to support herself and a family increases as the term of the sentence lengthens. One way to reduce the pressure is to have a relationship with a man with a steady job. That leaves one guy too many and you can guess who goes.

"She told you today in the Visiting Room?"

"Totally stunned me. I never expected it. We've been through so much together. I can't believe it."

He was referring to the investigation, indictment, and trial that resulted in his conviction. A jury pronounced him guilty of planting a "virus" that erased his employer's computer software system. He'd told me the legal fees cost him and his family four hundred thousand dollars and wiped out their savings and pension plans. Then, they sold their house and moved into an apartment to retain appellate lawyers. The legal arguments, initially considered very solid, were rejected as meritless by the Court of Appeals.

Rodney and I talked for a while. I listened as he spoke about future visits with his children, likely to be cut in half based on Mary's new sleeping arrangement. As he spoke, purpose and life returned to his voice. He was firing himself up from the depths of hell.

"I'm not going to let these bastards beat me," he said with conviction.

This was "warrior talk," with the "bastards" being the DOJ; the BOP and its caste of characters starting with the Assistant United States Attorney and moving down the food chain to Spooter in the Visiting Room.

I sat there another few minutes shoring up Rodney's defenses for the emotional struggle ahead. He rambled on about going back to the Law Library and filing his next appeal. He promised me that he was fine.

I decided it was a good time to leave since he was more like his old self.

"Let's meet in the Law Library tomorrow," I told him. "Let's see what we can do about your appeal."

This brightened him more.

"I'm gonna beat these people. You can bet on that! I'll fight through this."

He always swore that he was innocent and he'd expended countless hours in the Law Library researching legal issues relating to his case.

I nodded in agreement. "That's what warriors do," I said. "My wife moved in with another guy. I haven't seen or heard from her or my children in six years."

"Now it's happening to me."

"Seems so," I said.

I gave him a soft punch in the arm. "If you need me, you call me. I'll be in my hut down the hall."

"Thanks, Dan."

The rest of the night was typical for a Sunday. Actually, it was typical for any day that ended in a "y." My evening's ambition was to eat a snack of pretzel nuggets and to drink a soda by eight-thirty, hit the bathroom where I'd brush my teeth and discharge by eight forty-five, and then hop into my bunk with a book before the nine PM count. The last sound I wanted to hear was the word, "Clear" as announced by the hacks as they walked off the range.

Once again, victory was mine. As the word "Clear" died out, I put on my earphones and adjusted the volume for the light jazz station I listened to to ease myself to sleep. Tomorrow's workout would be chest, arms, back and three miles around the track.

"Be here in the morning," I told myself as a final thought.

Sleep was a welcome relief from all that is jail. No noise, no stupidity, no line cutting, no prejudice, no bad meals, no game playing; sleep is just you and the sandman. The only significant activities are the midnight; two-thirty, and five AM counts. I'd become so inured to the flashlight shinning in my face three times per night that I wasn't aware of it. That was, of course, unless the count doesn't clear.

When that happened, a special procedure known as a "bed book count" occurred. This requires all inmates to stand in their cubes and recite their names and U.S. Marshal's ID number as the hacks walked from cube to cube verifying the information with entries in their "bed book." In six years, I participated in three bed book counts.

Tonight was different.

I awoke for some reason.

I glanced at my watch. It was two-forty.

Joy at more hours of sleep.

Confusion over why I had woken.

Hacks were on the range. I could hear their boots and their voices. They were milling around for some reason.

I reached for my glasses and sat up.

I saw a couple of hacks three cubes away comparing count slips. They were shining their flashlights at their papers.

"Here comes a bed book count," I moaned to myself.

"Did you check the stairwell?" A voice near my cube said.

One of the hacks further down the range did a "one-eighty" and walked to the back exit door. Since I bunked in the cube across from the stairwell, he walked past me.

I watched the hack push open the back door.

He froze. "Holy Fuck!" He held the door ajar and yelled to the hacks up the range, "Call the 'LT' right now!"

I wondered what was up. What was in the stairwell that would require the presence of the Lieutenant? I climbed down from my bunk and walked toward the door.

As I approached, I saw the legs of a man hanging in the air. I edged closer.

A bed sheet was tied to the sprinkler pipe on one end and around an inmate's neck on the other. A plastic garbage bag was tied around his wrists. The hacks arrived and spoke into their walkie talkies requesting assistance. Panic was in their voices.

I recognized the sweatpants.

The khaki patch over the knee.

Rodney Crane!

"Get back in your cube," a hack ordered me.

I felt near collapse. Don't remember how I got back to my cube.

Two hacks cut Rodney down and tried to revive him; to no avail. He's been dead for too long. More hacks arrived, then an EMT team. I stood by my cube and stared at the ceiling. I questioned God. If God is so good and forgiving, why did He allow pain and suffering to exist? Why didn't He stop Rodney? Anger rose up in my chest.

When I'd left him after dinner, he was a warrior. It's the inmate code. We're warriors. Warriors fight and never give up. Rodney was a warrior. He spent countless hours in the Law Library researching his case. He turned himself into a decent jail house lawyer. He had a chance to beat the bastards at their own game. Why did he give in and give up.

Then, I thought about Stephanie. She'd have another tragic scene to color on a pumpkin. Another train wreck to untangle.

I looked over at Rodney being placed on the gurney and I wondered why he "hung it up?"

A short answer might be that inmates don't have any todays— inmates only have tomorrow. The hope that tomorrow would be better pulled us through and enabled us to endure all the bullshit. Inmates don't talk about the upcoming Thanksgiving. We talk about the first Thanksgiving after we get out. In the space of one visit, Rodney lost all his tomorrows. He only had the numbing pain of abandonment today.

All that was left was to have the EMTs roll Rodney's body out, complete the paperwork that said Rodney had died in transit to the hospital, and call Mary.

The BOP machine and its system would churn on. In a day or two somebody else would be in Rodney's bunk. The system didn't care whether Rodney was here or not because there was a pipeline of people coming through the system and the machine had to process them. You learned that people came and went but the machine ground on.

Rest in Peace, Bro.

35

Bad Choices

Closure. That's what people need to recover from a tragedy. Closure. That was what the victims of my crimes sought to make sense of their lives after their encounters with me. They entrusted me with their money and I stole it. How did they reconcile the fact that I'm supposed to be trustworthy and I violated that trust? How did I effectuate that reconciliation? How could I answer the question "Why did this happen?" and allow myself to move on?

As the years passed, I began to understand that there was more to life than me. I learned that happiness was derived from helping others and not from accumulating wealth. An expression provided substantial meaning and motivation: "What you do for yourself dies with you; what you do for others is eternal."

To make sense of my existence, and learn who I was and what I could do to better the world, I did like many other inmates, I turned to God. So, I went to church; attended Bible studies, and began to take the principles of the Bible to heart, especially, "Love thy neighbor as thyself." This was hard in prison since I was forced to love a melting pot of people including those who spoke Spanish, Ebonics or some other foreign language. Despite the linguistic and prejudicial hurdles, I sought opportunities to interact. I participated in programs sponsored by the Administrative Staff. I taught ACE courses (Adult Continuing Education). I researched legal issues for other inmates. I interacted with others and learned about them. The more I practiced my new lifestyle, the more I realized we are all more similar than dissimilar.

During this journey of self-analysis and self-improvement, I discovered a Camp secret. Not many people in America knew it, but the intrepid Counselor Hinkel had created a community outreach program that permitted him to escort inmates to high schools to discuss the evils of their criminality. For easily influenced teenagers, this was first-hand exposure to inmates who would relate the impact of incarceration on themselves, their families, and society. The program, a variation of "Scared Straight," was called "Bad Choices—Harsh Realities."

At first, the prospect of speaking before a high school assembly where I could help someone in the audience avoid the calamity that had become my life was intriguing. The ability to contribute to society renewed and uplifted my spirit.

But wait—

Spooter thought up "Bad Choices—Harsh Realities?"

Color me skeptical.

Spooter didn't have the brains God gave a thermos bottle. At least a thermos bottle knew the cold stuff was supposed to stay cold and the hot stuff was supposed to stay hot. Spooter couldn't do that.

"Bad Choices—Harsh Realities." It had to be a hoax. Hoaxes in prison were plentiful. Every couple of months, there was a rumor that Congress would reinstate parole or increase the amount of "good time" that an inmate could earn. Unfortunately, like almost everything an inmate touches, it was all bullshit.

Anyway, I applied a touch of reality to "Bad Choices—Harsh Realities."

The BOP was not designed to perform a civic duty, unless keeping bad guys off the street was a civic duty. Nope. The BOP was incarceration. Lock 'em up until there aren't any more of 'em is the philosophy. Oh sure, the mission statement might mention rehabilitation, but that was propaganda for budgetary purposes. I'd read enough legal cases to know that rehabilitation played no part in incarceration.

But, I kept thinking about "Bad Choices—Harsh Realities" and Spooter. The combination was improbable. Spooter was a complicated nit-wit. He was a poorly educated hick from West Virginia who'd escaped hillbilly status by joining the Army. He'd been an MP for twenty years and he collected a modest pension from his service to our country. Then he'd become a hack with the BOP.

His goal was to become a counselor in order to educate us lower-level primates. Spooter was willing to accept being transferred from institution to institution in order to *earn* a promotion to the exalted title of Federal Prison Camp Counselor, Catskill.

But the best advice was simple—to know Spooter was to avoid him.

On a good day, he was manic. In an instant he would snap at an inmate for the most trivial of infractions. Having an un-tucked shirttail could cost you extra duty. At the sight of something improperly done or misplaced during unit inspections, his anger could rage and he'd toss mattresses to the floor, throw laundry soap powder down the hallway, or heave lockers into the corridor. If the plastic chairs weren't stacked properly after a church service, he would erupt into a chair-throwing rampage.

Spooter's lack of impulse control wasn't limited to "his unit," which was Camp Two. The Visiting Room, the Chow Hall, the Law Library, the entire campground—nothing and no one were safe when, according to another unverified inmate rumor, Spooter's meds wore off.

Despite these volcanic outbursts, he had a compassionate side. To deal with Spooter in a safe manner, you had to approach him when he was sitting behind his desk in the Admin Office. And he needed to be addressed as "Counselor." He loved being called "Counselor." The title imported meaning and purpose into his life. You could see it on his face.

While the rumor of Spooter's program seemed farfetched, there was the possibility that the program existed. Carlton Skedrick was Spooter's Camp Two Head Unit Orderly. Skedrick, an ex-lawyer in his early sixties, was a respected and easy going guy who knew the inner workings of the camp. At this point in my bit, Camp Catskill was still predominately white and non-combative. Skedrick knew that most of the inmates wanted to pass Spooter's random inspections, and the best way to pass was to anticipate where he would be and make sure that part of camp would satisfy Spooter's standards. Skedrick always had someone watching Admin to alert him when Spooter left the building, a sort of *Hogan's Heroes* cat and mouse.

Skedrick confirmed the existence of "Bad Choices—Harsh Realities." He said Spooter had presented his program before two high school assemblies in the past year. He stressed that to be selected as a speaker, Spooter had to like you. Not the easiest of tasks.

While praiseworthy in its lofty ambition, "Bad Choices—Harsh Realities" had its detractors. According to Skedrick, the Administrative staff attempted to derail it. They believed incarceration and rehabilitation were incompatible. The thought of inmates being in a public place repulsed them. To keep the project from being killed, Spooter had to complete reams of paperwork, not his favorite endeavor but he muddled through with dogged persistence.

The biggest hurdle was Spooter's essay.

To qualify as a participant in the program, an inmate had to write a fifteen-hundred word essay on the impact of his crime on himself, his family, and society. Spooter wanted to know the emotional side of crime. I wrote an essay and read it to Spooter. Then for weeks, I rewrote it to satisfy his criticisms.

"Hole-meese. You has gots to have more remorsefulnesses. Ya needs ta scare them little kids more. Make them not do what you did."

After a while I became tired of rewriting. Then, to circumvent, I read the essay to Spooter, heard the changes he wanted, waited a few days, and then reread the same essay to him. He complimented the improvement and offered different changes.

After months of drafting an essay jam packed with remorseful prison clichés, Spooter declared me fit and ready to go.

My first trip was uneventful. I learned that, despite being incarcerated, I could still contribute to society. And, I knew the more I spoke in front of an audience, the more comfortable I would become with the process—standing at the podium, speaking into the microphone, and looking at the students—it was like being back in court. For me, it provided a boost of self-confidence.

And, oh God, it was exciting to leave the Camp, to see regular people driving around, to visit the little towns, and to look at different colored clothes. The air smelled different outside the camp. You forget how important little pleasures are until you don't have them.

Once, I was scheduled to speak at a high school in St. Clair, PA with Luther Sanchez and Paul Wright, aka "Animal." Sanchez was Spooter's head unit orderly and chief snitch. Since Sanchez kept the unit clean and ratted out illegal activities, Spooter rewarded him by allowing him into the program. That disappointed me. It wasn't that I didn't like Sanchez as much as I couldn't tolerate his constant whining. He'd been caught carrying a gun during a drug delivery. As his defense, he asserted he was doing a favor for a friend and didn't know he was carrying drugs. He thought it was a package. And he claimed he had a permit to carry the gun but could never produce it. He owned a nightclub in York, PA. From the way he described the interior, it sounded like a gay bar. The state and the feds tag-teamed him. The state prosecuted the drug crime and, once the state secured their conviction, the feds prosecuted him for being a felon in possession of a firearm. The result was nine years, and for a short, squat, Aztec looking guy who had an abundance of family support, his constant tears were hard to endure.

On this particular day, we'd been instructed to assemble at the Administrative Office at seven forty-five AM. I arrived on time and saw Spooter behind his desk sorting paperwork. Animal appeared with another inmate from whom he was negotiating the use of his commissary card to buy a twenty-ounce soda. When Wright stopped at the Admin door, the other inmate kept walking with his commissary card.

Sanchez was late because he was waiting for his pants to be pressed. He showed up about five of eight. He carried a Pepsi from the vending machines.

"This'll be the first time I've been off the grounds in six years. Can I have the window seat, please? Can I?" he begged.

I knew how he was feeling. I'd felt the same way my first time out. After being in prison for so long, even the smallest taste of freedom was exciting. What I didn't tell Sanchez was that the experience would also remind him of what he was missing, and how badly he'd screwed up.

Spooter noticed we were ready and spent another few minutes to wind up whatever paperwork he was processing. He came out into the hallway and said, "Alla ya'll run off to the bathroom, now. We ain't stoppin' for no bathroom breaks. Drain it or knot it."

At about eight-oh-five, the four of us departed through the squeaking metal door into the parking lot.

Sanchez opened his soda and took a swig. He offered it to Wright. "Wanna sip?"

Wright took the bottle from Sanchez and gulped a mouthful. He handed the soda back to Sanchez. Luther saw all the backwash and refused to take it.

"You don't want it?" asked Wright with an inquisitive look.

"No thanks. It might make me hurl."

Animal looked at me and said, "FNG, Dan, what can I say?"

"Fuck you," Sanchez said as a reply. "I'm a grizzled vet you cocksucker." Sanchez inquired, "What's an FNG?"

"Hey, lighten up. You're a fucking new guy," I said to calm him down. "You're the rookie on this gig."

By this time we'd reached the car, a white Ford compact.

"Alla ya'll hafta get in the back."

The back seat was too small for the three of us. However, no one volunteered to stay behind. I sat in the middle so Animal could belch out one window and Sanchez could pant out the other. Spooter slid behind the wheel and tried to put the key into the ignition. Before it became too embarrassing, I mentioned out loud, "On the newer models, the ignition is on the side of the column, Counselor. Not the dashboard. It's not like your pickup."

Spooter inserted the key and turned it. The engine sputtered lackluster.

Like all the vehicles in the motor pool, the car was on its last legs. Spooter reversed and we coughed out of the parking spot. At the first stop sign, Spooter fastened his seat belt and instructed us to do likewise. We were packed tighter than sardines and we couldn't move enough to have a hope of finding the straps.

"We're set, Counselor," lied Animal, and we were off into the Real World.

Or so we thought. Spooter drove down the hill to the Admin Building of the Medium Security facility. A fat white woman in a BOP uniform came out and shoehorned herself into the front seat. The vehicle sank under her weight. Breathing in heavy rasps, she pulled her seatbelt from the side. I heard it click into place.

"Why aren't these inmates in restraints, Spooter? What if they

227

run?"

Her statement surprised him.

"They won't even talk lest talked to first," was all he could muster.

"Did you requisition a weapon?" she asked.

Spooter's cheek twitched.

The fat woman sneered, "I secured one."

With that, she turned her head as far as she could toward the back seat.

"No one's gonna to escape on my watch." She held up a piece of menacing black steel and promised us, "I'm locked and loaded." Her hands had dimples where the knuckles should have been.

I was close to puking.

Spooter, unusually the diplomat, interjected, "Not these boys, Dee Dee."

We rumbled down the road and crossed over into civilization. Minutes passed as we stared at the first houses along the route and then a railroad crossing.

To break the uncomfortable silence, Spooter asked, "Say, how's your daughter doing with her horseback ridin' lesson? What's her name?"

"Johnnie Pearl and she's a coward!" cried Dee Dee, obviously upset

"Why does you sez that?"

"The other day the horse threw her and she hit her head against a tree and started bleeding. Then the little bitch cried and refused to get back on the horse."

"Was she hurt?"

Spooter was demonstrating a degree of compassion I'd never seen.

"She was bleeding good but that's no excuse. You have to suck it up. Life is hard. You gotta be tough. Can't let a little blood stop you." Dee Dee fell into silence.

I felt sorry for some kid I didn't know. I was doing eight years, but Johnnie Pearl had a life sentence with Dee Dee as a mother. Sucked to be her.

"How old is she now?" said Spooter.

"Just turned four."

And I thought my life was bad.

Spooter said, "Here's my speech, Dee Dee. I wrotes its myselfs."

No one believed that. He handed her a folder. "It's got the consent forms for the television stations, too."

Animal awoke from his slumber at that news. "We're gonna be on TV?" He held his hands up in a "V" for victory sign.

"Maybe," was all the confirmation Spooter gave him.

"An' here's streets map Cleeta done printed up on how to get there."

Dee Dee took the folder with her right hand and examined the contents in silence.

We merged onto the interstate as we collectively held our breath. Spooter drove like he was racing in the Daytona 500. The speed limit was meaningless. We zigged and zagged between cars, SUV's and eighteen wheelers. I prayed that I wouldn't die in the back seat of a fatal car crash.

Dee Dee directed Spooter to exit the interstate and we entered onto a two-lane winding, mountain road that led into the little town of St. Clair. The area was a ghost town that had boomed when coal was king and shriveled when the mines closed. Old, battered cars lined the streets, the houses were in disrepair, some abandoned and boarded up. The sidewalks were littered with trash and weeds. No one was around. It looked like a set from *The Twilight Zone*. We'd entered a new dimension.

Dee Dee directed Spooter using the map, turning left and right, around a curve and then a school appeared.

The building was old and elegantly constructed of brick in an 1890s design that indicated money had been spent to build something permanent. The town believed the mines would never close. It had decorative diamonds and squares of darker brick on the walls and around the windows. This building would be standing long after the wood frame houses were gone.

Spooter pulled into the parking lot, perhaps a third full. Maybe the town's population had dropped by two-thirds. Spooter must have thought the school, like the camp, was his turf. He parked in the space reserved for the Principal and killed the engine.

"Inmates out," he ordered.

Sanchez opened his door and lifted his knees out from being so cramped. He was rubber-legged for the first few steps. I followed him.

Animal and Spooter piled out, but Dee Dee was struggling to negotiate the removal of her girth. Spooter ran around the front of the car and held out his hand. She spurned the offer as if to say, "That won't do any good." He then took both her hands and started pulling. WD-40 came to mind and I turned away to hide a laugh.

Poor little Johnnie Pearl.

"Inmates," said Spooter after he pulled her out of the car. "Follow me. Dee Dee, you follows them."

That's the way we marched to the front door of the school. Spooter, Animal, Sanchez, me, and Dee Dee, probably with her hand on her gun.

Spooter pushed the intercom button beside the door. A voice said, "Yes?"

"I'm Counselor Hinkel from the prisons camp an' I'm here to puts on my pro-grim."

Silence. The voice must be checking the daily activities sheet.

"This one has a shank!" yelled Dee Dee.

She stepped away from us. Spooter turned to face the three of us. Animal, Sanchez and I were wondering who had the weapon.

Dee Dee blurted, "It's the tall one."

That would be me!!!! I was a head taller than the other two.

Dee Dee played hack. "I'm going to have him turn to me so you can restrain him and then secure the shank."

I raised my hands and turned slowly. I saw the gun barrel pointing at me. The feeling was hard to describe. My chest, heart and lungs were suddenly numb. I couldn't breathe. I don't think that I blinked.

"Meet Mr. Glock." The gun was inches from my face.

I couldn't cross my eyes close enough to see it clearly. I was afraid of the aggression on Dee Dee's face. I've had this dream dozens of times. I thought she was going to explode my head on the front steps of the school.

I took what I thought was my last breath.

"Hole-meese," Spooter asked from behind me. "What you gots in you pocket?"

"Sp—spee—speech—"

"What's a sp-spee-speech-?" said Dee Dee.

"My speech." I replied. "It's the speech I'm going to give today." I gulped, "If I make it that far."

Dee Dee wasn't buying the answer, "Why's it so big?"

I looked away from her, just to the side. She had a two-fisted grip on the gun.

"C—Counselor Hinkel," I tried to explain. "He knows my speech. It's fifteen pages. He's heard it. He's approved it."

Spooter patted me down.

"Is this it, Dee Dee?"

"Yep. That's it. Be careful."

Spooter removed the speech from my pocket and unfolded it.

Dee Dee didn't lower her gun. At that moment, I didn't want anything to upset her. She seemed intent on *wanting* to fire. Then, Sanchez proceeded not to help at all. He leaned over the handrail and hurled on a bush. Dee Dee drew a bead on him.

I dared to breathe but kept my arms up.

The hammer on the gun was cocked as she aimed at the coughing and choking Sanchez.

Spooter finished his investigation of the papers. He patted me down again as Dee Dee aimed at the gagging Sanchez.

"I think we's be okay now, Dee Dee. It's just his paper speech. These inmates is okay."

"You sure?"

"Yep. I's is sure."

Dee Dee uncocked the hammer and holstered the gun.

My knees buckled as I almost fainted.

Spooter commended her, "You done handle this very comfortable, Dee Dee. I'll mention you safety concern in my report."

I must have been as white as a sheet when I turned to Spooter. He handed my speech to me.

Sanchez straightened up and looked around. He wiped his sleeve across his mouth. He was so nervous about getting out of camp that, when the little creep saw the gun, up-chucking was his knee-jerk response. Or maybe he'd been carsick. He tried to look as if nothing had happened. I wanted to drop him onto the bush face first.

The door buzzer sounded and clicked open.

I looked toward heaven and breathed a Good Grief sigh.

A video camera was pointed at us, no doubt having caught everything on tape.

We wandered into the lobby. The Administrative counter was in front of us and we walked up to the receptionist. We signed the log and a student intern guided us to the auditorium.

The walk took less than a minute; no one said a word. Four people were awaiting our arrival. Two were men who stood around television cameras stationed on tripods. They wore sweatshirts, jeans, and sneakers. Both were short and middle-aged.

The other two were women dressed in business suits, quite petite, with short to mid-length coifed hairstyles. Excellent make-up. Mid-thirties. Absolutely fabulous.

As we approached, I stared in awe at the women.

The student intern said, "Here are the people from the prison."

All eyes fixed on those of us wearing khaki.

"This is Counselor Hinkel and Corrections Officer Hayes."

We inmates didn't merit an introduction.

One of the women held out her hand for Spooter to shake.

"Hi, I'm Lisa Fox from Channel 35 news. I'll be covering today's program."

She had teeth so white they looked unnatural. Like peppermint Life Savers. And not a hair out of place. A camera-ready porcelain doll.

The other woman walked up to Spooter.

"Good morning, I'm Tina Styres from Channel 16."

She asked for a description of the program we were presenting to the students. They explained that the two crews would tape the presentation for later editing.

I'd seen Tina Styres on television. She was one of the local news anchors. On the air, she was beautiful and affable, semi-smiling through each segment. In person she was different, more business-like, and intense. Her eyes were bright blue. She too had Life Saver teeth. I stared at her like a teenager.

Spooter told us to sit on the stage behind the podium. The cameramen positioned their equipment. The students came in and were chatty and loud. They were excited at seeing the TV crew and us, the criminals. A man came in wearing a suit and tie. He was middle-aged, bald, and reminded me of an organ grinder. The student's quieted down.

"I'm Principal David Piccolo of St. Clair High School," he said.

Spooter said, "I'm Counselor Spooter Hinkel from the Federal Prison Camp in Catskill County and this is Corrections Officer Dee Dee Hayes."

Spooter waived an arm in our direction.

"These heres be the inmates."

The Principal went to the microphone, made a few opening remarks and introduced "Counselor Hinkel."

Spooter went to the podium, put his file under the microphone, opened it, and started the show.

Spooter's speech was flawless. The prose perfect—the subjects and verbs matched, no adverb/adjective confusion, no inappropriate plural verbs. He'd had his speech edited, maybe by an inmate with a teaching background, or by Miz Buckles.

Spooter described the severe penalties for a life of crime. He listed the different levels of the federal prison system from Super-Max down to Minimum Security. He introduced each of us with a short description of who we were, what crimes we'd committed, and the sentences we were serving.

Then each of us went to the podium and presented our speech with Spooter standing at our side. Our presentations could not change. This was clearly explained to us in advance. Dee Dee sat on the left side of the stage behind the podium on two side-by-side folding metal chairs. The formal presentation lasted forty-five minutes.

At the end, there was a question and answer period. Experience indicated that there were never many questions. Spooter asked the audience for "kes-tions."

One boy held up his hand and said, "The guy who was in the gang and had a motorcycle. What kind of motorcycle did you have?"

Spooter, at the podium, turned around and said, "Inmate Hole-meese. What kind of motorcycle did you has?"

"I never had a motorcycle, Counselor Hinkel."

Spooter continued. "Inmate Sanchez. What kind of motorcycle did you has?"

"I have never had a motorcycle, Counselor Hinkel."

"Inmate Wright. What kind of motorcycle did you has?"

"Harley. There's no other kind."

And so it went.

"Is there sex in jail?" a girl asked. This was followed by laughter and snickering. The principal stood and held up his hands. He didn't say anything, but the kids quieted quickly. The power of this organ grinder was impressive.

A tall skinny, basketball player type said, "I'd like to ask the officer sitting in the back row something."

"Go 'head an' ask, son. Corrections Officer Hayes is here to help you."

"Where do you buy underwear that big?" he asked in a clear loud voice. "Jimmy Bob's mom cain't fine enny enny-where 'round here and I'm getting twenny-dollars to ask this question." The boy extended his hand to the boy sitting next to him. "Pay up!"

This brought the house down.

The principal shot to the podium and, with a surprising decibel level, out-shouted everyone in the room. It took him about ten seconds to restore order. Again, I was impressed.

"We will have order!!"

Dee Dee sat mute on her two folding chairs; her face bright red.

Spooter waited until the principal nodded to him to resume.

Spooter said, "Ahs thinks that Corrections Officer Hayes would be the best one to answer that question. Does you agree, Inmate Holemeese?"

He had to be kidding me. All I could muster was a feeble, "Why yes indeed, Counselor Hinkel. As usual, you know what would be best for one and all."

At this point, the principal, who'd been glaring at the student who'd asked the question, burst forth into a hail of laughter.

The student body erupted.

The principal shook his head back and forth, his little mouth now in an unnatural grin, eyes shut like a Buddha statue. He did his best to restore order.

He smiled as he walked around the auditorium, up and down the aisles, motioning with his hands for quiet and saying, "Okay, okay. Let's settle down, now. Let's have some respect for the Corrections Officers, and our other guests."

I heard kids say things like, "That was pretty fuckin' funny!" "Fuckin 'A'" "I'll fuckin' say it was." "Where does she buy her fuckin' underwear?" "She fuckin' makes it herself from parachutes."

"Okay, okay," the principal kept saying, not booming it out like Patton, but with a certain recognizable command. "Let's get ourselves back under control, now. Settle down, settle down."

He went on to say, "Ask not impertinent questions of our guests." It was a little poetic, as I recall. "Think about it. These inmates are being exposed to the outside world, so would you not think these inmates would be considered rehabilitated? Doesn't that thought lend itself to a host of inquiry?

"Now, let's have serious questions."

A pause of several seconds followed.

A boy raised his hand.

"Yes, Russell." The Principal nodded to Spooter. "Go ahead and ask Counselor Hinkel."

"If there's no bars, or fences, or gates, or locks at a Minimum Security facility," said the little burr-headed waif, his eyes overly narrow.

He was going to ask something stupid that he intended to defend as a legitimate question. I could see it coming and thought to myself, "Let's see if he's destined for a life of crime!"

"That's right, isn't it?" said the kid. He was at a critical point.

If his question was appropriate, this kid might grow up to be a politician, or a corporate executive.

"Well, if there's no locks, or cells, or bars—"

I could see him thinking.

"Has anyone ever tunneled out?"

He can take my place!

The room burst into guffawing laughter.

"Sit down, Russell!" the principal shouted.

This brought some shortening of the noise.

When it was quiet enough to hear, Spooter asked each of us in turn, "Has anyone ever tunnel out of camp?"

Each of us said, "No, Counselor Hinkel. No one ever has."

All of this was caught for prosperity by the two television cameras. Substantial editing would leave a lot of tape or digital electrons on a back-room floor, but the highlights would be good.

Eventually, Spooter thanked the school; the principal thanked Counselor Hinkel and Corrections Officer Hayes and the students returned to their classrooms.

The television announcers then asked if they could interview the inmates. Spooter agreed and directed us to stand by the door of the auditorium.

The interviewers started with Animal and Sanchez. I stood off to the side with Spooter.

Spooter had a sad expression on his face. I shifted closer. I heard him mutter, "It's my pro-grim and nobody evers wants to talk ter me. It's *my* pro-grim."

He was right.

Here was a *golden opportunity* for me to make Spooter's day and to rack up a bunch of brownie points. I awaited the right moment.

Wright had turned his baseball cap backwards. A sure sign the Animal was on the hunt. Lisa was about to ask him a question when he said, "You know they call me 'Animal.' Wanna know why?"

She recoiled.

"Hey, you got a boyfriend or something?"

Lisa said, "That's inappropriate!"

Animal went for the kill. His philosophy being you seldom get what you don't ask for.

"I was thinkin' you could come visit me. We could hook up and then you'd be my Visiting Room bitch. I'm down to forty-three months and then the 'Animal' is set free. Catch my drift?"

She swallowed hard. She turned to the cameraman and said, "He's hitting on me."

The cameraman said, "And I got it on tape. Wait 'til the station sees this."

I decided is was time to make Spooter's day.

"Tina?" I said. "Why don't you interview Counselor Hinkel? 'Bad Choices—Harsh Realities' is his program. He's done a lot of work on it and I don't think he's ever been interviewed. It'd be a television first and an honor for him."

She smiled.

"Counselor Hinkel," she said. "Would you grant me an interview, sir? Please?"

The contrast between Tina's Life Saver teeth and Spooter's gray inner tube teeth was hard to miss. Plus, Spooter didn't floss, ever. Chunks of white bread and baloney from God knows when were stuck between his teeth.

"Why shore, missy." He was pleased.

The cameraman positioned Spooter and Tina in front of the lens. She held the microphone to him and said, "We're rolling, Counselor. Could you spell your name for the record please?"

Spooter turned as white as fresh snow. Only his gray hair and eyebrows defined his pasty face now. Seconds passed.

Tina asked, "Is something wrong, Counselor?"

Spooter said, "I thought you was goin' to ask me a pro-grim kestion?"

"First you need to spell your name so we can put the caption under your picture. We do that in editing. Then you can talk about your program."

"Oh."

Spooter looked dazed. The little paperclip in his glasses jiggled back and forth. He trembled. His nervousness moved the clip that much faster. Was that sweat on his forehead?

"You can start any time you want," she prompted.

Spooter cleared his throat. He said, "I'm Counselor Spooter Hinkel and I am here to—"

"Cut!" Tina said. The cameraman took the camera from his shoulder. Tina took a nerve-calming moment to glance at her shoe and then at Spooter.

"Counselor. *Spell out* your full name. We have to have that information for the caption."

The cameraman said, "A beer says he can't do it."

Spooter gave the cameraman a look that would have curled any inmate into the fetal position. Tina, standing next to him, glanced at the cameraman and gave him a quick "you're on" nod.

She said cheerily, "Let's try again."

The cameraman put the camera on his shoulder.

Tina said, "Roll."

Spooter coughed, and then he stared at the light atop the camera. He said, "I am Counselor Spooter Hinkel."

He tried to peek at the name tag pinned to his shirt without touching it. A sneaky-peek he could not pull off.

He said, "That spell—"

He looked back at the camera with a resigned expression. "K-O-U-N- Z—no—make thatta S..."

Then he lifted the name tag on his shirt with his right index finger and turned it toward his face.

"No it's—C-O--U-"

Tina sighed to the cameraman. "I owe you a beer."

The camera came off his shoulder. Tina tried once more after the cameraman offered her a "double or nothing." The outcome didn't improve. Spooter could provide no sound bite that would not make him and the BOP look bad. Finally, Tina waved off the cameraman and mumbled, "Fuck it."

Spooter pressed on incoherently. Tina closed her notebook.

While Spooter was still attempting to spell Counselor, Tina came over to me. "I don't remember." She said. "How much time did you get?"

"Ninety-six months."

Her eyes narrowed. "That's not long enough."

Needless to say, we were out of there fast. Spooter booted me out of "Bad Choices—Harsh Realities" before we got to the car.

Just about everyone in camp watched the local news that evening. On both stations more time was devoted to the video showing CO Dee Dee Hayes pointing her gun at me; Spooter frisking me, and Sanchez puking than on "Bad Choices—Harsh Realities." The stations wanted to know why was a federal Corrections Officer pointing a gun at an inmate. Why was he frisked? What were the security concerns? They ended the segment by reporting that calls to the prison had not been returned. In the end, I was allowed back in the program a month later when Spooter had only one other inmate to go to a college to present the program. Before the presentation, he made me promise not to ask a media representative to interview him.

36

Smoking Banned

Prison resembled a mini-society, and all of society's ills are there. Drugs, violence, gambling, alcohol and sex are present (in one form or another) along with hatred and prejudice. I've started talking with some of the brothers who have a different skin pigment than mine, and I've realized that we share the same fears and dreams. I came to believe if we talked to each other, then we'd get along better.

Imagine a controlled environment with a population addicted to at least one drug since adolescence, and then the drug was taken away. To make matters worse, what if you couldn't smoke to ease the withdrawal process or relieve stress?

"Dat's not gonna woik," Ace Baldini informed everyone who would listen.

"They're asking for a riot. Maybe I'll get lucky and be sexually assaulted. Know whudah I mean?" This was from Frankie Bananas.

Luka Slobodo panicked. "What we gonna use for money?"

Bronco and Pill Line yapped away in Spangloricano.

Everyone is addicted to something. Alcohol. Work. Sex. Reading. Puzzles. Gardening. Whatever. Me, I'm addicted to the fog-lifting effects of coffee. I drank two twelve ounce cups each morning for breakfast. Nothing like a shot of caffeine to start the day.

One day the BOP announced that, in six months, cigarettes would no longer be sold from the commissary.

When I first heard this, I thought it was a joke. After I'd read the memo posted on the bulletin board, I thought it was an elaborate joke. According to the announcement, the ban was part of a lifestyle rehabilitation program designed to improve an inmates' chances of not smoking after release.

I thought someone must have told Counselor Hinkel that too many inmates were dying of lung cancer before completing their sentences, and he'd started a program to prevent inmates from dying before their entire sentences were served. Spooter didn't smoke, and it sounded like one of his brainstorms.

I was wrong, again. The smoking ban was initiated from the BOP headquarters in Washington, D.C. and was implemented throughout the country in all federal buildings.

I'd estimate that about a third of the inmates smoked. That would be about a hundred and thirty guys. And cigarettes were cash equivalents. Guys who never smoked bought them and kept them in their lockers for a rainy day. Slobodo must have had twenty packs, and he didn't smoke.

Kurt Steiner did. And he was more disliked than Luka Slobodo, a feat not easily accomplished. Steiner was arrogant, and thought he was above the rules. His "fuck everybody" attitude rubbed the other inmates the wrong way since it occasionally resulted in everyone losing a privilege. For example, one night the cop on duty recalled everyone back to their respective housing units and closed the compound after Steiner refused to obey a direct order. It made him very unpopular.

Steiner was in his forties, never married, no children, no friends, and ugly. His eyes were so close together that I don't think he could look through both binocular eyepieces at the same time. His teeth were large in his smallish head and were jumbled like a shark's. He'd been a "roadie" for a few off-studio TV shows, and then he'd self-published a book. He had enough contacts and credentials to claim he was a literary agent.

He was in for mail fraud.

"I'd put my name into the Literary Agent reference books. I used a Fifth Avenue, New York City address. It was a post office box. I'd answer the inquiries and tell the writers to send me their manuscripts."

Evidently there are lots of unpublished authors out there. He said his garage was full of manuscripts.

"After each manuscript got to be four or five months old, I'd send the stupid jerk a legitimate looking letter and Agent Contract for Representation. I told the dumb ass I wanted a one-year exclusive contract plus a three hundred and fifty dollar Agency Fee, as if that was the magic number to cover the costs of a best seller. The cover letter said I'd already had the manuscript vetted by two New York publishers. The three hundred and fifty-dollar fee would make the illiterate a millionaire."

A couple of times a week he rode the train into the city and picked up inquiries, new manuscripts, and checks ready to be deposited.

Steiner wasn't dumb, though. He never responded to anyone with an address closer than a couple of hundred miles. He didn't want anyone visiting him. And he kept a computer log of each payment with the name, address, and the gist of the book so that if the author called, he could talk about the manuscript with some authority. He'd send back letters enclosing Xerox copies of real Return Receipt Requested slips from publishers, the same receipts for all, occasionally updated. An answering machine recorded the author calls. He'd go to his computer, look up the author, read his quick summary of the book and review previous conversations. Then he'd call back and enthusiastically tell the author that his book was the next big seller. Good things would happen "very soon" he promised.

"I'd keep it short. I had a tape of phones ringing and voices yelling. After about a minute, I'd have to take another call and I'd hang up."

He'd keep them entertained for the contracted year with gladhanding.

"I was pulling down a half million a year on about fifteen hours a week. Some of the dumb fucks extended for another year. Same price.

"There's a sucker born every second," Steiner said.

The clincher was that about every third year, Steiner would pick a manuscript and have it published through a print-on-demand outfit. The book might not sell more than what the author could get his friends to buy, but it made The Kurt Steiner Literary Agency legitimate.

Or so he thought.

A retired postal inspector, and wanna-be author, grew suspicious, traveled from Arizona to New York, spied on the post office box, and followed Steiner home. The Feds procured a warrant for his computer, and the incriminating evidence was on the hard drive and laid out as if prepared by a German accountant. Steiner couldn't produce the original Return Receipt Request stubs for the manuscripts he supposedly sent to publishers; promises made through the U.S. Postal Service and not kept. That would be mail fraud.

Steiner probably could have negotiated his way out of the case by paying a fine and some restitution but he was arrogant. He told the investigating agent for the FBI to go fuck himself when the agent asked Steiner some routine questions. That pissed off the FBI agent, and the prosecutors dumped on him to teach him a lesson. He never admitted doing anything illegal. He went to trial, was convicted, and was sentenced to jail for forty-two months. He arrived to learn that the BOP had decided to ban smoking in federal facilities.

The BOP's plan was to notify inmates that, in six months, cigarettes no longer would be sold from the Commissary. The last day of cigarette sales was August thirty-first. Panic spread through the smokers, especially Kurt Steiner, who was seldom seen anywhere except in a designated smoking area. The only program offered to assist with nicotine withdrawal was Spooter's "No Smokin'" class that included two smoke breaks in the one hour session. You can figure out for yourself how effective that class was.

While supply lasted, each inmate could buy a maximum of two cartons of cigarettes each Wednesday. You could pick any brand as long as they were Winston or Newport.

"Steiner!" the Commissary Clerk yelled. I was two people behind him.

Steiner held up his ID card.

The Commissary Clerk verified Steiner's identity and handed his Commissary sheet to an orderly who scurried around frantically filling it. Sheer chaos. The orderly assembled Steiner's items on a table until everything on the list was collected. Then, in one massive dump, the order was handed to Steiner who had seconds to take everything off the top of the Dutch door before the items dropped to the floor. If anything fell, eager hands scooped it up, and claimed ownership by possession. Steiner had no way to check whether his order was completely filled because the next inmate was pushing him out of the way.

After Steiner stepped aside, the Commissary Clerk said to the inmate in front of me, "Yo, Gas Pump." Gas Pump earned his name because of his anal emissions. "You don't smoke."

"I'm gettin' them for Steiner."

That was the wrong thing to say with the Commissary Cop standing next to the door supervising the Commissary process.

Steiner was having inmates buy cigarettes for him so he could stash enough smokes to last the length of his sentence. He had six months to accomplish this. He should have told Gas Pump to claim that he was taking up the habit.

Steiner idled against the wall opposite the Commissary door so that he could take the cigarettes from Gas Pump. When the Commissary Cop heard Gas Pump, the game was over. He halted everything until Counselor Hinkel could be summoned. Twenty minutes passed until Spooter arrived. Everyone listened to him interrogate Gas Pump across the top of the half-door. Gas Pump told Spooter he'd been promised a radio, a watch, and a pair of sunglasses in exchange for two cartons of Winstons.

Spooter put the ka-bash on Steiner's fun.

"I'mma tella alla y'all right now," he announced. "Only smokers is gonna gets smokes. Iffin you doesn't smoke when you gets here to my camp, you ain't gonna start here in my camp. We gonna have no whorin'."

Someone in the crowd said, "That's 'hoarding,' you fucking moron."

The Counselor ignored the correction. He stood inside the door with the Commissary Cop and monitored the rest of the orders to be sure only known smokers purchased cigarettes. There were several inmates like Gas Pump in line. They couldn't lie because they'd each checked off the box to buy cigarettes on their Commissary sheets. There were a number of no-shows though. Spooter wrote down everyone's name who ordered cigarettes but didn't smoke, and he had the cigarettes pulled from their orders. These inmates would have to attend Spooter's "No Smokin'" class.

Steiner said to no one in particular, "I'd rather die than not be able to smoke."

"You'd have better luck getting a death certificate than a smoking permit."

"Fuck you, Holmes."

Steiner's next move was to determine whether the smoking ban extended to the staff. It did. Steiner went to the bucket for trying to bribe a hack to supply him with cigarettes. He realized how powerless inmates were.

When he returned from two weeks in the bucket, he was more determined than ever to acquire cigarettes.

Counselor Hinkel was relentless in shaking down Steiner's cube, throwing everything onto the floor and then confiscating whatever he arbitrarily considered contraband.

I don't remember Spooter ever being so focused on torturing one inmate, not even when someone claimed another inmate had a cell phone. Spooter never searched the woods for the cell phone, but he did when he searched for Steiner's cigarette "whore."

In six months, the deadline arrived. No more cigarettes were available at the Commissary and, except for Steiner, the ban passed uneventfully. In jail, you become accustomed to privileges being "taken away."

After Steiner consumed his personal stash, and traded his personal belongings for smokes, he became hostile with a hack who was smoking outside the Admin Building. That altercation resulted in his transfer to a Medium Security facility. No one in the Camp felt a sense of loss over his departure. You didn't morn the transfer of an asshole.

37

The Heat Seeker

I spoke to mom last night. Shannon is the starting pitcher in the annual 'Father-Daughter' softball game.
Cliff was going to play. Tears welled up in my eyes, I'd been replaced.
Now the concept of "family" was all the more important to me.
All I wanted to be was a good father.

Existence.
That's what life was called in prison.
I had twenty-four months to go.
Time was getting short.
The vets tell the FNG's to count the amount of time they've done and not how much is left. This advice was to prevent the FNG's from going crazy since time never passed fast enough.

At this point in my sentence, I was secure in every aspect of my existence. I was a regular, like a daily customer at the local diner. I hated to admit that I was comfortable and thought of my cube as my "home." How repulsive is that?

Even the cops recognized my veteran status, and shot the breeze with me. This was especially true at the Power House. The hacks knew I was dependable, and I ran the place using all the non-authority I had. I was a regular Radar O'Reilly.

The hacks at the Power House were good guys except for Corrections Officer Skorzeny. Work was a job for them. They showed up, did as little as possible, and went home. Their work detail was little more than an eight-hour sit. To keep the place running on an even keel, they weeded-out and transferred to other details the anti-socials no one could tolerate.

In short, at this point in my ninety-six-month sabbatical, I was Fully Institutionalized. I realized that there was a purpose to the BOP and that there were people who didn't deserve to be in society since they were a menace and a danger. Before my incarceration, I was one of them.

Of all the hacks at the Power House, my favorite was Mr. Colvin. He was a mountain of a man in his early thirties. He stood six-two and tipped the scales at a muscular two hundred forty pounds. He didn't pump weights and didn't inject chemicals into his body. He could fix anything except the water pumps, and we had a lot of water pumps. Mr. Colvin fixed a water pump by beating on it with a wrench. This wasn't a madman's beating. He banged on the top of it with a pipe wrench to see if it would perform. When it didn't, he banged the back. He'd shake it. He'd pick it up and drop it on the concrete. It was a thoughtful beating. "Do you want to work now?" he'd ask the pump. If the pump disrespected him, he resumed the abuse.

Mr. Colvin had been a Parade Magazine All-American high school linebacker and, after graduation, he enlisted and served ten years in the U.S. Navy. He'd had offers from a handful of college football teams but opted for the Navy. He often said, "Holmes, I could have gotten a free ride to about any college in the country and had a blast. Instead, I chose the Navy. Not the Naval Academy but the fucking Navy. Fucking genius that I am."

Time flew when Mr. Colvin supervised the Power House detail. He kept the mood light. If existence in prison could be compared to a movie, Mr. Colvin was R. P. McMurphy in *One Flew Over the Cuckoo's Nest*. He flat out didn't give a fuck about anything. He was mostly concerned about his next hunting or fishing trip. He never wore the required BOP gray shirt or BOP blue cap. Instead, he had a "Cabala's" hunting cap. He took grief from no one and was, at the same time, a gentle giant, unless someone or something pissed him off.

Mr. Colvin once caught somebody making a shank in the tool room. Instead of writing him a "shot," he took the inmate to his office, closed the door and performed live hamburger drills on the inmate; Mr. Colvin did the meat grinding. That inmate claimed he'd been beaten. Mr. Colvin countered that he worked with the inmate for weeks, and the inmate was clumsy. He said the inmate had fallen off a ladder at the back of the Power House into a pyramid of wood boxes. That explained the bruises. Whatever charge was being processed was dropped when Mr. Colvin had a private word with the inmate about the severity of the next beating if he did not recant.

But that incident was the exception rather than the rule. I liked Mr. Colvin and spent a lot of time with him.

Now, for a plant of its size, the BOP did not have a preventive maintenance program. There was one on paper, but it was never implemented. Equipment was fixed only when it broke. Or, if the equipment was irrevocably broken, it was replaced after a great deal of paperwork and waiting. This caused a major problem if the part was operationally vital.

The Power House was a series of electric fired boilers that heated water for the FPC and the FCI. It had miles of underground hot water lines. The compound was twenty-eight years old by this time. The main pipe exiting the Power House had a "T," directing hot water down to the FCI and up to the FPC. The water main had an expected life of ten years per industry bulletins. So, when I arrived, the plant was already twelve years past retirement.

The preventive maintenance program recommended chemical treatments to delay corrosion and fatigue. The suggested chemical, and the procedure for its application, were listed in the manufacturer's operating guide. Even though I filled out the paperwork to requisition the chemicals, we never received them. About this time the main hot water line sprang underground leaks and hundreds of gallons of hot water pumped out of the Power House never arrived at the FCI or FPC. The excess had to be going somewhere. But where?

Every hour, the plant was losing about five hundred gallons of water. If we increased water pressure, we might blow the entire system, so the officers decided to wait until the leak was visible. In the cold and snow of a mid-January, the camp's housing units became freezers because the pressure and water flow were insufficient to provide heat.

Everyone on the compound, cops, inmates, and staff, was on "steam alert," walking the length of the underground pipe to locate mushy ground. If a leak were discovered, the cops would make us shovel down to and repair the break.

I was in the Power House with Mr. Colvin the day after a fifteen inch snowstorm. He was in his office drinking coffee and watching his favorite television show: *Live with Regis and Kelly*. He often said of Kelly Ripa, "Holmes, I'd absolutely break her in half." Not something I personally wanted to witness. In any event, from nine to ten, Mr. Colvin was not to be disturbed regardless of the emergency.

On this day, Mr. Colvin rushed from his office at nine-ten.

"Let's go, Johnny Wad!," he ordered loudly going through the door to the parking lot without looking to see if I'd heard him.

I'd been there long enough to know that if he said, "Holmes," he wanted something mundane, like typing. If he called me "Holmesie," a joke was on the way, usually at the expense of some inmate. "Johnny Wad" was a reference to my so-called cousin John Holmes, the porn star, and I should be ready for an extraordinary event like turkey watching or deer counting but never anything that could be considered work.

I arose up from my desk and grabbed my winter coat. When I walked outside, Mr. Colvin was sitting in the driver's side of a flat bed pick-up truck. I slid into the passenger's seat.

He pointed to an inmate sitting on a bench in front of the Power House.

Mr. Colvin said, "I told limp-dick there to protect that bench since terrorists are trying to steal it, and it's his job to guard it while I go tell the Warden."

"Did he buy it?"

"He's sitting there, ain't he?"

I looked at the inmate and recognized an elderly Hispanic who was kindly referred to as "Poppi."

The inmate waived as Mr. Colvin started the vehicle.

"Know who he is?"

Mr. Colvin knew who he was as well as I.

"Nope," I played along.

"That's my main Hispanic bench-warmer, Manuel Labor. Not real bright. Can't work worth a shit, but he'll protect that bench like a mother fucker."

That would be true until we were out of sight and then he would be inside the Power House foraging for food.

"How's Kelly Ripa lookin' today, Mr. Colvin?"

"Fucking wearing red pants that must be painted on, Holmes. I'd do her in a second. I'd break her fucking back."

Mr. Colvin reversed the truck without looking behind. He shifted to drive and peeled out. As he entered the main road, he dropped something onto my lap.

"Take that."

I spread my knees—a knee-jerk reaction to avoid touching it—and it hit the floor.

It looked like a sci-fi ray gun blaster.

"What is it?"

"It measures ground temperature. If you aim it at a spot and the temperature is warmer than the surrounding area, you probably found the leak."

I picked it up. I hefted the device and pointed it out the window as I examined the gauges. I pressed the On/Off switch to On. Nothing happened. No gauges moved.

"How do you turn it on?" I asked fully aware that as a former lawyer, my ability with tools and devices was very limited.

"Holmesie. What do I always say about being a genius?"

"To be a genius, you have to be a little smarter than the equipment you're using."

Mr. Colvin laughed. "That piece of shit doesn't work. I took the batteries out and put them into my TV remote t'other night."

"Why do we have this gizmo if we know it doesn't work?"

"To make us look good in case my boss drags his sorry ass out in the cold to see if we've found anything."

"It's a prop?"

"Yeah. A fifteen-hundred dollar prop. Welcome to the federal government."

We barreled into the FPC parking lot on two wheels, and slid to a halt by plowing into a snow drift. The engine coughed once and died. Mr. Colvin got out. He left the keys in the ignition.

Not a good idea.

Leaving keys in a vehicle invited an inmate to escape.

I watched his back.

"Do you want me to grab the keys, Mr Colvin?"

His facial expression said "No."

"Not my truck, not my inmate stealing it, not my problem."

He walked across the field toward the woods. I carried the heat seeker.

The snow was deep here, maybe a foot and a half. Mr. Colvin didn't raise his feet up and down much; he bulled his way through the snow making it easier for me to follow. He headed into the field in a zigzag pattern as he looked at the snow hollows around the ground. There were no pipes anywhere in this area.

What were we doing here?

Mr. Colvin crouched down and looked at the ground where he could see it.

"Shoot here," he ordered.

"But this thing doesn't work," I shot back.

Mr. Colvin lifted his head from his study of the ground and said with an edge, "Just do it Holmes. It's a fucking prop. Just play along."

I pointed the heat seeker at the ground where he directed and said, "Zap!"

I checked the gauges. Nothing. I pointed at the ground again and again and again.

"Zap! Zap! Zap!"

Mr. Colvin walked in a circle around some low scrub. I stepped onto a little mound and pointed at a swale running beside it.

"Why don't I zap here a few times, Mr. Colvin?"

"Go for it," he said still looking at the ground. "Holmes rocks."

I pointed the heat seeker at the ground in front of me and said, "Bzzzzzzzzzztt!"

Mr. Colvin didn't notice.

I was cold just standing there. I headed over to where he was.

"What are we looking for?" I asked.

"Deer tracks." He pointed at indentations in the snow. "Deer have been here looking for food."

Deer tracks in this snow?

I noticed where he was pointing. Nothing there indicated "deer" to me.

I said, "Just thinking out loud, if the boss comes out and finds us zapping and buzzing the ground with a heat seeker without batteries, and we're nowhere near a pipe, is he going to say, 'Keep up the good work, boys?'"

"Nope. He's the one who wants to know if deer have been around here."

Somebody else's tax dollars at work was my only thought. We wandered around for another ten minutes. I tired of making sound effects and the cold was making me shiver.

Mr. Colvin said, "Okay, we're done. Let's go fuck around in back of the housing units."

"There's no pipes back there either."

"I'm gonna let you in on a little secret, Holmes. It's Wednesday and there's a leak. The plant operators decided to drag out locating the leak 'til Friday at four o'clock when we're gonna fire up the pumps full blast and turn the leak into a gusher. Then, we'll know where the leak is and we'll fix it on Saturday and Sunday at double time after we've collected our regular forty hours for this week's work. Got it?"

"Don't you th—"

"Yeah, I know. It sucks to be an inmate. But we have Christmas bills to pay."

Off he started to the back of Camp One.

I followed like a little puppy carrying the heat seeker.

As we mushed past Camp Two, Mr. Colvin stopped. He looked into a ground floor window on Range C. He'd seen something that bothered him.

"What's that, Holmes?" he asked.

I looked inside, shading my eyes with my hand for a better view. I didn't see anything that seemed out of place and told him so.

"The fuckin' curtain. Looks like the bunk is shaking. What the fuck is he doing in there?! If he jerks off any harder, he'll pull his dick off."

Now I knew what he was talking about. It was the bed sheet that was draped around Gay Cliff's bunk like a curtain.

"Welcome to the 'gayborhood', Mr. Colvin. I think the expression 'butt is not just a conjunction' covers the situation. Know what I mean?"

Mr. Colvin shook his head in disbelief.

I asked, "Are you thinking about going in there?"

Mr. Colvin said "I want to torture the queer by 'cuffin and stuffin' him."

"If his boyfriend, freaky Enrique, is there, he's already 'cuffed and stuffed.'"

A short pause ensued.

"I didn't see nothing," he snorted.

We walked away.

As we approached the rear door of Camp One, Mr. Colvin slowed. There were cigarette butts and burnt matches scattered on the snow. Something was wrong because smoking had been banned in federal prisons, and enough time had passed for the inmates to smoke up their stash. I couldn't help but smile. I knew Mr. Colvin was plotting something.

The metal door on the range was slightly ajar. Mr. Colvin examined the door and said, "Give me the gun."

I handed him the heat seeker.

"Follow me."

We approached the door.

Mr. Colvin took a deep breath.

He grabbed the knob, jerked the door open, jumped on the threshold, pointed the heat seeker inside, and yelled like a drill sergeant, "This is a raid!"

He traversed the room from left to right with the heat seeker.

"Nobody move! Put your hands in the air."

He stepped inside.

"I'm Ranger Hal and this is Deputy Dan. We're the smoke police. Don't anybody move or I'll electrocute your balls!"

When he said that, I was holding my breath, trying not to laugh.

"What are you doing?"

It seemed like nothing happened for the longest time. Mr. Colvin posed in an FBI shooting stance inside the door.

I took a step closer to look over his shoulder.

Two old black guys were sitting on the floor smoking cigarettes. I edged closer and could see fear in their eyes.

One of the men, hardly able to speak, said, "Don't shoot, boss. We just tryin' to relax a little. Know what I mean? We jus' sittin' here doin' a little somethin' somethin'. Tha's all. We ain't tryin' to hurt nobody. Don't write us up, boss, or dey bag us and ship us to da med um."

Mr. Colvin covered them with the menace of the heat seeker.

The inmates were shaking themselves to pieces. I imagined arms and legs falling off.

It was a staring contest.

Who would blink?

The cigarette burned the fingers of the man who'd spoken. He yelped, threw down the butt and put his fingers in his mouth. He closed his eyes thinking he would be phasered into oblivion.

Mr. Colvin held steady.

When the man deemed it safe to open his eyes. Mr. Colvin said, "Okay. You get one free pass. But if Deputy Dan here sees you smoking one more time, it's down the hill to the big house for you. All he's gotta do is tell me. That means whether you did it or not."

The two smokers looked as if they were saved.

Mr. Colvin turned to me.

"Let's go Deputy Dan. Our day of deterring crime has just begun."

I said, "Yes, Kemo Sabe."

I backed out and Mr. Colvin shut the door behind us.

Then he lost it.

"Did you see that, Holmes?" he laughed placing his hand on his chest. "I thought that one guy was going to piss his pants! I had to stop, or he was going to have a heart attack."

He bent over in a belly laugh.

I was laughing too; one of those laughs deep enough to have a health benefit. The image of the two guys sitting there shaking and wondering if Mr. Colvin was going to pull the trigger was worth being in jail. Well, not really; but, it was funny. They must have thought they'd be zapped into the Phantom Zone.

When Mr. Colvin caught his breath, he said, "All this fun, and they give me sixty-four grand a year plus benefits. What a great country!"

"You didn't take their cigarettes, Mr. Colvin."

"Who gives a fuck, Holmes!" He pointed up a rise toward the recreational area.

"What's up there?"

Before I could answer, he marched that way.

We arrived at the two bocce courts. This was sacred ground to the Italians among us where they sat all summer and traded tales about the days in the old country. Unlike the other recreational areas, the bocce courts, the score keeping area, and the benches were devoid of white flakes. Here grounds keeping reigned supreme and the space was meticulously maintained. The Italians cared for their beloved bocce courts by bribing the Hispanics to manicure them.

Mr. Colvin was amazed at the condition of the area given the amount of snowfall. He pointed at the courts.

"What the fuck is this, Holmes?"

"Bocce."

"Where's the goalie stand?"

"No, no. It's more like horseshoes."

Mr. Colvin studied the surface and looked at the balls lined up on their racks.

He said, "Being a redneck, I understand 'shoes. Where's the poles?" He picked up a small white ball. "What the fuck is this?"

"Well, that's sort of the pole. It's called a Bellini. You toss the Bellini to the other end of the court, and then the two teams toss as many balls as close to the Bellini as possible. That's how you score points."

Mr. Colvin rolled the ball around in his hand and looked at the court.

"Let's play."

"I thought we were looking for a leak?"

"The only leak you're gonna find is if you take one," he snapped. "Show me how to play. I can make it an order."

"You want to play bocce when it's freezing?"

"This is your government talking, Holmes. I got a lot of time to kill before my retirement. Let's play bocce and kill some time."

Here I was, middle of January, shivering cold, no heat or hot water

in the housing units for the upcoming weekend, and I'm playing bocce. What's wrong with this picture? Am I here being punished? Well,
yes I am.

"Do you want to be red or green?"

"I'll be red."

He beat me eleven to four.

"We need to get to Unicor, Holmes. You really suck at bocce, you
know that?"

"How do you know that I didn't throw the game to make you feel
good?"

He must not have liked that thought. He left the balls on the court,
picked up the heat seeker and headed for Unicor.

I followed like a puppy again, five steps behind.

We arrived at the drainpipe outside of Unicor. The snow was up to
our knees. My feet were numb in the worn out boots.

Mr. Colvin bent over and wiped away the snow that encrusted the
clean-out plug. He unscrewed it with a small crescent wrench he
pulled from his back pocket. He looked inside.

"Know what I'm doing, Holmesie?"

"Checking for escaping midgets?"

"Nope," he said not laughing. "I'm looking for drugs. When I was
the hack on patrol, I'd always check here 'cause it's where guys would
stash their shit."

"What would you do with it after you found it?"

He put his hand down the pipe and felt around. Better him than me.
It was a sanitary drain.

Finding nothing, he screwed the top back on. He looked at me and
said, "If it was weed, I'd take it home and smoke it. Anything else, I'd
spill it on the side of the road."

To me, that seemed like something he would do. I started laughing
and quoted one of his favorite lines.

"Fuck 'em all and feed 'em rice."

"Fuckin' A!" he laughed. "You're learning, Holmsie. You're gonna
do good on the outside someday."

He picked up the heat seeker.

"Let's see if we can locate the leak in the Admin Building."

We headed toward the squealing black metal door.

The Admin Building, especially the Admin Office, was the best maintained area of the compound except for the bocce courts. No less than five Hispanics expended a considerable amount of time and energy to keep it spotless. They didn't appreciate anyone dirtying the area. So when Mr. Colvin and I walked through the foyer, and then into the Admin Office, we dragged a trail of mud, slush, and snow behind us.

"What's up Fettuccini?"

This was Mr. Colvin's greeting for Mr. Federini, one of his friends

Mr. Federini was the Camp Two Case Manager. He was a good looking guy in his mid-thirties and was considered to be upwardly mobile. He was a Gulf War veteran and then joined the BOP. He served ten years as a hack before being promoted to "Case Manager."

He had been a cop in the Medium Security facility with Mr. Colvin.

Their mutual respect grew from working in the trenches of the Medium Security facility together and having had each other's back.

"What are you doing here, Dave?"

"Looking for a water leak. Seen any?"

Mr. Federini looked at me.

"Why isn't Holmes at the Power House?"

Mr. Colvin aimed the heat seeker at Mr. Federini and said, "That's Deputy Dan, Mister. Don't get that twisted, or I'll shoot."

Just then, Ms. Fowler, the Camp Unit Manager, walked out of her office into the secretarial area. Ms. Fowler was in her early-thirties. She was reasonably cute and liked to spend money on clothes. She was also cold and no-nonsense, a by-the-book and tough-as-nails type of person. Administration liked her. The inmates called her Nurse Ratchet.

Oh, and one other thing.

Mr. Colvin and Ms. Fowler did not get along.

"Hereeeee's Amy!" announced Mr. Colvin in his best Ed McMahon voice.

Ms. Fowler's usually tight face grew tighter.

"See, Holmesie. You were wrong. She doesn't ride a broom."

Her mouth became a slit, her eyes narrowed. This is what she would look like after botched plastic surgery and Botox.

Mr. Colvin said, "Oh! My mistake, Holmsie. You didn't say she was a witch. You said she was a bit—"

"What are you doing here, Colvin?" she snapped.

Mr. Colvin pointed the heat seeker at Ms. Fowler's crotch.

"We're looking for a leak." After a timely pause, he continued, "No fluids here. Dry as a desert."

Ms. Fowler spun around in a huff, sped back to her office, and slammed the door.

Mr. Colvin turned to me and laughed. "I'll bet she makes you pay for that, Holmes. She's pissed!"

Ms. Buckles came out of her office and said quite happily, "Dave, what are you doing here, baby?"

Mr. Colvin, who often said he'd like to bend her over, said, "Official business, Cleeta. Deputy Dan and I are hunting leaks."

She smiled. "Is that like hunting wabbits?"

Mr. Colvin pointed the heat seeker at Ms. Buckles and announced, "Holmes, stop the presses. We found the sweetest wabbit in Wabbitville."

The phone rang and Federini answered. After he hung up, he said "Play time's over. Get back to the Power House. Flynn is looking for you."

Ms. Buckles was smiling at Mr. Colvin as if more than a co-employee relationship existed.

Mr. Colvin looked at me.

"Holmes. Fun time is over. Let's get back."

We went back to the pick-up. It was still there with its nose stuck in the snow and the keys in the ignition. Mr. Colvin backed up without looking. We roared out and sped to the Power House in record time.

Mr. Flynn, Facilities Chief, met us at the door. No greeting. Just, "Any luck, Dave?"

Mr. Colvin contorted his face into a look of utter frustration.

"We walked every inch of the Camp and didn't find a funkin' thing, Pat. We nearly froze our asses off. Holmsie's pants are wet to the bottom of his coat."

Mr. Flynn was disappointed. He didn't care if I was wet or cold. He was hoping not to have the FCI and FPC without heat and hot water for two days.

"I appreciate your looking. The place is going to stink with no hot water."

That meant the pump system was going to be turned off for the weekend.

Sucked to be me.

Mr. Colvin said, "I think the ray gun is way over-rated, Pat."

38

The Messiah

When I was still on the street, I went to a psychologist to help me handle things better. On my first visit, after, just after I had been indicted, he asked me what I did. I started telling him "my story." He cut me off and said, "You're wasting time. Just tell me what you did." I started again and he cut me off again. Finally, he said, "Let me help you. Try, 'Hey, I stole a lot of money from my clients and I got caught. I fucked up.' Isn't that what happened?"

I've been at Camp Catskill for more than half my sentence now. I'm over the hump and gliding down hill. I have fourteen months left—not an impossible stretch considering the time I've already served. Trouble is, I can't see the light at the end of the tunnel.

Life at Camp was easy. "Doing easy time" applied to everyone who could accept the reality of their situation and adopt a routine. I knew the cops and how to avoid problems with them. At the Power House, I more or less was in charge of the operation. The cops were content to let the plant operate by itself as long as there were no problems. My job, as the trusted clerk, was to anticipate problems. The position provided a degree of operational freedom, within reason. So, to enjoy my lofty rank, I didn't abuse my situation. I stayed on top of preventative maintenance and parts ordering, and I handled administrative issues by filing the required paperwork. In essence, I was a vital clog in the operation of the Power House.

One of the clerk's requirements was to have a driver's license for the compound. This permitted me to drive the hacks around the institutional grounds. On a regular day, I picked up the cops in front of the administrative building for the Medium Security facility and drove them to their assigned work details. In the afternoon, I did the reverse.

While the cops were all business at their work details, the ride in the van showed a different side of their personality. Inside the van, the trip was a series of insults, body sounds, and practical jokes. Both male and female cops participated like frat house brothers. I was initiated into the humor on the first day when one of the cops stuck a finger in my direction and said, "Holmes, pull my finger. It's jammed." I complied and a gaseous explosion emitted from his ass that stunk out the van.

Since I'd arrived at the camp with my state driver's license, I was allowed to apply for, and was granted, the job of town driver. A town driver was needed due to budget constraints. Each fiscal year, a smaller amount of the federal budget was allocated to maintain the Federal Bureau of Prisons. So, instead of hacks being paid overtime to transport inmates to medical visits or to the bus station, inmates were used as drivers. To be eligible, an inmate had to have a valid driver's license, and be liked by the "right cops."

While motoring through Catskill County by myself was an immense pleasure, I had to be careful not to be caught "goofing off" since the hacks lived in the area and if one of them saw me eating at the diner or ordering a ninety-six ouncer at Starbucks, I would go straight to the hole. Also, on occasion, some gung-ho hack would follow me to be sure I stayed between the lines. And, as soon as I returned from a trip, I had to provide a urine sample to verify I had not ventured off the straight and narrow.

This particular adventure began on a Monday. Dinner had been marginal at best and I'd run a slow six miles counting the laps with my fingers. I showered and changed into fresh clothes. It started raining. Without warning, two cops arrived at my cube, cuffed my bunkie and escorted him to the bucket. Then two hacks cleaned out his desk, locker, and wall pin-ups. They provided no explanation. So, for about the sixth time in my prison experience, I had a cube to myself. I was enjoying the momentary privacy since there was an unending stream of inmates coming down the pipeline.

I always turned down other inmates who requested to bunk with me. I preferred "pot luck." My new bunkie could be a transfer from the FCI, a transfer from another prison, or a self-surrender. The risk was that the new guy would be an unknown—the devil you didn't know versus the devils you knew. Since the available bunk was the lower one, the odds were that my new bunkie would be an older, white-collar type.

At this point in the day, I was tired from running and was dehydrated. I was going to drink a gallon of lemonade and watch Monday Night Rasslin', specifically *"Raw is War."* One of my dreams was to be pinned by Stacy Keibler. Maybe my dream would come true tonight. Regardless, I would enjoy the solitude of one night without anyone fidgeting in the bunk below

Wrong again!!

From the desk in my cube, I saw the range door open and a tall black man came in. He was carrying a green duffel bag. Lucky me, my new bunkie. I stood up. Mine was the first cube on the left as he entered. He had a splotch on his face below his right eye. It was the size of a fifty-cent piece and was pinkish. He stood about six-four, well-built, and looked mean.

"Oh, no," I thought. "This sucks."

Three other blacks followed – each carrying two duffle bags. My bunkie had to be a transfer from a Medium Security facility.

Pink Splotch spotted the cube number. He didn't look at me. He put down his bag and turned to the others.

"Put the bags against the wall," he said in a deliberate and soft voice. "Let us join hands and give thanks."

My heart sank. A religious nitwit.

All four men joined hands in a circle. They stood silently and blocked the center aisle. They ignored two inmates who wanted to walk past. Seconds passed and then Pink Splotch said, "Oh, Jesus, I thanks You Lord for the good brothers here who helped me move in and made me welcome in this place. I thanks You Lord for the rain tonight that will help bring forth good food that will nourish and strengthen our bodies. I prays Lord that You will use me in a mighty way and allow me to be Your servant and chase the devil on outta this place so that the Camp will be a holy Camp, Lord. Jesus, in Your holy Name I do pray."

The four said, "Amen," and hugged one another.

When the hug-fest ended, the three bag-boys left. Pink Splotch watched them go and then, with all due deliberation, examined the cube as if I were invisible. Not once did he look at me during the next minute and a half.

I stared at Pink Splotch. He was two inches taller than I. He put his hand on the three-inch-thick gray and blue striped mattress. He pulled the chair out from under the desk. He opened the locker closest to the aisle. He looked at his bags as if wondering if his belongings would fit into the limited space available.

He finally looked at me and said solemnly, "I am The Messiah."

"No kidding."

Not a flicker of change came to his face. He didn't blink.

I'd encountered several Messiah's so far in my prison journey. They're all over the place. Go to jail and be saved. The fact is that the Bible seldom makes it home when they leave. After a while, it becomes very old. I decided to mess with this one and see how far I could push it.

"Can you tell me my name?"

He stared at me as if we were having a contest. I fixated on his pink splotch.

An inmate in another cube said, "Oh, my God!"

"Yes?" answered The Messiah.

Nothing fazed him.

I said, "This means I never have to go to confession again. You're omniscient and you're here."

He blinked once. Then he said, "You are wondering about this mark?" He pointed his finger at the pink splotch.

I didn't answer, but, he was right, I was curious.

He instructed me, "It is the mark of the Lamb. I have been chosen and cleansed. I am He. I am the One who is to come. I am the Alpha and the Omega. I am the bright and morning star. I have been ordained since the Beginning to separate the sheep from the wolves and lead the sheep back to my Father, the Good Shepherd..."

He continued rattling away with his apocryphal speech.

My thoughts wandered to Sister Josephine, the Chaplain. Sister Josephine was known as the Nun with a Gun for allegedly breaking up an inmate fight by pulling a Glock-9 from under her habit. She had once told the camp Bible Study group that an inmate at the FCI claimed to be The Messiah, but he had never attended authorized religious services. The Messiah conducted his own bible studies on the exercise yard and had quite a following. The Messiah's failure to obtain administrative approval for his services led to his group being classified as a 'cult' and the group was put on the BOP 'watch list.' After that, The Messiah began preaching in his cell.

"...so it ever shall be, until I come again unto My Father's everlasting kingdom..."

Great, I thought. As his bunkie, I'd be branded a Branch Davidian with my cube the home of a cult. I'd have to stop that branding of myself now.

"...lest there be terror in your hearts..."

A crack snapped down the range. The Messiah flinched. The noise didn't bother me; I had adjusted to the PA system.

Then I heard, "Attention in the Camp. Attention in the Camp. Inmate Dan Holmes. Inmate Dan Holmes. Report to Counselor Hinkel's office."

"Sorry, Pink Splotch," I said so all could hear. "That would be me. But you already knew that, didn't you?" I took off my sneakers and put on my boots.

"Can you tell me what Counselor Hinkel wants?" I asked as I tightened the laces.

I didn't take my eyes off him.

He didn't answer. He was full of shit.

I headed for the door.

39

Prisoner Pickup

I have two brothers. I have almost no relationship with one, who is very religious. With the other, I've had an on again; off again relationship.

The religious brother decided I was the "devil." He testified at my divorce hearing that I was unfit to be a parent. Needless to say, once the Judge heard that, I had no shot at visitation rights while I was in jail.

He and I are done.

You don't break blood.

The rain was light, and I ran down the hill to the Admin Building without seeing anyone. As I stood in front of the office door, C.O. Smith waved me in. Smith was average in height and build, with short hair dyed black. He was a BOP lifer who'd figured out that the way to lap up some overtime gravy was to work the off-shifts. He was approaching retirement; coasting home. Smith was gruff and his only rules were "don't fuck up my counts" and "leave me alone and I'll leave you alone." A liberation, so to speak.

"You Holmes?" he barked.

"Yes, sir."

"Go down below. Front desk at the FCI called for you."

I did an about-face and walked out, the shorter the encounter with Smith, the better.

The rain was still light.

When I walked into the lobby of the FCI, the cop handling Control yapped at me, "You Holmes?"

"Yes, sir," I answered. He was a fat, burly white cop with kinky permed hair. He had a parka over his shirt so I couldn't see his name tag.

"What's your number?"

I rattled off, "Five-three-seven-four-two-oh-six-six."

He matched that against a sheet on his desk.

He lifted a set of keys off the tabletop.

"Here." He held them out. "You got a pick-up at the bus terminal in fifteen minutes." I took the keys. "He's a transfer from Texas." He looked at the paper in front of him. "Name is John Reid."

"John Reid. That's the real life name of the Lone Ranger."

Fat burly cop said nothing.

"You know, the Lone Ranger and his Indian companion Tonto? The masked man with silver bullets? Rights wrongs in the Old We—"

"I don't give a shit, you dumb fuck!" he shouted. "Don't get lost. An' I gotta piss you when you get back."

True that. My bladder took note and started to tighten.

I headed for the van out front and climbed in. It started at the turn of the key. I flipped on the wipers, dialed in the soft rock station, backed out, and started toward the bus station. Before I left the prison grounds, I fastened the seat belt.

I drove straight to the depot. I didn't see any headlights following behind.

The town was raised on coal deposits. The coal had since petered out and the descendents staffed the county's major businesses—the two BOP facilities. The bus terminal was near the center of this derelict burg. At night, in the rain, it resembled more of a homeless shelter than a bus stop. And I was by myself—almost a free man.

I pulled into a space near the main entrance. One car was present. I looked at my watch. I didn't see any buses. In fact, no activity, period.

I waited about fifteen minutes. The humorless hack at the FCI would be expecting me back soon. Where was the bus? Where was John Reid?

I went inside and asked the woman behind the counter when the next bus was due. She was a chunky, bleach-blond, with a cigarette in her hand, and a bruise under her left eye. Without looking at me she said, "In an hour."

That cinched it. I had to go back. I didn't carry any money for a phone call, and if I didn't get back soon, there would be an APB issued with my name on it. Besides, I had enough verifiable information to defend myself if I returned right now.

I thanked the battered blond and left. Just outside, two soaked, straggly haired runts with backpacks approached me. One of the MTV rejects asked, "Hey dude, can we hitch a ride?"

"Sure," I said. "I'm going straight to the Catskill Federal Correctional Institution, then the Prison Camp."

Both kids stood still. The talking one asked, "You a cop?"

"No. I'm an inmate."

The kid tilted his head to one side undaunted and said, "Can you score us some drugs?"

"Go ask the lady inside. She's got lots of pain meds."

Like two addicts, they went through the entrance to ask her.

What was the Real World coming to?

I hopped into the van, headed back and parked in front of the FCI. I hustled through the rain to the Control Desk. I laid the keys in front of fat, burly cop.

"A no-show?"

I said, "No bus. No person. The ticket taker said the next bus was in an hour, so I came right back. Have you heard where he is?"

"No fucking clue and it's not my problem. You ready to piss?"

Upon hearing these words, my guts tightened. I ran six miles two hours ago. I knew that I couldn't piss; my shy bladder was bone dry.

"I'm dehydrated from running this afternoon. I need a big cup."

Fat, burly cop looked at his watch and laughed.

"You gonna piss off Smitty since I'm gonna have to hold you here for the nine-o'clock count. If I don't call him, it's gonna mess up his count, an' you know how he hates that."

Lucky me. No way could I produce bodily fluids fast enough not to mess up Smith's count.

"Well, officer. I'd hope you would call him."

"Don't know right now whether I will or not. Depends."

I didn't ask what it depended on.

It just sucked to be me.

A water fountain was in the corridor and I went to it and started gulping. In five minutes I was bloated. Waddling about, I could feel massive amounts of water sloshing around my stomach. Despite the water at the top of my system, the release valve was a long time away and it usually refused to function if someone was staring at it so they could "certify accuracy" with their very own signature on some federal piss form.

I wondered if The Messiah might direct some divine intervention my way. Maybe I should have been nicer to him.

The phone on the Control Desk rang. Fat, burly cop answered, listened for a breath or two, and said, "He'll be right there. Don't move."

He hung up and looked at me. "You're off the hook for now Holmes," he said. "That was your pick up. He's at the Chestnut Hill bus stop, not Catskill. Said he missed the bus stop and got off in Chestnut Hill. You know where that is?"

"Yes, sir," I grinned. "It's across the street from Trader Rob's Used Cars."

He smiled. "'Best tin in town,'" he said. "'Rob won't rob you.'"

I continued the jingle, "'So come on down. Best deal in town.'"

He ended it with, "'Just a good ol' boy.'"

We laughed at that. I said, "So, John Reid's at Chestnut Hill."

Fat, burly cop sat up in his chair. "He's off to a bad start, all right."

He picked up the keys and tossed them to me. "Better get moving. I don't want this guy wandering around too much, or the locals will pick him up."

"I'm on it," I said.

Outside it was raining harder, and I got wet before I slid into the van. Go pick up the guy and be loaded up to piss when I got back, I told myself. I turned the key, and reversed away from the FCI. I headed for Chestnut Hill, another old, abandoned coal-mining town without the savior of a prison. It was about twenty minutes from Camp. *Rasslin'* started at ten. If everything went right this time, I could watch all of it.

The ride was uneventful. I followed the signs for Trader Rob's. When I saw Trader Rob's neon, there were police cars with lights flashing on the side closest to the bus station. I pulled up next to them and kept the engine running so the wipers would work. Chestnut Hill cops had a man lying face down on the shoulder of the road. He was handcuffed. As I watched, two cops lifted him to his feet, walked him to one of the squad cars, and shoved him into the back seat.

"I think my man just got arrested," I thought to myself. "Great. Now, what do I do?"

I slid out of the van after some of the police cars drove away. I had to sort this out. If that was John Reid, I would have to go back to fat, burly cop empty-handed a second time. The sole police officer remaining was a stocky white guy about six feet tall with a shaved head and a hard expression. He wore his brown uniform proudly. The creases in his pants were crisp and tight. He had a Sam Brown belt full of gear.

In a friendly voice, I asked him, "How are you tonight, officer?"

He looked me over as I stood there in prison khaki and answered with a military snap, "Fine, sir. How may I assist you?"

The name tag on his parka read Skorzeny.

The color must have drained from my face. Was this cop related to our Skorzeny?—the most hated and reviled cop at the FPC and the FCI?

The world could not be that small.

"I'm—I'm looking for—for someone named Reid, John Reid. I'm supposed to transport him to—the Federal Correctional Institution Catskill."

His expression went darker than the surrounding night. His eyes became hard slits as he stood to his full height. He stared at the van.

"That your vehicle?"

"It belongs to the FCI Catskill. I'm the town driver."

His eyes bored into me. He shifted to Red Alert. Several seconds passed. He asked, "Can I see some ID?"

I felt a sudden bladder surge but caught it in time. I'd left my driver's license in my locker when I was paged to the office. All I had was my prison ID card, which I was never without. I reached into my pocket and handed it to him.

The cop held the plastic in the light, examined the photo, and then took a step backward. Tension filled the space between us. He glared at me. A game was being played where he'd become the hunter and I was the prey. His right hand reached for the gun butt on his Sam Brown.

"Turn around, spread your legs, and put your hands on top of the vehicle," he ordered.

The rain fell in hard sheets. It poured down my back and into my boxers. Now, I felt a real rush to pee but held it back. I assumed the position.

The situation was deteriorating. The rain, and the water I drank, was making me have to go. And, goddammit, I was going to miss Rasslin' for sure.

Officer Skorzeny patted me down none too gently. Then he pulled my right hand high behind my back, wrenching my shoulder. I heard the cuffs come out of his Sam Brown and then felt the cold, wet, hard steel snap tight on my wrist. Then my left hand was ratcheted up to my shoulder blades and likewise secured. Skorzeny then stepped back and ordered me to turn around. I'd been momentarily distracted by the process, but now I really felt the urge to pee. I squirmed as I was turned around.

"I have to take a leak," I said.

This seemed to confuse him. Then he looked as if he didn't believe me.

He ordered. "Get in the car."

"I'd let me pee before you put me in your nice clean squad car, officer."

"Get in!" he snapped.

I slid into the back seat as Skorzeny shielded my head from hitting the roof. The ride was bumpy as he used the steering wheel, accelerator, and brake to toss me around the back seat. The two minute ride ended when Skorzeny slammed on the brakes in front of the police station. I hit my head on the metal grill separating the front and back seats.

Skorzeny jumped out and opened the back door. "Get out."

I struggled to lift my feet out of the car and exit. Skorzeny grabbed my cuffs in his hand and guided me through the door to the police station on the side of the Chestnut Hill Municipal Building.

He escorted me to a gray metal desk where another officer, also in a brown uniform, was seated and was reading a newspaper. Our sudden appearance surprised him. This officer had a friendlier face than

Skorzeny.

"Sergeant, this one's an accomplice to the prison escapee we just brung in. This one had a van and was going to drive them both out of state. This one is a Catskill inmate and he done got a Catskill prison ID to prove it. He was drivin' a government van. He done come right up and asked right out for John Reid who we just done arrested. They both escaped from Catskill."

The desk sergeant looked at me.

"Why you twitching like that?"

Skorzeny said, "Says he gotta pee. He's lyin.'"

The sergeant now looked confused.

"Escaped, huh. Tell me about it again, Hans?"

Skorzeny said, "Got a Catskill prison ID on him and he's drivin' a van with no officer. He's wearin' prison khaki. Has the right kinda boots and all. An' Reid had a letter sayin' he was to report to FCI Catskill. They's done escaped! He ain't gotta pee. He shakin' like a leaf 'cause he got caught red handed an' he knows it."

I looked at the desk sergeant as he listened to Skorzeny. It dawned on me that the sergeant detested Hans Skorzeny as much as the Catskill cops and inmates hated his brother or cousin or whoever our Skorzeny was. The sergeant rocked back in his chair as if he knew he was hearing a bullshit story.

The sergeant said to me, "Could you explain what's going on here, or do you want a lawyer?"

I knew I'd have a fool for a client if I represented myself but I accepted my offer of representation anyway.

"My name is Dan Holmes. I'm an inmate at FPC Catskill serving a ninety-six month sentence. I have fourteen months to go. I'm the town driver. I was sent to pick up John Reid. Supposed to be at the Chestnut Hill bus station. I went to get him earlier at the Catskill station, but he was a no-show. I drove back to camp. I had to give a urine sample. I'd run six miles earlier today and I was dehydrated. I started drinking tons of water. While I was drinking all this water, the Control Officer received a call that Reid was at the Chestnut Hill station and he sent me to pick him up. When I got to the station, I saw the police cars and a guy getting cuffed and hauled away. I thought, 'That's my man,' and

I went over to ask this officer about it after everyone else left. And here we are."

The desk sergeant didn't move for a few seconds. Then he leaned forward, arms crossed, elbows on top of the desk and said, "Do you mean to tell me that the Federal Bureau of Prisons has inmates driving vehicles all over Catskill County and Chestnut Hill, and God only knows where else, without an escort, in order to pick up other inmates coming from Texas on a bus? You expect me to believe that?"

"Let me use the bathroom, and I'll give you the number to call to verify it. Otherwise, there is going to be an accident right here."

The desk sergeant said, "Lock 'em up, Hans and see if he pisses."

Skorzeny pushed me down the hall. At the end there was a metal door. We stopped and he pounded on the door with his fist.

Another officer opened the door from the inside. There were four holding cells.

"Put him in number three," said Skorzeny. "Take the cuffs off him."

The new officer, a short, stocky man with a flattop haircut, led me to a cell on the left. He eased me inside and locked the door. Then he took off the cuffs. As soon as I was free, I headed for the toilet.

Relief at last and none too soon. Then the smell of excrement and urine hit me. The cell was a pigsty.

After I finished, I felt more composed.

Skorzeny went back through the door to the desk sergeant. The flattop officer sat at his desk next to the metal door. The only other person in the room was a white man locked up in another cell. He was in his mid-forties and wearing gray sweats.

Like clockwork, I knew I would have to pee every ten minutes and I was glad to be where I was.

"Are you John Reid?"

His hair, a dusty blonde, was matted from the rain. His face was dirty, and he needed a meal and a shower.

He slowly and steadily turned his head and said, "You some kind of fucking prosecutor?"

That sounded like someone long familiar with doing time. He was probably hardened from years in the system; the kind of person who didn't like, and seldom answered, questions.

"Fine," I said.

Then to the officer near the door, I said, "I'd like to give someone the number for Counselor Hinkel at FPC Catskill when you have the chance."

The cop nodded in my direction without looking up.

I turned back to Reid across the room. The grin on his face said he was about to say something worthless or stupid or both.

"You a closet bitch pissing in front of me like that?"

That response told me he was a smacked ass at least. I decided to treat him that way until he proved me wrong. In a slow voice I said, "No. I was trying to drown your mother."

"You fucking jerk-off!" he screamed wildly. "I'm gonna break your fucking face. Nobody talks to me like that. You fucking soft-ass piece of shit."

I had him going now. Time to torque him up—I could be a rabid prison dog, too.

"Why don't you back up your mouth, asshole?" I told him. "Tell the cop you want to be in the same cell with me. I don't give a shit. I'm right here. I saw how bad a dude you were when the cops picked you off the street and slammed you into the squad car. Bad fucking dude that you are."

"Go fuck yourself, homo," was his answer. His voice was calm now.

His anger was an act.

"What's the number you want the Sergeant to call?" asked the man at the desk. I gave him the telephone number and Spooter's name and title. I repeated my name and that of John Reid.

The officer stood up with a piece of paper and walked out of the room.

"Yo, bad dude," I said to Reid cheerfully. "I was sent to pick you up. What happened back there?"

Reid looked at me for a moment and then said, "I'm a transfer from a medium in Texas. I've been on busses for three days. I'm dead tired and starving. I missed the stop where I was supposed to get off. Slept past it. When I realized I was at Chestnut Hill, in the middle of fuckin' nowhere, I decided to get off. Nothin' is movin' so I decide to flag down a cop and get some help. Cop asks me for ID. I tell him I ain't got none. I tell him the truth, that I'm a federal prisoner, busted broke and waiting for a van to take me to the prison. I showed him my transfer letter. Next thing I know, I got every fucking cop in the fucking county drawing down on me and telling me to get on the ground. Some fucking welcome, huh? Welcome to Pennsyl-fucking-tuckey. Next thing I know, I'm locked up here."

He looked around in disgust.

A long silence followed.

John Reid was lying on the metal slab that doubled as a bunk. We talked Rasslin' for a while. I thought Reid was bi-polar.

The metal door banged from the outside, and the inside cop opened it. The desk sergeant came in. He unlocked Reid's cell and then mine. We went outside to see fat, burly cop standing next to Chestnut Hill's Officer Skorzeny. Fat, burly cop still had a parka over his name tag. He looked at me and shook his head in disgust.

"They're mine all right. Did they behave?"

The desk sergeant said, "If they yours, go ahead and take them, but in my twenty-three years as a cop in Chestnut Hill, I have never once locked up two suspects who were already locked up. Get 'em outta here."

I looked at Skorzeny and said, as offhandedly as I could, "What's the first name of Corrections Officer Skorzeny up at Catskill?"

"Adolph."

"What?"

"Adolph."

I still didn't think I'd heard him correctly.

"His first name is Adolph? Like Hitler's Adolph?"

"Yep. All his life he's hated what his Daddy named him. It's on his report cards and his driver's license. But he'd be an asshole whatever his name was."

"A boy named Sue," I said.

"What's that?"

"It's the biggest kept secret in camp."

Reid and I walked out of the room. As we passed, fat, burly cop said, "Ready to piss for me when we get back, Holmes?"

"Not unless you taped Rasslin' for me."

I realized I was in a good mood. I knew Corrections Officer Skorzeny's first name was Adolph. Imagine that! I'd put my idle mind to work and come up with a way to use that information during some of my down time. I'd figure out how to humiliate Skorzeny to the max, give him a little payback for all the pain he'd caused to inmates and cops alike. Maybe ruin his career. Payback is a mo-fo.

40

The Letter

You knew a guy was going home, "getting short" as we said, when his routine changed. You could see him get edgy and moody. Suddenly, the reality of the moment overtook him, and most realized that they didn't do time; they wasted it.

I'd been at Camp Catskill for the better part of eighty-nine months when I received the letter.

I had about seven months to go. A mere pittance.

Camp Catskill had changed for the worst since my arrival. Plant and equipment were older and seedier. Deferred maintenance was a mounting problem. Since the inmates were assigned to work details, the quality of the labor was inconsistent, at best. Inmates were more attuned to going through the motions than being directed toward a goal. Replacement parts never arrived. The pumps in the Power House were on their last legs. The only item that shined as bright as when I arrived was the razor wire around the medium security facility.

As the brothers said, "The most majorest change" was that the predominately white collar, older, and quieter inmates became an increasingly lower percentage of the overall population.

The current crop of incoming inmates was younger and had drug-related résumés. They had a hip-hop outlook, and were bling-bling festooned.

Out of the four hundred inmates now in the camp, there only were a handful of men I could converse with. When they cycled out without being replaced, I grew more lonely and isolated.

I made a point to stay away from the newer inmates. My hiding places were the Power House and the Law Library.

On the street, the Law Library was the lawyer's sanctuary. A retreat away from the telephones where research was conducted in solitude among rows and rows of neatly arranged leather-bound books. I'm told computers are critical to effective research these days, but in my day, research meant books. Every case was filed currently. Copiers and computers were well maintained and operational. Clean. Neat.

The Law Library at Camp Catskill was part of the overall deferred maintenance program and a Program Statement, issued by the BOP, mandating allowable research materials.

Any non-approved items were contraband and were removed during the quarterly inventory review by the Educational Supervisor. This would include any information mailed by an attorney to an inmate that the inmate subsequently donated to the Law Library.

Generally speaking, the only reference materials available at Camp Catskill were the decisions by the Courts of Appeal for the various circuits, and these books were filed two to three months late.

Inmates loved to file appeals. There were five manual typewriters and one copier to assist them. The copier deducted ten cents per copy from the commissary card or 50 minutes of inmate pay at twelve cents an hour. Usually a few typewriters, and almost always the copier, were broken. Most inmates asserted that this was a conspiracy by the BOP to deny inmates access to the courts. Actually, the inmates broke the equipment trying to fix it. When the ribbons became faint, that was the cue to pound the keys as hard as possible. Preparing and filing a motion with a manual typewriter was a challenge.

I'd filed a motion with the court called a "2255." The thrust of my 2255 was that errors had occurred at sentencing and I was denied the effective assistance of counsel, as guaranteed by the Constitution. More specifically, I asserted that the four level enhancement for being a 'leader/organizer' of the scheme was applied improperly because all my crimes had been committed as a sole-proprietor. There was no leader/organizer. This enhancement increased my sentence by four years.

After I filed the motion I waited for the Sentencing Judge to respond; I sat in the Law Library and read cases that touched on the issues I'd raised in my 2255. To kill time, and help other guys, I prepared motions for them.

In truth, most inmate appellate motions are judicially worthless.

They overload an already overburdened system. But inmates had rights—and more importantly, inmates needed "hope," especially if he was "doing a big number" like I was.

I was finishing up in the Food Circus when Spooter called my name over the loudspeaker. It was raining heavily outside. We had a few laughs when a couple of new guys fell in the mud running down the hill.

I'd finished a forgettable dinner, eating only as much as necessary to survive until the next meal. The meals had been running together for a long time by then.

Spooter's page gave me a shiver. The request could range from being asked to speak at some school to going to the bucket because someone had snitched me out. I dumped my trash into the can, stacked the tray, plates and cutlery in the appropriate places on the kitchen window and left the chow hall. Institutionalized, I went to see the good Counselor.

He was sitting behind his desk in the open area of the Admin Office eating his dinner, a baloney sandwich on white bread and a bruised apple. I stood at the door and awaited his nod to enter.

He lifted his head and waived me in.

"Hole-meese," he said. "You gots a legal."

This was unexpected. I knew that I had that 2255 going, but I figured that Judge Smert had forgotten me.

I didn't have anything else in the works. What could it be?

Spooter opened a green, hard-covered book to a page where an envelope stuck out.

According to the return address, The Honorable Judge Emil N. Smert was sending me some love.

This was his formal denial.

I was emotionally unaffected. I wasn't angry. I wasn't disappointed. I only had seven months to go. After all I had endured, why let a little denial upset me?

I signed the book where Spooter had scrawled an "X." I don't know what Spooter thought when I said, "Thank you, Counselor. Good night."

In the hallway, I looked at the thin envelope in my hand. A denial didn't take more than one page. But neither did "Motion Granted." I felt a spark of hope.

I'd done seven and a half years and I'd had enough.

I had settled in and was comfortable.

I was beaten and had surrendered.

I couldn't fight any more.

But…

I wanted out—

Wanted to go home—

Bad—

Real bad—

I stood there holding the envelope in my fingers. The surroundings faded away and it became my central focus. The baby-blue walls and inmates walking past disappeared. The envelope was all I could see.

It was bad news.

But maybe not.

My name had been printed by a computer that addressed envelopes automatically after the letters had been signed. I didn't know that for sure. Technology had advanced. It was a new world out there; one I didn't know.

The envelope could open the door back to that world.

All the ambient inmate noise was gone. I stood in the main concourse outside Spooter's office surrounded by the barber shop, the craft room, the music room, the cardio-room and the commissary. Yet, I was all alone with that envelope. Just me and a stupid envelope from my sentencing judge from eighty-nine months ago.

Had to be a denial. The Judge had been very mad at me and rightfully so. No way was he granting me relief.

I'd spent countless hours doing research—reading case after case. I had filled more legal pads than anyone in camp. I'd read every case in every book back to 1975, the earliest present in the Law Library. I knew the issues of my case better than the Honorable Judge Emil N. Smert, the prosecutor and my criminal defense attorney, Steve.

And I believed I was right. I was right.

I'd worked hard to craft a document that was short, easy to read and easy to understand.

I filed it, and I meant for it to work.

The motion claimed that my attorney had not properly argued against the enhancement and that the enhancement had no merit.

Besides, filing the Motion was my little way of saying, "Take that!" to them. I was a warrior and that's what warriors do. Warriors fight. I believed in my position, and I argued for my freedom; my life. The passion I had for it as I stood there was returning.

I opened it.

My fingers were shaking along with my hands, arms, and shoulders.

I read the greeting. One page. A cover letter. I skipped to the second page and the caption of the document.

Motion Granted!

I read it again. The words didn't change.

I flipped back to the cover letter.

The court had granted an evidentiary hearing on my motion to be heard on the fifteenth of August.

The Ides of August.

Tears welled up in my eyes. I bit my lip. A drop fell onto the cover letter. I thought of my children whom I hadn't seen in eighty-nine months. And my Mom. I had to call my Mom right away.

I WAS GOING HOME!

My motion had been granted. My evidentiary hearing had been scheduled! I was going back to the District Court to renew the fight. I was leaving this fucking hellhole.

I leaned against the wall. Legs quivering.

I had to calm down. I didn't want to blow this. My mind raced from thought to thought making plans. I had to figure out how I'd be transported to court. Could I get a furlough? Who would represent me? Was Johnny Cochran available? I'd be entitled to have new counsel assigned to me since the right to counsel attaches when the motion is granted.

Jesus loves me!

I floated to the Law Library. I'd kill some time until the news spread. And news like this, rarely received, would spread quickly.

Four inmates sat around the conference table. Two Hispanics

played checkers, hurling chicken scratch at each other. There may have been a checker moved out of turn, or one that had lost its proper square. From the intensity of the voices, it seemed like a stabbing was close at hand.

I knew the two other guys, both named Steve. One was my current bunkie, Steve "Big Dog" Golden. Big Dog was fifty-two and from Philadelphia. He was six-two and weighed three-eighty, hence the moniker and his need for a lower bunk on the range. Big Dog was a fixture with Dr. Rushdi. He claimed to have almost every illness or disease known to man. He'd been an accountant who'd had a Series 7 license that enabled him to invest client funds. Unfortunately, Steve invested these funds in games of chance favoring the casinos in Atlantic City. And, like many other investors, Steve needed copious amounts of alcohol, white powder, and female companionship to assist in his final investment decisions. The result was a three-year prison sentence. The judge advised Big Dog to drop the gambling habit while in prison. Steve refused to play cards or otherwise gamble while incarcerated, but his blood pressure would boil when someone told him that investing in the stock market was no more than gambling on public companies. Big Dog studied the stock market and charted trends. That enabled him to have a new stock market tip every day.

The other inmate was a smallish, paranoid imp named Steve Scanlon. He was in his mid-fifties and was a newspaper freak. He read every word of five newspapers and then stored them in his locker and in boxes under the bed until his cube became a fire hazard. He was serving a thirty-month sentence for growing marijuana in his apartment. He argued that the weed was a medicinal necessity since smoking it eased his headaches. The Judge, unfortunately, didn't agree.

Big Dog and Steve were arguing. This bastion of intelligencia known as the Law Library was supposed to be quiet. The two Hispanics and the two Steves were growling at each other at near riot decibels.

"The mob hated Kennedy," Big Dog was screaming. "They wanted him dead because he was letting the Department of Justice and his brother Robert investigate their Chicago and New York operations. Gianconna hated his guts. That's who killed Kennedy."

"No, no, no, no. I researched this. The Russians and Cubans did it. They had three assassins. One behind the grassy knoll, one under the manhole cover, and Oswald in the School Book Depository."

Big Dog smiled at me.

"Now, tell Dan here. What publication of national reputation did you work for?"

Scanlon looked at me with the humble expression used when someone stands before a judge.

"I worked for an international daily that adheres to the same journalistic standards as *The Washington Post* and *The New York Times*."

"That's not informative," I noted.

Big Dog said, "Is this the outfit where you reported on the front page that aliens from Mars had landed in San Francisco?"

Scanlon snapped his head around at Big Dog.

"I had an excellent source on *that* story. He claimed he was an eyewitness. How was I supposed to know he was tripping LSD?" He put both elbows on the table and rested his chin on his fingers. "I stand by what I wrote. The only problem was the source was wrong."

Big Dog was all smiles. He'd out-mentaled Scanlon. Still, I needed to know the international daily where Scanlon worked.

"What paper did you write for?"

Counselor Hinkel appeared in the doorway. He looked at the five of us around the table.

He put his finger to his lips. "Shush!"

A chorus of weak, "Yes, sirs," followed.

Hinkel left.

"What paper did you work for?" Big Dog pressed.

Scanlon didn't want to answer. He slinked down into his seat.

"Star Magazine."

There's a jailhouse rule that you stomp on someone after you knock him down. Big Dog didn't miss this opportunity. In an all-out laugh he said, "We have a world class journalist sitting right here who reported that Martians were landing in San Francisco, and we're supposed to believe him when he tells us that the Cubans and the Russians killed JFK?"

Then a shadow darkened the door's threshold; it was Luka

Slobodo who looked at those present and limped in with a purpose.

"Dan," he said. "Muscle—" He thought for a second, and then tried again. "Muscle—Tuff, whatever it is."

"Thanks, Luka," I said back to him.

Big Dog didn't like secrets he didn't know.

"What's going on?" he asked.

"Dan here is going to be released tomorrow. Spooter told me. The 2236 I filed on his behalf has been granted without an evidentiary hearing."

Typical Luka. Taking credit for anything positive that happened and incorrect about the facts.

Big Dog smiled at me.

"Bunkie, you're leaving me! Why didn't you say so?"

"I came here to do that," I said. "But you two were engrossed in the who killed Kennedy debate; these other guys were exploring the mysteries of how checkers work, and I didn't want to break up the brainpower.

"I'm not being released. I have an evidentiary hearing on my '2255' scheduled for the fifteenth of August."

One of the checker players said, "You prepare me? I go."

I had ceased my practice of law about ten minutes ago, but before I could tell him, Slobodo said, "First, let's discuss my retainer. I take commissary or you can clean my cube and make my bed."

Just then, unfortunately for us, Hiram Custardi waddled in. He was built like an overstuffed sack of lard. Not many inmates liked this bald asshole, including me.

He'd once owned a large construction company. He was doing fourteen years for a huge real estate Ponzi scheme that had rocked the State of Maine to its core and effectively bankrupted the state teachers' pension fund. The total loss, which was an estimate due to its size, was in the upper several-hundred million dollar range.

Custardi started his professional career as a franchise salesman for McDonalds. Soon thereafter, with a partner, he started a small construction company. Over time, due to his ability to "sell and attract" investors, the company expanded. As it grew, so did his personal fortune. Near the end, his possessions included a castle in England; a yacht and a professional hockey team. Custardi was arrogant, egotistical and opinionated—not characteristics that endeared him to others. He wanted to go home like everyone else, but, in typical Custardi fashion, he was not pleased when another guy caught a break. Ostensibly, Custardi came in to huddle with Big Dog and learn his stock market pick of the day.

Big Dog said happily, "Hey, Custardi. My bunkie here's going back to court."

Custardi smiled at me. Through that oily grin of his he said, "A new case? Can I use it? What is it?"

His presence filled the room like a bad fart. He was so self-centered no one could stand him.

"I've been granted an evidentiary hearing for my 2255."

"Those things never work. There's no sense in going back and wasting your time."

Realizing there was nothing that could reduce his sentence, he slimed like a snail into a chair next to Big Dog.

"You got a favorite today, Big Dog?"

"I got nuthin' for you today." With that, Custardi rolled out of the room. He left silence behind him.

Big Dog said, "Why'd he say that? Why can't that slimy dick be happy for someone else?"

"Because he's an asshole," I said. No one disagreed.

The mood brightened when Seamus McMahon walked in.

Seamus was a seventyish patriarch of the Irish mob in New York. Simply put, he was the boss of bosses for the Northeast. He was doing ten years for his participation in a drug conspiracy. The DEA offered to drop the case if Seamus wore a wire and set up one of his cohorts. Seamus responded by telling the DEA agent to "go fuck yourself." He had the respect of everyone in Camp regardless of race, color, or creed, and he deserved it. He was a true gentleman, always willing to help out.

Big Dog said, "Hey, Seamus. You hear the news? Your lawyer here got an evidentiary hearing. He could be going home."

A huge smile broke across Seamus's face.

"Did you call your Mother? Give her the news?" he asked with that heavy Irish New York accent.

"In a few minutes I will."

I wanted to bask in the warmth radiating from Seamus and Big Dog.

Big Dog returned to his argument, "Hey, Seamus. Who killed Kennedy? The JFK Kennedy, not Robert. I say it was the Chicago mob and Scanlon here says it was Russians and Cubans. Who's right?"

A moment of reflective silence followed. "You're both wrong." He tapped his forefinger to his lips a few times. "What can I say?"

Big Dog and I laughed out loud. There was no way Seamus was providing that information, even if he knew.

Seamus started to leave when Scanlon said, "Eh, excuse me, Mr. McMahon. Hiram Custardi was just in here, and he said it's a waste of time for Dan to go back to court. What do you think?"

Seamus turned back and faced Scanlon. He raised the pointer finger of his right hand and said, "Danny boy here is Irish. There's two things Irish types like us do. We don't trust Jews, and we don't trust Day-go's. Custardi is the worst type of both of those. Trust me when I tell you, Danny may lose the war, but he'll take a lot of dem sons-a-bitches down with him. He'll make us all proud, won't you, Danny?"

Seamus was smiling.

The Frank Sinatra line in *Von Ryan's Express* came to mind.

"'If only one of us gets out, it's a victory.'" I smiled. "I'll never give up, Seamus. Never. I'll make you proud."

"That's my boy," Seamus smiled. "Custardi's a cunt."

He left. There was a silence while we picked up our thoughts and remembered what we'd been talking about.

Scanlon said to no one in particular, "Why don't the Irish like Jews?"

Big Dog said, "Because you're a fucking idiot, that's why!

I rapped the top of the table twice, stood up and started out to the phone banks to get in line to call Mom.

Big Dog and Scanlon resumed their Kennedy debate. Slobodo was negotiating a weekly allotment of sodas from the Hispanic for legal misrepresentation. The other Hispanic was yapping about two checkers being on the same square.

Everything had returned to lunacy; meaning, pretty much normal.

I reached the hallway outside as the two Steve's raised their voices at each other.

But I could ignore it…

It didn't bother me……

I didn't hear a thing…

I was going *home!*

41

Leaving

The next few days were a blur. I was a whirlwind driven by the prospect of freedom. I can tell you one lesson I learned from incarceration: Freedom is Paramount.

And I had a lot of things to do. I had to pack, groom a replacement for my job at the Power House, find a new Bunkie for Big Dog, sharpen my rusty courtroom skills, return all the property that had been issued to me by the BOP, and most important of all, request a furlough transfer.

The furlough transfer was critical. With it I could have Mom and Emily pick me up and drive me to the Courthouse, much preferable to being cuffed, shackled, and transported there on the BOP bus.

Truth be known, I'd never been escorted anywhere via "diesel therapy" but I'd heard the horror stories—long days riding around whatever circuit they were traversing and longer nights in holding cells hoping not to be stabbed by some lunatic inmate or bitten by bed bugs. The three square meals a day were bologna and cheese on white bread, usually stale since they were prepared well in advance.

And since I knew the Lord helped those who helped themselves, I begged the cops at the Power House to back my play for a furlough transfer. The request would be processed through Ms. Fowler, the Acting Camp Administrator. I pulled every lever I could to let Ms. Fowler know how important this was to me, and I prayed that she would grant me the furlough.

I was paged to her office.

She informed me that everyone had signed off on my request.

She opened a folder that lay on her desk. It had a stack of forms. She signed them, one by one, telling me what each one was. When she finished, she warned me that if I strayed from the written, predetermined route in any way, manner, shape, or form, then, "Forty-eight hours is all the time you have. It's generous. More than inmates get for a funeral. If you stray in any way, don't get caught. That's all I can say, Holmes." She shook her head slowly and repeated, "Don't get caught."

She handed me a folder containing my set of copies with original signatures of the approved furlough. I examined it carefully, making sure of its terms. The Warden, the Associate Warden, the Captain, and Ms. Fowler had all signed it. If I deviated in any way from the written schedule, they'd all be waiting for me when the U.S. Marshals brought me back.

If that happened, it would truly suck to be me. I thanked her for all her assistance.

She closed the folder on her desk.

"Don't thank me yet."

Oh God, what now—

"I don't appreciate that you had the Power House hacks push me for this furlough."

She scowled.

I stood there for what I thought was a long time. Finally, I said, "Yes, ma'am. This is end-of-the-world important to me. I didn't want to leave anything to chance. "

"Shut up."

She looked around her office and then fixed on me again. In a slow measured voice with thin slit eyes she said, "I'm going to leave a note for the Duty Office to wake you up at one o'clock tomorrow morning and have you come over here, take all the furniture out of this office, and then strip and wax this floor by hand." She leaned back in her chair and smiled. "When I get in at seven-thirty, it had better have the shine of a mirror. You got that, Holmes?"

"Yes, Ms. Fowler." I nodded. "I have that loud and clear."

"You may go."

I left.

In prison, pay-backs from staff are a mo-fo.

At one o'clock the bunk shook. A flashlight burned into my blinking eyes. Big Dog on the lower bunk mumbled, "What the fuck?"

This was my wake up call from the Range Cop.

"I'm up," I told him. I hopped down on the cold linoleum for him as proof. "It's okay Big Dog. This is for me." The Range Cop made a note on his clipboard and walked off.

I dressed and shuffled over the wet grass to the Admin Building. The Duty Officer saw me coming down the corridor. I didn't know him. He said, "Do you know where all the stuff is?"

"Yeah," I replied.

He opened the main door to the Admin Office from the corridor and then opened Ms. Fowler's office. He looked at his watch and noted the time on his clipboard. Then he disappeared to wherever the Duty Officer goes in the Admin Building at night.

I moved all the furniture out of Ms. Fowler's office into the common area with a hand truck, careful not to scratch the floor. I stacked most of it in a line between Ms. Fowler's office and the door to the corridor so that it would be hard for the Duty Officer to see me without coming inside and looking around the stacks. A small act of protest.

I dropped to my hands and knees and rubbed on the stripper. While the liquid soaked in and eradicated the built-up wax, I went to the storage closet, rolled out, and fired up the ancient stripper/buffing machine. By two-thirty the floor was cleaned, stripped, and mopped. I had to wait for the floor to dry. Instead of going to the soda and candy machines for a snack, I sat in the common area and watched the wet spots evaporate.

One coat of wax later and I'd be back in bed.

The Duty Officer walked around the makeshift barrier, held up a sheet of notebook paper for me to see and said, "Ms. Fowler says here she wants her floor done special. She wants five coats of wax, an' she wants you to wait an hour after the last coat before you buff it out so it look real good when she get here." He lowered the paper he'd been waving in front of me. "You got that?"

I should have expected as much. As it was, I was surviving on the adrenalin of freedom. Lack of sleep did not matter to me at this point. Freedom was my motivator.

"Yes, sir. I got that. Five coats of wax, let the last one dry for an hour, then buff it all out 'smoof as silk.' Then put the furniture back."

His mission accomplished, he turned and walked out of the office.

I knelt down and started applying the first coat. Before long my knees and back ached from all the leaning, and the back and forth movement. Then my hands got sore. About application three, my elbows hurt. Floor wax elbows, a new medical phenomena. Then it was my ankles. She'd timed this so that it would take me all night to do it.

She'd probably told the cop to see how long it took me to do one complete strip, clean, wax and buff job, and then to make me do it enough more times so that when I was done it was breakfast. If I'd dawdled, it might have been just two times. If I'd done it as fast as Waterbug would have, I'd have had to do eight.

So that was two people together in the same plan equals a Conspiracy under RICO rules. Anyway...

By six-thirty or so the floor glowed. I buffed the corners by hand so they matched what the machine had done everywhere else. I was stiff and I had a headache at the top of my spine near the back of my head. The floor looked better than the day construction was finished. It looked, I don't know, maybe a quarter inch to a half inch thicker, like some sort of shiny mat had been placed on it. God damn it looked good.

I put her furniture back, careful not to scratch the finish. I double checked to be sure there were no foot marks or scratches. I closed the door to her office and policed the common area. I put all the equipment and materials back where they belonged. All was well to my eye, a masterpiece of a floor shine second to none.

Breakfast was being served to the inmates now, but I decided to guard the common area so that nobody would walk into Ms. Fowler's office before she did. I didn't even leave to wash my hands or face. I wanted her to see the caked wax on my hands and fingernails.

At seven twenty-five Ms. Fowler marched through the main door. "How's it look, Holmes?"

"You'll be proud, Ms. Fowler. Really. It's the best wax job I've ever done at Camp Catskill."

Truth be told, it was the first wax job I'd ever done.

She opened the door to her office, turned on the light, and went behind the desk examining the floor. She surveyed the corners as she circled her desk. A drill sergeant's piercing eye on each tile.

"Hmm," she commented.

She stepped out from behind the desk and walked toward me. She stopped about three feet away, put out her heel, and dragged it back to her other toe leaving a ten inch slick of black shoe polish.

As I watched her heel drag across the floor, every bone in my aching body screamed, "No!"

"You call this clean, Holmes?"

I could not believe she'd done that right in front of me.

"Is this the quality of your work? No wonder you stole all that money if your wax job resembles your legal morals."

Now was not the time to panic.

"Don't tell me you can't see this mark?"

My body tightened. I prepared myself to absorb another beating. "Well, I'll be damned, Ms. Fowler. How could I have missed that?"

I got down on my hands and knees. I followed the mark from one end to the other. From one side I stole a glance at her newly polished shoes gleaming in the fluorescent light. I could smell shoe polish.

She was going to make me wax the floor again the next morning. No doubt about it.

"Well, flip me a fish," I quipped. "I might have to have my glasses checked."

I had to be careful. She could be setting me up. If I overreacted, she would cite me for insubordination and rip up my furlough transfer as punishment.

"I can't have this Holmes."

Her voice didn't have the meanness she'd probably rehearsed at home that morning.

"This is not acceptable. Not at all."

I stood up to speak.

"I couldn't agree more, Ms. Fowler. I can scour out that spot for you right now. Do you want to go get some coffee in the Chow Hall while I do it? I can wax out that spot in no time at all."

This was my best Uncle Tom.

"Or I could come back and do the whole thing over again starting at one o'clock tomorrow morning. Which do you prefer?"

I thought this was my best shot at her heart strings.

"Come back tomorrow and do it again."

Nope. She'd told the staff what she was going to do to me and she had to do it or lose face. Bureaucratic fascism.

"Try not to miss anything next time."

She looked around at the rest of the floor.

She'd be showing off that shoe polish streak and telling the story to everyone who came by the Admin Office all day.

"Mr. Dunne will be the cop again tomorrow. He's already told me he saw you apply the five coats as instructed. Be sure he tells me the same thing tomorrow."

"Yes, ma'am."

"You may go, Holmes."

"Yes, ma'am."

So I did it all again, but with rubber gloves and towels wrapped around my knees, and some aspirin I bummed from the always sick Big Dog.

When she arrived the next morning, I was standing guard in the common area. "Come into my office," she ordered. We walked inside.

She went behind her desk, turned to me, and in a soft, resigned voice said, "Get out of here Holmes."

The next week blew by in a daze. I'd packed and arranged for Mom and Emily to pick me up by eight o'clock. Just to be sure, I told Mom I wanted to see Emily's car in the parking lot not later than seven-forty-five. Another inmate, Doc Levin, was being transferred to a halfway house the same day, and I wanted to be out of R&D before him or I'd have to wait for Doc to be checked out and, given the pace at which Doc moved, that would take some time. I knew Doc from Friday nights at synagogue services. When Doc heard we were being transferred on the same date, he told me that his wife, brother, and son were going to pick him up. Given that Doc weighed about three hundred and eighty pounds and moved at a snail's pace, that sounded reasonable. He would need three people to help him into an SUV.

Anyway, the big day arrived at the speed of Christmas for an eight year-old. I hadn't told anyone that I was leaving but everyone knew. Somehow they always did.

I could not sleep until the last two hours. Some second, or more times through, guys had told me they had not been able to sleep for the last three nights prior to leaving. Such is the level of anxiety when one is released back into society. I wasn't that bad. But I did fidget, and fidget, and fidget.

When I did wake up, Big Dog was gone. Bunkie etiquette. He knew I'd be an emotional mess. He was right. My mind was jumping from the second I woke up.

I ate breakfast and then showered. As I started to dress in my new clothes an eerie sensation gripped me. I hadn't felt this uncomfortable in over two thousand, two hundred and eighty days. It had been that long since I dressed in other than prison khaki, but today, I was to be wearing the freedom tasting sweat suit and white socks that I had bought from the Commissary with the funds I saved from my twelve cents an hour job.

Putting on the newly purchased items was the first step in my self-reclamation. I stared at the sweat suit and slowly but surely fear began to envelop me. Then panic. It was as if I were swimming in the ocean and I saw a shark circling me. My heart pounded in my chest as the realization hit me. I had nowhere to go. If, no I mean, when I won my freedom today, I'd be released back into society with all my worldly possessions that now sat in front of me on top of my locker. I had no place to go. I had no clothes. I had no money. I had no job. And I had no phone. For God's sake, I didn't have a toothbrush to call my own. For the past seven years, everything I "owned" was the property of the Bureau of Prisons and I had turned all of it in. That left me with nothing except the fear of the unknown. How was I going to provide for myself? The only skill I had was as a lawyer and I'd been disbarred long ago. And I wasn't coordinated enough to learn a blue-collar skill now. I'd win my freedom today and be homeless.

The more I pondered my dilemma, the more I didn't want to leave. Fuck the courtroom appearance. I looked around and saw the sum total of my friends. Moon (a bald guy), Lefty (a guy missing three fingers on his right hand) and Shorty (a seven foot gentle giant)–I had formed relationships with them and they were the closest people to me in the world. I always knew that I would have to leave someday but I wasn't ready today. I struggled to calm myself, reclaim my composure. I looked from bunk to bunk and realized that these guys were my "family" and that I was closer to them than to anyone else in the world.

I stood there for a long time. I had to snap out of this jailhouse funk and reclaim my Warrior thoughts. Searching for a safe, comfortable "mental hideout" away from the terror rising in me, I started repeating the opening lines of my Courtroom speech.

That helped.

Soon I convinced myself that today was the start of a trip back to a better time when I honestly represented clients in criminal matters.

Piling good thought on top of good thought, I assured myself that I had the answers to all the questions the Judge would ask me. I had responses prepared that would addle and befuddle any witnesses brought against me. I had a closing argument that would leave the Honorable District Court no alternative but to order the execution of my immediate release. My performance would be comparable to being the winning quarterback at the Super Bowl. Damn! This was my Super Bowl. And I was ready.

Finally calm again, I closed the file that held my legal papers and put it in my shoebox with my other possessions. I had donated my radio, earphones, cooking utensils, and clothes to inmates who came in and didn't have the money to buy them.

Going down the hill I saw two cars in the Visitors Parking lot. None of the people standing around the cars were Mom or Emily. They looked like Doc Levin's body lifters. Mom and Emily had to be in the Visitors Room.

As I crossed toward the Admin Building a few inmates called out, "Good luck!" "You go, Holmes!" and things like that. I gave them a wave and a giddy smile. God this felt good. Other inmates looked at me with a jealous hatred. Generally inmates aren't supposed to "hate on" each other, but some guys can't get past themselves. I'd seen this before when other guys had left camp. I guess that's part of the reason those guys were here.

I hustled into the Admin Building. I was tempted to run down to the Visiting Room to make sure Mom and Emily were there, but decided to check out at R&D first.

The hacks at R&D were busy reading the newspaper. Their function was to ensure that I didn't take any Government issued property with me. Today, it appeared that their job was secondary to catching up on local news. While I waited for them to notice me, I looked down the concourse toward the black metal entrance door. Three people walked in and knocked at the Admin Office. They resembled Doc Levin, big and beefy.

No sign of Mom and Emily.

One of the cops put down his paper. "You Holmes?"

"Yes, sir. I am. Checking out to the Real World."

"What's your number?"

I rattled it off.

He handed me a form.

"You know where you're going?'

"Yeah."

"Your ride here, yet?"

"The car's in the lot," I lied. If I got outside and there was no one there, I'd walk.

"Got your shit."

I handed over my bedroll, pillow, sheets, towels and a wash cloth.

He checked off each item on a list.

"Here's your personal shit."

He produced a manila envelope, ripped off one end, and dumped a contact lens case and my false front tooth onto his desk. These were the items confiscated on my initial visit through R&D. To be honest, I'd forgotten about them.

I picked them up and dropped them into the shoebox.

"According to BOP records, you have twenty seven dollars and thirteen cents left in your Commissary account. Here it is." He produced an envelope and counted it out.

"You okay with that, inmate?"

"Yes, sir. So far so good."

"Okay, then. Sign here."

He handed me a clipboard. I signed the bottom line.

"Good luck."

I grabbed my shoebox and walked out of R&D. This was the last stop on my journey through the BOP. The next stop was Freedom. I was nearly waltzing down the main corridor in utter and complete elation. The distance to the front door was about a hundred feet. I felt I could cover the distance in a few giant leaps. I wouldn't even touch the linoleum. I'd fill my lungs and float effortlessly toward the black metal door. My self esteem, long ago deflated and dormant, was soaring. Until I met Mom and Emily, I'd let it fly. This was going to be "my day" where everything was going to lead to release. After seven years in jail, and in the face of everything it represented, a little self-confidence was a good thing. I'd walked this hallway over a thousand times since I began my sentence and I never felt as joyfully happy as I did at this moment.

At the Visitors Room I glanced through the glass in the door. The three people I'd seen earlier were there sitting on metal chairs. They looked at me with eyes like patients in a cancer doctor's waiting room.

Mom and Emily must be waiting outside.

I turned toward the Admin Office door and saw Spooter sitting behind the desk fighting the computer keyboard as only he could. I'd never see him again. What a complex, twisted fellow he was. How could the same person have such a violent temper, be capable of throwing whatever he could put his hands on in one instant, and in the next one set up a program to help children stay out of trouble? I silently mouthed, "Thanks," to him for letting me participate in his speaking program. I'll never know if I ever helped a single child, but that program gave me a sense of achievement and proved I could contribute to society in a positive manner after all my crimes. It had been a rare pleasure during my incarceration.

But that was all over. I had a new life. I pushed open the squealing black metal door for the last time. Standing there I slowly looked around and remembered those first moments after I was dropped off. Miz Buckles blowing cigarette smoke into my face, Slobodo introducing me to Spooter, the Italians waiting to welcome a mob figure, and Frankie Bananas. Seven years of memories and faces flashed before my eyes.

Admin maintained two lists of inmates. One list contained the names of inmates in the order of their release date. Inmates call it the "Next Guy To Go" list. An inmate always knows who is next to go and how many have to go before him. The second contains the names of inmates who had been at Camp the longest.

I was at the top of both lists. I was the next to go and had been at Camp Catskill longer than anyone else currently here. I was the last guy left out of all the guys who were here when I arrived.

Tears crept to my eyes. This never should have happened. I gulped a huge lungful of air and exhaled saying, "You can cross me off both those fucking lists." All the crimes I had done in my life. Cross them off as if they didn't happen. Sadly, it doesn't work that way.

Shoebox in hand, I stood on the concrete stoop. I looked at the two vehicles in the Visitors parking lot. Then, I surveyed the Staff area. None of those cars were Emily's Mercury Sable.

My breath caught in my throat along with a sinking stomach.

I'd spoken to Mom repeatedly about the time and the date. The weather was perfect, so that wasn't the holdup. Had something happened on the trip? Where could they be?

I'd walk to the courthouse from here if I had to.

Then Ms. Fowler's words about not deviating from the schedule popped into my head.

I couldn't walk anyway. If Mom and Emily didn't appear soon, I'd have to go back inside and tell Spooter my ride hadn't showed.

I didn't want to do that.

I walked toward the two vehicles in the Visitors lot. One was a beat up rusty van and the other looked like some big government SUV. I didn't recognize their make and model. There would be a lot of non-recognition I would have to deal with after seven years.

Then a car door opened and someone slid out of the rear passenger side door.

I hadn't seen anyone in either car. My vision had deteriorated to the point where everything was "blurry" at best.

Another face popped up in the rear window and stared at me.

Damn it. Where were Mom and Emily?

The person walking toward me and the face in the back seat of the car, could they be the U.S. Marshals sent to arrest me on some as of yet unknown charge. I'd seen it a few times in my seven year hiatus here. Just when an inmate thinks he has a shot at freedom, it is snatched from him in the form of another charge.

The guy from the SUV was walking purposefully toward me. I

stood still. Then a head popped up at the steering wheel.

These were U.S. Marshals here to Rendition me when I walked out the door.

The back door of the SUV opened and a girl climbed out. The first guy was about twenty feet away. He was coming at me. I could not move.

All of the emotions that flowed from the original Indictment rushed upon me like waves upon the sand. I closed my eyes and visualized the headlines in the newspaper. "Con Indicted for Additional Crimes." What chance would I have? A con caught committing another crime while incarcerated. I'd be road kill.

I decided I would surrender without incident.

"Hey, Dad!"

I opened my eyes.

This was from the guy standing ten feet away. I looked right at him.

Could this be Joe?

Joe was in Arizona. He and his brother and sister were in midterm exams all week. Mom told me that.

Oh my God. This *is* Joe!

The shoebox fell to the asphalt and spilled it meager contents. Joe ran into me and wrapped his arms and legs around me, all one hundred and twenty pounds of spindly kid that he was.

I heaved him up in the air.

"Joe! Joe! Is it you?" I gasped.

Holding him in the air, arms stretched out, reminded me of when he was a baby and he would laugh as I held him up in the house until his head rubbed against the ceiling. He loved when we played that game. When I put him down, we'd read a book or assemble a puzzle. When we finished, he'd always hug me and say, "I love you Daddy."

"Yeah, Dad. It's me!"

Two others ran at me from the car.

Seven years ago, they were like little colts taking those first steps in life with gangly and awkward movements. Their mature physical features were just starting to be outlined. Now at fifteen, thirteen and eleven, they were old enough to show their own physicality. Joe looked like me, tall and lean with big ears. Seven years ago he came up to my stomach. Now, the top of his head was at my eyes.

Shannon was blessed to be as eye catching as her mother. The women from my "in-laws" were athletically built and very attractive. She had shoulder length blonde hair and the prettiest brown eyes I've ever seen.

Brendan, at eleven, looked like a punk rocker. He had neither his mother nor his father in him at first glance. Spiked black hair with purple highlights, an earring, and a metal chain hanging from his hip were his "statement." But he was Brendan.

A group hug followed and tears flowed. All my memories were of their youth. I had missed their growing up. Some Dad I was.

Then the passenger side door opened and I could see the blur of a white-haired woman.

"Welcome home, Danny," Mom said to me.

I heard the words but, as she walked tentatively toward me, I felt like the earth was crumbling beneath my feet.

Mom was now eighty-eight years young. She'd lived to fulfill her promise to be here and see the day when her son would graduate from Federal Prison. Her presence was proof that she was too determined to do anything else but to be there the day I walked out. Even God, whom she loved and served, could not have wanted a different result.

Her hair was whiter than I remembered. Her walk a little less steady. Her posture a little less upright. But, she had a twinkle in her eye that told me she was the one responsible for the children being here. She must have worked on it for weeks ever since I told her about the hearing. I could see the triumph in her face. Ever the matriarch, despite the anger and bitterness between my ex-wife and myself, Mom knew the importance of family and she knew how important it was for me to have Joe, Shannon, and Brandon here.

A strange calm came upon me, like going into shock. "Daddy! Daddy! Daddy!" they were all saying. To me it seemed like slow motion. Emily watching us halfway between our little group and the SUV. She was taking pictures. I was speechless.

The courtroom appearance seemed irrelevant at the moment. All the anxiety from the years of fine-tuning a legal argument, the months of waiting for a response from the Honorable Court and the weeks of preparing myself to be "lawyer for a day" vanished in an instant. For years I prayed for the chance to be a father again. I'd asked God to please let me be the Dad that I never was, but wanted to be. The hugs told me that my petition to the Lord had been answered. When we let go of each other, my eyes were so thick with tears I couldn't see them. I removed my glasses and wiped my eyes on the sleeves of my sweats.

I tried to say something like, "How did you get here from Arizona?"

It came out, "How…"

Brendan, explaining their presence as only a "bad ass" could said, "We're gonna watch you kick ass in court."

Joe said, "He means we're taking you to the courtroom to watch you win."

Then the only noise was sobbing and the sound of a clicking camera. For a while it seemed as if we each waited for someone else to speak.

In my mind, I knew that I was standing at a crossroads and had to choose which one to take. I was a free man once again, that is, if I could convince the Court to grant my motion for release. Then true freedom would follow.

One way to go would be to follow the path someone like me never would take. Fuck the Courtroom and the restrictions detailed in the furlough. I could take everyone to the indoor water park in Harrisburg and ride the waves for a week. That's what I wanted to do. That would be the best thing I could do for them right now and they would never forget it. It would be a memory they would have forever. A warrior would do that. A dumb warrior.

The other path would be to follow the advice I presented as part of Spooter's speaking program. That is, in every matter, before acting, step back and think through the consequences. If you perform this simple exercise, usually, the right path is obvious.

Shannon broke the silence and asked, "Dad, what can we do after the courtroom stuff is over?"

Her big doe eyes begged for me to come up with something fun.

"Here's what we do. Let's go to the Courtroom and see if I can win the case fast. I'm told I'm the only case on the Docket, so it should start on time. Then we'll go to the indoor water park in Harrisburg and ride some waves!"

"Will the judge be okay with that?" Joe wanted to know.

I smiled as I hugged the three of them. I said, "I bet the judge will be really glad."

Epilogue

Justice

Well, the rest of the day was a good news versus bad news sort of thing.

The good news was that the ride to the Courtroom lasted about two hours. To me, it seemed like twenty minutes. In order to see my "long out of sight" children, I'd thought I'd have to beg for permission, and then crawl to Arizona, but instead, they were here. I was in awe of them. Within moments of starting down the road, they were chatting among themselves, all pumped with adrenaline.

I inspected each of them like they were newborn babies. To me they were. Joe, Shannon, and Brendan had grown and changed so much since I'd seen them last in the flesh. Sure, I had pictures, mailed to me by my Mom, but watching them interact and listening to the lilting sounds of their voices was hypnotic. I smiled at everything they said, and interjected a "Yes" or a "No" in the right places. It was a good while before I became conscious of the other two people in the car.

Mom was in front of me in the passenger seat. I felt shameful at having spent so much time adoring the three kids in the two back seats. I focused on Mom while Shannon talked about shoes.

It was apparent that her hair was whiter and thinner – as was she– though not so much that she looked sickly. Even though she visited me twice a year, she looked different from every time I'd seen her in the Visiting Room. She seemed shorter when we hugged in the parking lot. She felt frail. A lot more frail to tell the truth. Her skin was a dry, wrinkled texture that the indoor elderly develop. She was holding up as well as she could for where she was in life's journey. Most important, at eighty-eight, she still had her mind. I could tell that by how well she spoke and how animated she'd been before we left the parking lot.

On the other side of Mom was Emily, who always had brought

Mom to see me in her Taurus, then the Mercury Sable. She hadn't changed that much over the past seven years. Sure, she had aged and had lost a little of her edge physically but she was still one of the most principled individuals that I've ever met. Being a part of the reunion with my children, especially with Mom present, was the equivalent of her winning the lottery. Nothing meant more to her than family because, as she always said, "In the end that's all you got."

During the trip, I kept glancing back at Brendan.

And Shannon.

And Joe.

Words cannot adequately describe the emotional high I derived from being with them while we were in the car. I was elated. I felt so alive, and well, and good. I started thinking this entire scenario was too weird and I thought of the possibility that I was dreaming. I pinched myself.

This was real.

Finally, as we approached our destination, I focused on some courtroom images. Everything from a small office type with a low ceiling and six people present to the majestic cathedral style statehouse with every pew filled, plus balcony observers staring down at me. And, regardless of the legal complexity that reared its ugly head, I already had a planned response. For example, if the Honorable Judge Smert were now a pygmy, I had it covered.

To my dismay, the place was in the lower ten percent of the courtroom quality-chart that I'd envisioned. Nine people present. Mom, Emily, my three children, the Assistant U.S. Attorney assigned to the case, one clerk, one bailiff and, of course, me.

The absence of witnesses for the Government told me that the Assistant U.S. Attorney was confident that he could defeat my Motion based solely on the evidence presented in the submissions.

My legal mind shifted into overdrive. I didn't plan for this hearing to be little more than a pit stop during my incarceration. Processing the legal options available to me, including the pros and cons associated with each one, I knew I was mentally, physically and emotionally back in my "element" and that my heart was pumping harder and faster than it had in a long time.

The Honorable Judge Smert appeared from a side door, walked to the bench as though to my funeral and sat. The clerk announced, "All rise. The case of Holmes versus United States will now be heard."

The Honorable Judge fumbled through a file and then said he had made his decision based upon the written submissions.

"Motion Denied." He never looked at me. The hearing lasted less than fifteen seconds.

I jumped up.

"Motion for Reconsideration, your Honor." This was a reaction from a time when I was King of the Court.

This drew from the Honorable Judge, "I'll deny that Motion as well." He pronounced this with a soft falling voice, as though he had pronounced it many times before without regret. He stood and left.

I felt turned to stone.

After he disappeared, the Courtroom clerk, armed with her files, shuffled out of the Courtroom. The bailiff followed her leaving me and my army alone.

I hadn't planned on anything like this. Why had Judge Smert scheduled a hearing on my Motion if he was going to summarily dismiss it?

Despite the setback, I realized I still had that sharp mind I'd once had. I took pleasure in knowing that the Government had taken everything else from me over the past seven years except my mind. That sharp mind that was ready for anything that could happen in the Courtroom today. Even this!

I turned around and scanned the faces of my family. They were as stunned as I was.

"Well," I said, putting on a wry grin. "I don't think the Judge bothered to read the file." Then I smiled. "Do you?"

They relaxed a little.

"Under the rules," I said as I examined an imaginary watch. "We have thirty-six hours of freedom to do whatever we want. Who wants to eat ice-cream and hit the indoor water park?"

That brought Shannon back from the verge of tears.

I started dreaming that one day, way off in the future, my children would be telling my grandchildren how well their Daddy handled being completely shut down by a Federal Judge after so much traveling and so much hope. Dad hadn't lost his temper, hadn't cried like a twelve year-old girl, hadn't jabbed a pencil through his eye killing himself instantly. No, with one sentence, their Daddy pushed the Honorable Judge to the edge of rudeness, then turned to them and spoke of ice cream cones and water parks.

So that's exactly what we did. I walked back behind the gallery and hugged them. Then I joked about this not having been such a big deal; that seven more months, or even a year, was a snap for a professional such as I; that they could look forward to another trip East next year, and that we were going to have a good time no matter what happened.

My goal was to downplay the entire "proceeding" in order to mask my anger and disappointment over being "back handed" by a Judge.

And in about fifty years, if I made it to Mom's age, I'll muster the courage to ask my kids if my acting abilities were better than my legal skills.

Glossary

Bit – The sentence, as in, "I have a seventeen month bit."

BOP – The Federal Bureau of Prisons.

Bucket – Solitary confinement, also called segregation, located in the medium-security down the hill from the camp.

CCS-1 – All night duty doing janitorial work in the Medium-Security facility down the hill. This is the most hated and avoided Minimum-Security job.

Chillin' – Just lying on the bunk. Loitering of any kind. Chillin' is a prison job description.

CO – Corrections Officer

Compound Cop – The CO who constantly drives the perimeter of the FCI and FPC looking for intruders or escapees.

Cop – Informal name for a Corrections Officer. Also an inmate who informs on others to get favors from staff.

Cube – The double-bunk, double-desk and double-chair area in the range where inmates sleep.

Daisy – An effeminate inmate.

FCI – Federal Correctional Facility – formal name for Medium-Security facilities.

FNG – Fuckin' New Guy.

Food Circus – The entire Food Service operation for all meals.

FPC – Federal Prison Camp – formal name for Minimum Security facilities.

Hack – Informal name for a Corrections Officer.

Hole – Solitary confinement, also called segregation, located in the medium-security down the hill from the camp.

House – The cube where an inmate lives as in, "I'll stop by your house after dinner."

I-T-S – The Inmate Telephone System for outgoing inmate calls only.

Mandatory Four O'clock Stand Up Count – The formal daily count reported to the Bureau of Prisons in Washington, DC. Inmates stand to attention in their cubes as a detailed formal count is made.

OP Cop – Outside Patrol Cop.

PA Office – Practitioner Assistant's Office.

Pill Line – Where medications are dispensed to inmates based on prescriptions.

PITA – Pain in the Ass.

PYT – Pretty Young Thing.

Range – The single floor housing designation as in, "I'm on Range B in Camp Two."

R&D – Receiving and Dispatch, where inmates are checked into the facility and where they get checked out of the facility.

Rat – Someone on the street who informs on others to get a lighter sentence. Also someone in prison who informs on others to get favors from the staff.

Shot – Writing up an inmate for an infraction. Generally a shot will get an inmate sent to the bucket for two weeks.

Sleepers – Inmates who lie low about themselves but show surprising talent when pressed for performance.

The Street – The world outside prison.

Unicor – The plant facility in the Bureau of Prisons that manufactures items for use by the General Services Administration.

About the Authors

So, by now you're asking how did the co-authors meet?

Well, even though we grew up in different parts of the country and never would have met, we can thank the BOP for collaborating in the creation of this masterpiece by assigning us to serve our respective sentences at the same Federal Prison Camp.

You see, Sam was born and raised in Florida. He graduated from college and began a career in banking where he rose to Vice-President, Construction Loans. Then he changed career paths and worked as Chief Operating Officer for a real estate developer in Virginia. It was then that his life took a turn for the worse. He decided to be loyal to his employer when the employer committed bank fraud to try to secure takeout financing for his upside-down real estate portfolio. Sam did not call 911 and report the felonies as soon as he saw them, which is the letter of the law. His loyalty to an individual he liked and admired trumped his moral compass. When everything collapsed, Sam was indicted and pled guilty when the developer did not stand up and take responsibility for the frauds he alone had committed and authorized.

Dan grew up in Philadelphia, Pennsylvania and went to law school after graduating college. He worked hard and became successful in his trade and was on his way to enjoying the fruits of his labor. Unfortunately, Dan wasn't prepared for the many trials that life makes you endure and, in his moment of testing, Dan failed miserably.

So one day, as Dan was resting at his assigned prison work detail in the Power House, this guy walked in and, based upon his years of relevant work experience, was assigned the position of Tool Room clerk. That guy was Sam. After a short while, Dan noticed that Sam was writing. Turns out it was Sam's first novel. After Sam went home, Dan had another five years left to serve on his sentence, having been much more evil than Sam. Learning from Sam, and figuring it would be a fun way to kill five years, Dan wrote down the more interesting events of his prison experience. Then, once Dan collected a number of